Passages to
the Dream Shore

Passages to the Dream Shore

SHORT STORIES OF CONTEMPORARY HAWAII

Edited by

FRANK STEWART

A KOLOWALU BOOK

UNIVERSITY OF HAWAII PRESS

HONOLULU

Library of Congress Cataloging-in-Publication Data

Passages to the dream shore.

  1. Short stories, American—Hawaii.   2.   Hawaii—
Fiction.   3.   American fiction—20th century.   I.   Stewart,
Frank, 1946–
PS571.H3P37   1987   813'.01'0832969   87–13594
ISBN 0–8248–1122–4

CONTENTS

PREFACE

The physical beauty of Hawaii has always been apparent to travelers reaching these islands. The early Polynesian voyagers especially must have celebrated the sight of this spectacular landfall, perhaps 1,500 years ago. In the centuries following their settlement, waves of other travelers and immigrants have arrived. From East and West, tourists continue to come each year in growing numbers, lured in part by Edenic poster-images of the shining sand and clear, azure sky.

Those born here or who spend many years in the islands, however, inevitably learn that Hawaii is much richer and more varied than even the bright, dreamlike shore that travelers first encounter. The vegetation that flourishes here year round, the light that falls through the rain on stone and earth, the tastes and smells of island foods, the seasons, birds and mountains, city streets and rural towns—these are merely the surface of Hawaii's attraction. Ultimately, it's Hawaii's people and their ways that make this world so distinctive and so compelling.

No camera can fully capture the complexity and diversity of the lives here, no painting or object of art can render all the changing subtleties. Stories, however, have the power to show the passage of time, and especially how time impresses the island landscape into the hearts and thoughts of the people.

The stories in this collection are like that. They show the ways in which Hawaii, despite its idyllic surface, can be a place of war and hardship, of unhappiness and failure, as well as a place of great compassion, love, and self-sacrifice. They show that here, as in few other places in America, ancestry and memory are still vivid, the past is intertwined with the present, and for all its modernness Hawaii is a place that continues to be profoundly sacred.

Unlike previous anthologies of stories about the Pacific, this one is concerned primarily with contemporary Hawaii. The writers in the collection are all living, all the works were published or written in about the last ten years, in English, and nearly every author is a long-time resident of the state —most were born and raised here. The stories were chosen for the way that each in its own way portrays, through the emotional lives of the characters, Hawaii's individual yet universal qualities and for the way they demonstrate, as a group, how this powerful landscape has joined the destinies of many different peoples and voices.

In addition to these writers of short fiction, Hawaii has excellent novelists, journalists, essayists, dramatists, and poets. Many talented writers here compose song lyrics. The reader who wants to know more voices of Hawaii should listen to the music of the islands and search out the other forms of written and oral art as well.

Compiling this volume confirmed for me how indebted we readers and writers are to the editors of Hawaii's small, independent presses and literary magazines. Year after year, usually without any compensation or much recognition, these editors have put Hawaii's writers into print. They have, to a large extent, been the nurturers, if not the creators, of the contemporary literature of the region. Good examples of such editors are Darrell H. Y. Lum and Eric Chock; their magazine *Bamboo Ridge* has appeared consistently four times a year since 1978. In addition, numerous student editors of *Hawaii Review,* published by the University of Hawaii's student body, have done remarkable independent work over the years. The various other regional magazines and presses in the state which first published some of the work in this collection are *Hapa, The Paper, Honolulu,* Topgallant Publishing Co., and Petronium Press. Their existence has made this anthology possible.

Many friends helped me find the stories collected here. I'm grateful to all of them, and in particular to John Heckathorn of *Honolulu,* Michael McPherson, and Pat Matsueda. I'm also grateful to Robert Sparks at the University of Hawaii Press, who from the beginning was encouraging and supportive of this project and has been a supporter of Hawaii writing in general. Finally, I thank the University of Hawaii Department of English for allowing me time to complete this book.

Frank Stewart

ACKNOWLEDGMENTS

Grateful acknowledgment is made for permission to reprint the following stories:

Asa Baber, "The Surfer." Reprinted from *Hawaii Review* 10.

John Heckathorn, "Hanalei." Reprinted from *Honolulu*.

Steve Heller, "The Red Dust of Lanai." Reprinted from Steve Heller, *The Man Who Drank a Thousand Beers* (Kirksville, Mo.: The Chariton Review Press, 1984); first published in *Thicket*.

John Dominis Holt, "The Pool" and "God Sent You into That Gomorrah This Morning to Bring up the Truth." Reprinted from John Dominis Holt, *Princess of the Night Rides and Other Tales* (Honolulu: Topgallant Publishing Co., 1977).

Michael LaGory, "Seaside Idle." Reprinted from *The Paper* 2:3.

Lanning Lee, "Born and Bred." Reprinted from *Hawaii Review* 17.

Darrell H. Y. Lum, "Yahk Fahn, Auntie." Reprinted from Darrell H. Y. Lum, *Sun* (Honolulu: Bamboo Ridge Press, 1980); also published in *The Paper* 2:3. "Primo Doesn't Take Back Bottles Anymore." Reprinted from *Sun* (Honolulu: Bamboo Ridge Press, 1980); first published in Eric Chock et al., *Talk Story* (Honolulu: Petronium Press/Talk Story, Inc., 1978). "The Moiliili Bagman." Reprinted from *Hawaii Review* 13.

Ian MacMillan, "The Rock." Reprinted from Ian MacMillan, *Light and Power* (University of Missouri Press, 1980); first published in *Hawaii Review* 2:2.

Michael McPherson, "Beachboy." Reprinted from Michael McPherson, *Singing with the Owls* (Petronium Press, 1982); first published in *The Paper* 1:3. "That Was Last Year." Reprinted from *Hawaii Review* 14.

Ralph Anthony Misitano, "Deep Water." Reprinted from *Hawaii Review* 11.

Victoria Nelson, "Coming Back." Reprinted from *Hawaii Review* 14.

Susan Nunes, "A Small Obligation." Reprinted from Susan Nunes, *A Small Obligation* (Honolulu: Bamboo Ridge Press, 1982); first published in *Hawaii Review* 13.

Robert Onopa, "The Man Who Swam through Jelly fish, through Men-of-War." Reprinted from *Hapa* 2; first published in *TriQuarterly* 33.

Patsy S. Saiki, "Communion." Reprinted from *Bamboo Ridge* 6.

Marjorie Sinclair, "Secrets." Reprinted from *Hapa* 2.

Mary Wakayama, "Watching Fire." Reprinted from *Bamboo Ridge* 17.

Sylvia A. Watanabe, "The Seabirds." Reprinted from *Bamboo Ridge* 24.

Cedric Yamanaka, "What the Ironwood Whispered." Reprinted from *Hawaii Review* 18.

The Surfer

ASA BABER

During Rabbit's last weeks, when he knew and I knew that he was going to die, I sat with him at night.

I charted the times he was supposed to take Demerol and I gave him Thorazine when he needed it. The Thorazine was for the hiccups, which came when he tried to talk too much.

At night, Rabbit kept hearing a voice on the ridgeline at the top of the valley. I do not think the voice scared him so much as it interested him. He thought it was the spirit of his father calling to him.

Things like that happen in Hawaii.

Then one night I heard the voice, too, although I tried to pretend that I did not. "You're stoned," I said to Rabbit when he asked me about it. "You've got too many pills in you." But I jumped again when I heard the voice clearly. It sounded like the call of a wolf.

"That's him, brah," Rabbit smiled. He called me 'brah'—Hawaiian lingo for 'brother'—not cheaply, like the mod crowd in Waikiki, but with love.

"It's just a dog or something," I said.

"That's Seki. He knows. He's waiting for me, Bobby. He's waiting."

Seki, Rabbit's father, had shot himself through the heart with a .22 pistol ten years ago. That was right after Lowell, Rabbit's brother, had been killed in a chopper crash in Laos. Right after the burial ceremony in Punchbowl with flags and rifles and a full bird Colonel and the smell of smog and ash in the slow Kona wind.

"Seki doesn't want you to die," I said.

"Yeah, I know," Rabbit nodded. "But if I have to die, Seki's saying he'll take care of me."

I did not know what to say, so I went back to talking surfing because that helped both of us.

For a short time we were not in a shack in Palolo Valley with a tin roof that rattled in the wind and a ball of opium in the saucer on the table. We moved out of there in our minds, leaving the pain, and we got back to the water where we belonged, where we had grown up together.

I told Rabbit what he already knew: that the summer waves were good on the South Shore and that there was sewage and sharks off of Sand Island and that Kaisers was as crowded as Publics and that Secrets had some long, heavy lefts with real power.

"You been to Cunhas?" Rabbit asked.

"Not this summer," I said. "It needs five feet to show. I'm working Cliffs mostly."

"You hotdog," Rabbit said. His eyes were closed but he was smiling.

"Hey!" I said. It was one of our old jokes. I surfed Diamond Head but Rabbit had never liked it there. The tour buses stopped at the top of Kuilei Cliffs on the wide part of Kahala Avenue and all day long the tourists watched us through binoculars as if we were toys on exhibit.

"You haole hotdog."

"Howl-lee, howl-lee," I exaggerated the word. "How come you always call me a haole, huh? I was raised here, too."

Rabbit was having trouble swallowing, so I kept talking to cover for him. "You call me a haole? Ok, gook. Rabbit the gook. Here he is, folks. Rabbit the shy gook who surfs Secrets so nobody can see him. Awww." I pinched his thin cheeks. He tried to smile. His face was cold and there was something going on in his throat and chest that I did not understand. I waited to see if he was going to be sick but he got things under control. He was sweating.

"You think I could have another hit?" Rabbit asked later. "I don't know; maybe I shouldn't go out so stoned, huh? What do you think, Bobby?"

"It's been four hours," I lied. I propped him up so he could swallow another Demerol. As I helped him lie back on his pillows, I thought for a moment that he was one of my sons and that I was a full-time father again, nursing my children through the flu. It was a good feeling.

Sometimes I took a pill with Rabbit to try and float out of my own kind of pain. It was not Rabbit's pain of a diseased pancreas and a toxic bloodstream. But I missed my kids and I was losing my best friend and I had wasted my life. I was thirty-five years old and I should have been dead nine times over and I was burned out, wasted, like a spent shell casing. I knew there were as many kinds of pain as there were plants in the world, or trees or rocks or fish, and I knew that I was not coping with my pain as well as Rabbit was with his.

During those last days, as I watched Rabbit die slowly, I learned all over again that I am a racist and that I think there are genetic patterns, not in weaknesses but in strengths. Most Orientals handle pain better than most Caucasians.

Rabbit may have been a sansei, the grandson of Tatsuno Harada and the son of Seki Harada, but there was a reservoir of Japan in him. Maybe he was part samurai or part priest. Maybe sometime back in the sixteenth century one of his forbearers had left Kyoto and gone into the mountains to practice calligraphy while he waited to die.

I do not know the exact history of the Harada family, but I do know that Rabbit was able to rise above his pain.

Towards the end, he decided to go without pills.

One of the best surfers I had ever seen, Rabbit had shrunk to a skeleton's weight, two operations in five months, the victim of various exotic therapies, but he sat up in the middle of what was to be his final night and he handed me the Darvon and Demerol and Thorazine and Vitamin B Complex and Maalox and he said, "Wipe these out, brah."

"OK," I said. I moved the tray across the room.

"No. I mean out. Get rid of them." Rabbit waved his thin hands. He looked both old and child-like, the quilt around his shoulders, the gray sweatsuit covering his changed body, black felt slippers on his feet. He could have been a Montagnard or a tribal chief, say a chief who had signed a bad treaty and knew it.

"You sure?" I asked him. He did not answer. I took the tray into the kitchen and pretended to throw the bottles away. But when I walked into his room again, he was smiling at me.

"Bobby," he said, "I want them out of here. So do it."

I felt apart from him, and I knew that he had a special intuition now, something granted only to the dying, perhaps, and I did not argue with him. I walked through the garden and towards the road where I dumped the drugs in the trash pile.

It was past midnight and I stared up the valley towards the headwaters of the Waiomao Stream and I thought that I was on the moon, an astronaut in a deep crater close to the dark side of the moon, and I was almost dizzy as I tried to track the clouds crossing the ridge.

The thought that I was praying did not occur to me then, although I suppose I was, at least in my way: prayers to all the dead, of course, and to Buddha, to Jesus, to anything that might help, mixed with quick memories of the life that was passing in review.

Me, I am so twisted and scarred that I could not stand out there in the dark like that without also checking for trip wires, watching for ambushes, monitoring the ridgeline for the flash of tracers, and yes, I know it was peacetime Honolulu, 1977, but for some of us it is always other times and other places, too. Always.

"Roberto," I said to myself, "you were present just before the destruction of a whole people."

That line came to me without my asking. It was delivered to me, and it was an awesome thought. So was the fact that Rabbit was passing into certain shadows as I stood in his vegetable garden. He had planted these flowering, budding things but he would not be around to harvest them.

"The destruction of a whole people," I said to myself again, remembering Kroong as he listened to the sounds of the prowling tiger near Sar Lang and Baap Can weeping at the funeral of his son and Maang-the-Deputy slicing the tendons on the hocks of the buffalos before he cut their throats.

"Moi," the South Vietnamese called the Montagnards: "savages."

They are all gone now.

I was thinking about that when I heard the voice on the ridgeline again and I knew that Seki was telling me that Rabbit needed company. I walked back to the house.

"Bobby?" Rabbit whispered as I came into the room. He reached out for me. His eyes were closed.

"I'm here," I said. I held his hands. It was as if we were children in Manoa again, skipping school and planning where to surf for the day.

"Thanks, brah," Rabbit said.

"It's OK, brah."

"No pain," Rabbit said quietly.

I squeezed his hands. "All right."

I did not know what else to do, so I talked surfing again. Rabbit nodded sometimes.

I told him how next winter we would rent a house in Haleiwa and surf Sunset and the Bay and how he could ride the winter juice in The Pipeline and how Kapono, his sister, could come with us and surf Vals Reef and break the skeg on her board again at Kammieland. I took him all around Oahu one last time, even after I could see he was not breathing any more.

"Goodbye, brah," I said. "You did good. Number One." I hugged the stick figure that had been my best friend. I felt sad and tired, but I was also relieved that it was over.

After a while I walked back to the gate and hiked down to the dealer's house to use his phone. I called Kapono at the hospital. She said she would come right up but I told her to finish her shift. "I'll stay with him until you get here, lady," I said. "He wouldn't want any fuss." I went on to tell her we would take Rabbit's ashes out in the Hobie Cat the way he wanted, and we would sink the urn somewhere past the reef.

When I got off the phone, the dealer offered me a joint and we smoked it in silence.

"You want me to go with you?" he asked me as I got up to leave.

"No," I said, "that's OK. I'm not afraid of dead people. Some of them are my best friends."

The dealer had a poster of Jimi Hendrix on his front door and he had a vegetable garden in his yard with huge cabbage heads that looked like seaflowers in the early morning light.

I walked back up the path, past the grove of papaya trees and the palms and the high grasses. I was thinking that I was very old and that I probably did not deserve to be alive.

I decided that I did not want to be around when the valley was bought up and turned into a resort and the path was paved for tour buses and there were building cranes standing like metal birds on the tops of new condominiums.

Sitting on my Lightning Bolt tanker in the front yard, peeling old wax off the board, I heard sounds on the ridgeline.

There were two voices this time.

Hanalei

JOHN HECKATHORN

Every time I get divorced I cry, big blubbery bursts of tears, usually at dinner time. My soon-to-be-ex-wife Diane finds these tears at the table suspicious. I'm not upset she's leaving me, she insists; I'm upset that I won't have anyone to cook my dinner. An unfair allegation if I've ever heard one, because Diane is a horrid cook and because, despite all good sense, I am going to miss her, her ramrod-straight posture, as if life were a military school, and her curly hair cut short like a helmet around her head, and her full lips set like a prune in disapproval, usually of me. I've lived so long with her disapproval, I'm afraid I'll collapse once it's gone, undone by the sudden lack of opposition.

Divorce is misery, all that loss coming at once, lost people, lost hopes, and that sense of loss which comes from knowing that you've screwed up once again. I don't want you thinking that I get divorced all the time—just twice, as many times as I've been married. I realize I'm risking reader sympathy here: *Who is this guy?* I can hear you thinking, *What's wrong with him that he can't stay married?* And you're proving exactly the point I'd like to make. Get divorced once and everyone's ready to cut you a little slack: You married too young, you picked the wrong person, anyone can make a mistake. But get divorced twice by the time you're thirty-two and everyone thinks you're a criminal.

I'm trying not to let it bother me. The purpose of life, as far as I can tell, is not to stay married; it's to be happy as much of the time as possible. Again, that's as far as I can tell: I've been known to be wrong about these things.

Actually, now that I reflect on it, the purpose of life is to stay alive. It's better, almost everyone agrees, to be alive than otherwise. If, of course, you're facing terminal cancer, or the certainty of torture, or the destruction of everything that makes your life worth living, then killing yourself might be a reasonable alternative. But you can't be expecting me, just to prove I'm

6

a serious person, to start thinking about suicide. Which is why I say that the purpose of life is to be as happy as possible: The second you become persuaded otherwise, you begin entertaining gloomy thoughts.

Of course, lots of people lead long and satisfying lives immersed in deepest gloom, my soon-to-be-ex-wife Diane among them. These people do not commit suicide; they take deep pleasure in thinking the rest of us are shallow. What you need to be a successful suicide is not so much gloom as anger. Some months ago at the university where I work, someone's girlfriend went up to his room in the high-rise dorms and told him they were through. *We need to start seeing other people,* she probably said. *We're no good for each other anymore. I hope we can still be friends.* You've probably been through a similar scene; no matter which party you are, it's never pleasant. To show his displeasure, this particular broken-hearted lover plunged out his open window, ending up on a concrete courtyard eighteen floors below with a squashy-sounding thump.

Nice, yeah? A nice way of telling your girlfriend *I hate you* and making sure she hears it, for years and years, even in her dreams. Nice also because our brokenhearted lover stepped out of life in front of a stunned audience. The courtyard was filled with students on their way to class. A good number of them screamed. A few, especially those who had been closest to where he landed, stepped into the bushes to blow lunch. Some began to rush around aimlessly, but most stood stock still, shocked at the way death had jumped out at them in public. One of them happened to be Lisa Tanabe, a tall, intelligent young Japanese woman with short black hair and an astonishingly beautiful face. With the fascination of someone glued to the television screen, she listened to the shrieks and astonished curses give way to rumors, saw the firemen roll up and wrap the ex-boyfriend in a green plastic tarp. When the firemen unrolled a hose and began unceremoniously to spray the concrete clean of blood, Lisa hurried away and, without thinking much about it, ended up where she'd been headed in the first place—my 1:30 writing class.

She was a little late. She slipped into her seat in the front row, took out her notebook, and sat staring into space. She was usually bright-eyed and eager, but I assumed that her ongoing religious crisis had for the moment overwhelmed her. About a year earlier when her mother had suddenly died, Lisa had fallen into the hands of some evangelicals, who convinced her that the best way to escape her grief was to accept Jesus as her personal savior. They baptized her in the surf off Waikiki and told her that the point of life was to do what they said Jesus said she ought to do, which was to throw herself into making more converts for the evangelicals. Her only problem was that she was a normal, healthy twenty-one-year-old, who could hardly resist sleeping with her boyfriend, which the evangelicals assured her was exactly what Jesus didn't want her doing until she could marry.

So Lisa had some unhappy days, poised between the desires of the flesh and the prospect of eternal damnation. Thinking that she was no more damned than usual, I went about my business, explaining the rigors and joys of the English sentence, and everything was quiet until Charles produced the following example of a periodic sentence: "The cocktail glass, propelled off the lanai railing by a careless elbow, picking up speed according to Galileo's law of falling bodies, accelerating 32 feet per second, fell."

I didn't think it was a great sentence, but I liked the way it came down heavily on the verb *fell*. Janice put up her hand and said it would be a better sentence if Charles had left out Galileo's law of falling bodies, and several people agreed. Especially Lisa, who sat up very straight and said in a quiet, distinct voice, "He screamed all the way down."

It was like a poem: Nobody understood her, but it sounded like she knew what she was talking about. She said it once more, then broke down into quiet, decorous sobs. "They said he jumped on purpose. His girlfriend."

"Who?" I asked. I was still thinking about Galileo and the cocktail glass.

"I don't know!" said Lisa. "How should I know? He just jumped."

Then Carla spoke up. Carla, who up until that moment I had thought of as the girl with too much make-up who cut too many classes. She'd been inside the dorms when it happened, arriving in the courtyard in time to watch the ambulance drive off and the fireman hose down the concrete. Now she leaned forward and rubbed Lisa's shoulder, explaining to the rest of us what had happened. Lisa stopped crying a minute and gathered her books together. "I'm sorry, I'm sorry," she said.

Carla got up to walk her home. "It'll be all right," I said as they walked out the door—which convinced nobody, especially not Lisa. Halfway out the door, she turned, looking me straight in the eye, and said, "It bothers me he might be damned. They keep telling me suicides are damned."

"No," I said. But I lied. I think we're all damned. Consider what is going to happen to you even if you don't throw yourself out an eighteenth-story window in your early twenties. If you're lucky and don't catch some wasting disease at thirty; if the thugs and fools who run the world's countries don't shoot you or napalm you or unleash thermonuclear hell in your neighborhood; if your car doesn't blow a tire and send you spinning into a lane full of oncoming traffic; if no one throws you into prison for your political beliefs or into a concentration camp for perhaps no good reason at all; if none of the unimaginably awful things that happen to ordinary, perfectly nice human beings happen to you—what then?

You get inevitably older each day. You watch them bury your parents, your older friends, your contemporaries. Your dreams, being dreams, go mostly unfulfilled. Your children, if you're fortunate enough to have them in the first place, turn into people you never expected. You get old, get sick, and die.

And that's the best that can happen.

So I'd advise you to pause before condemning me as shallow when I say that the point of life is to be happy, to have a good time if at all possible. I don't want it to sound like I'm inviting you to a party. And I don't even want to sound like I'm telling you *how* to have a good time. Some people like their beef rare, some people like their fish raw. Some like girls, some like boys, and some like working themselves to death. Some like sleeping till noon, and some like getting up at dawn and running 10 miles.

Do what you want. All I know is that my idea of a good time, at the moment, is to sit here on this beach chair, my clipboard propped against my knees, writing one sentence after another.

Not your idea of a good time? You have to consider the setting.

This is a story about Hawaii, although you might be excused for not noticing that till now. It is a story about Hawaii because that's where I live, in Honolulu, and because that's where I am at the moment, not Honolulu, but the long white-sand beach of Hanalei Bay, about 30 feet from the water. It is the last weekend of October, starting to cloud over late in the afternoon, but still warm. Hanalei, for anyone who doesn't know, is on the North Shore of Kauai, which is the northernmost of the Hawaiian Islands—or at least the most northern of the islands anyone would want to go to, the rest being rocks and reefs now slipping slowly back into the ocean and being inched toward Siberia by the movement of the Pacific plate, having had their geological moment of glory as islands.

Hanalei has to be one of the great places on the earth. I haven't been to the Greek Isles, or to the South of France, or to Sri Lanka where the waves travel 6,000 miles from Antarctica without stop to crash onto the beach, but those places have to be great indeed to be better than right here: a nearly circular bay 2 miles across, with soft-sand beach sloping away gently into the bright blue water. The bay is at the end of a long, wet valley, still agricultural. It is peaceful, quiet, and nearly deserted at 3:30 on a Saturday afternoon. There are some houses dotted along the beach, small ones, but you can hardly see them. What you can see, starting about 60 or 70 feet from the shore and ascending the steep lava walls of the valley, are lawns and coconut palms and plumeria trees and flowering hibiscus bushes and ti plants and all manner of luxuriant vegetable life. I am surrounded by green, staring out at the blue sky and the blue water. I feel wonderful.

This is all, of course, too good to last. Not only is Kauai eroding an infinitesimal bit at a time, so that in a few million years it too will be a rock on its way to Siberia. But Hanalei itself doesn't have that long. Already the state Department of Transportation has plans for the narrow metal bridge which is the only way into the valley. They've let it go badly; now it's rusty and unsafe and due to be replaced by a multimillion-dollar multi-lane concrete monster, a bridge big enough to accommodate trucks and construction equipment. What then? Hotels, shopping centers, golf courses. Condominiums with quarter-of-a-million-dollar one-bedroom apartments. Rich people from the Mainland and Canada and Japan. High-rises up and down the bay.

Oh well, it will last until Thursday when I have to fly back to Honolulu. It will probably last long enough for me to come back a few more times in my life. When there isn't any Hanalei, I won't be around to notice.

Why am I here? First, because my friend Randy, who used to copy my geometry homework in high school, has become a millionaire selling guitar amplifiers and can afford a house on Hanalei Bay. He's too busy to use it much, having to stick close to the amplifier factory in California. Most of the time he rents his house out, but he called me and said his rental for October had fallen through and I was welcome to the house; just pick up the key from the real estate agent.

Second, I'm here for a few days because my soon-to-be-ex-wife Diane needs the space—sorry, that's the way Diane talks—she needs the space to pack up all her stuff from our condo in Honolulu and ship it back to New Jersey. Why anyone in their right mind would want to move from Hawaii to New Jersey is beyond me. But Diane is looking forward to it, having hated paradise from the moment she walked off United Airlines Flight 126 four years ago. She actually seems happy about having a one-way ticket to Newark Airport, but she needs the space to pack—and also, I'm guessing, to see her lover, whom I'm not supposed to know about. She hasn't been subtle. She haunts the mailbox. She says she's writing for jobs. But I doubt whether many firms write their prospective employees a handwritten letter each day. She was so anxious to get us off on time that I suspect her lover, whoever he is, flew in from New Jersey the same day the Beast and I flew over to Kauai.

The Beast, my two-year-old daughter Beatrice, is sound asleep now in a little tent improvised from an old blanket, a boogie board and a broken beach chair. On my other side, leaning against a back rest, sits my friend Willie, reading a book called *Blood and Money*. Willie frowns a little as she reads, concentrating, I guess. Every once in a while she gives a little chuckle of appreciation.

"You look like you're having a good time," she says, tipping her sunglasses down on her nose and looking over at me. "What's that you're writing? Another story?"

"So far it's seven pages on the purpose of life. I put in a section about that suicide Lisa saw last year, you know, the kid who threw himself out the dorm window."

"Don't remind me. I had to write a ten-page report for the chancellor on that one. He was in the College Opp program, and I had to explain why my advisers didn't prepare him better for college life. As if we could have known." She shakes her heavy head of curls. "This year I was tempted to put a little paragraph in the registration materials about always looking on the bright side."

"You can put my story in."

"Don't tell me you're giving people advice." She takes the clipboard from me and flips through the first few pages. "I like the voice," she says. "But when are you going to learn that the whole point of a story is desire, conflict, sex, violence?"

"What about happiness?" I asked.

"I don't think it's possible," says Willie. "It's almost impossible to write about a good character, and it's even more impossible to write about happiness. It'd be nice if you could do it. Wouldn't it be perfect if you could just capture a day at the beach like this, the sun rippling off the water, the trade winds against your skin, the smell of marijuana from the parking lot, the baby asleep, the sound of your pen scratching across your pad, then drinks, dinner, bed? But face it, Walt, happiness just isn't interesting."

She resumes reading her book about murder among the Texas millionaires. The Beast stirs, then falls asleep again. There are a couple of hours to cocktail time. Time enough for twenty or thirty sentences if I keep at it. Willie is an extraordinary-looking woman, and she has been my best friend for several years now. I wouldn't even put her in a story, not under her real name, anyway, if she hadn't been so superior about what to put in and what to leave out. Besides, anyone who has sat through all my ramblings on the purpose of life is good enough to be introduced to Willie.

Desire, conflict, sex, and violence. Willie sits next to me in her shiny purple one-piece bathing suit that shows off her large breasts. Diane, with her military posture, her chest flat except for her nipples standing at attention all day, was jealous of Willie's breasts, sure that I was waiting for the first opportunity to grab them. I have never been a devotee of huge breasts; they seem to me somehow uneconomical. On Willie, however, they look wonderful. She also has the world's most magnificent ass, which you can't see at the moment because she's sitting on it. What you can see of her is very nice, except for the five or six pounds around her middle which she could afford to lose. Willie would be outraged if she could read what I am telling you about her. It's sexist, she'd say, concerned only with her outward physical appearance. Besides, I could afford to lose five or six pounds myself.

Still you'd want to see Willie, her huge head of curly dark hair, her sunburnt face, peeling nose, and behind the sunglasses dark Scorpio eyes which sparkle with mischief, but reveal nothing, nothing at all.

For about two years I was in love with Willie, back when the two of us shared a tiny office and taught writing every semester. Since that time Willie and I have become assistant deans, she first, then me following her example, and we hardly see each other from week to week. Before we rose in the world, however, we fell in love. She was married, I was married, her husband was a bastard, my wife was pregnant. Finally, her huge, handsome husband left her. We saw each other every day; in fact, I do not think there was ever a period where I worked so hard, where I could hardly wait to get to the office every morning. We were hopelessly in love, we never said anything, not about that, anyway, although we spent hours and hours talking about everything else. Finally, one Friday afternoon when we were discussing how to teach the right-branching sentence, I threw my arms around Willie and started kissing her. "I think that was a mistake," said Willie. "Now we're really in the soup."

But nothing came of it, not really. Diane watched me like a hawk, and I was trying to be faithful. Only a creep, went my reasoning, would start up an affair while his wife was suffering through the Hawaiian heat carrying his child. Willie had some doubts about whether she ought to sleep with somebody married. And so, except for some fervent grapplings at odd moments, nothing happened. Once we took off all our clothes and got into bed—but it was the night after Beatrice was born, Diane was still in the hospital, and I couldn't, I just couldn't. So I got back up, put on my clothes, and left.

That was two-and-a-half years ago. Now the baby has grown into the Beast, the world's hungriest and most aggressive toddler. Now Diane is leaving me. "You can marry Willie now if you want," she says. Diane has a way of ignoring inconvenient facts. One of which is that Willie already has a new husband, Emerson Chang, who is at this moment skimming the waves of Hanalei Bay on his flashy-looking windsurfer with its bright orange sail. Willie and Emerson have been married about a year, after living together for almost that long, and they seem very happy. I didn't marry Willie when I had the chance because I was trying hard to stay married to Diane, whom I couldn't make happy no matter what I did, and who couldn't stand living in the best city in the United States, Honolulu, and who, despite all her anti-racist rhetoric, never could adjust to living in this most Asian of American towns, where even the most militant and anti-authoritarian woman social worker was just one more loud haole. Damn Diane, anyway.

Willie hits me on the arm. "I just saw Emerson's board fly up in the air and I can't see him anywhere."

"Isn't that him?" About a quarter-mile out I see Emerson's board. Emerson isn't on it. By straining hard, I can pick out his dark head bobbing as he swims back to the board.

"I think he's in trouble. Why don't you swim out and see how he's doing?"

"He looks all right. It's calm out there, and he's a better swimmer than I am."

"Walter!" says Willie in a stern tone. I set down my clipboard and pen, pick up my goggles, glance apprehensively at the Beast, sleeping blonde and pink under the shade of the blanket. "I'll watch her. Just go."

I stand up and start stepping across the hot sand. "Don't rush out there like you're going to rescue him," says Willie. "Just pretend you want some exercise and happen to be swimming in his direction. But don't be all day about it."

I'm not a bad swimmer, but it was a solid ten-minute swim out to where Emerson was. My heart was pounding, and my goggles were misted over by the time I found him. He'd gotten the windsurfer right-side up and was sitting on it, rubbing his eyes. "Hey, you all right?"

"Willie send you out to check on me?" asked Emerson. "I thought I was getting real radical. Then I leaned too far back and lost the board. I think it got me, or the sail got me, on its way back down, banged my head, and now I got something in my eye."

"Blood," I said. "That's blood. Looks like you've got a cut right there above your eyebrow."

"Shit. Willie's going to laugh at me."

"She's not going to laugh at you. She's worried."

"First she's going to make sure I'm OK, then she's going to laugh," said Emerson. "I went and brought this thing instead of my surfboard, thinking it was safer." He pulled himself up on the board and lifted the sail. I looked back toward shore; we were a long way out, and I wasn't looking forward to the swim in. "Hang on," said Emerson. I got a firm hold on the back of the board, Emerson set the sail, and suddenly I was yanked along the water like I'd been tied to a motorcycle.

When he first moved in with Willie, I used to hate Emerson Chang. Not only had he gone through Stanford Law sixth in his class, not only had he spurned the family firm until he'd proved himself on his own, not only did he run every morning and lift weights a couple nights a week, not only was he handsome, amiable, intelligent, modest, and good to Willie and her daughter, not only, in other words, was he almost infuriatingly perfect, but he also wrote stories, good tight little stories in pidgin, that seemed to capture the life of these Islands in a way I never could. As I got to know him better, I realized that he had some faults: He drank a bit more than was good for him, and argued with Willie all the time, although it is almost impossible not to argue with Willie.

The one thing Emerson was not, however, was talkative. Which led me to believe he'd been more shaken up by falling off the board than he was letting on. Because, despite the fact that it was terribly inconvenient, especially for me, to have a conversation while being towed in, Emerson wouldn't shut up.

"Willie's going to make fun, I just know it. Just like my mother, just like her. Chinese mothers are supposed to pamper their sons, but mine used to make fun of me whenever I didn't do what she wanted. She used to hate it when I surfed in high school. Good Chinese boys are not supposed to waste their time surfing; they're supposed to graduate top of their class from Iolani. So every time I got the smallest bit hurt, she'd start in making fun of me. I suppose now Willie's going to be on my case. You think you inevitably marry someone who's just like your mother?"

"Willie isn't like your mother," I said. But I swallowed a lot of water so it came out "Willie glug akkk spit mother."

"Yeah," said Emerson. "Just like my mother, except louder, of course. More merciless. They say if you get divorced you marry the same woman over and over. Is that true? You seem a lot happier now you're breaking up with Diane. But this is twice around for you, right? You must know a thing or two about the ways of the heart. How come you married your first wife?"

"Passion," I said.

"How come the second?"

"I thought I was being sensible."

"And neither worked," said Emerson. "Figures."

A gust of wind jerked the sail, the board leapt forward. Rather than be dragged choking through the water, I let go. Emerson, leaning back on the board, holding on to the sail with two hands, shot toward shore. I swam quietly after him.

When I finally reach shore, Emerson is sitting on the beach, being comforted by Willie. The Beast is awake and crying. "She just woke up," says Willie.

"Hello, Beatrice," I say. "What's wrong?"

"Juice," she says and stretches up her arms to be carried into the house. I heft her up into my arms. "You're getting too heavy to carry," I say. "Juice," she says.

"You all right?" I asked Emerson, who is holding a towel to his wound.

"Fine."

He looks a little pale, sitting on the sand, Willie's arms around him. I carry the Beast up to the house. Lisa, wearing a red bikini, looks up from the table where she is chopping vegetables for dinner and smiles, "Hello."

It is the same Lisa, Lisa Tanabe, who watched the suicide almost a year ago. Since then she's gotten out of school, broken up with her boyfriend, extricated herself from the clutches of the evangelicals, moved out of the house into her own apartment, and into my arms. We have been lovers for almost four weeks now, ever since I spotted her one evening at the McCully Zippy's, eating chili rice. I cannot look at her without feeling stunned. Her face is still astonishingly beautiful. The first time I ever took her out of one of the long, shoulderless, flowered sundresses she favors, I was shocked at how little there was of her, how nice what there was was. Her skin is honey-brown from the sun; she looks like long, sweet strand of butterscotch toffee.

What is she doing here? Making dinner. It's her turn. As I set the Beast down on her own two feet, Lisa's knife flashes diagonal slices from a daikon. All around her are little saucers full of cut green onions, bamboo shoots, bean curd, garlic, watercress, peppers, ginger, eggplant.

"Looks like a ton of food," I say.

"We'll eat."

"Lisa, Lisa," says the Beast, stamping her legs up and down on the carpet. "Juice, juice."

"You want juice?" says Lisa. "Hang on a minute."

"I'll get it."

Both Lisa and I go for the refrigerator. "You look wonderful," I say.

"A little burnt from all that tennis this morning." She points out the red on her shoulders. "I wish we could stay here forever. I can't believe that in a few days I'll be back writing publicity brochures for HMSA."

I put my arms around her when I see the Beast climbing a chair to get at the table. I figure she, insatiable, is about to grab a handful of food, but—and by this time I'm already moving Lisa aside and moving toward the table—she goes straight for the knife Lisa left on the cutting board. "Don't!" I scream, and defiantly Beatrice picks it up by the blade and holds on tight, pulling it away from my grasp. She screams, but she won't let go of the knife, so fixed is her intention of keeping it away from me. I don't want to fight her for the knife, for fear she'll cut herself worse. "Daddy," she screams at me angrily. She's telling me to leave her alone. Finally, she seems to realize I am not causing the pain in her hand and flings away the knife, which clatters to the table. A drop of blood, then another spatters onto the white daikon. I grab her hand; she is still fighting me; there is a cut straight across her palm. She hits me with her free fist, then throws herself into my arms.

I carry her over to the sink and unfold her hand under a stream of running water. She starts to sob. The cut is deep, but not too deep. I try to hand her to Lisa, so that I can get the bandages and the antibiotic cream out of my suitcase, but now she screams and won't let me go. Lisa goes to find the bandages. In walk Willie and Emerson. The Beast starts screaming all over again.

"More blood," says Emerson. "Must be some punk rock fashion. She OK?"

"I turned my back for two seconds and she grabbed the knife." I am thinking of what Diane will say.

"Kids always grab exactly what you don't want them to," says Willie.

"Want to be blood brothers?" Emerson asks the Beast. He uncovers the cut in his right eyebrow. It is still bleeding heavily. The Beast screams.

"Maybe I should have said blood sisters," says Emerson. "Blood persons. I think I better lie down. I feel a little woozy."

Lisa reappears with the plastic bag full of first aid stuff. I put cream on the Beast's wound and, fighting her to keep her hand open, wrap it in a clean white bandage, taping it down with adhesive tape. "All better," I say. "Hurts," says the Beast and begins picking at the ends of tape, trying to get the bandage off. "She going to be OK?" asks Lisa.

"I think so." But by the time I get the kid into the shower to clean up the rest of her and get the sand and blood off me, I am sure that if I don't take Beatrice to the doctor, Diane will fix me with a stare so chilly that my heart will freeze. After our shower, Lisa reading the kid a story on the couch, I sit down with the skinny Kauai phone book and start calling doctors. It is Saturday afternoon and after a dozen phone calls, I have managed to contact a dozen answering services or, more probably, the same answering service a dozen times. At last I get a cheerful-sounding doctor named Honey, whose office is in Princeville. He takes checks and credit cards, he says, and will wait for us in his office. We shouldn't have any trouble finding it.

"We're going to take Beatrice to the doctor," I tell Willie.

"Wait a minute," says Willie. "We're coming with you."

Dr. Honey, when we found his office sandwiched between the gift shops and resort boutiques, was in his youthful fifties, slim, tanned, dressed for tennis. He had a vaguely British accent and a rapid, businesslike manner. He only glanced at Beatrice's cut hand, although unwrapping the bandage was enough to send the Beast, who was calm all the way here in the rental car, into hysterics once again. "Clean wound, not too deep. You scrubbed it up well, I suppose. No problem. Now, now, don't cry. You're a pretty little girl. Healthy lungs, though." He re-wrapped the bandage around her hand, then turned to Emerson, who was half-leaning against the wall, trying to look casual. "Let's get you on the table. You're going to need a few stitches along that eyebrow. Surfboard?"

"Windsurfer," said Emerson.

"Leaves the same kind of marks."

Emerson, pale, climbed onto the green vinyl examining table and lay down, crackling the paper cover underneath him. "I'm going to ask you all to leave," said the doctor to the rest of us. "Can't stitch with a steady hand if I'm worried about one of you fainting on me." He gestured at the door.

For the next half-hour I pace the tiny waiting room, my arms growing heavy as I carry Beatrice back and forth, trying to keep her calm. The moment I stop moving, she resumes her crying. Willie, too, is restless, sitting down, flipping through a magazine, jumping back up, pacing to the door through which she can hear Emerson's muffled voice. Lisa is busy cutting pictures out of a magazine with her nail scissors. "What are you doing?" I ask. When she hands the pictures to the Beast, the baby quiets immediately. I let her down to the floor and she arranges the photos in patterns on the carpet.

"Where's Pretoria?" Lisa asks, pointing to the doctor's framed medical diploma.

"South Africa."

Emerson emerges through the doorway, a neat square of tape over his shaved eyebrow. "Very stylish," says Willie.

"I need the checkbook." Willie hands it to him out of her purse. "How much do I owe you?" he asks the doctor.

"About ninety should do it," says Dr. Honey amiably.

Scowling, Emerson writes out the check. "Thank you," says the good doctor. "Always glad to help someone out. Remember: No alcohol, and if you have any of these symptoms, call my service right away." He hands Willie a mimeographed half-sheet of paper titled *Warning Signs of a Concussion*. "If he starts acting loony, bring him back, won't you?"

"Maybe we should just leave him," says Willie. "Otherwise we'll have to make a dozen trips."

Emerson glares at her. The doctor looks puzzled, then realizing it's a joke, laughs harshly, sending Beatrice back into tears.

"Why did you come here from South Africa?" Lisa asks the doctor as we are leaving.

"Had to get out before the blood bath. Besides, it's paradise here." He smiles at Emerson. "Of course, no place is perfectly safe."

That night, the Beast asleep in her own room, Lisa's five-course Chinese dinner all consumed, we sat at the table talking story. Emerson was wearing sunglasses to hide the growing bruise around his eye. Willie started teasing him about going Hollywood. Emerson mentioned her weight. Willie countered with what a pig he'd been at his cousin Nalani's wedding. As long as they were talking about Nalani's wedding, Emerson said, they might discuss Willie's unpleasant remarks to his Auntie Ethel. "I think 'Stuff it, you old fool' was a bit harsh, don't you? I mean, she's a sixty-year-old woman with four grandchildren. You could show a little respect."

"Haoles aren't filial," said Willie.

Lisa's small foot banged my shin under the table.

"We're not talking about ancestor worship here," said Emerson. "We're talking about common courtesy."

"Lisa and I are going to take a walk," I said.

"Have fun," said Willie, waving us away. She poured herself another glass of wine and turned to Emerson. "If you think I'm going to sit there and let her lecture me about how selfish I am for not having more children—I don't care if she is your aunt, Emerson."

I checked the Beast—sleeping soundly—and stepped outside with Lisa. The night was still, the beach empty, the only sound the soft susurrus of the surf. Overhead hung a plump yellow moon, nearly close enough to touch. As we crossed the beach, the moon seemed to hang more and more heavily above our heads.

"The moon is famous," said Lisa.

It struck me funny. Of course the moon was famous. It was the same moon everywhere, looming over Bayonne, New Jersey, lowering over Wiesbaden, dominating the night sky of Jakarta, Beijing, Osaka. The moon, goddess of all our lunacy, well known in all times and places.

"No," said Lisa. "The moon at Hanalei is famous." She began singing a song in Hawaiian: "Ku'u Ipo Ka He'e Pu'e One."

"Is that about the moon at Hanalei?" I asked.

Lisa smiled. "I forget the song about the moon. This one means, 'My love is an octopus on the sands of the beach.' Funny, yeah? My love is an octopus."

Tangled in each other's arms, we walk along the waterline under a moon as large and threatening as love. The water is warm, and finally I cannot resist stripping off my shorts and launching myself into the water. When I look back, Lisa starts to lift her dress, hesitates—there is no one more modest, in public, than Lisa—then with a quick scan round the deserted beach, pulling it over her head, dropping it on the sand, she runs for the water, arms crossed over her small breasts. As we swim, tiny microorganisms in the froth around us phosphoresce and our bodies are outlined with light.

When we return dripping to the house, Willie and Emerson have retired to their room, their voices still raised in a good-natured quarrel. Lisa and I shower, slip into bed. With two arms and two legs apiece we turn ourselves into love's eight-limbed octopus until, tired, we fall asleep.

Morning, bright and cheerful. I wake up before seven, without a trace of tiredness or a hangover. Lisa breathes softly on the pillow next to me. I listen to the sounds of early morning and realize that Beatrice is awake, playing in her bed. She is a good kid and has learned that adults are unpredictable when roused too early in the morning. She always amuses herself for a while before demanding everyone else wake up. I struggle out of bed and fetch her. "Daddy!" she screams and launches herself out of the bed into my arms.

I get both of us cleaned up and outside in our swimming suits before we wake anyone else. Once I set her down, the Beast runs toward the water, her little buns bouncing in her red Wonder Woman swimsuit. In the early morning light she looks cherubic, round and pink, and filled with joyous energy. But I am not one to confuse children, especially my own, with angels. Beatrice is as human a creature as I have ever encountered: vain, greedy for her own pleasure, impatient, ignorant. She doesn't understand that the waves to which she runs so eagerly can drown her. Or that knives will cut her, that falling off the porch will break her small bones, that cars will destroy her with a quick bump. She does not understand on this tender morning that love is an octopus ready at any moment to seize her heart and pull it under.

Nor does she understand that she is soon to be shuttled 5,000 miles every six months from one parent to the other. Diane is worried that living in Hawaii will distort her picture of the world. Diane has a point. What do you tell a child who has run across the sands at Hanalei that will prepare her for New Jersey?

I run after her across the beach, one of my strides covering as much of the white sand as four of hers. Within moments I am beside her, scooping her up into my arms. "No," she cries and beats on me with her bandaged fist. "Got you," I say and tickle her stomach. She shrieks and throws her arms around my neck. "Leggo," she says and clings tighter. I carry her toward the gentle line of surf.

There is much also I do not understand. I do not understand why this small creature clinging to my neck loves me so uncritically, and why my love for her seems to transcend the pain of our circumstances. I do not understand why all of a sudden I have Lisa, the most tender and beautiful of lovers, lying sexy and asleep back in the house. I do not understand why there should be a place as perfect as Hanalei Bay, radiant in the still cool morning air. And I do not understand why I, of all the world's miserable hundred millions, should be standing here, my daughter around my neck, fresh croissants and coffee waiting for me back in the house, surf curling round my toes, happy.

The Red Dust of Lanai

STEVE HELLER

Shigeo Masuda wheels his battered green jeep into the tiny parking lane in front of the Lanai Lodge. He swings out of the vehicle with the rough grace of a sturdy young man who has just put in a full day in the pineapple fields. Antomino is waiting for him sprawled in a wicker chair on the glassed-in porch.

"One hot day down on the plain, eh?" he greets Shigeo falling into a chair beside him.

"You said it." Shigeo rubs the back of his still grimy neck for the hundredth time today. It has been a tough afternoon operating the boom spray. Twice the main tank developed leaks, drenching a quarter acre of ratoon crops with hundreds of gallons of insecticide. The smell lingers with him where he sweats feverishly beneath the tanks to cease the drain of valuable chemicals. But he knows Antomino understands and will say nothing.

"You want to smoke?" Antomino offers him one of the blunt black cigars he always carries in the pocket of his flowered shirt. Shigeo shakes his head. Tobacco in the late afternoon makes his throat parched and raspy. Antomino shrugs and lights one for himself. Antomino is in his late fifties, lean and tan with an expression that seems at once good natured and calm.

Shigeo regards the relaxed figure intently. He thinks of Antomino as someone he can count on. It was Antomino who taught him how to hunt wild goats in the island's cavernous gulches—how to patiently squeeze off a good shot instead of firing excitedly at the first sighting. And it was Antomino who gave young Shigeo the keys to his own jeep to challenge the steepest rocky trails of Mount Lanaihale shortly after his father died—a bizarre feeling of detachment that engulfed Shigeo's mind like a narcotic.

Later, when he began to work in the pineapple fields after school, he grew accustomed to seeing the Filipino's enormous rust-colored flatbed truck rumble by, raising above the fields copper red clouds that slowly melted into the sky. And it seemed Shigeo could never drive down Frazier Avenue in the evening without noticing the red tip of Antomino's cigar in the shadow of the tremendous Norfolk pine blackening his small front yard.

In the past couple of years, however, Shigeo has encountered Antomino only occasionally at the lodge. The Filipino sold his tiny square iron-roofed house and is now living on the island of Maui. The transition has become important to Shigeo.

Antomino leans back after a preliminary series of puffs on the black cigar. His forehead contains four deep wrinkles that squeeze together whenever he lifts his eyebrows.

"Things pretty quiet here, eh?" he asks.

"Yeah, the same. You go Maui again soon?" Shigeo's eyes follow the wisps of smoke upward. He wishes the drifting haze could soothe the taut muscles in his neck and back.

"Maybe tomorrow. Maybe next day." The Filipino flips an ash neatly into the empty paper cup on the table beside him. He says no more, but watches Shigeo closely.

"Tell me, Antomino," Shigeo says finally. "You drive a truck here twenty years. You buy a house. You raise kids. Now you run round like hell. Why?"

Antomino crosses his legs and watches another guest emerge from the south wing and walk past the two men to the small indoor window marked "Office and Bar," where she orders a beer. He looks back at Shigeo and his expression grows more distant—the way he looks when talking about the old days.

"You know most of it," he begins. "Before Anita die she say, 'Take care Ernesto.' This I promise. This I have always done. But then Ernesto—he four, five years older than you—he join the Army, go fight Vietnam. He get back OK, but now he go school one more time Los Angeles. Get on the GI Bill. So I say, 'Antomino, you released from your bond. The Army take care of Ernesto now.' So I look around and say, 'Now time to start over. Now time to see old friends. Now time to start something new.' "

He pauses as the lady walks past again with a can of Olympia. She sits down at the end of the porch and stares out. Antomino looks down abstractly at his feet for a moment, then continues.

"So one day I go back Maui. I grow up there, you know. I go back Wailuku only second time twenty years. Stay two, three days. Never see nobody I know. Then one day I go this little bar on Mill Street, name I forget. New place. Most the old places gone now. But this place I find old friend from before the war—Herbert, Hobart, something Gonsalves—I never know his real name. We call him Turkey, cause he's always squawking about something. Used to live Paia. That guy was a gambler and a good pool player. But when he was Paia he never work. Lay the pipe—odd job like that. Just like chain gang. Would be rich a couple months, you know."

He shakes his head and grins at Shigeo, who nods. Shigeo has only been to Maui twice to visit his cousin. He knows the place mostly from Antomino's stories.

"He was a terror, that bugger," Antomino goes on. "Used to get two, three wahines, go drink Wailuku. One time we all go one hotel Wailuku. Drive down from Paia. Who the hell was in the car—Lureen, I think. This before I know Anita. Turkey, he go pass out—drive the car right off the pier. Shee, that car was in bad shape! Top all smashed. Rest of us, we're OK, but Turkey, he cut his leg bad. When I see that blood I thought he die for sure. That one tough bugger. We wrap his leg up and he say, 'Go back hotel— make love now!' Crazy, you know."

Antomino punctuates this judgement with a wink.

"But Turkey, he settle down later. Get him skinny Filipino wife. Pretty wahine. They all the time together still. They move Wailuku, and Turkey, he get himself a taxi car. Drive rich tourists all over hell. Fifteen years ago now. Now he got whole fleet taxi cars. So he say to me, 'Antomino, what you do now? You still drive that truck Lanai?' I say yes. I already tell him Anita dead four years. He tell me, 'maybe time now you come back with us, eh?' I say, 'maybe so.' "

The wrinkles squeeze together as he looks through the window glass.

"I think it over long time, you know. Twenty-two years I been Lanai. Drive the truck. Make good friends—know *everybody*. Hunt on the mountain. Have a damn good time. But I think about it and I decide this island just no damn good without Anita. I decide maybe I start over. Drive the taxi car. Once a while I come back Lanai. But it's not the same for me."

Silent a moment, he looks at Shigeo and smiles. "You stay for dinner?"

The question breaks off the young man's thought and he jerks his head slightly before answering.

"No, uh, I can't. Six o'clock I meet Maxine. She move to Honolulu next week, you know."

Shigeo looks at the older man. Slowly, through a slight tightening of the stomach muscles and a moist chill on his arms and shoulders, Shigeo feels his own image brought into focus. *Hold it steady now and remember just to squeeze. Wait till the bugger raise his head . . . OK, he see you.* Awareness of the change in body chemistry slowly dissolves, but the link remains. Antomino regards him steadily and responds.

"Maxine go school some more, eh?"

"Yeah, she go to the university—be big businesswoman."

Antomino nods. "She want you to go Oahu with her?"

"Yeah," Shigeo answers, meeting Antomino's eyes. "She like me to go."

A pause. The woman at the end of the porch has finished her beer, but Antomino takes no notice of her.

"You worried about Oahu not the same like here, eh?"

Shigeo says nothing, but Antomino continues.

"One thing I know—everything change no matter where you go. Lanai not the same for me now. Anita and me, we meet over here when I come drive the truck for Dole. After that we together all the time, you know? Anita and Ernesto, they always the best part of this place for me. Lanai not the same without them. But when I go back Maui, I go back something not the same too, you know? More people, more problem—just like Oahu. But I think maybe drive the cab I forget, eh?" He shakes his head. "Those days gone for good, but I remember still. Lanai, Maui, neither one the same for me now. So maybe better I never leave. Maybe not. Who can say?"

Shigeo rubs his eyes. His back is beginning to ache where he sprained it working underneath the boom spray tank.

"What would you do if you go Oahu?" Antomino asks. "Go school somemore too?"

Shigeo laughs. "I wonder, you know. Maybe take agriculture—become great scientist. Or maybe business—become a tourist. Ride around in your taxi car."

They both laugh. Shigeo looks through the glass at the lengthening shadows of the Norfolk pines outside.

"I got to go," Shigeo says finally, standing up. "Maybe I come by tomorrow after dinner. You still be around?"

Antomino looks at the lady in the chair. "Maybe I be here."

Shigeo smiles, then pushes open the white doors.

The air is cool as it blows through the evergreen branches above him. Shigeo is thankful for the elevation and the pine trees of Lanai City that create the mood of a cool mountain village. It was hot today down on the dry pineapple plain of the Palawai Basin. On his seat atop the boom spray he felt the dust settle on his body as it mixed with the insecticide coating his skin and the sweat working up underneath, until it formed a grimy film that completely clothed him. He must have seen at least ten pheasants and countless quail today. From his vantage point on the boom spray he would line them up in imaginary rifle sights. Twenty birds had fallen on the red roads and rusty-green pineapple leaves of the basin—a good haul.

He swings into the jeep, and, after considerable gear grinding, starts down the brief hill to the heart of Lanai City. Sides are being chosen for some sort of frisbee game in the park where he is to meet Maxine later. Mrs. Hirayama waves as he passes Lui's and the "Dis 'n Dat" Store turning onto Ilima Avenue.

Shigeo has often wondered what will happen to the tiny business district and the twenty-five hundred people it supports when they build the hotel. It could go up any time now. But this island is different, they say. The company has a plan. "Limited growth," they call it. The basic character of the island will remain the same. Hunting, fishing, agriculture. They all say that. They are phasing out pineapple on Molokai. But the company only leases those lands, he reasons. It's more expensive to operate there than on Lanai.

Shigeo's small two-bedroom house lies near the end of the street back toward the highway into town. A note on the door says his mother is at the Pine Isle Market where she has worked once or twice a week since his father died. He sheds his clothes as he heads for the bathroom and a needed shower. Standing in the tub, he lets the water spray weakly at first, watching the dirt peel off his skin in brown-edged waves.

Maxine has not arrived when Shigeo pulls up in front of the bowling alley on the south side of the tiny park. Feeling refreshed, he props his feet on the passenger seat and watches the kids toss a couple of frisbees around. Shigeo figures he knows most everyone on the island except some of the younger kids, so he watches with curiosity, trying to pick out unfamiliar faces.

He is distracted a few moments later when he sees Kiyono emerge from Lui's and cross the street toward him. Kiyono is about the same age as Shigeo; shirtless with a deep tan and wearing plastic sunglasses. Kiyono operates a crane on the dock at Kaumalapau Harbor. His uncle had the job until he ripped the ligaments in both knees and had to take early retirement. This is the busy season on the the dock; today probably well over a million pineapples were loaded on barges headed for the big cannery in Honolulu.

Shigeo raises his hand in greeting as the shirtless figure walks silently over to the jeep and leans in the passenger side. Kiyono speaks first.

"Ey, how come you don't throw the frisbee, man?" he asks, glancing back at the kids in the park.

"Bad arm," Shigeo pleads, rubbing his shoulder.

"That's OK," Kiyono laughs. "Everybody too tired for play tonight. Hey, you see that big buck Richard shoot yesterday?"

Shigeo shakes his head.

"Big bugger. Must go one-eighty. Tomorrow I go hunt the big ones Kuahua Gulch. You want to come?"

Shigeo stares into the shadowy reflections of the plastic sunglasses. He and Kiyono often hunt the small axis deer in the brushlands in and above the gulches that dissect the northern arm of the mountain. Their fawn-like spotting helps them blend into the surrounds, and it is a good hunter who can catch a buck silhouetted against the horizon for an open shot. Shigeo has brought down three with his Remington.

"Mmmm. Maybe," he says at last. "Tomorrow Saturday. Maxine may like us do something. I ask her and let you know."

Shigeo always asks.

Kiyono gives a shrugs that says "no big thing," and begins punching at the glove compartment button.

"Maxine still go Honolulu?" he asks as it will not fall open.

"Yeah, she go."

Kiyono says nothing, but gives up on the glove box and watches the frisbee game, which appears to be breaking up.

"I see you later, man," he says finally. "I think that's her coming now."

Shigeo nods as he watches Maxine approach from across the park, a slim figure in light blue shorts and a blue print blouse that ties around the middle. Charcoal brown hair hangs long behind her back. She approaches with a well-measured pace that exhibits neither reluctance nor enthusiasm. Shigeo has noticed this quality before: Control. A grip on the drives and passions that could wrench the course of her life from her own hands. "Tough wahine. She wear you down." That's what his friends all told him when they first started seeing each other.

Yet it was not always so. Sure, she would listen to him with a kind of respectful detachment when he described the things he loves about Lanai. And she firmly put him off that day at Manele Beach when he reached for her beneath the swelling surface of the waves.

But there were other times. Like the late afternoon when the storm caught them jeeping the rugged Munro Trail high atop Mount Lanaihale, where the planted pine trees draw moisture from the clouds to replenish the dry plains below. The wind blew cold as they huddled amid thrashing tree ferns and she sought the warmth of his body tensing beneath the damp canvas cloth covering them. The wind that day seemed to drive them shivering deep into the moist earth of the mountain's crown.

Lately the sober image is stronger. Her decision to leave for the University of Hawaii is well reasoned and firm. "No future here," she complains. "Not for me to pick pineapples and run cash registers." Shigeo's swelling sense of loss is compounded by the sting of these arguments.

He moves his feet as Maxine climbs into the jeep. They regard each other silently for a moment. Her smile, soft through gently curving lips, subdues the more intense expression of her eyes. Anxiety, affection, strength—Shigeo feels conflicting patterns of force impress his body in a bizarre mesh.

"Where you want to go?" he asks quietly.

"I don't know. You pick."

"Manele Bay?"

"Oh, Linda and Yoshiro down there." She looks at Shigeo, who says nothing. The frustration in her voice is quick and sharp. "No place to go on this island. Nothing to do and everybody watch."

Her words are a trigger mechanism. Shigeo feels the conflict snap on with a short electrical burst that could swell into anger momentarily. His voice is firm. "We'll go Garden of the Gods."

"It's hot and dirty there," she protests.

"Nobody around and we can watch the sunset," he says, intending to argue the point no further.

Maxine makes no reply, but begins to put her hair up with a clip. Shigeo reaches for the keys.

The Garden of the Gods lies seven miles north of the city, past the cultivated land. Shigeo wheels the jeep expertly over the rough red pineapple roads, boiling up red clouds of dust that pursue the vehicle like the trail of a rocket blast. By the time they pass through a brief forest of ironwood and eucalyptus trees and into the small canyon of the Garden itself, the fine particles of dust have swept over their skin and clothing like smoke, working down into pores and garment fiber like a stain. Shigeo drives over the reddish-brown iron-rich volcanic sand and around the boulders and occasional gray scrub brush atop the low gully ridges, until he reaches Three Mormon Rock, a gray silhouette of three hatted figures staring solemnly across the channel at the island of Molokai.

He pulls the jeep off the trail, laying blurry tread marks across the rippled sand. Shigeo is at home here in the natural rock garden. He will sometimes come here alone in the late afternoon to watch the setting sun splash prismatic colors across the canyon like a rainbow pressed into the earth.

He leans back into the seat and surveys the arid canyon. The sun is low in the sky and its glare offers no view toward the sea. Maxine, sitting upright, looks vacantly through the windshield. Shigeo's eyes return to her rigid figure. He takes her hand.

"Want to talk?"

With her other hand Maxine reaches into her purse for some kleenex. Finding none, she wipes the dirt off her face with her hand, leaving white finger marks on her forehead.

"Have you thought about going to Honolulu?" she asks, finally looking back at Shigeo.

He does not want to talk about this. He wants to stare into her eyes and call to life the sensations that underlie their relationship. But she resists. The image remains impassive, though Shigeo can see a flicker of intensity in her eyes. Honolulu? School? Shigeo hates school with its chalky words and numbers. What is there for him? Here he has his work and his respect. Only last week Lorenzo said he was in line to become supervisor of the boom spray operation. That means more money and responsibility.

"Have you thought about it?" she repeats.

"Yeah, I think about it a lot." He squints into the sun. "But I don't know. I don't see what good it do me."

"What good to stay here?" she snaps back. "You going to spray bugs the rest of your life? Let them run you round: 'Over here, over there, Shigeo!' And what happens when they don't plant the pineapple anymore? You going to guide tourists around?"

Shigeo exhales slowly, releasing some of the anger welling up inside. Maxine watches him for a time before the softness returns to her eyes.

"I want us together," she says.

Shigeo leans forward and finds her lips moist, pressing urgently. He moves with strength, enveloping her with his arms, pressing against her. The weight of his embrace forces her breath and she gasps. He rocks back and freezes for a moment on the fingermarks on her forehead. *Drive up the high trail where the stones shake away everything you know. Let the mountain take you.* Her eyes are open and pleading. His awareness poised over an invisible precipice, he sinks slowly back into the driver's seat.

Gutted. Minutes pass before resolve fills the void and his muscles regain control. He looks over at Maxine holding her head in her hands.

"Let's go back," is all he can say.

The jeep erupts into life and Shigeo winds it around the shadow of the Three Mormans back toward the trail home. The sun still well above the horizon, he wheels the jeep through ironwood and eucalyptus and back into the pineapple fields when a white puff of steam escapes from the hood.

"Shit!" He pulls to a quick stop in the dust and raises the hood, now more gray than green. The whine from the radiator cap is now clearly audible as steam sprays out around the neck.

"Overheated," he says, walking around to reach the plastic water jug in the back. "We got to wait a few minutes."

Maxine says nothing, but stares in frustration at the propped hood. Shigeo walks around to the front again and listens to the decreasing whine.

Leading the tourists around. No, it can't come to that.

He looks over the fields. On this side of the road the pineapple stretches all the way to the horizon, but there are no other jeeps or trucks in sight. Out of habit he leans over and begins to inspect the rusty-green leaves for mealy bugs.

On a nearly mature plant he spots an ant carrying a dust speckled mealy bug down the leaf of a shoot growing beneath the fruit itself. He remembers how amazed he was when he learned how the ants cleverly move the bugs from plant to plant—before signs of the wilting disease they produce begin to show. This could be an old bug, however, being carried off to slaughter because it no longer secretes the sweet substance the ants love to eat.

It doesn't matter, though. He will have to spray here in a few days.

The whine has stopped. He tests the pressure cap with an oily rag. The boiling subsided, he empties the precious two gallons of water into the thirsty radiator. He climbs back into the driver's seat without a word. Maxine is smiling now, and Shigeo returns her affectionate glance as the jeep lurches forward once again. As they drive toward Lanai City, an oasis of pine trees on the edge of the plain, he knows what he will do.

Tomorrow he and Kiyono will go hunting.

The Pool

JOHN DOMINIS HOLT

It was perhaps as large as a good-sized house. It tended to be round in shape. At the far southern end of Kawela Bay, it sat open to the wind, the sun. Scattered clumps of coconut grew around it, splashing shade with the look of Rorschach ink blots here and there at the edges of the water.

Fresh water fed into it from underground arteries, blended with warmer water pushed in by the tide from the sea through a volcanic umbilical cord. "The lagoon," as we called it, had a definitive link to the sea, being joined as it was by virtue of this unique tubular connection.

We were always afraid of "the lagoon." For one thing it was alleged to be so deep as to be way beyond anyone's imagination—like the idea of endless space to the universe or the unending possibilities of time. Its dark blue-green waters were testament to the fact of the pool being deep according to our elders. We accepted their calculation, but not entirely. It was deep to be sure, but not depthless.

Within "the lagoon," huge ulua, a local variety of pompano or crevalle, would suddenly appear in ravenous groups of three or four, chasing mullet in from the sea. Once in the confines of this small body of water the mullet were no match for the larger, carnivorous predators. Ulua could grow to the size of three or four feet and weigh nearly a hundred pounds. The mullet feasts by ulua in the lagoon were wild and unpleasant scenes. We would watch as children, both enthralled and frightened, as mullet leaped for their lives in glittering silvery schools of forty or fifty fish, some to fall with deadly precision into the jaws of the larger fish. The waters swirled then and sometimes became bloody. The old folks said this would attract sharks. They would wait at the opening of the tube in the ocean to prey on the ulua, whose bellies now were fat from feasting on mullet. These tumultuous invasions were not frequent, but they were reason enough to keep us from swimming in "the lagoon." Perhaps most fearful to us were the tales we heard offered by assorted adults that a goddess of ancient times inhabited these strange blue-green waters. Some knew her name and mentioned it. I have forgotten what it was. She was said to be a creature of unearthly beauty, a queen of the Polynesian spirit world, who revealed herself at times in the forms of great strands of limu, a special seaweed growing only in brackish water, her appearance depending on tides, the moon, winds, and certain cosmic manifestations we could not completely understand because they were mentioned in Hawaiian.

I wandered by the hour in the area of "the lagoon" and on the reefs nearby with an ancient, bearded sage who was our caretaker. His hut of clapboard and corrugated roofing sat near an old kuula, a fisherman's shrine, half-hidden under some hau bushes. His people had been fishermen from time immemorial. Some of his relatives lived a short distance down the coast toward Waimea Bay. Infrequent visits were made upon the old man by these ohana; usually three or four young men came to consult him about fishing. His knowledge of the North Shore and its inhabitants in the sea was vast. Once or twice a year he paid a ritual visit to their little house standing in its tiny lawn surrounded by taro patches and sheltered at the front by clumps of coconut and lauhala trees. He spent hours explaining in Hawaiian, and in his own unique use of pidgin, the lore of the region, mentioning with distaste his wine-drinking nephews. I was only four or five years of age at the time. Much of his old-world ramblings is now lost to me.

But I do remember him mentioning that the sea entrance to "the lagoon" was too deep for him to take me to it. He was too old now to dive to those depths. He secretly led me to the kuula, a built-up rock shrine, round in shape, where we took small reef fish and crustacea we had speared. We would pray; the old man in Hawaiian, I in a mixture of the old native tongue and English. It was being impressed upon us now we must speak perfect English. The use of Hawaiian was discouraged. After prayers we would leave offerings on the kuula walls, walk to "the lagoon" where more prayers were said and the remaining bits of fish thrown into the pool as offerings to the beautiful goddess.

All of these activities fell within a definitive framework of time and circumstance. These were not helter-skelter rituals. I obeyed without question and I declared it untrue when confronted by my mother—whose father, a half-white, had lived for years as a recluse in the native style in Iao Valley—that the old man of Kawela was teaching me pagan ways.

In horror one day I heard the old man say "hemo ia oe kou lole—take off your clothes," which consisted of a pair of chopped-off dungarees.

"Hemo ia oe kou lole e holo oe a i'a i ka lua wai—take off your clothes and swim like a fish across the pool." My body froze and goose bumps formed everywhere on my skin.

"Awiwi—hurry."

I stood in sullen defiance, thinking: He is an old man, a servant. He cannot order me to do anything, anything.

"Au, keiki, Au! Swim, child, swim! Do not be afraid. They are with us."

I remained motionless.

"Auwe, heaha keia keiki kane? He kaika mahine puiwa paha?—What is this child, a frightened girl?"

Thoughts came to me of past fishing expeditions when I clung to the old man's back and he dove with me into holes filled with lobsters and certain crabs. He would choose as time allowed, pluck them from the coral walls, hand me two. Then, I could cling to him with only the use of my legs. In time I learned to rise to the surface alone, clinging with all my might to the two lobsters the old man had handed me. What excitement the first of these expeditions created! I leaped and danced around the crawling catch. We went down for a second take. Again two were brought up. On the reef above they were crushed, one then left as an offering on the kuula walls, the other fed to the akua in the pool. I was four or five then and wild with joy.

There were other days when he took me to great caverns swarming with fish of such brilliant colors you were nearly blinded by the reds, yellows, greens, blues and stripes. Above on the reef he would name them for me. Patiently he named them, these reef fish, aglow in cavern waters: the lau'ipala; the manini; the uhu; the ala'ihi; the kihikihi with its black, yellow and white stripes; the humuhumu with its blue patch on throat and vibrant yellow and red fins.

On one very special day, a sacred day in his life and mine as well—for I was linked to the family gods, the aumakua—he took me, clinging to his back, to the great sandy places under the sharp lava edges of Oahu's North Shore, to the places where the great sharks lazed in the light of day. Breaks in the lava walls sent shafts of light to sandy ocean floors and there we could see the sometimes-dreaded monsters rolling from side to side in harmless, peaceful rest. Shooting up to the surface, the old man would breathlessly tell me the names of this or that shark—names given them by his contemporaries.

"Why names?" I would ask wonderingly.

"Are they not our parents, our guardians—our aumakua? Did you not see the old chief covered with limu and barnacles? He is the chief, the heir of Kamohoalii. I used to feed him myself and clean the opala from his eyes. Now a younger member of my clan does that."

I could not absorb these calm, reassuring concerns of denizens I had been taught to dread from early years.

But had I not been down in their resting place, close enough to see yellow eyes, to almost feel the roughness of their skin scraping like sandpaper across my arms?

My dreams were wild for several nights and my parents, worried, held several conferences with the old man. He was chastened, but at my insistence we went several times more to the holes under coral ledges to see the aumakua lazing in the daytime hours.

And now, frozen at the edge of the green pool, I looked hatefully at this magnificent relic of a Hawaii that was long vanished. I loved him. There was no question I loved him deeply. Ours was a special kind of love of a man for a child.

I was blond-haired. Exposed for weeks to the summer sun when we made long stays at Kawela, I became almost platinum blond.

The old man was bearded, tall and thin. Still muscular. He was pure Hawaiian. Blond though my hair might be and my skin fair, I was nonetheless three-eighths Hawaiian. I think this captured the old man's fancy—often he would say to me in pidgin, "You one haole boy, yet you one Hawaiian. I know you Hawaiian—you mama hapa-haole, you papa hapa-haole. How come you so white? You hair ke'oke'o?" He would laugh, draw me close to him and rub his scruffy beard against my face as though in doing this he would rub some of his brownness off and ink forever the dark rich tones of a calabash into my pale skin.

It was love that finally led me to loosen the buttons of my shorts and kick them off and race plunging into the green pool. I swam with all the speed I could and reached in what seemed a very long time the opposite side. When I turned around, the old man was bent over with laughter. I had never seen him laugh with such gustatory abandon.

"Look you mea lii-lii. All dry up. Like one laho poka'o ka'o—like an old man's balls and penis. No can see now." He pointed and made fun of my privates, shrivelled from a combination of cold water and fear. I turned away from him and raced home, naked.

Four days later I walked past the pool, across the sharp lava flats to the old man's hut. Flies buzzed in legion. The stench was unbearable. I opened the door. Lying face up and straight across his little bed, the old man lay in the first stages of putrefaction. Sometime during my absence the old man had died. At midday? In the cool of night? In the late afternoon, the time of lengthening shadows and the gathering of the brilliant array of gold-orange and red off the coast of Kaena to the south facing the sea of Kanaloa? When did the old man die? Why did he die? Tears began to stream down my cheeks.

I shut the door of the shack and went to sit in the shade of the hau branches near the kuula—my heart was pounding so I could hardly breathe. What should I do? Tears rolled in little salty rivulets down my cheeks. I enjoyed the taste when the moisture entered my mouth at the corners of my lips.

What should I do? Some instinct compelled me not to go home and tell my family of the death of the old man and the putrefaction that filled the cottage. Perhaps I was too stunned—perhaps it was perversity.

The family was gathering for a large weekend revel. Aunts, uncles, cousins —all the generations coming together. Usually I enjoyed these congregations of the family. There would be masses of food, music, games and the great lauhala mats spread on the lawn near the sand beach. Someone would make a bonfire and the talk would begin. I would sit at the edges of the inner circle of elders as they ruminated on past events. Old chiefs, kings, queens, great house parties—scandals and gossip of one sort or another would billow up from the central core of adults and leap into the air like flames. I absorbed the heat of this talk and greedily absorbed my heritage for they spoke of family members and their circles of friends, mostly people from royalist families, the Hawaiian and part-Hawaiian aristocracy during the last days of the Monarchy. I heard of this carriage or that barouche or landau, this house or that garden, this beautiful woman in love with so-and-so, or that abiding "good and patient" soul whose handsome husband dashed about town in a splendid uniform, lavishing on his paramour a beautiful house, a carriage and team, and flowing silk holokus fitted finely to her ample figure. O, the tales that steamed up from those gatherings on lauhala mats at Kawela's shores!

One of my great-aunts, an aberration of sorts, came once in a while for the weekend. She brought a paid companion and her Hawaiian maid. She looked like Ethel Barrymore and talked with an English accent. Her gossip was spicy, often vicious, and I loved it. She fascinated me as caged baboons fascinate some people who go to zoos. She was also forbidding. I thought she had strange powers.

Often the old man had joined us during these family gatherings, and I would sit on his lap until I fell asleep.

There was something of great warmth and unforgettable charm in these gatherings. Even as the talk raged over romances, land dealings and money transactions long passed, I revelled in hearing about them and loved everyone there, particularly those who talked. There was an immense feeling of comfort and safety, of lovingness for me on those long nights of talk.

But now under the hau branches I scorned my family. I hated them. I held them responsible, for some unknown reason—a child's special reason I suppose; inexplicable and slightly irrational.

I decided not to tell them of the old man's death but to run down the path along the beach to the house where his relatives lived. I would tell them. They must rescue him from his rotting state; they must take him from the tomb of his stench-filled shack. I ran down along the beach, sometimes taking the path pressed into winding shape from human use in the middle of grass and pohuehue vines.

The men were at home, mending fishing nets. This was a good sign. I ran to the rickety steps leading upward to the porch where they sat working at their nets.

"The old man is dead," I said forcefully.

One of the young men looked down at me.

"Ma'ke."

"Yes, he's ma'ke. His body is stink. He ma'ke long time." They put down their mending tools and came in a body to the top of the stairs.

"How you know?" one of them asked.

"We just came back from Punalu'u. I went to the old man's house. I saw plenny flies. I open the door and see him covered with flies. It was steenk." I spoke partly in pidgin to give greater credibility to my message.

They fussed around, called into the house, held a brief conference and faced me again.

"You wen' tell anybody?"

"No, nobody."

The four men took the path at a run. I was under the hau bushes, catching my breath, when they flew past me heading back to their house. I sat for what seemed like hours in the shade of hau. My sister appeared at the side of the pool. I ran to fend her off. She caught the stench from the shack.

"Something stinks."

"The old man has fish drying outside his shack."

"Where is he?"

"Down on the reef fishing."

"When are you coming home?"

"Pretty soon."

"Mamma is looking for you—Uncle Willson is here with those brats," she referred to his adopted grandchildren. Uncle Willson was a grand old relic. Something quite unreal. He was brimming always with stories of the past.

"Aunt Emily has arrived with Miss Rhodes and that other one," my sister added, referring to the maid whom she hated.

The cottages would be bulging and perhaps tents would be set up for the servants.

My sister swung around abruptly and took the path back to our cottage. She was always purposeful in her movements.

"Tell Mamma I'll be home soon and kiss Uncle Willson and Aunt Emily for me."

"Don't stay too long. You'll get sunburned."

I walked past the pool. It seemed purer in its color today. Deep blue, deep green. I was crying again. The stench filled the air with a stronger, punishing aroma as the sun rose high and began the afternoon descent beyond Kaena Point. I walked along the reef; the tide was rising. I peeked into holes the old man had shown me, watched idly the masses of fish swimming in joyous aimlessness it seemed.

What ruled their lives? There was life and death among them. They were continually in danger of being devoured by larger fish. Some grew old and died; I suppose they die of old age.

Death. Such an angry, total thing. There was no escaping it. I looked back at the shack and shook my fists. The old man's nephews had returned with gleaming cans. They poured the liquid which filled them all around the little house. I rushed backed to the hau bushes as two of them threw lighted torches of newspaper at different places around the shack. Soon it was in flames which leaped to the sky; as the dry wood caught fire, it crackled angrily. The flies buzzed at a distance from the blaze as though waiting for it to die down. The heat was intense. The smell of burning rotting flesh unbearable.

I ran from the hau bushes toward the pool. One of the men saw me and yelled, "Go home, boy. Go home."

"Git da hell outa hea, you goddam haole," another one shouted. I was angry and stunned in not being accepted as a Hawaiian by the old man's nephews.

I ran around the pool at the side we seldom crossed. My family was massing nearby to watch the fiery spectacle.

"What's happening, son?" my father asked with more than usual kindness.

I ran to my mother and hugged her thighs.

"The old man is dead. I found him. He was stinking. I ran down to tell his family."

"And now the bastards are burning him up," my father said. "It's against the law."

Aunt Emily had arrived on the arms of her companion and maid. Her handsome face pointed its powerful features to the center of the burning mass.

"What is happening?" she asked in Hawaiian.

"Our caretaker died. Been dead for several days. The boy found him."

"What are they doing?"

"It's illegal. They're cremating him without going through the usual procedures."

Aunt Emily blasted forth with a number of her original and unrepeatable castigations. Everyone listened. They were gems of Hawaiian metaphor.

Uncle Willson and his man servant arrived.

"The poor old bastard finally died. He was the best fisherman of these parts in his younger days. No one could beat him. As a boy he was chosen to go down to the caverns and select the shark to be taken to use for the making of drums. His family were fishermen. One branch was famed as kahunas. He was a marvel in his day."

"But Willy," Aunt Emily was saying in a commanding tone. "Those brutes are burning his body. The boy here says it was rotten. He'd been dead for several days. The whole thing's a matter for the Board of Health authorities. The police should be called."

"No, no!" I screamed.

"Emily dear," Great Uncle Willson intervened. "He is one of us. His ohana, those young men, are a part of us. Leave them alone. They are doing what they think best."

I had gone from my mother to my nurse Kulia, a round, happy sweet-smelling Hawaiian woman.

"No cry, baby. No cry. We all gotta die sometime. Da ole man was real old."

"Not that old," I whimpered.

Aunt Emily cast one of her iciest looks at me.

"Stop that snivelling. Stop it this instant. What utter foolishness to cry that way over a dirty, bearded old drunk."

She turned to my mother.

"This child was allowed to be too much with that old brute. I think his attachment was quite unnatural—quite unnatural."

"Another one of your theories, Aunt Emily," my mother snapped.

"Not a thing but good common sense. Look at him clinging to Kulia and whimpering like a girl."

Kulia took me away. We walked on the beach.

How I hated Aunt Emily's Ethel Barrymore profile and her English accent.

Late that day, in the early evening, the old man's nephews came back and carried off his charred remains in the empty cans of kerosene. No one ever found out what they did with them.

When did the old man die? Why did he die? This I will never know. We called him Bobada, but I remember from something Great Uncle Willson said on the night the shack was burned that Bobada's real name was Pali Kapihe.

"God Sent You into That Gomorrah This Morning to Bring up the Truth"

JOHN DOMINIS HOLT

The men had come to capture alligators that were—according to a friend of a friend of the telephone operator at the Forestry Office—thriving in the entanglement of jungle and swamp in our deep gulch.

"Please come in," I offered. "Come in, and sit down! This needs some explanation!"

"There is no need for explanation. We just want the alligators. We've brought fish nets and a couple of guns that we'll use, if it is necessary. You know, of course, that it is illegal to keep alligators in Hawaii?"

"I am perfectly aware of this, and I am afraid you would feel pretty silly if you went down into the gulch with all your gear, only to discover that there are no alligators—no, not one!"

"We've heard from good authority that there *are* alligators here," volunteered the tall thin haole in the group of four men.

They came in now, wearing the gray look of patient suspicion. As logically as I could, I reconstructed the saga of Pauline's alligators: perhaps in not as full detail as this reportage, for I doubt if their patience would have endured some of the more abstract or surmised elements concerning Pauline's bizarre *idee fixe*. However, it is still a puzzle to me how they could have left us with the same sober and patient mien that they wore upon their arrival, after having been convinced, finally, that, perhaps, there were no alligators in Halekoa gulch.

Our property was a large one, substantially covered with tropical growth. Several mango trees—immense, dark, and brooding—occupied a space between the two main dwellings: one, our house; the other, an arrangement for guests. It was past a hundred years since the oval hirsute seeds of mango had been put into the dark island earth by a horticultural-minded ancestor, to grow above ferns and ginger into the giants they had become. In their advanced state of age they had assumed majestical elegance—mammoth sentinels, watching over the life of the murky and wet gulch, no-man's-land for

39

the children of the family for generations. The large pond, choked in spots with the growth of pink lotus and water lilies of many colors, reflected portions of the forms of one group of the mango trees, a cluster of four growing at the mauka, or upper, end of the property.

Water oozed from a number of unpredictable spots in the basin of the gulch. The area was so lavishly endowed with artesian springs that the two large ponds were never dry. This abundance of water created the perfect environment for the growth of aquaceous plants and should have provided a sumptuous haven for exotic waterfowl, snakes, and other reptilia, had such creatures been extant in the islands of Hawaii.

The gulch also provided a treasure trove of possibilities for the imaginative, the speculatively inclined. Its darkness, the lavish vegetation, its wetness gave to it an aura of the mysterious, promising all sorts of vaporous happenings should one wish to explore the nebulous twistings of growth: hau, guava, Java plum, and miles of maile pilau, that odoriferous and malignant vine which grows with such vigor—such tenacity—in almost every *milieu* of growing condition in the islands. I, myself, had nurtured for years a secret hope that we would someday find a small colony of proboscis monkeys, quietly undergoing existence in one of the darker corners of the area. Usually only the gardeners penetrated the muck and thickened growth of the gulch, venturing into it to cut stalks of bamboo or to collect the massive waxy and powerfully symbolic blossoms of torch ginger.

Sections of the amorphous tangle had been wrested gradually from nature and brought into the orbit of the garden scheme. My grandfather had begun a botanical collection: mainly fruiting trees, bamboo varieties, and water-loving plants. It had assumed a sort of catch-as-catch-can order as his scheme took shape. New paths and stone steps were set along the steep banks of the house side of the gulch. A wide grass passage was kept meticulously groomed around the ponds; and whole areas of the marshy bottom of the gulch began to burst with the growth of numerous ginger varieties, and other stranger plants imported from distant, impossible places—the warm tropical corners of the earth around.

Gradually, one whole side of the gulch had been developed into gardens. Cunning elusive paths meandered through groves of two or so dozen varieties of bamboo, or under the spreading round-leafed canopy of *Macaranga grandifolia,* or through densely massed *Monstera deliciosia,* clinging to the sharp banks. At one section, the paths wandered through a marvelous jungle of *Ravanela,* the traveler's palm of Madagascar, whose massive leaves from a distance suggest the foliage of a giant banana.

Our old friend, Pauline Irwin, could not resist imbuing the gulch with a

Then, too, she gave whole nations of people specific physical or emotional attributes, based on the observations she had made of individual representatives with whom she had been in contact, or from something she had read. The English were haughty and austere, tall and stately, built on the prototypes of Wellington, Melbourne, Queen Elizabeth, and the gorgeous ladies of Gainsborough's canvases; but they all suffered from anaemia and certain respiratory diseases. The dumpy plainness of the nuns at the Priory and their superb good health had done nothing to destroy the illusion. The Chinese people, who came from regions bordering the great rivers, had skins that were scaly because of the abundance of a very scaly fish in their diet. The people of India were all thin and bony because their religious beliefs compelled them to sit around in temples all day to fast and smell incense. Nothing cast a nation lower, in Pauline's estimation, than if some of its people burned incense in connection with worship. Combining the inhalation of aromatic essences with spiritual worship bore for Pauline a most obscene connotation.

Houses suffered brutally under Pauline's sensitive urges and responses. Every house in which she had spent any length of time unleashed certain strong emotions in Pauline. Although there would be many details connected with each in her mind, they fell into two general categories: the ghostly, and the non-ghostly. Armed with the category into which she placed a particular house, she would extol or condemn, taking great pains to describe the emotions she had felt at each visit. A house was "clean" if it did not effulge ghostliness; it was lepo, or soiled, if it did. A certain house in Nuuanu, where she had spent weekends with an elderly cousin, was the "Queen's bed's house." There she had slept in a massive, ornate bed, which a Hawaiian Queen had brought from Paris in the 1860s, and was not told its history until the following morning. She lived in horror of her cousin's house ever after. "That awful house of my cousin Kalani, and that awful bed!" Forty years later, she still squirmed with fear, speaking of the house, the bed. In another house, there could be a room, or a passageway, or a door, that contained the supernatural element. "Victoria Arlington's old house is haunted! Makaʻu loa ke ia hale! A frightening house! The door leading from the bedroom hall to the living room opens mysteriously at night—even after it has been shut tightly! I saw it happen twice!" Pauline had repeatedly told of her experience in the Arlington house, concerning one of its hall doors.

It had been generally conceded that in the conglomerate of oddities of thinking that filled Pauline's mind, her fear of our gulch at Halekoa was just another oddity, like her insisting the fruit of the *Monstera deliciosia* contained seven distinct flavors miraculously intact in the single fruit: lemon, lime, pineapple, strawberry, orange, banana, and one other which she could never remember.

So, when Cousin Aileen went into the gulch that day, determined to explore every cranny and nook in search of ginger blossoms, papyrus, and water lily blooms, it was natural that Pauline should declare Aileen insane, on the spot:

"Have you lost your mind—to go into that Gomorrah? Why, my dear, it is infested with evil things!"

"I have wanted to explore it for years! It's been such a hotbed of mystery! I've never been down to the other side of the gulch—only on the grass paths. This is my chance! Besides, we need flowers for the New Year's party!"

"I'll buy flowers from the florist for the party!" Pauline offered quickly.

"O, no! You *can't* just *buy* some of the treasures that grow down there. It's like Africa, or the jungles of Brazil—all those choice, imported plants!"

"And they're all poisonous—evil—like so much that is found in Africa and Brazil."

"Really, Pauline," Aileen snorted in exasperation. Then, seizing the moment, she suggested, "Since I'm determined to go down into that gulch, I promise to bring you a detailed account of everything—*everything!*"

"That's fine. I'm going to stand watch at the top of the trail and wait for you to return. If anything happens, you be sure to yell for help. I've been told one's hair can turn white in a moment with fright, and you have such beautiful hair! I would just hate to see it change color now." Pauline became a little breathless with the anticipation of inevitable disaster. Her bronchi rattled under the impetus. "Really, Aileen, to do this at your age. You ought to be ashamed!" She wheezed and coughed, producing sounds like those made by antiquated gas waterheaters in London.

"I've told you a thousand times, we've all told you, there is nothing to be afraid of in that gulch. Nothing!" My mother had come upon the scene, and, overhearing Pauline's last dire remarks, she had felt compelled to make again the statement of reassurance she had made hundreds of times before. "It's absolutely safe, Pauline! Absolutely!"

"That's what you think, Emma Newton! I lived in this valley as a young girl with my old uncle and his wife—for many a summer! You know, Uncle Henry, he could tell, you remember, if the telephone rang at certain times— even before answering it—that it would be a call telling us that someone had died. Well, he ordered us to keep strictly away from this gulch. *You* only came here after you were married. You don't know the true history of this place!" Then, as if she were struck by a divine power with profoundly revealing insight, she said softly, but emphatically, "Why, do you know, there is even a bed of quicksand in that gulch!"

In all the years—the centuries of man's inhabiting of the Hawaiian Archipelago—there is no evidence that anyone has ever discovered the existence of such sand, *anywhere,* on any of the islands that comprise the chain. Mud? Yes. Sand? Yes. But quicksand?

My mother went about her business, leaving Pauline to her odd prognostications and Aileen to her foraging. So many times she had patiently attempted to divest Pauline Irwin of some of her untenable fancies, fearing that someday they would lead her, willy-nilly, into madness; but Pauline stubbornly kept the lurid impaled on some cornice of her mind. It had become a part of the fabric of her awareness at all times. She lived for the noble purpose of surviving the fearful. Life was an endless concatenate of bizarre threats from the world of the occult. To live was largely a matter of meeting the challenge of these threats; it was a fixed element of one's sense of responsibility.

She believed that hairy children—part ape, part human—inhabited the jungles of Sumatra. Somewhere, she had read, and believed, an account of mermaids being seen off the coast of Patagonia; and, years before, an aging British countess, who had passed through Hawaii after an exploring trip through Australia, had mentioned to Pauline the possibility of Paleozoic monsters being still extant in the vast interior of that distant continent. After being given this fascinating morsel of intelligence, Pauline suffered perserverating thoughts in which a giant beast kept dipping its vast head into slimy water, bringing up stringy bunches of seaweed after each thrust—a clear-cut image, exceeding the chimaera impressionism of a dream.

And, yes, there were sea monsters, and werewolves; and every phony charlatanic story resulting from the excavation of Tutankhamen's tomb Pauline accepted as the truth, *carte blanche.* She was an encyclopaedia of information of the sort which endlessly filled the pages of the *American Weekly* for a generation, or so, in the late Victorian times.

But for us, the most absurd of Pauline's soaring fantasies was her belief that there were alligators in the gulch at Halekoa. For years she had mentioned, always rather furtively, the possibility of this being so. Her obsession had begun from something her great-aunt had told her when Pauline was a little girl and would come to visit her relatives in the valley of Halekoa. The old woman had whispered something to the effect that my great-grandfather had brought giant lizards from somewhere in the Orient and had planted them in the gulch of his property which lay across the street from theirs.

Roaming, adventurous Englishmen were specialists in collecting exotica. Some of the old alii, Hawaiian nobility, who had traveled to England had returned to Hawaii, telling of the odd collections of plants and animals they had seen at the estates of the great lords whom they visited. After years of attempting to discourage Pauline in this belief that my grandfather had planted alligators in his gulch, members of the family circle tacitly agreed to allow her the fiction. My cousin, Aileen Ragsdale, in later years had remarked, "It's a wonder she hasn't carried this gruesome illusion outside the family." Oddly enough, she had not.

And then, on this day preceding our annual New Year's party, Aileen set out upon her venture of flower gathering in the gulch, taking two of the gardeners as a sort of gunbearer and his assistant *entourage!* Pauline had insisted that Aileen not go unprotected on this safari. Carrying *machetes,* pruning shears, and sharp sickles—all implements useful in gathering up the kind of tropical bloomage Aileen was so determined to collect—the little caravan made its descent into the dark marsh.

"Please take good care of yourself, my dear," Pauline had called out wistfully. "And remember, if anything happens, you must call for my help."

She envisioned the gaping, dripping jaws of a massive reptile, lying hidden in the ooze of the lower pond, poised for a quick attack upon Aileen: an image which flushed up in her mind the memory of what the peeress of Britain had told her of prehistoric creatures roaming the interior of the Australian continent.

But Aileen's venture into the gulch this morning was in keeping with her background. It was in line with the bizarre and radical antics of some of her forefathers. And the fact that my family should maintain such a property as the gulch kept intact the purity of idiosyncratic tendency, so far as we, the Newtons, were concerned. We were strange creatures, all!

I could walk the trails, and oversee care of the extensive plantings of exotic, luxuriant, moisture-loving vegetation, without evincing more than a small statement of caution from Pauline. I was young and strong and could resist any lurking dangers. Besides, it was my duty! Anyway, I was male; and, being so, a little of original sin lurked, also, in me.

We were curious families: the Archers and my family, the Newtons. All kinds of funny people were in both families, and now they had been joined again, for the first time in sixty years, with the marriage of my sister Cordelia to Aileen Archer Ragsdale's eldest son Archer Ragsdale. Pauline had heard, most of her life, of the antics of the old governor, Aileen's grandfather, and various other Archer antecedents. Then, too, there was all the talk of my great uncles; especially Uncle Timothy Newton, who had lost an eye brawling in some tavern when he was a young boy at school, which necessitated forever after his wearing a black eye-patch.

Pauline shivered when she thought of the old Newton ranch at Mikilua: the strange menagerie that had collected there, of monkeys, peacocks, macaws, and what had seemed to her to be an army of vicious dogs. She had visited the ranch only twice, as the guest of my great aunts, who had been her classmates at the Priory school. Her memory of the sprawling house, its huge rooms, and the great trees which surrounded that structure was filled with almost hysterical terror.

But Aileen Archer's gesture on that morning, as she descended into the gulch, provided a *coup de grace*. Bolstered by her reminiscences, Pauline Irwin could stand at the top of the trail and weave the pattern of attributes characterizing the Archer and Newton families. There was no other way to release the annoyance. These annoying attributes related comfortably to the rest of the legendary myths that saturated her mind.

If the gulch was possessed of evil, and Satan sat over it all, it was only natural for Pauline to see an element of satanic verisimilitude in Aileen's act; or, so far as we were concerned, in the raw cruel fact that we should want to continue to own the property of which the gulch was so intrinsic a part. The thoughts occurred to her again, and again; and her mind, like a great sponge, soaked up images which they had released. These occurred with such vehemence, with such divinely instigated force, that she was helpless to suppress any of the unflattering attributes of character which this imagery cast upon the Archer and Newton families.

She plucked a fragment of laua'e fern and brought it to her nose. Its sweet fragrance soothed her briefly. The olfactory stimulus diverted her thoughts temporarily away from speculations regarding the peculiarities of the two families. "They are very peculiar people—of one stripe, they are!" Helpless, again, to effect any further restraints of her thoughts, Pauline gave in to the urge to dwell further upon the Archer and Newton oddities of behavior.

She thought of Aileen's Grandfather Archer's famous gardens in Waikiki. She had been there a number of times before the old house was torn down and its ponds drained off. Her ears, in remembering Ua-hania, were filled with the eerie screechings of peacocks and her vision crowded with the shadows cast upon the ground by the swaying branches of enormous India banyan trees. Automatically struck by their resemblance in size to the trees she remembered at Ua-hania, she looked into the great old mango trees above her. How dark and brooding they were!

"Evil things! They should be cut down!" she thought. "Or at least thinned out!"

She started to count the aged fruit trees, then stopped. Somewhere from the recesses of her mind, a thought leaped out, telling her that it was bad luck to count. Bad luck to count . . . "Aileen," she called out. "Are you all right?" There was no answer.

Then, with a force to equal loud peals of thunder, flashing of lightning, and the cruel push of rushing waters, her thoughts shaped into a new design:

Today she would know! Aileen would tell her the truth. She was a very straightforward woman. She would know, for a fact, today, if there were alligators in that loathsome gulch. And if there were alligators in the gulch of Halekoa, it would be the final triumph of her having faithfully kept this macabre truth dancing on the fringes of her mind for all these years.

When Aileen returned, at last, weighted down by armloads of ginger and heliconia, she presented a picture of bucolic excellence.

The gardeners who had accompanied her followed, carrying stalks of papyrus, and a number of huge lotus blossoms, and pads that would dry fast and wrinkle up into fascinating clusters.

"Thank God, you're safe, Aileen! I was worried sick!"

Pauline had stood watch at the head of the trail for more than an hour. She quivered with hope for the report verifying her precious knowledge of one kind of the gulch's inhabitants.

Aileen, muddy and wet all over, put down her waxy surrealist burden. "I left my cigarettes here, someplace." She rustled her hands searchingly through some of the laua'e fern leaves.

"No, they are here." Pauline pointed to a moss-covered rock. "I picked them up and put them there."

Aileen recovered the cigarettes, took one slowly from the package, tamped one end of it on her thumb, and then, with further deliberation and what seemed to Pauline needless ceremony, placed it between her lips and lighted up. The whole act, although not taking more than a brief minute of time to accomplish, seemed to Pauline to consume an hour.

"Tell me, for God's sake, tell me! What did you see?"

Aileen inhaled a deep draw of smoke, and blew it out slowly. She asked a gardener to take the flowers to the house. When he had gone, she turned to Pauline, took another draw on her cigarette, and, after exhaling the smoke, said, "I saw an alligator. In fact, I saw two. One was on the trail, the other in one of the pools."

Praise God from whom all blessings flow! Here was verification! Her old tutu had told the truth! "Aileen, how marvelous! I mean, how horrible! But tell me— the one on the trail—did you touch it?"

"I certainly did! It was only about three feet long. I turned it over with this stick!" She pointed to a stick she had cast aside when she had searched for her cigarettes.

Pauline's eyes followed the gesture. Quickly the thoughts came, and the words rushed out: "Tell me, then, tell me, was it a boy, or a girl?"

Aileen, at this point, could barely prevent a telltale smile from shaping on her face. "So far as I could tell, it was a boy! A bouncing sturdy little boy alligator!"

Pauline was near crying; her eyes were moist, but, somehow, there was no evidence of an impending asthmatic attack. In spite of her state of joyous triumph, the affliction had won a temporary respite.

"At last, I know this to be the truth!" Her voice cracked, and she firmed herself within to suppress the tears of triumph. Then she said chokingly, "God sent you into that Gomorrah this morning to bring up the truth! I have always known something evil went on down there—and now, you have come back, having run smack into an alligator. And what, pray tell, could be more evil?" She gave the entangled composite of the gulch, the great mango trees, a vicious leer that was at once reproachful and triumphant.

"Let's hurry back to the house, my dear. I must tell Emma and, besides, you ought to be getting out of those wet clothes."

The tall haole had sat expressionless as I related the fantasy of Pauline and the alligators. No matter to what lengths of detail and logic I went in an attempt to explain away this strangely-tinged matter, hoping to preserve some dignity for ourselves and the Forestry Office men, they did not accept anything I said by word, smile, grunt, or any other visual or auditory kind of response.

Adventure had been promised—adventure in fulfilling the routine demands of duty—and now—

"I'm sorry you came all the way down here and went through all the trouble of loading your gear."

They rose in a chorus.

At the door, the tall thin haole—he had not offered us his name—stopped short, paused, and said quietly, and very knowingly:

"I have learned, if you ever do run into an alligator, and you want to subdue him, pinch the fleshy section at the side of his jaws—the place where the upper and lower jaws meet. Just take hold of the corner like this"—he demonstrated by pinching the corner of his own mouth—"and hold on firmly. This immobilizes the alligator."

And, with this parting gift of precious information, he turned away, and walked toward the station wagon where his three silent companions had already found places in which to settle comfortably for the long ride back into Honolulu.

The Resurrection Man

CRAIG HOWES

Kona

Isaiah had been walking behind the bulldozer, checking for bones, so when it went over the ridge he didn't see the *ohana* members right away. They were sitting directly between the survey stakes marking the sides of the road corridor, and they certainly weren't going to move just yet. The dozer stopped, its blade rearing up, and Walter, the driver, told Isaiah to get Curtis from the workshed. It was a quarter-mile back, and Isaiah walked slowly, since he knew the boss would be mad. He also knew what was coming next, and that made him feel bad.

About fifteen minutes later they walked back up the slope—Curtis, the construction foreman, in the lead, the police in the middle, and Isaiah well back. Walter was still sitting on his rig, smoking, looking anywhere but in front of the blade. Sitting quietly, their *ti* leaves and *lau hala* mats ranged around them, the *ohana* didn't even look up as the police moved toward them. This was the third time the police had removed the Hawaiians from this site, so there wasn't need to say much.

Then came the moment that always made Isaiah feel worst. Ben rose from the ground and lifted his arms slightly—not pleading, not threatening, simply gesturing. The police stopped. After what seemed like an hour the sisters behind Ben got up and started walking down the ridge to the police vans below. Ben followed them down, eyes ahead, the police never touching him, and Arnold, the *ohana* lawyer, walked beside the police, talking about the road, about trespassing, about T.V.

Standing to one side, not with the crew, not with the *ohana*, Isaiah watched everyone climb into the vans. Only Arnold didn't get in: he'd been standing outside the stakes so he could bail everyone out and talk to reporters. The vans headed off down to the paved shore road, and Curtis ordered Walter back to work. The front of the dozer dropped, then started

50

scraping again, tumbling the mats and leaves over and over, mixing them with the powdery red soil that rose like a wave from the blade's edge.

Isaiah felt bad a lot these days—mixed up. He felt bad every time the *ohana* climbed up to the ledge and sat down in front of Walter's bulldozer. He felt worse when he went into town and no one would talk to him. He even felt bad when he did his job. Isaiah didn't like walking up each morning, seeing the flat roadbed gouged across the slope, the line ending at the blade of the bulldozer that would draw the ledge farther on by late afternoon. He could quit, go back to laying net some, but $8.50 an hour was more than he'd made in a long time. He refocused his eyes on the red spray spilling from Walter's metal blade.

About 3:30, the first body came up. The dozer dropped into a shallow dip, with bigger rocks than usual strewn over the surface. Walter stopped in front of a large boulder, revved his rig, and surged ahead. Seconds later, Isaiah saw some brownish sticks spill from the blade. He walked over and picked up a piece of rotten branch, maybe an inch wide and five long. He threw it down. Only then did he notice the five teeth sticking out of another piece nearby.

"Waltah!"

Isaiah didn't pick this piece up, or the other pieces he saw, curved like shards from a bowl—or a skull. Walter brought the rig to a halt and climbed down the side. He stopped abruptly when he saw what Isaiah had found.

"Shit! No more driving, maybe two days. Da boss be real piss off; a dead Hawaiian more hassle than a live one on a road. Go tell Curtis."

Isaiah stumbled down the hill, thinking through every unsolved murder, every ghost story, every scrap of local history he knew. Was he in trouble? Walter hadn't seemed scared, though he'd stayed back when he saw those bones. God, he'd touched them! When he burst into the foreman's trailer, Isaiah was more confused than he'd been up top.

Curtis *was* pissed.

"Three days, maybe four, maybe a bunch, if it's anything like that time on Molokai," he said when they'd climbed back up to the job site and looked at the pieces of bone Walter's rig had scattered over the rocky surface.

"You've got good eyes, don't you? Walter didn't see the bones, did you Walter?"

"Not paid to look. Just drive."

"Stay here and watch the bones, Isaiah."

Curtis and Walter walked away, talking low. Isaiah looked at the fragment of jaw. He wiped a finger on his workpants, then put it in his mouth and felt along the sides of his own teeth. They were slippery, and felt hard. The teeth on the ground were brown and dry; one tooth was missing from the jaw. Isaiah moved his finger to where the dentist had pulled one of his molars. The hole felt small—this person must have been huge.

Curtis came back. He stared at Isaiah for a second.

"You're Hawaiian, aren't you?" he asked, and he didn't want to hear yes.

"My mother's side. My father Portagee, but my mother half through her mother, then Hawaiian back long time."

"Shit!" Curtis said this right to Isaiah, blue eyes staring into brown. "We'll have to phone those bastards who did the impact statement. Otherwise we'll have a Hawaiian convention up here." He walked down the hill, muttering.

Isaiah turned to Walter.

"What's Curtis talkin' about?"

"Archaeologists. They'll dig da buggahs up and move 'em, so we can grade. Maui one time, da guy told me, go ahead dig 'em up with one backhoe. Real fast . . . but no Hawaiians watching that time. Eh, next time, you stay blind, brah. We work faster."

When Isaiah arrived for work the next morning, someone else was there: a tall, thin *haole*. He wore a white, straw hat; and he needed it, since without it his pale, freckled skin would have peeled like old paint. His boots were as beaten up as Isaiah's or Walter's, though more broken down at the back from squatting a lot. He didn't look like a worker—more like someone you'd see painting pictures of the bay—but he seemed at home on the site. His name was Hal, Curtis said.

Walter was pointed out the bones from the day before to him. "This was one big guy," the archaeologist said, looking down at the jawbone. Isaiah was pleased; he guessed that yesterday. Then Curtis stuck his head in.

"So you're going to move him, and O.K. the grading?"

"Not yet. I want to find out if he's got company. Those big rocks on the surface aren't landfall, and if this guy was underneath one, they might be grave markers. I'll start looking now, and have some idea by tomorrow afternoon. Would you guys move that big boulder for me?"

Walter grumbled as he and Isaiah walked toward several large rocks. "They were under rocks on Maui. Plenny hard work now."

The two men put on their work gloves, to guard against centipedes and scorpions, then pried the boulder out of the ground, picking up shovels when their hands couldn't budge it any further. When it finally rolled out, Isaiah held his breath, scared he would see a skull staring back at him. There was nothing.

Hal squatted beside the hole. With a trowel, he carefully scraped about an inch of dirt from the sides. After examining the walls carefully, he scooped the dirt into a bucket.

"Have either of you guys ever screened?"

"One time on Maui," Walter said. He picked up the bucket and walked over to a wooden frame with wire mesh stretched over it that Hal had brought. After dumping the dirt in, he picked the frame up and shook it, as if panning for gold. The dust sifted through, turning Walter's pants red.

For the rest of the morning Isaiah carried the buckets from Hal to Walter. He wished he could be two places at once, to watch Hal slowly widen the hole, and to watch Walter screen until only bits of lava and shell were left in the frame. Soon Isaiah was almost running, since he found he could watch the screening and still make it back in time to get the next bucket full of dirt. Around 11:30 he was peering over Walter's shoulder, looking at all the tiny *pipipi* shells turning up, when he noticed one piece that was even smaller than the others. Walter tossed this stuff away, but Isaiah picked up the piece he'd noticed. A tooth. Half-afraid of causing more trouble, he walked over to Hal and held out his hand.

"Maybe da guy's tooth, yeh?"

Hal took the tooth from Isaiah. He removed an envelope and a roll of toilet paper from his pack. After wrapping up the tooth and placing it in the envelope, he wrote some numbers on the outside. "That's a baby tooth, so I don't think it's the big guy's. You've got good eyes. Why don't you screen for awhile?"

Walter was mad; he'd been able to smoke a cigarette between buckets. He didn't seem too happy about Isaiah's eyes either, muttering as he passed, "You better blind, brah."

Work now went more slowly, because Hal was using a brush instead of a trowel. After lunch, Isaiah screened out a shark's tooth, some fragments of volcanic glass, and his first false alarm: a small piece of bone that Hal said was probably dog. But he put both the tooth and the bone into envelopes. When Isaiah asked why, Hal said that archaeologists liked to know what people ate, "and that shark didn't walk up here." Isaiah was soon screening as fast as he could, then walking over to the hole. He felt something was going to happen.

About two, it did. Hal was smoothing down the sides of the pit when some lighter-colored dirt fell away. Carefully touching his brush to the place, with round swoops he slowly exposed a light-brown spot that within fifteen minutes bulged an inch from the wall. "I'll bet you a beer that's your *keiki*, Isaiah. Walter, go get Curtis."

Hal covered the baby's skull with a garbage bag, and whistled as Curtis came slowly up the hill.

By four the next day, Hal had put in five test pits, all under big rocks. He was only going to do three at first, but he found bodies in two of them so quickly that he tested a couple more. More things went into envelopes—shells, other animal bones, the white bone fishhook Isaiah found in the screen. With a tape measure and survey map, Hal marked out the pits with string. Isaiah caught onto the terms right away. The first hole was now C-4, and the one with the two *keiki* bones sticking out of the walls was C-12. The only pit with nothing in it was D-9, and that was funny, since the rig Walter drove was a D-9.

None of this made Curtis very happy.

"How many do you think are here?"

"I don't know, but it's going to take some time and more people to find out. I've got seven bodies exposed, and I've just been fishing. All I can guarantee right now is that any road going through here as it is now is going to have bodies under it."

"How long?"

"Can't say. I don't have X-ray vision like Isaiah here. I phoned back to Oahu last night and told them they'd better get a crew ready. You're just lucky your accountants had to budget for this."

Curtis was heading down the hill when Hal called to him.

"By the way, I want Isaiah and Walter working on this. They can help screen and move rocks. We're as worried about the locals as you are, and a couple on the crew are good public relations. Besides, Walter's got some experience, and Isaiah's a hard worker."

Curtis didn't say anything, but when the other archaeologists arrived, Isaiah was at the airport to help load the shovels, brushes, and boxes into the jeep.

That dig was the most exciting thing that had ever happened to Isaiah. Most of the crew were female, which set him back at first. He'd never thought he'd see a *haole* woman in work boots, the dust caked on her face. Isaiah was also amazed at how much these archaeologists talked. For the first couple of days he thought they were all Portagee; always gabbing, yelling back and forth about a bone, about a new layer in the earth—"stratigraphy," they called it—or teasing each other but never meaning it. They each knew one thing best. Lucy knew the bones; Eileen, the bottles, the fishhooks, what they called "artifacts"; Mort, the kinds of dirt. Isaiah soon knew who to call when something turned up in the screen. "Hey Eileen, I got one button!"

Isaiah liked the bodies themselves best, or "the folks," as the archaeologists called them. The bones were brittle and often crumbled when moved, so each body was brushed clean, measured, and photographed before the archaeologists lifted the bones out of the earth, wrapped them in newspapers, and placed them in long cardboard boxes like the ones flower shops put anthuriums in. Isaiah thought he'd be scared but he wasn't, even when they removed the garbage bags covering the half-exposed bodies each morning, and he saw beetles running out of the eyeholes in the skulls, or when they found one body in a coffin with the backbones scattered and a rat skeleton lying next to the hips. Sometimes he wanted to cry when he looked at a completed *keiki* burial, the little skeleton all curled up sleeping on the dirt, or when he saw the little woman with the *keiki* lying below her ribs, and Lucy said she died when she was pregnant.

After awhile, Hal let Isaiah actually get into the hole and dig. Toothbrush and dental pick in hand, he soon found himself slowly uncovering a leg bone. Hal said, "The body you find is yours to finish." He watched for a bit, but after lunch he went back to his own work, and Isaiah was left alone. He was afraid of doing something wrong, but he soon stopped worrying, and concentrated on uncovering the body slowly. People who worked too fast were called "butchers."

Isaiah soon was digging all the time. He found he could slip his brush down between the ribs without breaking them, and he quickly learned how to work his way slowly around the body, brushing until it lay on its own little table of dirt. Sometimes the bodies were a mess, the bones were scattered through the soil. Three bodies might be mixed up, and starting from the edges, Hal and Lucy and Isaiah would work slowly with their brushes, meeting over the knot of bones at the center.

The summer slowly passed, and Isaiah worked on. He was amazed that for three whole months now some very dead Hawaiians had been able to stop both Curtis and the road. Hal told Isaiah that by law any construction project had to pay for an "Environmental Impact Statement"—a report that described what the development was going to destroy—and if any signs of human bones or buildings turned up, then the contractors had to bring in archaeologists. Curtis once suggested that things might go faster if they just dug a big hole on the other side of the survey stakes and dumped everything into it. But the archaeologists kept brushing, screening, measuring, and photographing, slowly revealing Isaiah's past.

And with each day, Isaiah felt more strongly that it was his past, and not the archaeologists', that was being uncovered. The others treated the folks with respect—no dead body jokes, no fooling around with the bones—but Isaiah knew he was closer to these bodies than anyone else. As a child he'd heard stories about long-ago Hawaii, and he'd thought sometimes about those ancient people fishing, or planting taro on the stone terraces still dotting the slopes. But the early Hawaiians had seemed unreal and flat to him—people painted on a wall or tapped into a rock, who would disappear when they turned their shoulders to the sun. Now he held their bodies in his hands.

Sometimes he thought about what he'd look like buried, and whether he'd want Hal digging him up. Isaiah decided he wouldn't. If anyone brought him back to the surface, he'd want it to be someone like himself—another Hawaiian, or at least part, who had laid net off the reef, who might be family, who would be glad to know that he'd been there too. Isaiah started thinking that whenever someone built a road, or a house, or a 7-11 store, everyone should have to stop for three months to think about the people—and not just the Hawaiians—uncovered and moved elsewhere.

On the last day, after Hal felt certain all the bodies had been found, Isaiah drove up to a church nearby for the reburial. He didn't have to go, but he wanted to see the end, since he'd been there for the beginning. Only a couple of the archaeologists attended; the rest had returned to Oahu. The little wooden boxes were lying side by side in a long trench Walter had dug with his backhoe in the corner of the cemetery. Though most contained the bones of people buried long before Cook came to Hawaii, the minister said the bodies were "asleep in Christ," and he spoke about shepherds and pastures, although the church stood on a rocky slope looking out on the bay so far below. Walter turned on the backhoe, and with a roar it pushed the pile of dirt back down into the hole. Tears streamed down Isaiah's face, and he turned his head away for shame.

He was still wearing his work pants, and when the others turned to leave, he walked over to the new mound and turned his pockets inside out. Three months of dust drifted down, placing his people under the dirt they had been under so long.

On his way back to town Isaiah stopped at Ishikawa store and bought a shovel, a bucket, a whisk broom, and three toothbrushes.

East Maui

Hal was puzzled. He stood on a slope side, looking down at a body the backhoe had uncovered. Around him were boulders, grouped around the body almost like a miniature Stonehenge. This was the second time in a week he'd been here, the construction site of an office building for real-estate agents, dentists, and doctors. The similarities between this burial and the last one, some hundred feet away, were too striking to be merely accidental. Once again the bones seemed almost too clean. No clumps of dirt adhered to the shaft ends, no roots coiled around the long bones. And yet the bones were old—probably prehistoric. Hal guessed that the test pits he would dig under the surrounding rocks would turn up nothing, that this body was a single burial like the last one. He'd taken two days to test the area around the other burial, but with this one he'd just put in a couple of pits, and if nothing turned up he'd give the O.K. for construction to continue.

He squatted down to begin removing the body, glancing idly at the survey stake a few feet away marking the front corner of the construction site. Suddenly, he had a hunch he couldn't wait to test out. He borrowed a survey map from the foreman, and sure enough, the stake he'd noticed near the first burial marked the back corner of the site. Hal walked quickly to the other back corner. He found what he was looking for immediately: a few boulders scattered over the surface, circling a big one well set into the ground. He pushed the rock and almost fell over when, with no resistance whatever, it flipped out of the hole. With his brush, Hal moved easily down through the four inches of recently disturbed fill that covered the skull.

He stood up and stared seaward. Either the ancient Hawaiians had seen the corners of the construction site in a vision, or someone was using the survey markers to map out his own cemetary. Hal didn't even bother checking the fourth corner but headed immediately for the phone.

Leeward Oahu

It was a sunny day at Barber's Point—just a few clouds coasting down from the mountains. A fleet of limousines and military vehicles lined the sides of the dirt road, down near the shore. A hundred people were clustered together on the dead coral, some wearing three-piece suits, other decked out in full-dress military uniforms. After the endless introductions and expressions of thanks, the governor, a red carnation *lei* draped over his charcoal-grey suit, lifted the microphone from the portable P.A., and spoke.

"I think it's a wonderful thing that this project is now ready to go ahead. The people of Hawaii join me in congratulating those who have worked so hard to make this project possible. It's good to see we can work together, but in Hawaii, people have always worked together to make a special place. *Mahalo* to Colonel Frisbort and the many men who have worked so hard to make this a reality, and *mahalo* to those people, in government and in the business community, for their efforts. When the Hawaii Military Center for Business and Technology is completed, we will have something we can all be proud of."

There was a flurry of activity as reporters gathered around a piece of ground marked off with stakes and plastic streamers. The governor walked to his position between the colonel and the bank president. An aide presented each man with a silver spade, then they lifted their heads for the photographers, smiled, and drove their shovels into the earth.

The governor had never seen a skull before.

Hawaii Nei

The next two months would be remembered as the summer of the dead bodies. They turned up everywhere: in condo developments on Maui; just under the sand that bulldozers pushed seaward to extend Waikiki; even in the valleys, where city workers dug ditches to carry the runoff from upstream. Construction companies hired security guards to watch sites round the clock. The Carpenters' Union offered a reward of $10,000 for information leading to the arrest of the "The Undertaker," as the media now called him. Composite drawings of any suspicious character seen buying a shovel appeared on the front page of the newspapers—almost all looked like Jimi Hendrix. Callers on phone-in shows could talk of nothing else; everyone from Martians to the former mayor was a suspect. People threw chicken bones into uncut lawns, hoping to teach lazy neighbors a lesson. Children buried each other under palm fronds, then played construction worker. Two fly-by-night mortuary companies offered to bury people in concrete, and crematoriums doubled their business. Honolulu went into a frenzy when police arrested a man burying his just-murdered wife in a playground sandbox. Within a month, over thirty bodies appeared—all in construction sites. Within six weeks, reporters from every major newspaper on the Mainland had filed stories.

As the first person to have figured out The Undertaker's ways, Hal found himself in the thick of things. Crackpot callers threatened him with death; others reported seeing armies of people marching past their front doors, carrying bodies and shovels. Many confessed to the crime—these calls usually came from asthmatic old men.

Despite these distractions, Hal had figured out some patterns. The "victims" had all been dead for at least fifty years, so The Undertaker was a graverobber, not a murderer. Nor were the bodies all Hawaiian; in fact, they seemed to represent every ethnic background—the long, robust bones of

Polynesia; the slender bones of the East; the gold teeth and slightly curved long bones of Europe and white America.

The Undertaker was also very selective in his targets. Although Honolulu had the largest count, all the other islands had incidents—except Lanai, whose residents seemed almost disappointed. Most of the bodies were buried where they'd be uncovered immediately—the governor's experience was the most embarrassing example—but a couple had been stumbled upon only by accident. This promised new discoveries extending far into the future, each one stirring up again the complex feelings now pulsing through the islands.

What puzzled Hal most was where The Undertaker was getting his bodies from. Each one was clean and complete, with no evidence of the previous resting place other than the reddish color of the Hawaiian bones, buried without a coffin before or shortly after Cook. The bones were neatly placed in the earth, resembling the ancient Hawaiian bundle burials. Hal checked out the study collections at museums and at the medical school, but nothing was missing. These bones must be coming out of the ground, and someone was removing them carefully.

Hal also felt sure that The Undertaker had ended his campaign. Nothing suggested that any bodies had been buried after the first ones were discovered, and nothing was coming out of high-visibility locations any more. Hal felt frustrated at repeating "I don't know" to every question coming from the police, the press, the governor. But one thing he was sure of—The Undertaker had singlehandedly created the biggest flap about development Hawaii had ever seen. At times Hal had to catch himself from admiring his opponent; he often wondered why no one had thought of this before.

Kona, toward Kohala

Some time later, Isaiah was driving along the highway, getting ready to make the turn up to his tin roof shack; up the slope he saw a jeep and three police cars parked out front. Hal was sitting on the hood of the jeep. Isaiah turned off his signal and kept driving. Miles up the coast, the sun drooped to his left, and the wind stopped blowing down from the mountain. At this time of day everything seemed sharper: he could make out every branch, every thorn on the *kiawe* trees.

He pulled off the main road, taking a dirt road upward, then turned up a side path almost hidden by brush. After bumping along for a few hundred feet, he came to an old metal gate held shut by a rusty orange chain. Isaiah had cut through the lock long before. He got out, opened the gate, and drove the car through. He picked up a rusty old padlock from off the dash, walked back to the gate, and locked it for good. He hadn't driven up here for about a month, and the path was once again almost hidden by weeds and tall grass. He drove up the path to where it ended, a few feet from the edge of a high ridge. He looked down at the canopy of trees hiding the valley floor from view. Putting the car in neutral, he reached in and let off the parking brake, then pushed. The car plunged out of sight; he stood there until he couldn't hear any more noise. No one would find him now.

He climbed upward past small terraces—some ancient house sites, some little farming plots, covered with lantana and *kiawe*. He carefully avoided a long open slope, burned out by a brush fire. You could see it from the road, now hundreds of feet below. When he reached the rocky overhang, Isaiah found his way to a sharp cleft, the only path through. As he came closer to his goal, the trees were larger, the undergrowth more tangled. He could hear the songs of those Hawaiian birds that now only lived high on the upper slopes. Up here the ground became dangerous. Cracks, sometimes only three feet across but hundreds of feet deep, lay hidden beneath the ferns and fallen leaves.

Although he had made this climb many, many times before, he was always surprised when he scrambled up the final rock face and stood on the terrace. Before him stretched the man-made plain, hidden from the road far below by the large trees growing on the seaside edge. But this time he felt relieved as well as surprised. He now understood what the old Hawaiians must have felt when they climbed here, this place of safety high on the mountainside. There were many such *puʻuhonua* in the islands: places where the breaker of a *kapu* could run to and find shelter, shielded by the power of the *aliʻi*. If Isaiah had heard the undergrowth below crackling, then seen someone stumbling and surging to the top, he could have urged him on—with laughs, with cries, with his hands, throwing rock after rock down at anyone pursuing the climber, gaining on the victim but too late to catch him.

The *heiau* and some house sites were grouped to his right, just in front of the place where the slope began rising again. Isaiah had cleared off most of the scrub, and the dark lava platforms stood out in the fading light. At the far end he'd replanted some of the farming terraces, even planting some fruit trees in a little grove. The water, clean and clear this high up, ran down the side of the platform. He wouldn't starve, even if he stayed here for years.

Isaiah now knew many places in the islands. Old graveyards, overgrown and abandoned, the wooden churches caved in or carried off in pieces for lumber. Many nights he'd spent among the headstones in the high grass, working with his tools and his flashlight, removing and bundling the bodies as Hal had taught him. All worksites by the ocean were familiar to him, and roads, moving along the sides of slopes—each one a new resting place for his people. He now knew airports very well, and how hard it was to get three or four long flower boxes onto interisland jets.

He'd hidden this, his masterpiece, most carefully, for he loved and feared for this place of safety most. He would be the last person to hide here; he knew that someday this place too would be found. First the helicopters would come, hovering. People from Isaiah's town, $8.50 an hour, would walk beside the bulldozers edging their way up from the road below, plowing toward this place, pushing the red dirt wave before them. Many Curtises, many Walters, paid by people with vacant or hidden faces, would cut down the big trees so the new owners and tourists could see the ocean. They'd leave the *heiau* standing out beside the pool, and waiters would tell the story of the Hawaiians and their "Cities of Refuge"—odd tales that books and time had turned into ancient history.

Isaiah looked at the plain once more. The entire surface was strewn with boulders. The Chinese he'd carried up and reburied here slept neatly in rows; his Hawaiians rested under rocks spreading out in circles. He'd put the *haoles* six feet under. The people he'd come upon by surprise when digging in churchyards he reburied the same way he'd found them—no marker, no surface sign. He'd replanted some small trees to mark out the areas, and the seeds had already taken hold, wrapping some of the boulders in vines.

He hadn't been able to figure out where they would start grading, so he'd made the best guess he could. He wanted to be the first silent figure to greet them—his people had taught him that watchmen needn't shout. All were ready. Chinese and Portuguese, Filipino and Japanese, even the *haoles*, brought here by Isaiah, not by sugar, pineapple, or God. And the Hawaiians. All would now silently resist, turning their faces to the light when the pursuers broke through, climbing in pieces onto the dozer blade, making each turn of the caterpillar track wrench a spirit out of the soil, demanding more time, laying true claim to this, their place. Isaiah's place. One hundred souls stripped to the essentials, waiting.

At one point near the edge of the plain, you can just see the bay if you look between the thick trunks of the *koa*. Isaiah had dug a hole for himself there and found roots. He liked to think of the roots slowly winding around him, inching onward to find water, passing between his ribs, through his eyes. Two plywood sheets piled high with dirt hung suspended, propped up by two-by-fours standing at attention in the hole. Someday, Isaiah would inch his body feet-first down between the supports. Then without hesitating, he would push the props away and embrace the red converging wave.

But not now. Not yet.

Complete with Fireworks
above Magic Island

CHRISTINE KIRK-KUWAYE

"Yoo hoo, Margaret!"

Clink, clink. The sound of metal on glass?

"You home?"

That sound.

"Marge? It's me, Hazel. You sleeping in there?"

Margaret was in that limbo place, dreaming that the plane she and Deirdre were in was falling apart, clink, clink. She sat up on the couch, legs apart, feet pointed in different directions, and tried to figure this out.

"Marge, you okay? I know you're in there. It's Hazel."

Margaret cleared her throat. "Yes, Hazel, I'm coming." She stood and stumbled to the door.

"Whew," Hazel said when she saw her, "you really had me worried. I thought you were dead or worse."

"What's worse?"

"Hey, you don't look so good."

Margaret nodded. Ever since she had sent her daughter to live with her ex-husband, Deirdre's father, in Kamuela, she'd had trouble staying awake.

Hazel frowned. "No good to be alone on a holiday."

Margaret stepped aside, motioning for Hazel to come in. The woman plopped herself down in the middle of the couch and stuck her legs straight out in front of her. "I'm gonna die with all this New Year's stuff to do. Take it from me, Marge, don't ever start a tradition. Pretty soon you can't stop it."

"Making a lot of food again this year?"

Hazel shook her head from side to side, which was Hazel's way of saying yes. She pulled a long face, meaning, Margaret knew, that she loved it.

"I can help, just give me a few minutes. Wash my face, run a comb through this mess." She touched her hair; it felt as if it were standing on end.

"Nah. I'm on break. My girl and Clyde Jr. helping out. Sit."

Instead Margaret walked to the kitchenette and opened the refrigerator. "What would you like? I've got soda, diet—" She put her head in deeper, moved items around. "—and a couple of beers." She stood up and faced Hazel.

"Get me water, no ice. Makes my teeth ache." Margaret brought two glasses of water, one with ice, one without. "Ooo, this hits the spot."

Margaret could hear the liquid pass down Hazel's throat while she sat there staring, waiting, and tried to pull herself completely back from sleep. She attempted to stifle a yawn. "Oh, these afternoon naps."

"A real Sleeping Beauty, you. Me, I never sleep in the daytime. Bad habit to start, you know. But I'm too busy to sleep anyway, too much to do."

"Well, it's not like I don't have things to do." Margaret listened to the last of her sentence drift away.

"Sure you do, honey," Hazel said, her voice full of sympathy. "But now with Deirdre gone. Well. It's just you."

"You wanted to talk to me?" Margaret stood to open the curtains, but the light was so intense that she changed her mind and sat down on the couch next to Hazel.

"You're invited to a party!"

"Party?"

"Sure. Remember those things?"

"Uh." Margaret was unsure whether to answer this question or to ask the next one.

"See what I mean? You need some people, some action." The thought of people in action made Margaret feel even more tired. "It'll be fun. Our place," meaning Hazel and Clyde Shimabukuro's. "Come late, around nine or so."

"Well," Margaret said, waking and sinking at the same time, "that's pretty late. Deirdre may call and—"

"Aw, don't be a party pooper. What you need more sleep for? You slept all afternoon. And Deirdre, if she calls and you're not home, she'll call back." Hazel patted Margaret's hand and smiled. "What you do the last day of the year is important. It tells what you'll do for the rest of the next year."

"Oh, I didn't know that." Margaret thought this might be another of Hazel's Okinawan proverbs. Hazel's comments were often fraught with pith.

"Sure. Lemme use your phone."

Margaret excused herself to the bathroom. "Put Dewey on the phone," Margaret heard Hazel command as the bathroom door softly closed.

This room, now that Deirdre's things were gone, looked like a lonely motel bathroom, nothing on the back of the toilet to indicate that anyone of permanence used it. When Deirdre had been here, every available space had been filled with bottles and tubes, cylinders and palettes; shampoos, cream rinses, eyeliner, mascara, eyeshadow, blush—at seventeen, Deirdre had prepared herself carefully for the world's gaze. Margaret, years ago, had given up the fight.

She thought she probably needed to urinate, so she pulled up her muumuu and tugged down her panties. Out of habit, she looked at the crotch of her underwear. Although her period seemed late (she'd stopped counting days long ago), she wasn't concerned. Its absence could only mean menopause, still early at her age but not out of the question. She thought about menopause. She'd always believed that when her time came she would feel a deep sense of loss, the closing of the Great Chapter. Here and now as she sat on the toilet in her empty bathroom, she just felt tired.

"Marge," Hazel's voice crooned on the other side of the door, "come on out, I've got a surprise." Margaret could hear something beyond, bags rustling, thumps of solid but not heavy objects on her kitchenette table.

It looked as if Deirdre had returned. Bottles, tubes, compacts, palettes, a long tubular thing with a cord, something that looked like a ray gun from a science fiction movie, and a lime-green plastic box. Behind it all stood Hazel and Dewey, mother beaming, daughter looking glum as she eyed Margaret standing frumpy in the shortie muumuu that once had been alive with deep purple orchids but now was a ghostly patterned blue-gray.

"It's my treat." Hazel raced from behind the table to enfold Margaret's soft body against her sinewy one. "Dewey's gonna fix you up for tonight."

Hazel explained what Dewey would perform. Dewey only interrupted to say, "I dunno, Ma. I don't know if I get enough time." Hazel said that was nonsense and they argued, then negotiated. Margaret was sure that Dewey thought the task beyond human possibility. But they finally settled on a tint —"Gotta cover the gray"—and a perm—"Geeve em some body." Dewey reluctantly agreed to attempt a makeup job as well. "Ma, no time for one manacure."

"My girl's gonna work wonders," Hazel promised and was gone, upstairs to her apartment, in a moment.

Dewey, now Miss DewAnne, near-professional cosmetologist, near-graduate of the Hollywood Beauty College, was ready to begin. Miss DewAnne explained: "Firse, I wash em, den condition. Ooo, you sure need dat"— tweaking a section of Margaret's hair as if it were diseased and contagious— "Den da tint, perm, blow dry. And"—stepping back to get a good view, frowning, shaking her head, squinting her big brown eyes—"den da face."

Margaret's head was positioned face first into the kitchenette sink, where the scraps of her scrambled egg and toast breakfast still lingered in the In-sink-erator. The water poured down and around, first too cold, then too hot, but finally just right.

Margaret tried to make conversation, just as one would in a real salon, but Miss DewAnne was incommunicado, tiny sponge headphones pressed against her ears. What Margaret tried to tell her was that the conditioner smelled evil, then that the girl should watch the scissors so close to her earlobes. Later, it was out of fear of being blinded that Margaret abandoned speech and resorted to body language: she had to tip her head back as far as it would go to keep the red-hot chemical rivulet that was traveling down her forehead, balancing on her eyebrow, from plunging into the socket of her eye.

Miss DewAnne's motions eventually became soothing, careful, and not ungentle tuggings at Margaret's scalp, as the girl bedded swatches of hair in rustling papers and then firmly wound each swatch around a plastic perm curler. The sun had already set by the time Miss DewAnne moved Margaret to the couch and, on the end table behind her, placed the lime-green plastic box that when probed, expelled a tube, a shower cap affair, and an electric cord. She had a dreamless sleep while the hot air breathed on her head. What finally awoke her was the smell of what she thought was hair on fire.

"Can I see?" Margaret shouted, carefully forming the words with her lips so Miss DewAnne could read them if she were deaf to the sound.

"Not yet!"

Margaret reached up, hoping to see it with her fingers.

"Don't touch. Juss wait." The girl stepped back, took Margaret's chin by two fingers and a thumb, turned her head one way, then the other. Margaret couldn't read the expressionless face.

"What time now?" Miss DewAnne asked.

"Stove! Clock!" Margaret shouted.

"Well, I gotta make dis quick. I gotta date tonight." She pulled off the earphones; Margaret could hear the music from the contraption hanging around the girl's neck. "My muddah," Miss DewAnne said, disgust in her voice. Margaret, having herself lived so long with a teenager, felt cowed.

"Dewey, DewAnne," Margaret said, now in her normal tone, "I certainly appreciate all your efforts," although Margaret did wonder just how she might look. "Now you run along and get ready. I'll look fine without the makeup."

"You crazy? Ma gon kill me if you go up dere lie dis."

For years Margaret secretly had longed to visit a Merle Norman shop (they advertised complete make-overs, promised to make any woman beautiful), but she'd always told herself she couldn't afford it. The real reason, of course, had been fear, fear of humiliation, fear of making Merle a liar. But this, what Dewey had done, far surpassed her expectations; face *and* hair, more than she'd ever dreamed.

Dewey hadn't so much dyed her hair as simply turned silver strands to gold. Yesterday (was it just hours ago?) she would have been certain that she knew her own natural hair color, but now the woman who looked back at Margaret from the medicine chest mirror had hair that glowed auburn as if it were hiding a warm fire just under the surface. A long-wilted permanent, remnant of an attempt months ago to "do something with this hair," had been replaced with curls that licked and kissed the edges of her face. She touched one near her temple—it bounced with new life under her fingers.

This face! My face? Margaret thought. What had become of the pale middle-aged woman with vertical lines like fence pickets between her eyebrows, shaded pockets under the eyes? How she wished Deirdre were here. "See," Margaret imagined herself saying, "see how wonderful you will look when you're my age." And feel! It was as if she had slept a hundred years and had arrived at the moment of total wakefulness, refreshed, perhaps reborn.

All this sleeping over the past month had not been bad for her figure either. She pulled the faded muumuu taut against her body and examined her shape. It was soft, perhaps a bit flabby, but it was definitely thinner. She released the muumuu and it bagged around her. She went to the kitchen, found the scissors, and in front of the full-length mirror behind the bedroom door, watched herself cut the shoulders loose and the ugly blue-gray tatter fall around her ankles.

"Rags, all of it rags," she said to her clothes in the closet. She certainly couldn't wear just anything with this hair and this face. Her black dress seemed the best choice except it would be too dressy for the Shimabukuros'. In fact, it would be depressing, sitting in Hazel's living room (the TV never off), nibbling sushi, picking at the black beans (for fertility! Margaret giggled), forcing herself to eat just a little bit of seaweed, twigs they seemed to Margaret, encrusted with crunchy opaque fish eggs that Clyde always insisted she sample.

At the other end of the closet was where Deirdre had kept her things, empty now except for what Deirdre had chosen to abandon: a pair of designer jeans that had been too large, a blouse that had not been to her taste. Exactly what Margaret had had in mind: casual yet—well, yes—youngish.

Once showered and dressed, she cursed herself for her self-denial: not even a squirt of cologne in the place. She shot several bursts of Pine Woods Air Freshener at the bathroom ceiling, let the mist settle down upon her, and hoped no one would recognize the scent.

As she locked her apartment, then slowly ascended the stairs (Don't over-heat, she cautioned herself), a duet gamboled in her head—she felt pretty and her prince might come! She couldn't stop humming even as she, Margaret Foster transformed, stood at the open door of the Shimabukuro residence. Looking in, she saw Clyde Jr. belly down in front of the TV, his rapt face a ghastly gray-blue from the screen's light. And just beyond at the table, Clyde Sr.'s face frowned at the fan of cards he held, while Hazel, out of view, shouted from the kitchen, "I call and raise two." But before she could step over the threshold, she heard a toilet flush and a man, a stranger, stumbled into the living room from the direction of the hall. He bumped into the chair across from Clyde Sr. and sat down.

She cleared her throat and Clyde Sr. looked up. "Hazel, somebody at da doa," he shouted and studied his cards again.

Hazel, her hands dripping on the front of her muumuu, the carpet, her bare feet, came forward. She shrieked and clapped her hands to the sides of her face. "It's Margaret, Clydie. Just look at what Dewey's done to her!"

Things happened quickly: Margaret was swept into the room; Clyde Sr. dropped his cards, faces up, on the table; the stranger looked up, confused. Clyde Jr. glanced up, then turned his face back to the screen. A rush of sounds from Hazel; sounds of some sort from Clyde Sr.; and the man sat, turning his head toward one voice then another. Until, "Margaret Foster. Hosei Oshiro. Marge, Hosei," Hazel said, stepping back, hands on her hips.

The man cocked his head, smiled. He held out his hand in Margaret's general direction. She took the warm, fleshy hand in hers. "Nice to meet you, Jose," she said and took the fourth seat at the card table.

"I can see your cards, old man," Hazel said. Clyde Sr. made an apologetic sound and slapped his hand on the faces. "Aw," he said, "we deal em again now dat Marge's heah." He scooped all the cards on the table toward him and began slowly shuffling.

"You boys start without us. We got things to do in the kitchen."

In the kitchen, Hazel made Margaret stand up straighter, turn slowly, show a profile, then stay still under the bright ceiling light. "Well, she sure did a good job, Marge. I've never seen anything like it." So it is true, Margaret thought, for Hazel simply could not get over it: the transforma-tion, beauty where dreariness hand been, a glow (Hazel mentioned that). "The wonders of modern makeup," Hazel sighed.

Clyde Sr.'s voice bellowed from the living room.

"Keep your pants on, old man." Hazel began slicing sushi. Margaret offered to help, but Hazel insisted she was a guest. Hazel looked around for a platter. "Reach up in that cupboard, the one above the sink, yeah, that one, and get me the blue plate with the fish on it." Margaret did so. "Then get the beers out of the fridge and some glasses, yeah, that's right."

"Hazel," Margaret said, touching the hair that nestled on the back of her neck. "That man, Jose. Is he a relative?"

Hazel noisily pushed jars and Tupperware containers around in the refrigerator. "Nah, not really. Calabash. He's an old friend of Clydie's family from the Big Island, here for the holidays. He's thinking of living in Honolulu, you know." Hazel grinned then nudged Margaret's elbow with her own. "Handsome guy, huh?"

Margaret wouldn't say he was handsome. He was an older Oriental man, clean, neatly dressed. She'd found his right hand nice; it was warm and looked as if most of its life it had performed some sort of labor. But, she supposed, he might be considered nice looking. "Yes, nice looking," Margaret mumbled.

"I told Clydie you'd say that. I just knew it!" Hazel pinched Margaret's arm with two wet bony fingers. It had been very long ago, but Margaret felt a vaguely familiar uneasiness, like the time her best girlfriend in the twelfth grade insisted on introducing her to—

"Drink your beer while it's cold. Tonight's New Year's Eve, we gotta celebrate." Hazel spooned out *nishime,* then pushed the bowl aside. "Widower."

"Pardon?"

"Wife died, oh, three years ago? Clydie would remember. Anyway, Hosei has three grown daughters and he's a grampa. But all the girls and their families are on the mainland. Couldn't find work or something in Kamuela, so—"

"Kamuela? Jose's from Kamuela?" Margaret thought of Deirdre, thoroughly urban Deirdre, on a little farm in Kamuela. It had seemed best for the girl to be sent there, but she hadn't thought about how it might really be for Deirdre. Even Jose's daughters, born and raised there, couldn't take it.

"Yeah, that's what I said. Anyway, now he's retired, has his pension, some land. I guess he has to decide whether to sell and move to Honolulu." Hazel grabbed a slab of raw fish and began slicing out the blood section. "Maybe you can help him decide, eh, Marge?"

Poor Deirdre, out on some godforsaken farm, no teenagers her age, nowhere to wear her pretty clothes. Probably can't even listen to a rock station out there in the wilderness. Margaret knew Deirdre had always had a flair for dramatics. Maybe she'd run away, maybe she'd get mixed up with some country boy—oh god, Margaret thought, maybe she'd try to kill herself.

"That's why we invited him," Hazel said and smiled slyly.

Margaret took a long drink of her beer; she could almost hear it splashing in her empty stomach. She looked at Hazel. "He hates Kamuela too?"

"What Dewey do, perm your brains? I've been telling you why he's here." Clyde Jr. came in looking for a soda. "Get outta my kitchen, boy," Hazel shouted and gave him a swat.

"Aw, Ma," he said and stood at the open door of the refrigerator, letting all the cold air escape. He began opening jars and picking out food with his fingers, then only half closing the lids and sliding the jars back in. He finally found a soda and stood there shaking it.

"Darn kid. Old man, get this boy outta here."

Clyde Sr. came in and Clyde Jr. walked past him. "Hey, watchu doin in heah, havin one party or what?" Hazel loaded Clyde Sr.'s arms with platters and bowls and balanced two unopened beers and two glasses on top of everything. Clyde Sr. walked stiffly, carefully out.

"My family's gonna drive me to drink," Hazel said and took a long swig of beer.

"Why is he here, Hazel?" Margaret was sure she didn't want to hear why, for she had a terrible feeling she knew already.

"Why, Marge, Hosei's your date. Second surprise!"

Margaret tried hard to play poker. She'd never been any good at cards, and poker had never made any sense to her, so many variations, so much to remember, so much to watch. And then she had to bet, too. And Deirdre was on her mind, although in the back of it now, and the beer on her empty stomach and the enchantment of her looks all made her feel dizzy. The game played around her. She took cards, discarded others, pushed blue or white or red chips in front of her, but her mind was working on a memory of a phrase; she would almost have it and it would slip away. Her mind raced yet went nowhere.

Hosei only spoke to bet and Margaret noticed he had the oddest way of holding his cards, eye level and not far from the end of his nose. Margaret's attention drifted toward the inert body of Clyde Jr. and the show that so transfixed him, something about war and a submarine. It starred Clark Gable and Burt Lancaster, two of her favorites. The way she looked tonight and the way she felt about the way she looked tonight, she would not have been too shy if Clark (had he still been alive) or Burt (she'd never believed he was gay) was sitting in the Shimabukuro living room waiting to be her date. The scene changed and she recognized Don Rickles. Hosei carefully counted out four red chips.

"What time now?" Clyde Sr. asked.

"Look at the clock," Hazel said, not looking up from her cards.

"I no have my driving glasses, Haze."

She grumbled and went into the kitchen, called out the time, and brought back four more beers.

"We bettah go soon," Clyde Sr. said.

"Aw, take it easy. We got plenty of time."

"Nah, we gotta go early, get da good place."

Margaret wondered if this was all there was: the elaborate preparation so she might sit in the Shimabukuro living room with the TV on, a few hands of poker to play, more beers than she cared for to drink, a few bits of food to leave her unfilled. She decided she could always call Deirdre, see how she was doing, wish her a Happy New Year. "Well," Margaret said, seeing that another round had ended, "I better get back to my place. It's been real nice." She stood. "And nice to meet you, Jose," offering her hand this time.

Hosei made a motion to take it, but Hazel interrupted. "Where you going?" Hazel leaned over and patted the seat of Margaret's chair. "Sit down, Marge. We're all gonna see the fireworks."

"Fireworks?" Margaret knew that this was the first year of the ban on fireworks. While the Shimabukuros had complained bitterly that this would be the first year they couldn't burn their traditional ten-thousand string— suspended from a wooden pole at the edge of the apartment parking lot, illegal even before the ban—Margaret secretly had been delighted: no deafening noise, no smoke, no sticky red papers that clung to her slippers the morning after.

"Yeah," Hazel said, "at least those buggahs promised a good show for the whole city and we're gonna watch it. Right, Clydie?"

"Dat's why we gotta go early, get da good place."

"Well," Margaret said, hoping to still make an exit, "I think I'll pass." She had already decided that the new Margaret would not go to waste: she'd sleep sitting up, go out early the next morning somewhere, wander around. She imagined people gazing at her admiringly.

Hazel stood up and pinched Margaret's shoulder, hard. "Help me in the kitchen."

In the kitchen Hazel hissed, "What's the matter with you? Poor Hosei sitting out there and you want to go home? This man came all the way from the Big Island! And you, we told him all about you, how nice you are, how alone you are. Do you want to hurt his feelings, a nice man like that?"

Margaret felt a light sweat break out on her upper lip. "Hazel, I had no idea."

"What's with you anyway? I told you he was your date."

"Well, I know you said that, but Jose just sits there. He doesn't say anything and well—I just thought that it didn't much matter whether—" It sounded weak, cringing, Margaret knew.

"He's shy, that's all. Give him some time."

Margaret looked down at her hands, noticing the ragged cuticles, the uneven nails.

"Now say you're staying. Say it, Marge."

"I'm staying."

"Good. Now take out the beers."

Margaret did beg off from another round of cards and excused herself to the bathroom. She'd take her time in here, she decided, let them play their cards. She washed her hands slowly, refusing to look into the mirror. She wanted to save that, savor the experience once again of seeing that image. And when she finally did look up, she saw a faint pink streak, crooked and evil, that squirmed down the right side of her forehead and disappeared into her eyebrow where it was transformed into a patch of shining gold hair. She realized how close she had come to being blinded, all in the name of beauty.

She passed Hosei in the hall and saw Clyde Sr. disappearing into the bedroom. "Hazel, look at me." If she let herself go, she knew she would shriek.

Hazel, gathering up the cards, stacking the chips, glanced up. "You look terrific, Marge. Wasn't that a nice surprise?"

"No, look at me. My forehead, my eyebrow."

Hazel looked, squinted her eyes. "What?"

Margaret pointed to her forehead, the glistening patch of eyebrow.

"Well, I can hardly see it and in the dark you can't see it at all."

Hosei ambled in, stood in the center of the living room and looked in the direction of the TV, but Clyde Jr. turned it off and headed toward his room.

"Hosei," Hazel said, "doesn't Marge look pretty?"

Hosei turned and peered in their direction, then moved closer. "Well, she looks nice to me, but maybe she always looks nice. This is the first time we've met." He grinned, obviously hoping he was saying the right thing. "She smells nice."

"Marge, isn't that sweet of Hosei to say?"

The plan, Margaret learned once they were in the car, was to drive slowly, Clyde Sr.'s only operating speed, up Tantalus Drive to some lookout point that Hazel and Clyde had determined days before. They would watch the fireworks the City and County was offering the public from Magic Island. Hazel was enthusiastic. She'd heard it was to be the most spectacular ever seen in Hawaii, something about a rapid-fire bursting of varicolored chrysan-themum-shaped fireballs. Some rock station, which they wouldn't listen to, of course, promised to play a medley of tunes that would throb in synch with the visual display.

Margaret was not enthusiastic. And she was still not a little upset about her eyebrow, the facial scar, about agreeing to go with them, about missing the call she'd surely get from Deirdre. At the thought of Deirdre, these feelings gave way to depression and shame. What kind of mother was she not to be there when her only child called?

"Damn keeds," Clyde Sr. said at the sound of squealing brakes. "Dey gonna kill somebody. Shouldn't even be allowed to get license."

Margaret saw Deirdre dying in a car wreck somewhere on a deserted Big Island road. Would her father wonder where she was when she didn't show up hours after she should have been home?

"And after," Hazel was saying, "we can come back to our place—Watch the traffic, old man!" Clyde Sr. braked the car to a complete stop. Margaret looked at the rising road ahead of them, the beginning of the climb and the snaking curves.

"You wanna drive?" Clyde Sr. grumbled at Hazel who was leaning forward, nose nearly to the windshield glass.

"Go now," she said. "Take it easy on the curves and watch for oncoming cars."

Clyde Sr. guided the car upward, past the rows of houses on both sides of the road, slowing nearly to a stop each time he came to a cluster of parked cars. "Damn keeds," he said, looking from left to right and left again, waiting, perhaps, for the children to spitefully fling themselves in front of his barely moving car.

"Come on, old man," Hazel ordered, giving his shoulder a poke. "We're gonna miss the whole thing."

"Oh my," Margaret said, seeing the dark mountain forest ahead of them, "it's been along time since I've been up here." She worried at how the streetlights ended at the last house just ahead.

"Put on you brights," Hazel told Clyde Sr.

"I was juss gonna do dat."

"Isn't this great?" Hazel said, her face turned toward Margaret and Hosei in the backseat.

"It sure is," Hosei said.

"Great," Margaret said.

Several times Hazel told Clyde Sr. to pull onto the dark shoulder to let the train of cars that kept accumulating behind them pass. Hazel insisted that she counted the curves and knew they would be there at any moment; Clyde Sr. believed that they had a way to go yet. He said he'd memorized the terrain. "Get one tree wit all da bark falling off."

"Here it is! Stop, old man."

"Nah, it's furdah up." But he pressed the brake, causing another train of cars to jerk to a halt, and slowly pulled the car onto the apron. "Dis not it," Clyde Sr. said and turned off the engine. Hazel flung open her door and bounded out into the darkness. The three sat in the pitch blackness in silence, waiting.

Her pale face appeared outside Margaret's window, making Margaret jump and give a little scream. "Open up," Hazel's muffled voice called, as she rapped on the glass with her knuckles. Margaret's heart was racing and she could feel the prickliness of perspiration in her armpits. She rolled down the window just a few inches. Hazel's fingers, like a bird's talons, perched there. "Come on out, we're here."

"Give me a minute?" Margaret begged.

Hazel started to insist, but Hosei spoke up. "Hazel, you and Clyde go ahead. I'll sit with Margaret for a while. We'd like to sit and just smell the cool fragrance. Right, Margaret?" And it was true, there was a wonderful cool fragrance in the air, something so sweet and clean that it made her realize how pathetic Pine Woods Air Freshener was in its attempt at imitation. "That tree that Clyde kept talking about," Hosei said, "that's what you smell. We have those in Kamuela."

Oh, Deirdre, Margaret thought. Her heart, calmer now, began to sink. "My girl's in Kamuela," she said, apropos of nothing. "I miss her."

"It gets easier after a while," he said. "I know it's hard at first, but you have to let them go sometime, no?"

"Maybe you've seen her?" Margaret felt hopeful. "She's tall—well, not *too* tall, five-seven, dark brown hair, auburn really, big brown eyes. She doesn't look much like me really; she looks a little Hawaiian, more like her father. Nice willowy figure. A happy girl, really, except for once in a while—"

"Can't say that I've seen her. But you can be sure that she'll be happy there."

"Not *my* girl. She's a real city kid. Likes lots of things to do. Shopping. A real clothes horse. And concerts! If I were made of money—"

"Oh, she'll love it. You'll see. Nobody can resist Kamuela."

"Your children certainly could."

"My girls? Oh, they didn't want to leave. Cried days before they did, you know. Just couldn't find work is all. The first chance they get, they'll be back."

"Well, what's so great about Kamuela?" Margaret, even as the words escaped, was aware that this wasn't like her, assaulting a stranger. She wanted to blame the beer.

"It's hard to explain, except to say that Kamuela's special, a little magic even." He sighed. "We have space, green space. The air, well, it almost snaps it's so clean. Some Honolulu folks came two years ago and cleared a space for themselves, but didn't cut any big trees, and built their house by hand."

"Just like pioneers." Margaret thought things looked worse by the minute for Deirdre.

"That's right. Funny you should say that, Margaret. Those same people have a pet turkey."

"Are you thinking of the Pilgrims, Jose?"

He gave his forehead a quick slap. "Must be getting old. But the important thing is your girl. If she's like you, she'll see the beauty." And from across the darkness between them, a warm calloused hand found hers.

She wanted to (didn't want to) pull her hand away. "You don't understand. She's my only child, my whole family."

"I see. But maybe it's time for you to start your new life. You have to think about yourself and look around you, Margaret." She did and saw utter darkness, made bearable only by the lovely scent from the peeling tree. "I can tell you're a fine woman."

"But you don't even know me."

"Oh, no," he said quietly. "I know. I know."

Outside the car, Margaret felt buoyant, her mind remarkably clear. "Now, won't this be lovely, Jose? Here we'll be standing on the edge of the mountain, looking down at the city and all those lovely colored lights bursting above. Whoosh!" Had she felt this good at seventeen, she wondered?

She plunged forward toward the voices and faint outlines of Clyde Sr. and Hazel. "Do you know that the last firework display I watched was—let me see—" She was trying to tread carefully, not catch her foot on a vine, a root, or topple into an unseen gully. "That's right! It was the Fourth of July, the bicentennial year. Deirdre was ten and William, that's my ex-husband, was working—needed the overtime—and she and I, we went down to—where was it?" And in the lull, she heard a thud and a rustle. She looked back, her eyes somewhat adjusted to the darkness now, and could see that he had vanished. She stood still, listening, and a gust of night wind pushed against her. "Jose? Jose, are you there?" A sudden mountain shower tumbled down upon her head and shoulders, dampening her clothes. She could taste the makeup at the edges of her mouth. "Jose!"

"I'm here, Margaret."

"Oh, thank god," she whispered. "I'm coming. Don't move." She began retracing her steps, staring down at the ground although she could see nothing, nothing at all. Her foot bumped into something soft. She heard a stifled groan. "Oh, I'm sorry," she said, bending over and feeling for him. She touched an arm, a back, some hair. Her face burned in embarrassment.

"No, no, that's fine. I'm okay. Just a little fall. Happens all the time."

She helped him up, then stood back. "Is something wrong? I mean, you fall often?" Was he dying, she thought? Some disease that affected the muscles, made him lose control?

"Oh, yes." He sounded better. "It's just one of the hazards of being blind."

"Oh, I know what you mean." Margaret laughed. "Sometimes I stumble around just like a blind person myself."

"No, Margaret. I *am* blind."

Margaret wished the mountain to open up beneath her feet. And in that moment of humiliation, her soft curls turning into sopping coils, her makeup running and smearing, gradually revealing the old Margaret underneath, she remembered the phrase from her high school days that she had been searching for. It is what people called people like Jose and herself: blind dates. She groaned.

"Legally blind, but not totally blind. Don't apologize." He reached out and touched her clammy arm.

"Oh, I see. Oh, no, Jose, I'm sorry. I can't seem to say anything right."

"No, no. I say, 'I see,' see?" He placed his arm atop hers. "Let's lean on each other."

At the edge of the mountain, she looked down into the valley, which was pitch black right below but gradually became sprinkled then encrusted with street lights as she looked farther out. She described the lights to Hosei, trying her best to allow him to see through her words what she saw. She talked of jewels, black velvet cloth with pinholes of light, clusters of stars. Under the thick scent of the peeling tree she could smell herself, a blend of chemicals not entirely unpleasant.

"Nice," Hosei said. "Sounds very lovely, Margaret. Go on." She described the sea and the sky, which were one and the same, it seemed from up here.

"Get over here, you two," Hazel shouted from nearer the edge of the mountain. "It's gonna start."

Margaret looked off toward the direction of Magic Island and the first burst erupted—a perfect orb that was a duet of ocean blue and moon white stars.

"Hosei can you see," Clyde Sr. sang. Hazel punched his arm.

Margaret looked to Hosei who was facing west. "Here," she whispered, gently turning his body eastward toward Magic Island.

And as the four of them stood there, their eyes filled with the sky fire, Margaret felt a familiar churning in her lower parts, and she knew her old red friend was here, slowly spreading its presence on the crotch of her panties. She was too happy to care about the mess it would leave. Right along with the other two, she and Hosei laughed and ooed and whooped at each burst of light.

"Everybody make their resolutions," called Hazel.

"Hmph," mumbled Clyde Sr.

"To the first year of a new life," whispered Hosei.

Margaret would figure something out, at least she knew that she wanted to know more about him, his girls. Perhaps she might even consider seeing Kamuela for herself. Besides, she was more than just a little curious to know how an Oriental man from a place like Kamuela came to have a Spanish name.

Seaside Idle

MICHAEL LAGORY

Fate is an aloof passerby, heedless of our wishes as she takes her steady course. Or so it seemed to Damon Hookele this December afternoon. Even on a day when he had done things right, his modest designs were failing, for every single traffic light was green. He was used to having too little time, especially at the garage when his employer, Mr. Wong, was present. Today he had time to spare in returning from lunch. He had ordered only saimin and Coke, in order to take a leisurely drive through the heart of Waikiki. Mildly annoyed, mostly wistful, he considered ironically that Kalakaua Avenue was one of the two streets in Honolulu on which the lights were synchronized, yet it was the one street on which he *wanted* to stop frequently. "Who drives on Kalakaua fo' any reason?" he thought. "No can pahk. Nowhere to get. Only for look." It was in order to look that he had driven this way, but the moving traffic was hardly leaving him a chance. Sighing a conciliatory sigh, he reflected that there is nothing one can do about traffic lights but heed their vicissitudes. He held a fatalistic respect for traffic lights, whether due to superstition, weakness of will, or the ancestral blood of helmsmen who found direction in the lights of heaven.

Kapiolani Boulevard was a much faster route back to work, but he was in a mood to "cruise Kalakaua," as he would say to his comrade Ricky. Waikiki sometimes left him bored, sometimes disgusted. Deep down, though, he loved this street. Damon loved streets. He knew the roads well enough to go an entire month without driving the same route from home to the station. The bad thing was that every route led to King Wong (as Ricky called him), whose idea of a greeting was a stern glance at his wristwatch. Escaped from the station, Damon could indulge his present mood: sentimental, unaggressive, inclined to laugh at himself. The kind of mood in which he would hold elevator doors for little old ladies, pump gas for people in the Self-Service lane when King Wong was not watching, or yield right-of-way in intersections to haoles.

His mood had been enhanced by a song he had heard while eating in the parking lot of the K.C. Drive Inn. He had turned the radio to his hapa-haole auntie's station. "To Each His Own" was playing. Damon had always chided Auntie for her old-fashioned tastes. "Besides," he would reason with her, "dat's haole music."

> *A rose must remain*
> *With the sun and the rain*
> *Or its lovely promise won't come true*

"To Each His Own" had been one of her favorites. Damon turned off the radio when a tire advertisement came on, and made a mental note to change the tuner back to his FM station before Ricky rode in the car. But he was still whistling the song as he passed the waterfall windows of the Mitsukoshi Building.

He had another motive for choosing this route. He hoped to be able to match the story Ricky had been telling all week of a pretty woman in the passenger seat of a Datsun 280Z. Both young men had seen her waiting one car back in Full Service, but as usual Ricky beat Damon to the squeegee. "Premium!" Ricky had gloated; and although Damon knew his friend liked to exaggerate, he swallowed his envy and listened repeatedly to the details with sportsmanlike attention. Today he had seen one candidate, talking to a pedicab driver in front of the Royal Hawaiian Shopping Center. Her calves, Damon had noted, resembled those of Trish Stacy, Miss May 1975. Yet with a generous estimation, he could only report that she was an Octane 92. "Like Ricky says," he thought, "I too hones' fo' my own good."

His best chance, he decided, would be at the corner of Kalakaua and Kaiulani avenues. Close to the beach, it offers more bikinis and the well-dressed Hyatt Regency shoppers. He was gauging his chances of stopping there when he noticed a yellow light before him at Seaside Avenue. He was glad to stop, even though he would be two cars from the crosswalk. Traffic lights were his favorite part of driving. They gave him a pleasant feeling of suspension, a calm half-minute of helpless and meaningless immobility, utterly devoid of will, a brief time shared with a handful of individuals from the complicated mass of the city, each with a unique motive and direction, yet brought together at random, never to meet again, frozen as a unit in temporary aimlessness. "Aim is not native to your mentality," Mr. Smith had said one day in exasperation, in the semester Damon spent at a private school during the ninth grade. It was not a pleasant memory; everyone had looked at him and laughed.

Since his view of the crosswalk was not good, he turned his attention to the other waiting drivers. An Oriental woman in a European car with tinted windows was studying her rear-view mirror and doing something to her face. Directly to the left, a haole in an aloha shirt Damon had seen in the window at Ross Sutherland was staring at the traffic light; veins were visible in his right hand, which held the steering wheel. A youth in a van behind Damon bobbed his head and fingered the frets of an imaginary guitar. He obviously was not listening to Auntie's station. "Prob'ly dat new Stones song," guessed the observer, judging by the rhythm of the rapt musician's head. Behind the van, a teenage truant jaywalked with an air of serene defiance.

At the door of a travel agency, a tourist struggled with an armful of packages. Some rolls of wrapping paper protruding from the packages had become caught in the swinging doors. Had Ricky been in the car, Damon would have hooted boisterously, or speculated sardonically whether the paper was destined for a Hawaiian calendar or tapa placemats. For Ricky, life was a pageant of human fallibility, upon which he gazed and pronounced wry judgment, car by car, from his post in the Full Service lane. Fallibility, as well as certain other aptitudes, which Ricky judged in terms of octane ratios.

Alone in his Chevy, however, Damon responded to the shopper's fallibility only with the surprising recollection of the season. In Waikiki, he thought, you can hardly tell it is Christmas. Perhaps it is because a bit more glitter in December goes unnoticed. Or perhaps it is because Waikiki is calculated to conceal from tourists all traces of regular mainland life. In Waikiki, he sensed, life is a constant holiday; everyone there is vacationing—is on *time off*—except for those who serve, or those who watch, the vacationers. The crowd, like the skyline, is always being recycled. Even the smell of Waikiki is timeless—an atmosphere compacted of air-conditioned department stores and popcorn theaters, of ocean salt and suntan oil, of tour-bus diesel and plumeria. For Damon, it was a sentimental smell, like the smell of grade-school classrooms; and there was something soothingly constant, like the lull of waves, in this haven of fashion and transience.

He sensed the same soothing constancy in the even rumble of his Chevy's engine. He liked listening to it idle, turning at its own pace, independent, calm, without direction, dragging no weight, in suspension. Gears disengaged, gauges still, throttle closed. He contemplated the abstract beauty of the internal combustion engine. A taste of saimin returned to his palate, accompanied by the strains of a violin that blended with the quiet music of the engine. Calm revolutions pulsing through his being, Damon waited calmly for the green.

It was only indirectly that he noticed the lady. What had been visible of the crosswalk pageant included little to draw his eye. There was a quintet of tourists who bumped into one another's elbows while they gaped at the tops of high rises; a pair of lumpy local women wobbling under packages; someone dancing in a gorilla costume; and a pink military couple, holding hands an arm's length apart, looking like a canoe and its outrigger. Observing that something had drawn the Ross Sutherland man's eyes from the lights, Damon looked to the right of the cars in front of him. His eyes focused on a head of deep blonde, almost orange hair. Its ringlets, falling wildly along a white-clad bosom, put him in mind of Miss July 1979, Blanche Bergere, whose name, as he recalled, Ricky had pronounced "burger." As the ringlets swirled past to his left, and his view became increasingly a rear view, the thoughts of Blanche's centerfold led him to contemplations of an entirely physical nature.

Generally, the nature of Damon's contemplations of women was physical in inverse proportion to the intimacy of his acquaintance with them. Screened from them on either side of a windshield, or by the flat sheen of a photograph, the lecher in him rose like a vampire from the tomb. Eye contact, though, was crucifix enough to still the lecher; a word—one open, unthreatened word—could drive it meekly, indeed willingly, back beneath its lid. The aloof, private arrogance of desire was put to rout, banished from his eye, by the sight of something bright red falling from the lovely pedestrian's hair or shoulders. It fell lightly to the street, unnoticed by her, as she passed on toward the curb. It appeared to be cloth—a ribbon or handkerchief, or perhaps a scarf, like the red scarves Auntie used to wear. For moments he was transfixed by the fallen object; glancing again toward the woman, he saw, framed against the palm trees and the concrete, an apparition in white, gliding across the avenue with the buoyant certitude of a whitecap seen upon a distant wave. The white dress rippled in creaseless but ever-changing folds, and from under its low hem, against tanned ankles that were slender but softly rounded, freckles gleamed a deeper gold. Her motion was like that of morning clouds, young, fresh, collected, and stately. Yet in the poised measure of the lady's pace were serenity and wisdom beyond the scope of youth. Something about the dropped scarf perfected the vision, humanized the goddess, whether by hinting at her vulnerability, or merely by showing her withdrawn, unconscious, into a private, delimited, individual world.

Dozens of thoughts raced through Damon's head in the next few seconds. A compulsion to call her seized him. But what would he say? "Hey, you"? "Lady"? "Excuse me"? All would sound ridiculous. He had settled upon "Hey, excuse me" when he judged she was too far away to hear him. He sounded his horn, but no one noticed, not even the man in the car beside him. No one notices horns on Kalakaua Avenue. Jumping from his car to retrieve the scarf would not work; the red "no crossing" light was already blinking; traffic would be moving within seconds. He felt vaguely offended that none of the other pedestrians had noticed, or cared; yet he also felt glad that they had not, and sensed that there was something selfish in his gladness. He saw the lady turn right at the curb, and a gallant urge to retrieve her handkerchief blazed within him. The light turned green.

His heart sank as the scarlet token disappeared under a moving car, but it emerged untouched. However, the next car's wheels bore directly toward it, as if aimed from heaven by the gods at the symbol of Damon's hope. Meanwhile, he inched his Chevy forward, pulling to the left to gain a better view. A horn sounded behind him, but he did not notice. Miraculously, the tires missed the crimson prize by inches. He passed close enough to see that it was not cloth at all, but a beautiful, blushing flower, a hibiscus; apparently, it had fallen from her hair. As he drove on, he watched through his mirror as the lady moved along the sidewalk, and car after ponderous, brutal car threatened the blossom's delicate life, not a one veering to avoid it.

Life thrusts opportunity before us when we are least prepared to receive it: this was the gist of the confused, rueful meditations that swarmed within the gallant's fevered brain. Over the ashes of the lecher, the knight-errant in Damon mounted its steed to joust with the man of common sense.

"Here is the chance of your life! Run and seize that flower!"

"Oh, sure brah—whatchu goin' do? Stop da cah in da meedle o' da road an' swing over da cahs like Spiderman?"

"No one else picked up the flower. If I took the trouble to stop, she would know I really care."

"She goin' teenk you lolo! Or one otta 'Boulevard Romeo,' like King Wong says. Was on'y one flowah. Can peek one li' dat annywheah."

"But if I retrieve something like a flower, something perishable, it will be even more romantic."

"Maybe she stay married."

"She must be one of those rich tourist wives, trapped against her will in an unhappy marriage that stifles her individuality."

"Whassamatta you ack like one keed? Grow op, Damon."

"She had come to the tropic Eden starved for romance, yearning for the raw, primal vigor of a tawny-skinned native."

"Try look youself! Stink like gas, greasy hands, 'Wong's Garage' on da shirt."

"Excuse me, Miss . . . no, it was really nothing at all."

"Da flowah prob'ly flat awready. Or da wind wen' blow 'em away."

"I was blind to the danger; my will was taken captive. It was the only thing my heart would permit me to do."

"How you goin' find her in da crowd?"

"I vowed I would find you, though my search should last a lifetime."

"Gotta change five tires; King Wong goin' get all huhu."

"For better and for worse, for richer and for poorer."

By the time Sir Damon won the argument, the lady had turned into Duke's Lane, the flower was long gone from sight, and he was too far to stop and walk back to Seaside. His only choice was to take a side street to the left, and circle all the way back via Kuhio Avenue. Parking was always a problem. Realizing that he had received change after paying for his saimin, he said, "Awright, brah!" and made the "shaka" sign to a puzzled little boy in the car to his left. He began looking at his hair in the mirror. Then he reconsidered; it was too risky to try to find an open meter close to Seaside. He reviewed the possible lots in his mind. Every second that passed decreased the chances of the flower's survival. He determined to stop in the street, along the right-hand curb of Kalakaua Avenue, where taxis park in front of stores and hotels.

Minutes later, Damon was waiting for a group of doddering Japanese tourists to clear out of his way on Royal Hawaiian Avenue. As the moment of his rendezvous drew nearer, he thought of his forecast for that morning. As usual, there was nothing about romance. Always someone else's sign foretold romance; never his. "Planning ahead can help you foresee the future," he recalled. "See things from both sides before acting. Do not ignore good advice. Strive for increased happiness." That last sentence may have had something to do with romance. But maybe it meant the way to increase happiness was to mind his own business. Maybe it was just these sorts of silly distractions that got in the way of his happiness, that kept someone his age a servant to King Wong. "My mentality," he reflected, "always getting plenny distractions." The Japanese tourists passed, and Damon hastened on. His watch showed four minutes until the end of lunch.

Soon he was parked on Kalakaua behind a Rolls Royce that he recognized as that of Jim Nabors. Damon turned on his blinkers and rushed from his car, declining two offers of pakalolo and one religious pamphlet on his way to the light at Seaside. Cars whizzed past, and he could see no sign either of the hibiscus lady or her flower. Had it blown away? Nothing lay along the far curb except a discarded travel brochure. A crowd gathered; Damon rushed ahead of them when the light changed, then lingered in the lane where the flower had been, combing the pavement for a trace. Elbows jostled him, and a voice with a southern accent asked if he had lost something.

The crowd passed, the traffic light began to blink, and Damon realized he was alone in the street, himself now the object of drivers' idle stares. Eyes behind glass, neutral judges of his folly, anatomized him, as if his greasy coveralls were lingerie. The meridian sun glared off the row of windshields, and Damon turned away squinting. It was then that he saw something one lane away. He walked over and bent toward it, then stopped at an oblique angle to the pavement, with hand extended. At his foot there lay—the size and shape of a bottle cap—a flattened, wrinkled wad of gravel-soiled vermilion.

All of Waikiki is a pageant; and Damon felt at once exiled from, and frozen helpless within, the grand parade. The driver of a Porsche in the lane next to Damon's was the first to lose patience and drive past the young man blocking traffic, standing still, it seemed to the motorist, in drug-induced intoxication, or perhaps in youthful serene defiance, ignoring the alarum of horns. When he looked up, Damon paused again, unable to determine to which curb he should retreat. He formed a one-man traffic island, with autos streaming past him in the lanes on either side.

When the light changed, he was able to return to his car. With one more change of lights, he was able to drive perpendicular to the street, in order to reach the left-hand curb and look down Duke's Lane. Far back amid the crowds and the glittering strings of coral, lava, and shells, a blonde woman in white sat at the counter of a small lei stand. Damon rolled to a stop and stared. He glanced at his watch and smiled a smile partly wistful, partly amused. The light turned green behind him, but he continued to stare down Duke's Lane, glimpsing flashes of white crowned with gold in the intermittent partings of the crowd. The taste of saimin returned to his palate; the words "To each his own" to his ears; and a faint, warm twinge to his heart. Deaf to the horns sounding behind him, he switched the dial of the silent radio to Ricky's FM station, and slipped his Chevrolet back into gear.

Born and Bred

LANNING LEE

Every afternoon at 5:00 P.M., Sergeant Stillman would exercise his homing pigeons. The tradition continued during the five years I was in school on the mainland, and I remember the unexpected pleasure I felt watching that v-shaped flock cut its way through the early evening sky on my first day back in town. I recalled my own birds, and I wondered how the sergeant and Auntie Clara were getting along these days. As the months passed, that aerial display became a source of great relief for me. I looked forward to that time of day, needing it badly. The afternoon of the fire was the last time I would ever find any solace in the daily departure, flight, and sure return of those remarkable birds.

Honolulu was depressingly hot the summer I came back, but my optimism was high. Surely some lucrative job opportunity waited for me on the horizon. After several weeks of diligent hunting, however, my initial enthusiasm wore thin. Soon I began going through the interview ritual just to look good for my folks. I wanted to appear sincere for all my concerned friends and relatives.

Getting out of bed became a struggle for me. If I wasn't too hungover to make it downtown, I made perfunctory showings at the far-from "prospective" places of employment by day. By night I shot pool and hit the bars. With or without friends, it made less and less difference with time. The only thing of importance any more was being home, awake, at 5:00 P.M. Those pigeons mattered a great deal to me.

The night of the fire, drunk and weaving up the hill at 3:00 A.M., I passed the last fire and police vehicles on their way down. After parking in my garage, I was convinced by the heavy smell of smoke and water that the blaze had been nearby. I walked unsteadily down the dead-end street where both Clara and the sergeant lived.

Coming to Clara's lot, I could see that the house had burned completely to the ground. Small wisps of steam rose in the still night air. The front yard, site of her once immaculate vegetable garden, was now a trampled soup of mud and ashes. Even the spectacular bamboo forest in back had been reduced to a rubbled expanse of short, broken stumps.

As I stood swaying slightly in silence over the ruins, I became aware of soft sobbing noises behind me. Turning, I saw Sergeant Stillman sitting on his bench beneath the Norfolk pine. He was barely visible in the shadow of the enormous tree.

"Sarge," I called.

He didn't answer.

Climbing the narrow stone stairway from the street to his yard above, I called to him again. He must have heard me, though he still did not respond. The crying had stopped.

I went to the bench and sat beside him. He was staring down at Clara's lot, mesmerized by the scene. His close-cropped gray hair was streaked with ash, and so were his undershirt and khaki pants. He looked weak and tired.

"Where's Auntie Clara?" I asked, though I somehow sensed what had happened.

The old man wiped his face with a blackened hand, smearing more ash and grime across it.

"I tried to go in and get her . . . but I . . . too late."

He shook his head slowly.

I began to cry for Auntie Clara too.

Clara Wang wasn't really my aunt. After she stopped being mean to me, she invited me to call her Auntie Clara.

When our neighborhood gang was very young, the funny little Chinese lady hated us, I think. Her bamboo forest had been prime territory for playing "army," and we used to drive Clara crazy by tearing around through her massive, overgrown jungle. Half the challenge of our mock battles was to avoid being detected by her, but she always caught us anyway because of the noise made when we ran through the thick layer of dead leaves.

"Hey you kids!" she'd scream. "Get out my yard. I gon call cops if you kids doan get out!"

She always said the same thing. Scared silly, we'd take off through the stream bed behind, straight for home. Home safe, we'd wait for the screaming of sirens telling us that the police had converged on the scene of the crime. It never happened, and sooner or later we were back in her yard, daring her to discover us again.

When we grew out of the playing war stage, and into the cigarette experimentation age, we'd still hang out in Clara's back yard. She'd yell at us, but we reacted differently in those days. We still exited via the stream, but we walked off casually, laughing loudly in order to spite her.

All her animosity, however, seemed to disappear after Ben died. With her husband gone, she channeled all her attention, all her energy, into her vegetable garden.

One day we were tiptoeing past her house when she came rushing out to us. "You boys like boiled peanut?" she asked, smiling.

We had never seen that expression on her face. We relaxed our "get ready to shag it" stance, shrugged our shoulders, and said, "Sure, Mrs. Wang. You bet."

"You wait hea."

She ran into the house and came flying back with a cut-down beer case full of boiled peanuts.

"Sit down," she encouraged, pointing to the driveway.

We sat and ate. No one said a word, partly because we were a little uneasy, partly because the peanuts were so good that we ate non-stop until they were gone.

"Soda? You like soda, yeah? Try wait."

Again she zipped into the house and hustled back with Diamond Head strawberries for each of us.

We thanked her as we stood to leave.

"You come back any time, okay? I always give you something good, okay?"

"Okay." We smiled and walked away.

I was the only one in the group who took Clara up on her offer. She kept her word. Every time I felt hungry before dinner, I'd walk up to her house. She always had boiled soy beans, or shredded mango, or cuttlefish, or something for me. I'd sit there munching away while she blended fruit and vegetable matter into her garden.

Once while we were out there, a slug happened to be oozing by on the curb. Clara got up on her little chicken legs, walked over and grabbed it, and then proceeded to work the creature into the soil with her very sharp weeder.

I stopped crunching on the potato chips she'd provided. Clara noticed the lapse in my activity and purred, "Das good for my lettuce, you know."

"Really?" I shuddered, making a mental note never to eat the Manoa lettuce which had looked so good just moments before.

"Sure. Das organic, you know. Make da vegetables come beeg."

I had a sudden inspiration to do something nice for Clara.

"Hey, Auntie Clara. You want my pigeon droppings for your garden?"

"Oh boy! Dat would be real good for dem, you know."

I ran home and returned with a heaping coffee can full of the treasured manure I'd scraped from the bottom of the coop.

"Eh, tanks yeah," she beamed as she quickly mixed the stuff into the soil.

"You like soy bean? I jus wen boil um today."

Looking skeptically at the soy plants in the middle of the heavily fertilized garden, I hastily declined.

"Gotta go, Auntie Clara. Sorry. I'll bring you droppings next time."

"Eh, Clayton," she called as I walked away. "Mo betta you bring me some birds. I cook for you. Ono, you know."

I turned and looked at her as if she must have been kidding me. It seemed too weird to be real. She was smiling enthusiastically.

"Sure thing," I said, walking away with visions of slug sections, bird droppings, and barbecued pigeons.

Not long after that, I decided that I'd had it with the homing pigeon hobby. I packed all my birds and sent them air freight to a cousin who lived in Kona. Clara, I believe, missed the droppings, and I know she was disappointed that I hadn't offered her any birds to eat.

A few days later, as I approached Clara's house, I noticed a California orange crate propped up with a stick, standing in her driveway. A long string trailed from the stick to the garage. I walked into the dark building, and there sat Clara, peering intently past me at the contraption outside.

"I get food inside, I goin catch da bugga."

"What?" I asked, turning toward the crate.

There, a foot away from the trap, walking right into it, was my Silver Bar. I was amazed. He'd flown all the way back from the Big Island.

I was about to speak when Clara pulled the string.

"I get um, I get um," she screeched, jumping up on her pencil legs and spinning around.

"Sit on da box, Clayton, sit on da box."

The happy hunter raced into her house. I knew the pigeon couldn't lift the crate, but I sat on the box anyway. I was confused. The thought of releasing him crossed my mind, but Auntie Clara came charging back. She carried a large kitchen knife in her hand.

"Get up, Clayton, get up," she screamed.

I rose slowly and stepped backward. Swiftly she knelt, lifted the crate just high enough to reach underneath, and immediately produced my Silver Bar. Walking quickly to the garden, she stooped over the Chinese peas and easily slit the bird's throat with one deft stroke. The animal jerked in her bony hand as she drained its blood into the soil, muttering all the while about a good harvest down the road.

Stunned and sick, I started to make my way for home.

"Eh!" she called. "You like eat dis bugga wit me tonight?"

"No thanks," I gestured over my shoulder. "See you later."

The steam had stopped rising from the pile of debris. Sarge and I sat watching the sun come up. I was stone cold sober, and so was he.

"Gotta go, Sarge. I've got some job interviews this morning."

As I stood to leave, he grabbed my hand.

"I'm going to miss her. Did you know that I really . . . I really did like Clar—Mrs. Wang?"

"I know, Sarge," I replied.

I went toward the stairway. He spoke again:

"Come with me. I'm going to take the birds to Waianae. Follow me out there, please." He looked so pathetic, so drained. I could hear the pigeons stirring in back. I really didn't want to go.

"Okay."

By the time I drove up, he'd loaded the birds into the bed of his truck. The beat up black shotgun case leaned against the door. He took that old gun everywhere.

Sergeant Stillman, an Indiana native, moved into the Nakamoto house across the street from Clara. Twice stationed at Schofield, he'd become attached to Hawaii. A veteran of both the Korean and Vietnam wars, he settled in Honolulu after his retirement. The sergeant looked like a man who might have enjoyed the battles he had fought, though he only mentioned his wartime activities to me once. That was the first day I met him.

One afternoon, not long after the demise of my Silver Bar, I was eating in Clara's driveway while she plowed through her garden. The Nakamoto's front door opened, and out came a large haole man. He held a gun case in one hand, and some rags in the other. He sat on the front step, removed the weapon from its case, and started cleaning it.

"Who's that, Auntie Clara?" I asked, wondering where Mrs. Nakamoto might be.

Clara coughed and spat into the dirt. "New neighbor. Always watch me. Always look down here. Make me nervous." She kept digging in the dirt, muttering to herself.

"Where's Mrs. Nakamoto?"

"Hale Nani. Long time now. You neva know?"

I watched him polish the rifle. I had never seen a gun up close so I considered going over to say hello.

Suddenly he put his work aside. He stood up, walked down the stairs and crossed the street. He stuck out his hand and said, "Sergeant Stillman, Army, retired."

I wiped the shredded mango residue from my hand and shook his. "I'm Clayton. Pleased to meet you." He had quite a grip.

The sergeant stared at Clara for an uncomfortably long time. She seemed oblivious. Finally he took two steps toward her and said louder than necessary, "Sergeant Stillman, Army, retired. Pleased to meet you ma'am."

Auntie Clara looked at him, then at me, and returned to business. The sergeant's face reddened, and I noticed that he slid his hands up and down his pants in a nervous kind of way.

"That's Mrs. Wang." I tried to help. I felt embarrassed.

"Pleased to meet you people. Excuse me. Back to work." He walked quickly back across the street. I followed him.

He started to polish his gun. It was powerful looking.

"I'm sorry about Mrs. Wang."

"No need to apologize, Clayton. I shouldn't have acted so foolishly. All things in good time." He looked down at her, his eyes distant, sad.

I reached out and touched his gun.

"Ever see one of these?" he asked, returning his attention to me. He held the thing up for my inspection.

"No sir," I replied. I'd never said "sir" in my life, but his military air demanded it somehow.

"A Browning Citori trap model shotgun. Over and under 12 gauge. A more beautiful piece of weaponry you'll hardly find."

"Yes sir," I nodded, not really understanding all that he said, but enthusiastic because he seemed so.

"This sweetheart would cost you a bundle, but I picked it up in Nam for a song."

"A song?"

"Yes. Simply picked it up. Easily done. Nice, huh?"

"Very nice," I replied, wondering what he was smiling about.

"I used to kill a great deal of time over there. Trap shooting beer bottles, . . . skeet shooting ration tins."

He'd stopped smiling. He was looking way beyond me somewhere.

"Excuse me, Clayton. Got to fix dinner."

I went back to Clara's driveway. She was still puttering away.

"Auntie Clara. Why didn't you say hello?"

The old woman stopped her digging and turned slowly toward me.

"Why you go up dere? Why you talk so much? You sit. Eat your mango seed."

I ate; she worked. Finally, she jammed her weeder into the ground and, without another word, got up and went into her house. I figured that would be it for the afternoon. As I walked away, I turned back and looked up at the sergeant's house. I could see him staring down at Clara's lot.

I liked Sergeant Stillman from the very beginning, though I didn't quite know what to make out of his preoccupation with Auntie Clara. He seemed like a very kind man. Whenever I went to Clara's he'd talk to me. He'd try to make conversation with Clara too, but she'd never respond. Still, that didn't stop him from trying to get some kind of response out of her.

The Nakamoto's yard had always been in pretty bad shape. That began to change. Sergeant Stillman chopped, mowed, and weeded that place into perfect condition. He always did this work when Clara did hers. I supposed that Clara would admire his yardwork, so I couldn't understand why she never did compliment him on it. One day I asked her about it:

"Auntie Clara. Isn't Sarge's yard nice and neat?"

She gave me one of her hard looks. Then she looked up toward his lot. "Hmph. Dat man drink too much." She kept on working.

I'd never thought about it much before, but she was right about the drinking. Whenever I'd talk to him he did smell of alcohol. With the passage of time, his drinking got worse.

One day he had really been putting it away. He leaned precariously against the Norfolk. I wondered if he'd fall over on me. He was observing Clara, as usual.

"She doesn't like my yard."

"Sure she does, Sarge. She admires it very much," I forced myself to lie.

"She doesn't tell me."

I didn't know what to say.

"Clayton. A fine woman like Mrs. Wang should have someone to take care of her, don't you think?"

"She used to. Her husband died a few years ago, and I guess she misses him very much."

The sergeant leaned heavily on his knees. He looked really unhappy now. I guessed I'd said the wrong thing. Down in the valley, a flock of homing pigeons was flying.

"I used to have birds too," I said. "Auntie Clara loved to mix the droppings into her garden."

"You don't say?" The sergeant brightened up and sat forward on the bench. "I admire those birds, Clayton. The troops could have used a lesson or two from them. True precision."

Stillman stared down at Auntie Clara.

"Young man, do you still have your coop?"

"Yes sir."

"You don't suppose that I could buy it from you, do you?"

I had a sudden inspiration to do something nice for him.

"You can have it for nothing, Sarge. For a song."

He turned and stared at me for a second. Then he smiled.

"Now?" he asked. "Today?"

Together we broke my coop down. Together we reassembled it. I told him about old Mr. Izawa in Kalihi Valley. How he would sell good young birds cheap. The sergeant was so excited that he went right over there the next day.

A couple of weeks later I went down the dead end street, and there, on Clara's sidewalk, sat a large cardboard box full of pigeon manure.

"Psst. Psst," Clara called to me from the dark garage. I walked inside.

"Eh Clayton!" she demanded, obviously upset. "Why you give him your coop? How come you tell him I like da droppings? What you tink you?"

I was very uneasy.

"I'm sorry Auntie Clara."

"Sorry my foot. You Clayton. Ho you. Look what you wen do! Get outta my garage! Doan eva come back!"

She turned and stomped off.

I felt terrible. Losing Auntie Clara was like losing a real relative. After that I never saw her in the garden again. It went untended. She didn't even harvest the crop that was already flourishing.

Every day I'd go by in hopes of finding Clara out there. I wanted to apologize to her. The box of manure just sat there, deteriorating. One night I went over very late and threw the mess away.

Even Sergeant Stillman must have given up on Clara. Even he stopped coming outside after a while. The only tangible evidence that anyone was still alive came at 5:00 P.M. every afternoon. Those pigeons flew like clockwork right up until the day I left for college.

The sun was pretty high by the time we reached the end of the road. Sarge, dressed in Army jacket, cap, and black boots, still wearing the ash covered undershirt and pants, walked ahead of me on the unpaved road. The shotgun case under his arm, he carried a single caged bird in each hand. They must have been special to him. I struggled behind with two large cages containing eight to ten birds apiece.

We walked a good distance in silence.

"This way," he said finally. We turned off into the bushes and headed uphill. The brush was high and dense, and the trails were narrow. I hoped he knew the path well because I would have been easily lost.

We climbed for the longest time, twisting and turning our way to wherever it was he wanted to go. I had decided to ask for a break, but we emerged into a clearing. It was the end of the line, a kind of rock outcrop which looked out at the wide Pacific.

"Here," he said, setting down the cages and gun on a large, flat stone. I gladly dropped the cages there.

He went off to some bushes on the side. When he returned, he carried a gallon jug. We sat together.

"Good stuff," he said, patting the bottle and looking into it longingly. After uncorking it, he began to swallow hard.

"Here," he said, handing me the liquor.

The mash was potent, but I forced down a few mouthfuls. We drank in turn until I had had too much.

Then he broke the silence:

"Clayton," he almost whispered, pausing a long time to stare out to sea. "You must take all the time you need to find that job."

He drank some more, then spoke again:

"Don't ever settle for just anything. You must never be locked into a routine that consumes your life."

I lay down beside him, dizzy and fatigued. I closed my eyes.

"Don't ever tie yourself down, boy. Do you understand me?"

I think I answered in the affirmative.

When I came to, the sun was sinking. I stood and saw that the sergeant had a second bottle on the way to empty.

"Better let them go, Sarge."

"You do it. But leave the two Red Checks for me."

I walked over and undid the latches of the larger cages. Stepping back to avoid the crush, I lifted the covers. The homing pigeons rose in a low roar of wing flapping and rushing air. They headed straight for the setting sun, circled overhead three times, and then headed for town.

"Excuse me, Sarge. Bathroom." I went down the trail several yards.

I was coming back to the outcrop when I heard the explosion. I ran and stopped at the clearing entrance. Stillman sat with the shotgun cradled in his arms. The dying light shone in his eyes, and he smiled a wicked smile.

"What you shooting at?" I asked softly, shivering at the sight.

"Here," he said, getting slowly to his feet. "I'll show you."

Moving to the flat rock, he stooped and undid the catch of the single cage. The other carrier lay on its side, a few yards to the right.

Positioning the shotgun at his side, he kicked the last cage over. The startled Red Check flopped on the ground momentarily, and then shot straight for the last speck of sun. Stillman swiftly raised the weapon to his shoulder, sighted, and fired. Instantly the bird disintegrated into a cloud of feathers.

I stopped breathing for several seconds. The sergeant scanned the horizon. Once again he smiled that peculiar smile. He murmured:

"If I could see far enough, you know, Korea would be just about over there."

He gestured with the barrel of the gun.

"And Nam," he pivoted slightly, "right about there."

We stood in silence. The sun was gone.

"Oh, Clara," I heard him sigh.

"Sarge. We'd better go." I was scared.

The sound of the gun breaking open startled me. The spent shells jingled on the ground. I heard him reload.

"We better split now, Sarge," I pleaded.

"You go, Clayton. I'll stay here—kill time."

"I'll get lost, Sarge. I can't see."

"No you won't. You go downhill from here. All the trails lead to the bottom."

The sound of the gun closing made me sweat.

"Please, Sarge," I begged.

"Get out of here, Clayton!" he yelled.

I jumped, turned, and started to move down the trail as quickly as possible.

"Take good care of those birds," was the last thing I heard him say.

I wanted to get to my car in a hurry. I had to call the police. I had to help. The way out was difficult. I was cut up by the dense brush. Getting out wasn't nearly as easy as he'd made it seem.

When I did finally make the road, I ran like crazy for the beginning of the pavement. Just as I reached the parking area, I heard the final explosion.

They sent Sergeant Stillman's body back to Indiana. The day after he shot himself, I went to his house, crated the pigeons, locked up the coop, and sent them off to my cousin in Kona.

I came home from the airport and collapsed on my bed. Just as I began to drift off, I woke myself, got up, and walked over to the sergeant's house. I unlocked the coop door, propped it open, and filled the two troughs with seed and water.

The homing instinct is incredibly strong. Those birds will travel unbelievable distances to return to the familiar confines of home. They can't really seem to help themselves. If any of them did happen to make it back, I wanted to be sure it felt welcome, comfortable. Still, I hoped that I would never see any of them ever again.

Yahk Fahn, Auntie

DARRELL H. Y. LUM

Jimmy would sit at the table with his fork and his father would spoon out the rice. Jimmy always got the plate with the chip in it and was always served last. That meant he got the bottom of the pot where the rice was brown and clumpy and soggy sometimes if it wasn't cooked long enough. Jimmy once asked how come he was always last. His father would look up from his spooning and say, "Because you're the littlest. When you're not the littlest then you won't get served last." Jimmy said, "Oh," and thought about that for awhile. It wasn't until later when he was sitting around and thinking about things that he figured out that he would always be the littlest because everybody was bigger than he. Or at least it would be a long time before he wasn't the littlest. His father probably hadn't thought of that but that was okay. Besides now that he was big enough to use a glass cup instead of his old chewed up plastic one and sometimes pour his own milk he didn't really mind being last for the rice.

Once Jimmy asked Auntie Tsu when he would be an uncle. Aunt Tsu laughed at first but explained that when she got married and had children then she would let Jimmy be an honorary uncle. He asked her right the next day if she were married yet but Auntie Tsu was busy and just said, "No," and looked away. Jimmy was confused for a long time about Auntie because his mother had said that she wasn't really his aunt. He asked his mother how come and she said Auntie came from China, that she ran away with grandmother and came to live with them when po-po died. But when Jimmy asked why, his mother was busy.

Once in awhile they would go to eat at a restaurant and Jimmy would be sure to announce, "I not going sit at the high chair."

"Okay, okay. What do you want to eat," his father would ask. Jimmy would always answer, "Chow mein kind," because they came in plates not bowls.

"Yum cha, Jimmy," Auntie Tsu would urge.

"I want Coca-Cola, I no like tea."

"Jimmy, the tea is very good," Auntie would persist.

"Don't force him if he doesn't want to," his mother would say. "But no Coke. You already had one before lunch."

Jimmy would pout and stab his fork at his noodles but secretly triumph over Auntie Tsu. She can have her lousy tea he would think and busy himself with his fork making such a racket that sometimes the other people in the restaurant would look and his father would quietly say, "One more sound out of you and that fork Jimmy. . . ." His father would never finish his sentences when he spoke to Jimmy like that. Jimmy would always imagine horrible things and he would always stop.

He stood watching them crank the coffin down. They said Auntie was asking for him just before she died. She had died before he had gotten a chance to see her. He must've been in L.A. changing planes. Jimmy stood in line and watched the rest of the family toss a clump of dirt into the hole and poke a stick of wispy incense into the burner. He followed their actions feeling clumsy and conspicuous.

The feast for Auntie Tsu was arranged before the gravestone; chicken, eggs, and pork, five bowls of rice and a cup of tea beside each one. He imagined one bowl was for Auntie and the rest was for the family. Jimmy watched an uncle tip each bowl and toss a bit of food on the ground. When he was through the scene looked as if Auntie had nibbled at the chicken and had a bite of rice. Auntie must be smiling Jimmy thought because his mother could never make chicken as well as Auntie could. Jimmy wondered which bowl was his. He thought he saw one of them with a tiny chip but he wasn't sure.

It was a good funeral with wailers and flutes and lots of relatives and crying. But Jimmy was tired and wished he understood the chants and the bells and the burning paper. A Caucasian man tried to take pictures but some uncle threatened him and chased him away. Jimmy clutched a piece of candy and a lee-see, a quarter wrapped in red paper which someone said was, "From your Auntie to sweeten the sorrow."

There was a party after the funeral where one uncle stripped to his undershirt and solemnly urged everyone to eat. Jimmy sat down and when the food came, everyone ate. There was no fork at the table. Jimmy meant to ask the waitress but by then everyone at the table had noticed that he wasn't eating.

"I'm not very hungry, excuse me." He made for the door but another unknown relative intercepted him and handed him a bowl and a pair of chopsticks. "You're supposed to keep these and the armband," he told Jimmy.

Jimmy walked back to the car in the wake of his father's explanation to the group, "He's had a long trip back."

Why had he come back? Seven years. He hadn't come back for seven years. He watched his hands drop the bowl, the chopsticks following, and he wished he understood why.

"Jimmy, yahk fahn lo!" Auntie Tsu would call. Jimmy would usually refuse to answer and pretend not to hear. He knew perfectly well that it meant to come and eat but he always waited for Auntie to come downstairs and mutter, "Lo-lo," and tell him to hurry and get inside before dinner got cold. She always said that even when they had cold ginger chicken.

"Use your chopsticks, Jimmy," Auntie would say. She would pick a particularly juicy piece of chicken and reach across the table and plunk it down on top of his rice.

"No, I no like."

"I don't want to, Jimmy," his mother would correct gently. Jimmy would take his plate and put his mouth to the edge and shovel the food into his mouth with a fork. He liked when everyone ate from plates. But when Auntie Tsu cooked, they used bowls and drank tea. Jimmy would always get angry when Auntie would forget his favorite chipped plate and only leave chopsticks and a bowl at his place. Jimmy would get his plate from the top shelf and push the tea away all the while crying silently with little hiccups. Auntie would say she was sorry she forgot and pick something good from the table and deposit it in Jimmy's plate. Jimmy would keep on pouting until he was sure everybody at the table knew how he felt about the matter and then eat Auntie's morsel.

His mother and father and Auntie would always talk Chinese when there was something they didn't want Jimmy to hear. Sometimes when Jimmy asked what they said his father would say, "If you did a little studying for Chinese school you'd know."

"Huh!" Jimmy would say. "All we ever do is write the same old stuff and say the same old stuff and read the same old stuff." Sometimes though, when Auntie Tsu said something that sounded interesting, Jimmy would say it to himself over and over so he wouldn't forget and listen for it in Chinese school. He never asked anybody because he was afraid it might be something bad or dirty and he didn't want anyone to think his Auntie Tsu said bad things. Because of this, he never found out what they meant because the teachers at school never talked about the same things as Auntie Tsu.

Jimmy never learned much in Chinese school because he always wrote things in American. He did his homework by writing the first strokes of each character down the page, then the second, and the third instead of completing each character one at a time. His assembly line characters were always poorly spaced but he was always the first to finish.

It was windy the next day when Jimmy walked through Chinatown, his nose curling at the suddenly familiar sounds and smells. The wind blew steadily until the old men sitting on crates in the storefronts had to fold their newspapers and go inside. The wind smelled of salted things, fish, cabbage, and duck from the corner grocery where his mother used to poke around the bins to choose a salted fish worthy of being cleaned and soaked and steamed. The old storefront was just as he remembered it, plastered with "Kent with the Micronite Filter" posters and the torn green awnings that were lowered each afternoon to keep the sun out of the dark smelly interior.

Jimmy turned the corner and walked into a restaurant. The greasy menu was written in two languages and Jimmy held it trying to remember the words. The waitress brought a glass of water, slapped a pair of chopsticks down on a napkin and stood with pad in hand waiting for his order.

"Uh . . . one order of chow mein, uh . . . gee yuk chow mein?" Jimmy ordered.

"Yut gwo order gee yuk chow mein," she repeated.

He mixed some soy sauce and hot mustard in a little dish and listened as his order was relayed to the kitchen, "Gee yuk chow mein." The response through the swinging doors was a lazy "Wai," accompanied by a splattering of oil.

The steaming noodles were delivered to his table about five minutes later and were deposited along with the check on the table's edge. The tiny mountain of noodles topped with pork, broccoli, and gravy fogged his glasses as he bent over the plate. He fumbled with the chopsticks for awhile managing to catapult a few pieces of meat into his mouth before he gave up. He flagged the waitress down, asked for a fork and absently complained that his teacup was badly cracked and chipped. She brought him a fork and went away.

When Auntie Tsu would take him to the temple, Jimmy would have to kneel and pray before the gilt Buddha. He bowed three times and made the praying motions until his aunt, satisfied as to his reverence, would give him a coin wrapped in red paper. He would have to wait until Auntie finished lighting the incense and stick the bunch into the sandfilled holder before she allowed him to go across the street to spend his lee-see. Auntie Tsu stayed in the temple to talk to the round-faced monk with the shaven head. The monk always smiled, a wan, kindly smile and sometimes would teach Auntie a new chant. Jimmy thought that his aunt could chant the best of all the ladies there. He didn't understand what everything meant but then again he never asked. He was afraid that he was supposed to know and that he wouldn't get any more lee-see if he asked.

He left the restaurant, wandering through the street rediscovering the wrinkled men and dirty children who played in the leaning balconies of the tenement houses shouting epithets in Chinese. An old woman carrying a worn shopping bag recognized him from the funeral and asked him something in a whining voice. Her eyes were wet and she clung to his shirt tugging at the sleeve. She kept pointing and gesturing and Jimmy kept saying, "Me no talk Chinee, no talk Chinee." He gave her a dollar and fled.

Jimmy watched her sit, carefully sweeping her hands across her rump first then settling down like a hen coming to roost. He watched her eyebrows dance as she talked in a careful Midwestern tone slipping occasionally into a local accent. He said, "Yes, that's right," so that she would continue. She blinked a lot, her eyelids scotch taped into a Caucasian double fold. Haole. Chinese eyes trying to be haole . . . Caucasian eyes. Jimmy looked around and every table had the same haole-ed oriental. Ironed flat straight hair and carefully made up noses to make it look as if there really were a bridge. He ordered another scotch. She had a mai tai. She giggled and lowered her eyes and crossed and recrossed her legs, her nylons swishing. He was supposed to take her hand now and suggest they go somewhere but he didn't feel like it. He knew the signals. He had learned them in the Army. Only there it had been Chicano chicks and a few Puerto Ricans. But they all looked about the same and always crossed their legs when the time came. Instead he ordered dinner.

They waited. Jimmy's dinner came in several bowls of painted porcelain and a large wooden tub of rice; hers came on a single platter, steak and potato. The waitress offered Jimmy a fork but he waved her off and gamely struggled with his chopsticks while she loitered over her meal quizzing him on New York and the fashions. He scooped out more rice. It had been a long time since he had rice. Or at least rice that stuck together and could be spooned in clumps. Haole rice always had butter in it and fell into the plate in a loose pile. He served himself then looked up to see her watching. Without asking, he scooped some rice over her baked potato.

Auntie Tsu would have laughed because she had once written to ask whether he had met a nice Chinese girl in New York. And here he was back home with a nice Chinese girl and a baked potato.

"Yahk fahn, Auntie," Jimmy said softly.

Primo Doesn't
Take Back Bottles Anymore

DARRELL H. Y. LUM

"Four cases, that's one dollar and seventy-six cents, Rosa." Harry of Receiving Bottle Empties wrote up the ticket for Rosa and made change from the register. Rosa K. dropped his load of empty Primo bottles on the counter and figured out his profit. If he walked home he could save a quarter busfare. Rosa used to list his occupation as "construction laborer" whenever he got picked up by some rookie cop for being a "suspicious person" rummaging through garbage cans. But now that he only collected empties to turn in at the brewery, he figured himself to be a "collector." It was forty cents a case, even more for the bigger bottles.

"Thanks, eh, I see you," Rosa said and shuffled out of the brewery, the money carefully folded into his handkerchief and jammed into his front pocket. He hoped that Harry wouldn't check the last case until he left. It was short three bottles. The three unbroken ones he should have gotten if that old lady hadn't caught him.

Harry checked the cases and smiled as he filled the empty slots in Rosa's last case with some extra bottles he always saved for Rosa. He remembered the first time Rosa had come in all shabby and ragged, a pair of tattered jeans buttoned underneath his pot belly and a silken aloha shirt with hula girls and Diamond Head and "Honolulu-Paradise" written all over it.

"Sorry man, read the sign, can't refund any amount less than three dollars. Come back when you have seven cases," Harry had said.

"Look, bruddah, I no can carry all dis back home, I nevah know about the rules. C'mon give a guy a break. As means I no mo busfare home."

"Okay, look I'll cash in your three cases now and add 'em to the next guy's load. But just this once. My boss finds out and I'm in trouble, you understand?"

Rosa had smiled and had given him a little thumb and pinkie wave. "Thanks, eh," he had said. Since then Rosa had been coming in every week with his pickings in his arms, catching the bus to the brewery and walking home to save the quarter. Sometimes he brought something for Harry, some seaweed, a small bass, a little opihi in a smelly shopping bag along with his empties.

We used to have kick haole ass day in school. One time this one kid, little ass buggah with one big mouth, his father was one manager of someplace or something. He went come inside the bathroom, cocky and smart mouth, went push Willy so I went kick the shit out of him. Nothing on the face so no can see the marks, just in the balls. The little shit started cry. He say, "I going tell my father . . . I going tell my father. . . ." So I tole him, "Look boo, you tell you faddah and you going get somemore." Yeah, we used to think we was big stuff. Go smoke in front the teacher for see what she do. She no can do nothing. One time she call my muddah though, and my faddah beat me up bad. He tell I gotta get one education. I nevah go school for one week. The social worker had for take me hospital. Willy, he just one mahu. The kids used to tease me that my bruddah one tilly, but I take care of them. Willy, he wanna be one mahu, he be one mahu, as okay. One time Willy and his frens go make one mahu day in school, come all dress up. Whooo, make the girls jealous.

Rosa peered through his dark glasses out at the large metal garbage bin of the apartment building. He had to squint because the flimsy lenses did little to cut the glare. He had found them outside the theatre about two months ago when there was a 3-D movie. It was a good pair with plastic frames and looked like regular sunglasses except for the small print at the top of the frame which said, "For 3-D Panavision only. Do not use as sunglasses." The garbage bins looked a funny shade of white, the glasses cancelling the green paint of the metal. Large bins rarely held empties because only places like business offices and schools used them. But this was an apartment building and it was sure to have at least a case or two of empties. If someone asked him he could always say that he lost something in the bin. Rosa figured that apartment building garbage was surely anybody's. No one could tell whose garbage was whose. His search yielded a case of Miller, two six-packs of Schlitz, and only one six-pack of Primo. "Fucking haoles only drink shit," he muttered and stuffed the Primos into his shopping bag.

I used to think all the haoles look at me funny so I kick their asses and they still look at me funny. I wasn't that bad though. When I make "search take" on one guy, I everytime give 'em back busfare. Bye' m' bye they gotta call their faddah for come pick them up after school.

The entry on the police record said, "Assault and Battery, Petty Theft, Item—Bottles, empty, six dozen; Bottles, unopened, approximately one

dozen; Location—Jay's Bar and Grill, suspect apprehended boarding Munici-
pal bus (Aala Park) 10:55 P.M., owner James Nakayama reported prowler in
back of premises, scuffle ensued; Damage—Two dozen empty bottles, broken, one dozen unopened Primo brand beer, approximate cost $3.50; Pre-
vious Record—Rosario Kamahele, A & B, Central Intermediate School,
enrolled student, grade 9, nineteen years old, charged as adult on request of
school authorities and referred to Department of Social Services; Present
Occupation—Unemployed laborer." The sergeant at the desk had said that he
was an unemployed laborer when Rosa was brought in and booked. The lady
at the welfare office had also told him that after he got kicked out of the
ninth grade of his third and final school. He was just a kid then, a smart ass
kid who beat up on anybody who didn't pay protection money. He was the
bull of the school and ruler of the second floor lavatory. Some haole kid had
told his father and the judge had sent him away to the Boys Home for three
months. When he got out he joined the union and was a laborer. He almost
became a carpenter's apprentice when he and half the crew got laid off. That
was when he started collecting bottles. For awhile the money from empties
was all he had to live on until the welfare came.

*After I come out of the Home, the judge tell me I join the Army or go work, 'cause I
too old for go back ninth grade. The judge he say I can go night school with older people so I no beat up people no more and then he assign me one social worker, one haole
lady, Miss Prussy, for check up on me. I tell Miss Prussy that I like live with Willy,
that I gotta take care Willy. She say I no can, that mahus, that home-saxtuals like
live with their own kind. I tell her, ". . . but that my bruddah." She tell I gotta get one
healthy family relationship and atta-tude. So Miss Prussy she find me one place with
one Portogee family and man they thought I was one servant. Rosa do this, Rosa do
that or we going tell the social worker for cut your check down. So one time I get fed
up and I say, "Shove it," and I split.*

The sticky smell of stale beer at the brewery always made Rosa thirst for a
"tall, cool one." A dollar seventy-six was enough for a six-pack and still leave
extra for busfare. Almazon, the Filipino bookie, expected his ten bucks
today. Almazon sold everything from lucky number chances to a "social
worker home," a place where guys like Rosa could claim legal residence in a
respectable home for the social worker's visits. Ten bucks a month to Almazon kept the family quiet.

*The one time that I was scared for beef one haole after school was with this six-foot
guy from California. He was in the smart class. I went tell one of my guys for let him*

know I wanted for see him, to tell him who was the big shit around Central. He was one show off too, that guy. He had his driver's permit and drove one car to school everyday. The day I was supposed to beef 'em I went skip class and went send Willy for steal some booze for me. Willy come back with Mama's bourbon inside one empty jelly bottle. Willy say the guys was talking that the haole's faddah was one marine. I tell, "So what," and drink the liquor down real fast and started for punch the wall of the lav for practice. The wall was hollow cement tiles and the pipes inside 'em went make one "tonk" everytime I punch the wall. I thought of all the haoles in the whole world and I went punch the wall somemore. Willy, he come scared and say something about Mama and I say to him, "Fucking mahu!" and Willy come real quiet. As the first time I call Willy that and he come real quiet. That make me more piss off and I punch the wall somemore until my hand it start for bleed and I no can feel no sore but I still punch the wall and then the teacher come and tell me for stop and I no can stop and my hand it keep making one fist and keep going and then I cry and Willy, he cry too, but Willy cry easy. I no cry, I no supposed to cry, but I cry. And then the teacher he take me to the dispensary and I try punch the nurse and get blood on top her nurse dress. . . . They say that the haole was looking for me after school for beef me and I wasn't there. . . .

Rosa got off the bus with a stinking paper sack and one case of empties under his arm. He had spent most of the week picking opihi from the rocks at low tide and only had had enough time to collect one case of empties. But he had a mayonnaise jar of opihi to give to Harry.

Workmen were painting over the old red brick of the brewery when Rosa shuffled up with his load. The "Receiving Bottle Empties" sign was painted over and the old smells were replaced by those of fresh paint and turpentine. Harry had acted brusquely last week and had mumbled something about bums who trade in bottles below the minimum refund amount and get employees in trouble and new management and aluminum cans but Rosa had just smiled and walked out quickly because his cases were short again.

One of the painters noticed his empties and said, "Eh, man, you can't bring back empties anymore. The new man doesn't want them. Ought to just throw them away."

Rosa felt an old rage and the tight clenching of his fists, the punching feeling. He turned to the painter and said, "Why you paint over the sign, why you no want my bottles, why you do that, I bring something for Harry today, and you do that, where Harry my fren', Harry my fren' he no do that. . . ."

The painter shook his head and said, "Not me, fella, why don't you talk to the boss." He turned and left. Rosa walked around in little circles, clenching and unclenching his fists, finally stopping before the blanked-out sign. A brush and paint can sat on the ground before him. Rosa grabbed the brush and in several quick motions wrote "F-O-C-K" on the sign. The paint was the same color as the sign but the work was visible as the sun glistened off the dripping letters. Rosa crossed the street and sat at the bus stop watching his word dry in the afternoon heat. The painter never came back and the word disappeared as the sun dried the glistenings and the streaks melted away.

The Moiliili Bag Man

DARRELL H. Y. LUM

One time by da Humane Society, had one bummy guy at da drive-in. He was eating from da rubbish can. Yeah. My fren tell, "Ass da Moiliili Bag Man dat. Try look, get anykine plastic bag hanging from his belt. I tink he got um from Star Market."

Da Bag Man was looking through da rubbish can and eating da leftovers. Yeah, da throw way awready kine. Mostly he was looking fo da plate lunches, fo da extra rice. He no care, da guy. We was looking at him from our table and da girl behind da counter stay shaking her head watching da Bag Man. Little while more, da cook guy wit one dirty apron and one broom and dustpan came outside from da kitchen part fo sweep rubbish. Da cook guy was so stink man, cause he jes go empty da dustpan, all dirt and rubbish la dat, right in da can dat da Bag Man was looking. Da Bag Man no say nutting . . . but da cook guy was stink, yeah? He could tell da Bag Man was still yet using da can.

Da Bag man never know what fo do. He jes went stand dere by da can. Den he went check his bags: cigarette bag wit planny butts and bus up kine cigarettes, someting else in one nudda one, and look like one half orange, peeled awready in one nudda one.

Russo, das my fren, told me dat people sometimes go give da Bag Man money jes so dat he go away from dem. Even if he not boddering dem, dey give um money. I guess dey no like look at him or someting. Funny yeah?

Anyway, I no can tell if da Bag Man is happy or sad or piss off or anyting l'dat cause he get one moosetash and skinny kine beard wit only little bit strands, stay hide his mout. But his eyes, da Bag Man's eyes, stay always busy . . . looking, looking, looking.

I look back at him, and to me, he ack like he little bit shame. We stay da only small kids sitting down at da tables, me and Russo, but da Bag Man ack like he no like know us.

Had one nudda guy in one tee shirt dat was sitting at da table next to us

105

was watching da Bag Man too. He was eating one plate lunch and afterwards he went take his plate over to da Bag Man. Still had little bit everyting on top, even had bar-ba-que meat left.

"Brah," day guy tell, "you like help me finish? I stay full awready."

Da Bag Man no tell nutting, only nod his head and take da plate. I thought he would eat um real fast . . . gobble um up, you know. But was funny, he went put um down and go to da counter fo get one napkin and make um nice by his place . . . da fork on top da napkin. Even he took da plate out of da box, made um jes like real restaurant. I wanted fo give him someting too but I only had my cup wit little bit ice left. I awready went drink up all da Coke and was chewing da ice. Da Bag Man was looking at me now, not at me, but at my cup. I nevah know what fo do cause j'like I selfish if I keep my cup but nevah have nutting inside awready, so shame eh if you give somebody someting but stay empty. But I nevah know what fo do cause I had to go awready. I thought I could jes leave da cup on da table or be like da tee shirt guy and tell, "Brah, hea."

So I went get up and walk half way and den turn back like I went foget throw away my cup. I went look at da Bag Man and say, "You like um?"

Da Bag Man nevah say nutting still yet but I knew he wanted um so I jes went leave um on his table. I was curious fo see what he was going do wit um so I went make like I was fussing around wit someting on my bike. He went get out his handachief from his front pants pocket and unwrap um. Had all his coins inside um and he went take out fifteen cents. Den he went take da cup to da window and point to da sign dat went say, "Refills—15¢"

"Coke," he told da girl. Sly da guy! When I went pass him on my bike, I thought I saw him make one "shaka" sign to me. Wasn't up in da air, was down by his leg, j'like he was saying, "Tanks, eh" to me.

Da next time I went see da Bag Man was by da shave ice place, Goodie Goodie Drive In. He was jes grinding one plate lunch, man. I dunno if he went buy um. I doubt it though. I thought I saw his busy eyes recanize me, but I dunno. I jes went nod my head, jes in case he was telling "hi."

Aftah dat, j'like everyplace I go, he stay. Da Bag Man stay. One time me and my bruddah went Bellows Beach fo bodysurf and da Bag Man was dere. I heard my bruddah folks calling him Waimanalo Eddie but was him, da Moiliili Bag Man.

Was jes like I knew him by heart awready. I mean, j'like we was frens. I seen him by da Boy Scout camp checking tings out. One ting about Boy Scouts, dey get plenny food, dey no run out, dem. But you know what, dey nevah know how fo cook rice. Dey went jam um up and had to dump um cause was too mooshy and wasn't right. Da Bag Man was right dere even befo one scoop rice went inside da rubbish can. Could tell he was happy, boy. J'like he was dancing. His okole was wiggling and he was holding out his plastic bag fo da throw way rice.

All da small kids, da Cub Scouts, started fo come around da Bag Man and ask him questions. "What you going do wit dat?" "How come you get so much tings in da bags?" One real small kid, wasn't even one Cub Scout, went tell, "You one bum?"

Da Bag Man jes went smile and tell, "Dis fo my cat. He like dis kine rice." Den da scout mastah went try fo get all da kids fo go back by him. "Come ova hea. Da man jes going take da food fo his pigs or someting, buta kaukau. Come. I show you how fo make da fire so da ting no piu," he went tell dem. But of course nobody was listening, dey still like hang around da Bag Man. Finally da Bag Man had to tell, "Eh, you fahdah stay calling you guys. Tanks, eh."

Aftah dat, I nevah see da Bag Man fo long time. I nevah see him so I nevah even tink about him until one day, me and Russo went go Ala Moana beach and we went go fuss around by da end of da canal, by da pond part where sometimes get da guys wit da radio dat control da boats. Dose guys get piss off man, if you blast dey boats wit rocks. Heh, heh, good fun though sometimes.

But nevah have boats dis time so me and Russo was playing try-come, try-come. Ass when you try fo get da uddah guy come by you fo look at someting, but only stay bullshet like, "Try come, try come look dis doo-doo stay look like one hairy hot dog." And you try jazz um up so dat da uddah guy like come by you instead of him trying fo make you go by him.

So Russo went tell, "Try come, try come. Get one ma-ke man stay in da bushes. He stay ma-ke on anykine *food,* la dat!"

Shet. I knew no can be. Dat Russo, he such a bull-liar. So I was going tell him some interesting stuff about doo-doo but Russo went tell real scared, "Da *ma-ke* man leg went move!" So I went by him.

"He only sleeping, stupit," I went tell Russo real soft, jes in case da guy was really sleeping.

"No, he *ma-ke* die dead," Russo went say.

"How you know?"

"I know. Maybe somebody went murder him!"

By now Russo was making up anykine stories and talking mo loud and I knew wasn't *ma-ke* man cause da legs was moving somemore and could hear sombody talking from inside da bushes.

"Sucka. Sucking kids, beat it befo I smash your face."

Was da Bag Man. He was blinking his eyes real plenny and den he went look at us, stink eye. Russo was getting chicken and was backing up little by little, but I jes went stay.

"Howsit," da Bag Man went tell me. Den he went check his bags, jes making sure was all still dere.

We jes went look at each udda but dis time da Bag Man's eyes wasn't so busy. He jes started fo rip up one coconut leaf. Was sharp, man. He had one super long fingernail on his thumb dat was jes right fo rip da coconut leaf into skinny strips yeah, and little while mo he went make one bird out of da coconut leaf. He nevah say nutting. He jes went stick um behind his ear. He went look at me, den at Russo, den at me again. I thought he was going scold us or someting but he jes went start making one nudda bird. Only dis time he nevah go so fast. In fack, he went real slow, j'like he was teaching me how. When he was pau he went give um to me and den he jes went split, even befo I went tell um tanks.

When I went home, I went put da Bag Man's bird on top my bureau and even if I nevah see him long time aftah dat Ala Moana park time, I went tink of him everytime I saw da bird dere on top da bureau. Sometimes I try practice make birds but I couldn't do um like da Bag Man. I could almost do um but mines came out funny kine. I used to wonder if da Bag Man was in Waimanalo or if he was grinding food at da drive-in or if he was making birds too at Ala Moana.

And den one day I was fussing around wit his bird, was all brown and coming had-it. Nevah have nutting fo do so I went try make da bird again. I kept looking at da Bag Man's bird and den back at mines one. Back and fort. Back and fort. I had to laugh cause must've been funny. Must've looked like da Bag Man's busy eyes . . . looking, looking, looking.

Den, shet, was so easy. I went make um! Came out perfeck! I went make my bird look exact like his one. I went get somemore coconut leaf and try one mo time cause even I nevah believe. Da stuff came out again!

I wanted fo go Waimanalo or Ala Moana or drive-in right away . . . but I nevah see him aftah dat time at Ala Moana park. And everyplace I go, I stay looking, looking, looking. But if I was to see him, I would make one bird fo him and den hold my hand down wit da shaka sign and make, "Tanks, eh."

The Rock

IAN MACMILLAN

Calder hits the water with the gleeful vigor of a boy, resisting the shocking cold by churning his legs in a burst of muscular energy. He aims himself at the mysterious, giant rock rising out of the deep water at the mouth of the bay. It is over a mile from shore and halfway there are the crushing breakers which will curl on him with unpredictable ferocity. He has been told more than once that sharks infest the area of the rock, and he has been toying with the idea of cautious approach now for six or seven trips out. Today he has decided that he will make it all the way. He has only been diving four months, but his equipment—fins, mask, snorkel, and spear—all show the satisfying scratches and salt stains of frequent use. He churns along using more force than he needs to because he likes to resist the gentle and powerful motions of the water, likes to challenge its vast, soft bulk.

There is something else—it is the quick and surrealistic, silent pastel brutality of the ocean. Perpetually amazed by it, he regards himself as a humble alien in the last real wilderness, moving in clumsy slow motion in an environment where survival depends on absolute attention. He has been eyeing the rock for months, has been venturing out farther and farther, through the violent and turbulent waves and into the relative calm of the twenty feet of water outside of the reef. He has gone as far as two-thirds of the way without encountering anything odd except very large and dangerous looking moray eels and some different fish. He is drawn to the rock, trudges along using more energy than he needs to use, enjoying the mummified fear somewhere at the back of his mind thinking, stripped almost naked for it. Stripped down to nothing but a goddamned pathetic bathing suit almost a mile offshore in a place whose only sound is the hum and the ticking of a buzzing confusion of life and me, the humble alien, who trades in gravity for its opposite, goggle-eyed and frightened and enjoying every second.

Calder is a New Yorker in Hawaii. He got his year here through a few tricky manipulations of influence, losing a casual friend or two and probably gaining back two or three who would turn out to be more valuable than the ones lost. He designs air-conditioning systems, and he was here only three weeks before he settled into his normal, lazy routine, a continuation of what he did in New York, almost nothing in the morning, drink a little too much at lunch, occupy a house a small notch above his means. Until he discovered the water, there was little that interested him here after the initial one week introduction to what he decided was a corrupted paradise. Not considering the water, here he lived in the moist laziness of a perpetual New York summer without the familiar urban discomforts. Half the secretaries were oriental, half the men you dealt with were oriental, you could not get the *New York Times* when it was fresh enough to read. In the evening you drank either your own or someone else's Scotch, or you entertained at your house or were entertained at someone else's.

The rilled sand passes under him slowly and he feels like a slow motion bird, his eyes darting into the corners of his limited field of vision and his legs churning along with more energy than he needs to move at a good pace. He raises his head out into the noisy wind and eyes the enlarging rock. Feels the fear and the eerie hollowness of the unexpected lying out there, jaws open, just beyond the pastel limit of his vision. Thinking, nobody near, so vulnerable, out of yell's reach, close to obliteration without a trace.

Calder is thirty-two and not usually inclined to introspection, but the water and its ticking silence and its pastel madness of life and his own freakish isolation almost a mile out turn his mind into itself with him thinking nearly without words, naked and alone with fear and tense-jawed excitement you really feel *here,* don't you, really, breathing hard enough to hurt your lungs. He slows down, gasping through the snorkel, through the little death rattle of collected water at the bottom of the U, thinking, I can really breathe— Jesus, I can really. . . .

When he discovered the water he stopped smoking. He had smoked all his adult life and quit with the convert's zeal. One could not pay him a hundred dollars to smoke. Once after four days he bought a pack and tried one cigarette, crushed the rest of the pack and cast it into a sewer. He felt ten pounds lighter. His face broke out with pimples as if he were fifteen again and sexual desire bloomed in a sort of innocent lust. His wife accepted the benefits of this change with good-natured amazement. The feeling drove him out of his office on warm afternoons and up to the university cafeteria to sit by the window and watch the braless girls ride by all perky-assed and jiggly and lean on their ten-speed bicycles. Just to watch, because they all seemed so beautiful. He had never realized how beautiful they really were.

Stranger yet than chemical innocence and lust was memory. It was reborn.

He could remember with glassy clarity things he had forgotten by the time he was sixteen. Refreshed and weightless in the morning he would shower erect and happy and amazed at his head, and he would go and guzzle half a can of orange juice from the pie-shaped hole in the can, standing with his hand on his hip in the falling coolness of the open refrigerator. He has not been smoking two months now.

Having stopped smoking with his new memory and isolated in the freakish ticking silence and the bluegreen madness of the ocean, he began a kind of brooding consideration of his life and his new obsession with the rock, now closer, the forbidding and barren gray-brown protrusion with the waves crashing against it sending fans of spray fifty feet into the air. In rhythm with the churning of his legs his mind chants the questions to itself, why the water, why the rock at the mouth of the bay. It is not danger itself. It is something else. He has begun to think of it as friction. Resistance. This is what he seeks in the surrealistic madness of the ocean. Resistance. Without it what else is there that you could call life? Somewhere along the line I have negated resistance. And reclaimed it now in the soft but infinitely powerful resistance of water. Chanting, forming the words into the black tube of his snorkel, he thinks, resistance and conflict. I have not felt like this in years. It was a frictionless rise, right up the line, you scratch my back I'll scratch yours. And now, in half-conscious and boyish daydreams he invites the shark, dreads it but secretly hopes for its attack, his thumb gently resting on the crude trigger of his spear. He knows he is defenseless if one comes at him yet he cannot turn back, knows he will push until something comes to him.

He thinks that his memory did it to him. After he stopped smoking, he started recalling the time when he was a boy on a piss-poor farm, his chin like numb putty from the cold, herding the cows from the barn to the watervat, chopping wood trembling with hunger, his hands numbly locked on the axehandle, shivering, still hungry at night, his body tensed up so much that in the morning his stomach muscles would ache. Although those days on that worthless farm were miserable, he remembers them now with an obsessive clarity, and he feels a funny sentimentality as if somehow those were better days. He thinks of the present with idle contentment, but above that in some loftier recess of his mind there lies a peculiar membrane of disgust.

At home after work he will sometimes sit, drink in hand, in his hip colonial living room and moodily regard the denim-clad crotch of his wife Emma. She will most likely read a magazine, her own drink sweating on the glass-topped table. He loves her. She is strong and attractive and slatternly. It is a kind of sexy laziness. He will sit, sniffing at the vague odor of sweet jungle decay which seems to hang in and around the house. His eyebrows will draw together and he will think: lazy, everything is too lazy. How did we get here? Why do you just sit?

He does not choose to seek excitement in the lights of Waikiki. Unlike his colleagues, who come to work on Mondays with stories about stewardesses and oriental beachgirls and hookers, Calder finds the attractive depths of moral depravity uninteresting. He has made his slips, but the adventure he would have expected never materialized. His latest was here, on a lunch period—a secretary who would lean over his desk delivering letters and memos, moving in a way which suggested to him a certain substantial mammary heft. It was lunch in her apartment, and after a series of ridiculously obvious mutual suggestions she was naked and hanging on his neck. No conquest. It just—happened, and that was it. And sitting, he can hardly remember it. He can remember with more clarity his first time at sixteen, on wet and dead hay stubble in March at two in the morning, the moon casting his own shadow on the pale body of a girl a year older than him, a girl he had to fight a bigger kid to claim as his. He can remember being cold and bruised, and his shadow moving on her.

At work or at home or at lunch he would sometimes sit and find himself working his knees together and apart together and apart like a boy being denied the shuddering relief of the bathroom. Wrong, something's just— wrong. He would find himself sweating in his air-conditioned office, an air- conditioning system that he himself helped to design. Air conditioning, he thinks, trudging along in the water, slowing down now with deep breaths of satisfaction, air conditioning is the essence of the whole thing. But the water makes him shiver so hard that on the beach after being in for three hours he knows he will sit with the towel around his shoulders and tremble and he will remember again himself a boy trying to talk with a frozen chin, useless putty, remember the terrible itch after warming up leaning against the wood stove above the cherry-hot metal and rotating so as not to overdo one side. He can see the line of his life as forward movement without friction or resistance. How did he come to make so much money when he was not sure that in the last seven or eight years he actually did any work? There is only the nebulous, conglomerate picture of himself behind desk or shoulder-to-shoulder with the right friends in the apartments or townhouses near Hunter or down the street from. . . .

He missed—his spear disappears off into the sand and he tenses himself up. A parrotfish, big. Missed by only an inch or so. He is secretly glad that he missed, because he would have been burdened by the fish and he wants to go to the rock. Outside of that, his freezer has five of them stacked and wrapped in foil, no more than a nuisance to Emma who prefers supermarket fish imported frozen from the Bahamas or California. This has always bothered him because he feels a strong pride about his fishing. Retrieving his spear is a matter of diving down fifteen feet and finding the little trench it made before getting covered by the sand. He grabs the spear out of the sand and slowly ascending, slides it back through the handle and catches its notched rear end in the surgical tubing sling which, attached to the crude handle, makes the primitive rubber tension that provides the spear's thrust. It is held in place by a simple trigger that binds it in the handle, cocked and ready to fire again. He has no use for the new, technological air guns because they make fishing too easy.

He chuckles into the snorkel, thinking of Emma. One night, almost as if inviting a conflict, he told her about the secretary. Fired up on his Scotch at midnight a week ago he talked away about freedom and restriction and about how she was so liberal about things like that and knowing he should keep his mouth shut because he didn't want to spoil anything, he fell into this almost experimentally pushy interrogation. "Well, suppose I went off now and again and found some girl—" And she, in that wise, blond frankness of hers, said well who am I to tell you what to do? What if I went out and found some. . . . He went on with, well, I know how women are supposed to feel about this stuff and. . . . Don't worry about me, she said. And he stopped then, thinking, very smart. Build a fence around a pony and he'll jump it and run. Take it away and he'll stay. Very smart.

So he told her, gave her a five-sentence, objective picture of what happened, and then stood there and waited calmly for whatever she had for him. She looked at the floor. "Oh I see, I see what—that's what you're getting at. Well, interesting, interesting." When he walked toward her, across the glass-shiny kitchen floor, she took a little step of her own, as if not aware of his existence but really evading him. So then she was crying to herself, and he cursed himself for letting her know, thought, now you've done it, now you've taken care of it. Six years. No children. How easy it would be for her now to just—the speculations raced through his head, sending a shudder of odd exhilaration through him.

"Only once?"

"Yeah," he said. And she thought about it.

Finally she threw her hands up as if in annoyance and said, "Ah what the hell, it's the twentieth century after all, just be careful, okay?" Then she went off to bed, leaving him standing there in the kitchen looking out the window at the silhouette of the house next door, a carbon copy of his own, squat and comfortable and dark, surrounded by the sweetly decaying plumeria trees.

When he went to bed ten minutes later, apprehensive and cautious, she was hot and lying there in the rumpled bed in her slovenly nakedness and latched onto him and breathed her hot breath on his face and pulled him down on her liquid and softly demanding body. And he looked at her and said, "What—what's the—" and then chuckled to himself in morbid amazement and gave in.

Calder takes very seriously what he is doing, even against the soft and reasonable protests of his wife, who will not go with him to the beach when he plans his excursions. He even enjoys her fear. The last time she went with him, along with some other people from work, they were all worried sick that he would not come back because he was gone for two hours. And Emma said, "It really scares me you know, please don't go out so far . . . you go out so far I can't even see you."

He looks down and nods when she says this, knowing that he will not be able to resist going even farther the next time.

"I just don't understand why," she said. "They don't either," and she poked her thumb over her shoulder. "There's some sort of a—a blindness I don't understand. You say you won't and you do." She held her shoulders up in a sustained shrug.

And he nodded and looked down at the sand. He cannot explain it yet, but is secretly warm inside that she should be afraid. But outside of that there is the gnawing shadow of an understanding suggesting itself—he almost sees something he doesn't like, that in his obsession for the rock there is a certain puerile and egotistical and boyish motivation. There is evidence that he is almost afraid to examine too closely. Once on a short excursion he lost his spear in a cave and foolishly went in after it, knowing that the ocean could decide to drown him in there. Fishing around reef caves was dangerous any way because one slip, one moment of loss of concentration could mean being badly bruised or even knocked out on the coral, because of the dangerously unpredictable nature of the waves. In the ticking blackness of the cave he retrieved his spear and tried to return to the light and a wave came in and then some strange current, which played with his life for ten seconds while he fought off the powerful impulse to breathe. Finally the current released him and he sprung to the silver surface of the water and exploded coughing into the noisy air, and coughing his throat raw he went right into the beach and sat trembling on his towel, thinking, I almost died there, I almost did not come out.

And later, he had some people over as usual and told them the details of his scrape, not at the moment recognizing that he was romanticizing it somewhat. And Emma, wise, sloppy Emma, said, "See what John Wayne's done to my husband?'' Everyone laughed, Calder the loudest, and in the awkward silence that followed he sat in a haze of warm shame, as if Emma had insulted him.

And he thinks, what *has* John Wayne done to me? He deliberately passes up a lobster, sees the black feelers peeking out from under a blob of dead coral. Maybe she is right. Some blindness I don't understand. More evidence: heading for this same rock a few weeks ago he found himself halfway, outside of the crashing breakers, and he felt frightened and happy and looked goggle-eyed at the fish and the sleepy, deadly eels and the rilled sand, thinking, this is far, this is way, way out. Nobody, nobody would—and he turned and saw something off in the distance. He raised his head out into the cold air and saw something protruding from the water and began to back away, muttering with fear into the snorkel. It turned out to be a boy. Local. There was another boy farther off, and when he realized this he moaned, sick of himself, and returned to the beach. Boys. It seemed to prove the dilettantish nature of his adventure. And it was the same day that he looked at the ominous rock off the bay and thought, all right, boys, there, I have to go there.

He slows down and thinks, yes, there is something hokey about this, about me. He is thirty-two, idly resisting the half-conscious impulse to consider himself somebody's Christ. Why? he thinks. All right, so let's find out. He is convinced that the ocean holds for him some personal secret that only making it to the rock will reveal.

There is Martin, too, one of the right friends to have, also from New York. He is the one who said to Calder, "You want St. Johns or Honolulu?" Martin now pokes fun at him, calls him Lloyd Bridges, that guy from the old underwater TV show, or sometimes he says at work: "Ask Jacques Cousteau over there. . . ." Calder resents Martin's joking, because he knows that the question of what John Wayne has done to him is important and touchy and personal. Emma, you wise bitch. You who look like a turn of the century New Orleans whore in the morning all hoarse and sexy, you are a wise bitch. How could he explain it to her? Resistance is life, therefore where there is none, then there is no life. The human has purged resistance from his life. What would she say? Aw, up yours honey, come to bed. Those hot, enveloping thighs and the great squash of breast that seems in the process of running off her chest. They seem to negate him.

He stops and puts his head out of the water and scans the mountains, the beautiful dark mountains with their outrageously green peaks in the clouds. He slowly treads water, his jaw quivering with cold. Then he looks at the minute dots of the houses, the crawly feeling at the back of his neck. He is not alert, and in principle, if he were a fish he would be dead. Living in the ocean means for them remaining perpetually alert. Or the shark, living for him means constant movement or suffocation. The eel sits in his hole and waits in perpetual readiness. God. He looks scornfully at the houses nestled under the mountains and shakes his head and snorts, thinks of himself sitting in his hip colonial living room which is decorated to make a social chameleon of him, a place with no balls. He thinks, that is the most indecisive room I have ever seen.

"All right," he says into the snorkel. He looks at the rock, scanning the water near it for the black triangle of a shark's dorsal fin. Only four or five hundred yards. Today's the day. His fear and excitement balance each other out. No one can help him now. He knows he is foolish, that this is not necessary and if Emma knew, she'd probably call the rescue squad. He looks up again, his face whipped by the cold wind, thinking, god it's big. It rises fifty or more feet out of the water, a fractured cube, threatening and monolithic and raw. The water sloshes against it in huge swells and he knows he cannot get too close. He sees also that the water under him is forty or more feet deep, which means he cannot use his spear. In front of him and down the bottom goes, off into the frightening blue distance. He is cold, shivering now but all the time enjoying it with his tense belly and back and the shudders in the throat and jaw. With the water getting deeper and the rock looming and his eyes darting around in the limit of his vision for the shape of a shark, almost as if it is the shape of proof that he lives at all, thinks okay, Emma, okay, what do you say now? The plot is thickening, honey. We'll move the cameras in when he comes at you.

He thinks enfolded in the pastel silence of the water with the blue nothingness below him, once you get there what will it mean? Behind this a more threatening thought comes to him, as if he is grimacing at himself in the mirror—he really is hokey, he really is a boy. This is almost too much for him. Trudging along slowly with exhaustion approaching, it is almost as if the excursion is ruined. He is shivering but inside he feels hot with shame. He has had this thought many times before, but today it wells up like a wave in his mind and he cannot easily rid himself of it. He looks up and sees his magnificent rock and now the fear begins to outweigh the excitement. Now the mask hurts his upper lip and the fins are chafing his Achilles tendons and his throat is salt raw as if someone has run a woodrasp down it. Now he is tired and wonders if he should try the last few hundred yards. He looks up and sees that the land jut at the mouth of the bay is actually closer to the rock than his point of entry. He decides he should head for it, the humiliating thought gaining ground in his mind. Another time sonny. Tomorrow maybe. He hangs exhausted in the water and looks down at the blue-gray nothingness of what must be sixty feet of water, hangs blank and tired and thinks, tomorrow Lloydo, tomorrow Jacques. This is enough. He is too far out. Jesus, he thinks, I got to get back in. I really got to get back in. Head for the jut. He will have to go through scary, unfamiliar territory.

But he does not go in. Hanging suspended in the water and now a little angry he thinks, why waste it just because someone implies that you are an irresponsible fool? Nothing to lose out here but doubt, boy. Sullenly biting down on the mouthpiece and disregarding the exhaustion that drags him down he churns on toward the rock, grimly forcing himself on despite the fear which now lies dormant somewhere, shadowed out by his brooding anger at anyone or anything which would influence him not to go as far as he goddamned well pleased.

He is rewarded quickly. Off in the distance, against the soft blue of the ocean, the reef around the rock begins to materialize like a photograph in a chemical solution. The reef is a hundred yards into the ocean around the rock, and it seems alive with fish, and scanning the picture whose clarity increases steadily, Calder sees nothing indicating danger. It is all beauty. It sends a shudder of excitement through him like ponderous electricity. It is incredible—he has never seen anything like this in his life. The yellows and pinks and the fish in schools and the fish alone, going on about their business. It is as if he has crossed a desert and come out into a beautiful town.

He spends ten minutes in a gawking, amazed inspection of part of the reef before he decides to fish for a few minutes. In his excitement he misses the first shot at a large parrotfish in a hole and he stays down, looking into the hole with his body inverted, and grabs for the rear end of his spear which lies across a crevasse full of little silver fish. He almost has the spear when the spotted eel flashes on his hand. There is no pain, only momentary shock in which Calder even feels the eel's tongue on the palm and sees that its teeth are buried as far as they will go, and in that same, peculiarly objective expanded half-second he sees the little malevolent eye buried in the fat, bulbous head staring back at him sleepily. He jerks his hand out of its mouth so that the teeth painlessly shred the palm and back and he springs off the coral-head already taking water into his throat and he curls up around his shredded hand like a leaf in a fire. He rises to the surface blowing air from the snorkel in a yell and then hangs there waiting for the pain which does not come up beyond a cold and wretched discomfort. Wailing softly with each breath he looks at his hand. The slashes are closed with blood escaping in little billows, like smoke. He gasps his breaths numbed with fear and trembling wretchedly and clasps his hand to his chest, thinking, oh, Jesus so far out, and blood escaping, Jesus.

Still without feeling much pain he turns and scans the water again and begins swimming backwards, frightened at the little billows of blood which disperse into the water. No defense, none at all. Get in. He looks up again at the jut of land, and rejecting the hollow fear of what must lie behind him and against his exhaustion he churns with all he has toward the jut. Before going two hundred yards he stops, gasping, cold and giddy and hopelessly tired. Before he can control it, bile scalds his throat and the inside of his nose, and he floats, eyes shut, trying to hold back the dreamy nausea which robs him of balance and strength. In order to keep from throwing up he hangs still, holding his hand against his chest, letting the ocean do to him what it will. For a moment he has a strange feeling, a strong impulse to just hang there forever, just die there enfolded in the water.

He needs to concentrate on something. Floating in aimless exhaustion is terrifying. He looks again at the hand, bringing it off his chest as if it were incredibly fragile. Still, the little billows, the seepage, and a kind of morbid interest in what the eel did makes him gently open one cut. It is even worse than he expects, like razors right into the muscles, all the way in, and the heel of his hand is partially severed, a one-inch chip in the flesh. He chokes with fear again and trudges on cautiously, because of his stomach, half-consciously muttering into the snorkel, Jesus god bad, my god my god, and he is too tired to glance back for the shark he is sure is on its way to finish the job. He can only chuckle with hopeless exhaustion and watch the rilled sand pass under him and curse with his teeth clenched when the ocean gently holds him back with one of its exasperating currents.

It is almost as if he sleeps, trudging along in the blue-green silence, as if he is at peace with his hand and now must simply go home. He has no idea how much time it takes him to make it any distance and he does not care. The fear has crystallized at the back of his head so that whatever feeling it is when some pair of jaws clamp on his neck will make him respond by simply drawing his shoulders up and wincing slightly. For long stretches he swims with his eyes closed, almost not caring if he is going in the right direction. His mind cocoons itself in a half-dream and it is only the growing pain that keeps him aware. Then the powerful breakers wake him up and carry him violently toward the shore so that he must raise his head out to get air. The sea is all foam, tossing him and pushing him and washing over him, all toward the beach, and he lies, his hand clasped to his chest, intent only on getting the air he needs when the ocean will permit it. Before reaching the calm water he has the wind blasted out of him by a high piece of coral that lays open the skin on his ribs. He continues on, a little hopeful because he is inside the reef, and the searing pain of the blow on his ribs wakes him up. And with horribly gradual progress, the bottom comes up to meet him.

On the shore he plows up to dry sand, still holding his hand, and falls back. He is almost too tired to keep going, but the recognition that he has made it to shore gives him a temporary energy and the noise of the land wakes him up and the blood streams from his hand because it is now not held in by the pressure of the water. With his good hand he pulls the fins off holding the bad hand aloft so that the blood runs down his arm over his elbow and toward his armpit. Gasping more air than he needs he is driven by a sullen fear as if something could still chase him and he begins trotting along the beach toward his car which is a mile away, and he fights the sand which slows him down.

A man intercepts him bearing a towel, which Calder numbly wraps around his hand, and the man leads him into the bushes saying. "Oh, Jesus the bugger got you . . . oh, Jesus . . ." and Calder hardly hears him. It is as if Calder is still in the silent ticking ocean and numbly he follows staring glassy-eyed at his own feet in the sand and then on grass and finally wet and shivering and salty he finds himself sitting in the front seat of the man's car, holding his wrapped hand against his injured side.

The bleeding has almost stopped and blood crusts his wrist and forearm and soaks into the towel. Now he sees that the man is Japanese, old, and keeps glancing at Calder's wrapped hand. Calder looks around, at the ocean, and at the white line streaming into the hood of the car. It is as if he wakes up suddenly. He pulls the towel away and peeks at his hand. It is cupped against his side so that the seeping blood collects in the palm. He is suddenly apprehensive about going home, as if he were a boy who had injured himself doing something he shouldn't have done.

But he snorts angrily at that thought, and turns to the man. "Have you . . . have you ever been out there, by that rock?" His voice crackles, almost as if the question is urgent.

"Not for me," the man says, laughing.

"It's . . . it's beautiful," Calder says, "I've never seen anything like that in my life."

Now he is relaxed, calm, almost content sitting there hunched around his hand, and he thinks, against what reason would tell him to think, if this is the blindness they make it out to be, then I aim to keep it. He takes another look at his cupped hand and at the brilliant little pool of blood in the palm. He holds it as if it is something valuable he has found in the ocean.

Beachboy

MICHAEL MCPHERSON

Chick lived for years in the studio over my grandfather's garage on Maunaloa Avenue, on the planted hillside overlooking Waikiki. After the old man died, I lived in his house for a while, the small one in the back he'd built after his kids had grown. Chick was a tall, long-limbed, barrel-chested Hawaiian with enormous hands and feet, an example of a body type with whose number that race is uncommonly blessed, the prototype swimmer. He was *seventy-two years young* when I met him that summer, and he had long since retired as Beach Captain at the Royal Hawaiian, first ukulele in the Monarch Room and all of that had changed long before I was in high school, though the hotel was still furnishing Chick's linen and, he told me, he got some interesting phone calls.

Chick was out raking leaves one afternoon when I came home from classes at the UH and we got to talking in the yard about how the old man had gone around and propped up all the lateral branches of his avocado trees with lumber. The old man would support anything those avocado trees wanted to do. His sons he packed off to Annapolis and West Point. Anyway, pretty soon Chick says why don't you come on up for a beer. His place was filled with photographs, most of them framed, of his children and their children, a little smiling tribe of Hawaiian-Chinese and Hawaiian-Chinese-Portuguese and other blends of the island races, and here and there were pictures of a striking blonde woman, fortyish and just dynamite-looking all her life, one of those.

Oh, that's Dorothy, says Chick, *she calls me every day from Reno, her boyfriend owns half Reno, hotels, you know. She came here after the war with her husband, Jack, he was a millionaire. We had good times in those days. Jack got killed in Korea, fighter pilot. Dorothy, she likes to keep in touch, reminds her of the old days.*

So we sat around his place and had a few beers. It was a cheerful little room, filled with little smiling faces and well lighted from high frame windows. Perhaps because of his build, it seemed as though Chick could reach anything in the room easily, almost without getting up. Here and there among the family photographs were mementos of faraway places, like Japanese laminated wood coasters with familiar designs on them, maybe great works of art reproduced in miniature, I'm not sure. Chick always answered his phone, *I'm ready,* and a good part of the time it was Shorty or Webster or another of the handful of very wealthy old men who still met in the distant cities of the world to carry on the party that had begun on the beach at the Royal so many years ago, before the war, and they would have a ticket waiting for Chick at the airport and off he'd go.

It was hard to settle down in those days, Chick says. Even sitting around in his undershirt, seventy-two years of late nights, long flights and gravity cannot erode the wealth of charm, the nugget emanating from within the original beachboy.

Land was cheap then. Seven cents a square foot in Waikiki. Hell, it was a swamp. What did I care, huh? I had a car. Me, a Hawaiian, I had a car. I had spendin' cash. I tell you, it was all right. But when I got married, I settled down. I bought a place on 8th Avenue, just around the corner, paid eight hundred dollars for it. Yeah, eight hundred. Couldn't make it, though. Still, I love my wife, my family, I love 'em all. But the beach, the wine and the good times, well. So I gave her the place when we split up, then two years ago I'm walking down the street in Tokyo and there's my wife, bang! So she tells me, "I sold the old place." I said, "How much?" and she tells me, "twenty-eight thousand," and I said, "twenty-eight thousand!" I said, "twenty-eight thousand, where's my eight hundred?"!

So we had a couple of beers and pretty soon the phone rings and Chick answers, *I'm ready,* and from the way he's talking I can tell it's a lady this time and finally I figure out it's Dorothy, the knockout blonde, making her daily call from poolside in Nevada to try one more time to persuade Chick not to break his legs falling down the narrow, termite-ridden staircase alongside the garage.

Yeah, he says to me afterwards, *she wants me to move down to her penthouse in the Foster Towers, right across from the beach, you know? She wants to take care of old Chick, for old times. So I can do the backstroke into my golden years, huh? Hell, I'm seventy-two years young. Ha! Ha!*

It wasn't long after that that my uncles all decided to tear down the garage and the back house and develop the property, and Dorothy got Chick down to the Foster Towers, right on the beach. I moved to Kalihi and later I moved again and then last week I was in town and I got to thinking about old Chick and his little room filled with familiar objects and I asked my old man about him and he said Chick died four years ago. They're all going, the old timers. And the beach, well, what can you say since they tore down Joe's? They haven't tore down the beach yet, and guys like Leroy are still there, they're getting to be the older generation now. I saw Leroy the other day down on Kalakaua with his face frozen and a little bulge back where his crazy shirt meets his hang-ten trunks, waiting to cross the street. That's mostly what the beach is anymore is the street. But out where the blue water begins, in that deep azure where in the sunlight you can see the reef falling away and sometimes even the sudden silver flash of a bottom feeder turning, out past the hundred-foot hole holding Kui's bones, way out there Chick them are doing the backstroke into their golden years.

That Was Last Year

MICHAEL MCPHERSON

Mel played the gaji on the sakura and it really pissed me off because I had forgotten he could do that. I may never learn to play the game properly, anyway. It's hard to learn such a subtle game at my age, especially having to play
against someone who's been playing most of his life.

"Aw fuck, Mel, that stinks."

Mel chuckled and looked around the curtain to see if a nurse or aide or anybody was coming. He'd been inside Maui Memorial, a good place to die, for
over three weeks already and had pretty much refined his routine for getting
loaded. Anything becomes normal if you do it long enough. He brought out
the little plastic container and straw from under the blanket and passed them
over to me.

"Here," he said.

I took a big blow and passed it back to him.

"They ever say any more about this?" I asked, and held out the stash. I
was rushing real nice.

"Oh no," Mel said, and planted the straw in his left nostril. He took a
blow. "I told the nurse to send the head man down here any time he wants
to talk about it, but not to fuck with my rights or I'll tear this place apart."

Mel hadn't actually torn apart much of anything lately, not since he'd been
shot in the spine and lost all the feeling below his arms. One time a few
months back he nodded out and the cigarette he'd been smoking rolled down
and burned a hole in his chest the size of a quarter and so deep it took weeks
to heal. He also had done a fair job of tearing up his kidneys over the past
year or so, which is how he came to warrant time in this circle of hell.

"They didn't find any stash?"

It figured that they didn't, or they wouldn't be so casual. They had to
know what we were doing, with all the snorting and laughing and interrupt-
ing each other all the time.

"Fuck no," he said, laughing and patting the small canvas travel bag at his side, "nobody opens Mel's bag, if they even touch it they treat it like a shrine. Where I go, it goes. It's your play."

He had blocked my last chance for a yaku, and it looked like I was going to get basa'd again. I hate like hell to lose at anything.

"If that little chimpo hadn't of snitched, they would know nothing," he continued. "I'd like to walk in, wherever the little asshole is now, with Eggs and B.J., you know and just tell him, 'we'll meet again.' "

Being hapa, Takahaole, and growing up in Wailuku without a father had toughened Mel early. His Japanese grandfather, the first of his family to settle in these islands, had been a renegade, a samurai with a taste for drink and womanly virtues who had come to Maui at the turn of the century and partied a succession of small businesses into oblivion. It pleased Mel that through the lean times his grandfather had never stooped to wear the yoke of the plantation; for better or worse he had remained his own man. Mel's mother had been valedictorian of her class at Baldwin High School, and several of her classmates had gone on to become judges, state senators, local power brokers. They'd all had hopes for Mel. His mother sent him down to the Hongwanji in the afternoons to learn her ancestors' language; he learned some Japanese, but since he was the only one there who looked like a haole, he had to fight his way out of the place every day. By the time he graduated and was awarded a full academic scholarship to study Chemistry at UH he had a name on the street, a jacket full of imaginative felonies and was regarded as the foremost firearms and powder man on Maui outside of old Judge Webber. One time he even hit the armory on Market Street, a long block from his mother's house, and took the National Guard's entire arsenal, but they caught up with him after that dummy Dickie Souza left a sack of grenades hanging from the cliff at Pauwela and they didn't go off, only Dickie's mouth did.

"Now, don't be vindictive," I suggested, "after all, his uncle is a lieutenant, he's not some fucking VASCAR patrol. The boy believed a crime was being committed in the next bed, it was his *obligation*. You of all people should understand."

"Finking is not an obligation, Alvin." He said it with more weariness than conviction.

"Aw, he's fucking up somehow to be in here, right, and he's so square the only comfort he's got is to be a good citizen and turn you in, make his uncle proud."

"Fuck him. I've known his uncle from high school. He's an asshole."

"Yeah, well, it's not like you to be thinking so small. You're just sour 'cuz they cut off your demerol."

"You're right about that."

Some of the family of the guy in the next bed, Jimmy, came in and sat down on the other side of the curtain. It was weird how they had put Mel in Jimmy's room after the chimpo had gotten him removed from the new wing. The old wing was enough to keep you sick; the staff didn't deny it. They had put Mel in the room next door to Jimmy's right after the kidney surgery, then a few days later when he was feeling stronger the good looking Japanee nurse asked him if he wanted to move by the window. He said yeah, and the bed by the window in his room was empty, but instead they moved him into Jimmy's room. Mel hadn't seen Jimmy in years, since long before Mel got shot. They went way back to childhood, when Jimmy and his brothers and a couple more of the kids from Hopoi Camp were some of the best athletes in Wailuku. Mel liked to be with the Flip kids back then; they accepted him on face value, he didn't have to be proving it all the time. When he saw his first chicken fight up at the camp, saw the knives and blood and everything, he and his brother ran hard around the punawai and halfway down the cane haul road before the kids from the camp caught up with them and said come back, everything's okay and don't worry, the cops won't come.

"It's your move, Alvin. Sometimes you have to feed."

"You know what, Mel, this game is fucked. Your mountain is always miraculous, mine is a zero. Real Buddhahead game. Nothing changes."

Jimmy had cancer. It was bad, because they'd finally cut him and found that his lymph glands were pretty far gone. He slept a lot, and sometimes his family would sit around the bed and watch him. Mel's TV, which was mounted on a high table between them, was on most of the time during the day. Mel had to tell him what the good stuff was for his pain, Jimmy didn't know anything about dope. Once Mel had gotten him on a program Jimmy would get nicely morphed out, lie back and drift in and out of conversations in his mind, sometimes talking like he was talking to a haole, other times in a soft melodious pidgin. One time he was talking to Mel's brother and later Mel asked him about it but Jimmy couldn't remember where he'd been.

The guy was a hero from what I could see, and Mel said he was like that all the time, didn't want people to worry about him. Mel told me one of the guys who grew up in the camp had called Jimmy from Boston and Jimmy told him that Mel was there and kept asking him if he wanted to talk to Mel. Another time Jimmy told Mel that if his hair started to go he would just shave it, he wasn't going to sit there and watch it fall out. These local Flips are tough, it's hard to beat them for heart; even the Japs have to admit it.

The good looking nurse caught us more or less sleeping on the job. She popped around the curtain and pulled it taut behind her. Good thing the stash was back under the blanket, but she was probably cool anyway.

"Who's winning?"

I kind of grunted, it was the best I could do.

"My friend here is learning," Mel offered magnanimously.

"Where's the Japanese guy with the funny name, he don't come to see you no more?"

"You mean Eggs?"

"Huh?"

"Eggs. *Tamago.*"

"Yeah. I dunno."

"That's Muneo's son."

She brightened. That's what she'd wanted to confirm.

"Eh, my boyfriend, he thinks he knows who ratted."

The week before the vice had taken down a 6–5 setup in the county building, up a couple of floors from their hole in the basement. An elevator case. Clearly they had some very good information, because they came away with $44,000 cash and reams of names and numbers. So she and her honey liked to gamble. Get a little thrill to hear the Old Man's name so personal, met his only son. She was okay. You have to give people a little excitement, it's part of the job.

"Yeah," Mel nodded, "he'll give himself up some way, you know, like in a Russian novel."

"Hah?"

"Uh, guilty conscience . . . it's hard to keep people from finding out something like that, you know."

"Uh-huh. I know what you mean. You need anything?"

"Yeah. Somebody who plays faster than my friend here."

"Sure, Mr. Richard. Bumbye."

She was very sexy. Nurses in uniform have a tremendous edge that way, it seems to me, but anyway it worked for her. A friend of mine had done a full page article in the *Maui News* about hanafuda, including the best diagram of the yakus Mel had ever seen, an "S" shape with the three sets of banner cards below. It was a photograph of the actual cards, very clever. I always unfold it and lay it across Mel's legs while we play so I can refer to it and know what's going on. Looking at it didn't make my hand get any better, though, and it was pretty clear that either this play or the next I was going to have to give Mel the moon.

A gust of rain pelted the window; a dark overcast stretched down to the harbor, twin spits of man-hewn rock jutting like teeth against a windy white ocean. Just inside the mouth a pair of tugs wrestled a Young Brothers barge in toward Pier 2. Christmas presents. The most depressing time of the year, some shrink wrote in a magazine. The hospitals fill up with drunks.

Mel had told me a weird story about waking up at five or so in the morning to some commotion in the hall, an excitement of nurses squeaking by and the hard footsteps of the man. Right away he felt the cops out there, the weight of them; their heavy shadows flickering in the hall pulled him suddenly from a dream of glass rattling in wind. He was lying on his right side, facing the lighted doorway, the only position in which he could sleep. Behind him he heard a faint shuffling from the darkness outside the window; he could vaguely sense something out there feeding a swirl of commotion around itself. It was a strange moment, Mel had told me, waking into such electrified air; the dream energy had surged, flashing his eyelids back, and back, between dreams. Jimmy lay in deep sleep, sedated. Moments passed and the energy died down, moved away toward the old wing. Mel thought he heard voices in the distance over the rattle of wind on the panes. After a while two nurses came into the room; they tiptoed to look down from the window beside Mel's bed. Then one of them saw he was awake and told him that a woman from the other side of the ward had gotten out a window onto the ledge and as far as the concrete column right outside Mel's bed, which she couldn't get past. She had huddled against that cold member in the darkness while the nurses and cops looked for her, had crouched in her small darkness just inches from where Mel lay dreaming, and she had waited. After a while she wandered, and eventually the nurse with the best heart talked her down, got her back in the window. They transferred her to the psych ward right now, marched her across the lawn in the grey morning light. The psych ward is on the ground floor; jumping out the windows over there is pretty safe.

The rain continued to roll in long droplets down the window. Suicide season. Tourists here. Mel took out the stash and opened it up.

"Haole Boy called me yesterday," he began, sticking the straw up there, "and I told the asshole I'm not going to do it for him."

"Well that's good," I said, "a thing like that could get real messy over nothing. You've got lunatics involved. A lot of hard time hanging over somebody's wounded pride."

He passed it over and I took another blow.

"I know," Mel replied, "like five grand is going to break him, sitting on all that land his mother bought for him. He told me that, told me it was really hurting him, and in the same breath he tells me that he cracked up his eleven grand Harley again. I asked him, and if the guy doesn't pay, is he gonna go over there and blow up his house? Eh, I don't have legs, who does he think is gonna do that kind of job for free?"

"If he were capable of that, why would he call you? If he wants respect, let *him* claim it."

I could understand why Sherlock Homes liked this stuff so much. It sure makes you smart.

"Hey, you can't believe all the shit he brings up," Mel remembered, "favors he's done for me, like the two hundred he sent me to cop smack for him. . . ."

"That was a favor! Believe me, I know the style."

"I told him I'd send the two hundred back, but then you should have heard him whining about having my picture up on his wall."

"Yeah," I'd seen it there myself, "that's just to scare the neighbors. When he steps in shit, your phone rings. Lucky for you."

"Right," Mel said, but I could tell he was not really sure. "But the other guy does owe him the money," he continued, "and he's a punk, I had to straighten him out about something else once. Now look, the two jerkoffs stay up for days whiffing and jacking each other up, and finally Toad goes berserk and takes it out on his old lady, pa-toota, tunes her up so bad she flies back to California, then he refuses to pay what he owes on account of it's all the other guy's fault. I hate these weaklings, they make me sick."

"The way I remember this one," I pointed out in all fairness, "first he was scared somebody would kill him for starting a fire in their wastebasket; then, after you assure him he's clear, he wants to go back and put pressure on the guy. Not him, of course. You."

"Well," Mel leaned back and reflected, "the other thing is the asshole has told so many people about the plastic that it's no longer any use to me. It could be traced. The people who lost it. . . ."

There was a commotion as somebody entered the room; a doctor stuck his head around the curtain, gave us a strange look and pulled the curtain tight in front of him. He was there to talk to Jimmy. Some of Jimmy's family were sitting around; his wife and kids were so quiet sometimes we forgot they were there.

"It's not what we thought," the doctor blurted out, "it's worse. Your whole stomach lining is affected."

We couldn't see anybody because of the curtain, but the doctor's voice sounded shaky, especially on "worse." Mel and I just sat still and looked at each other.

"Mr. Deloso," the doctor said, "you should look at the time you have not as time you're dying, but as time you're living."

There was a thick silence after he said that. It was a nice thing to say, but it just couldn't stand up to the coming down, the weight of amazement and hopelessness. Finally Jimmy spoke in an even, gentle voice.

"How long?"

The doctor stammered a little. He was young, and he was pretty shook up.

"Well, Mr. Deloso," he said, "it kind of depends on you. Uh, I've seen people just give up and go real fast, you know, in a week. Others have a will to go on living and live for years. Five years, maybe. The way things are going in the world, who knows if any of us will be around that long, huh? We're all going to die. . . ."

I played the moon and Mel picked it up. It made his yaku, but neither of us said anything.

I checked Mel out of that dump on December 19. He and Jimmy said their goodbyes, and after I helped Mel transfer into the car I went back up for the TV and some other stuff. On the way up I thought about what I should say to Jimmy. Everything I could say sounded terrible, "Merry Christmas" worst of all. I decided finally that "Take it easy" was the best, and that's what I said to him. He looked at me with his clear gentle eyes and said, "You too." I wonder what my eyes must have looked like to him. Whatever they looked like, I was forgiven. Mel had wanted to leave the TV for him, but actually it belonged to another friend.

Mel called Jimmy a few times after that, to ask him how he felt, what kind of dope was he using, and to try to encourage Jimmy to make it through chemotherapy, to see his home again and not to die in Maui Memorial. Then the afternoon of New Year's Eve I stopped by Mel's place on the way to the airport and New Year's with my family in Honolulu and found him just lying there and staring at the ceiling. He said that Jimmy's wife had called after lunch to say that Jimmy had died in his sleep the night before, and to thank Mel and invite his mother to the funeral. Then he told me that our friend had called a couple of hours later to whine some more about couldn't he get his money collected. It was bad timing, Mel figured. Mel was feeling pretty bad and I just kind of sat around with him for an hour or so before I had to catch my plane. It's always a thrill sitting on the end of the runway when the pilot starts leaning on those turbines and then when he gooses it you get that rush of everything flying by, like you're really going somewhere.

(In memory of R.B., bad boy/good friend, 1943–1983.)

Deep Water

RALPH ANTHONY MISITANO

An old man pushes his small dory down the sand to the water's edge. He pauses, and scans the cluttered vessel's interior. He begins a mental inventory of his gear. Curled in the aft section are two cords of rope, a half-dozen links of heavy duty chain, and positioned so to balance each other's weight are six empty wooden kegs. Wiping the perspiration from his bronzed and wrinkled forehead, he walks to the bow and takes the lid off a large plastic trash barrel. The stench is immediate as the old man inspects the heap of fetid fish heads that he begged from the sport fishermen down the coast. Replacing the lid, he glances under the single bench and spies his old baseball bat. Strapped to his waist is a long knife in a stained-leather sheath. The morning sun is just at the horizon and already the old man can tell it is going to be a very hot day. Convinced that he has everything, he stows his lunch and jug of drinking water under the bow, walks behind the boat and pushes off. He seats himself behind the oars, and with a brisk offshore wind whipping through his thick white beard, begins pulling for the outside reef.

As he rows out across the lagoon, the old man's arms and shoulders become pumped full of blood, and patches of sweat begin to show through his faded workshirt. He doesn't tire though, for this is a trip he has made nearly everyday for the better part of his life, and the many miles logged behind the oars have kept him in virtually the same splendid physical condition as when he was a young man. He picks up his pace, feeling energized at his muscle's response to the straining of the oars. He doesn't bother to look where he is going. He knows that very soon he will pick up the channel current that is borne by the huge volumes of water that pour over the reef with the swell. The water, needing to return to the sea, seeks the deep trough that runs between the opening in the reef that fringes the lagoon. The reef then extends seaward for several miles before bending around to follow the shoreline. On days such as this, with the seas running six to eight feet, a powerful swift current forms inside the lagoon, that once encountered, will jet him through the opening in the reef, past the breaking waves, to where the bottom slopes off to many thousand feet. Feeling the acceleration, he slows his stroke, just touching the surface of the water with his oars. He is now with the current and as he lets up he sighs through pursed lips and feels the pounding in his chest start to subside. The sound of the waves crashing on the reef is deafening as he approaches the channel opening. First appearing in the corners of his eyes, then emerging into full view before him, the swell lifts up as it encounters the steeply rising sea bed. The wind, whipping offshore, creates a feathering of spray off the peak of the wave before it topples and crashes onto the reef. A shower of spray and droplets rain down over the old man as he picks up his stroke. He knows another wave is coming up behind him and the current is now slowing as it begins to meet and blend with the deeper water. He pulls hard now, feeling himself lift up, up and over. He continues rowing hard as he watches the backside of the wave move away from him. Only after he is sure that he is safely past the reef does he stop and rest on his oars. His friend, the current, is gone now. The wind seems to have slowed, causing the surface of the water to take on a smooth glassy appearance. He rests for only the time it takes to maneuver a little turn, then begins a long deep stroke, moving off in a southerly direction following the reef to the spot where he will begin his day's work.

Jonah wasn't always a shark fisherman. As always during this part of the trip his mind drifted back to the days when he fished for the great marlin and to days when he would fill his boat to the point of near sinking with bonita and dolphin. It brought him peace when he remembered those times long ago. He and his father would spend days roaming over the deep waters outside the reef. They would follow the sea birds, stop here and there to put out their hand lines in hope of hitting a passing school of skipjack, or dolphin fish; and always, they would set one deep line, baited with their finest sardine and pray that a fat marlin would take it.

As he continued his journey along the reef, the old man remembered one day when he and his father hooked an enormous marlin, bigger than any before. As he raced around cutting the other lines free, his father positioned himself at the bow and began taking in the slack. They then let the fish pull their boat where it may be, keeping the line taut, and waited for it to tire. What fun it was being pulled along, waiting for the great fish to break the surface with a spectacular leap. He remembered feeling sorry for the fish as he watched it grow weaker with each display and finally, totally exhausted and near death, be pulled close alongside and clubbed until motionless with his father's baseball bat. It then became a race against time to get their catch lashed to the side of the boat and into shore before the sharks arrived. While his father began making for the safety of the shallow water over the inner reef, the small boy scanned the water's surface, searching for the first ominous sign of pursuit. The sharks, always nearby, attracted by the fury of the struggle and the scent of blood in the water, began to gather and circle the boat. While his father strained away at the oars, pulling for shore as fast as he could, the boy watched the sharks cruise by, closing their circle. He watched their dark dorsal fins slice the surface of the water, following in its wake by the scythe-like tail fins, as they drew closer. Finally, a huge tiger attacked. Coming straight up from below, jaws gaping, it plowed the belly of their fish. Thrashed once, twice, then swam off shaking its head and swallowing, streaming entrails through a cloud of blood. At this signal the others moved in. They attacked swiftly and the water began to churn with their frenzy. This was the young boy's cue to take the baseball bat, and while his father pumped furiously away at the oars, he knelt at the rail and swung down at the attacking sharks. He battered them as they swam up with their mouths open, jaws thrusting forward, their white teeth gleaming. Again and again he brought the bat down, causing great explosions of red spray and fragments of fish. Then suddenly, for some unknown reason, the sharks disappeared. The water became calm again, save for the dip of his father's oars. The young boy sat back and with wide eyes looked to his father who simply nodded and continued rowing. Reassured that he did well the young boy returned his searching eyes to the calm water, still holding with both hands his father's baseball bat, the same bat that now rested securely under the old man as he continued rowing towards his destination.

The sun is at his shoulder now and the reflection off the water causes the old man to squint, making deep creases at the corners of his eyes. The wind has become but a slight breeze, and once he rounds the point he will be shielded from the swell. The surface will be totally flat then, a good day for rowing.

Those were good days the old man thought, remembering the bountiful catches and the many battles with sharks. The sharks were the hated enemy that always lurked beneath him. Dark shadows in the sea that would appear out of nowhere and steal a hooked fish before it could be boated, or strip the flesh from a marlin before it could be brought to shore. The old man gazed into a dazzling blue sky and watched a great frigate bird as it soared high above him. The bird seemed to be scanning the water's surface, perhaps searching for a school of small fish. "Yes!, the bait-fish," that's when it all began. His mind took him back again. Back some twenty years, to the days of prosperity for him and other fishermen of the small village. He remembered how the men of the village would gather each morning before sunrise and divide into groups. They would fan out over the lagoon in their small boats, and using large seine nets, encircle and trap the wandering schools of anchovie and sardines. They would then maneuver the circle of net close to shore and one-by-one, all of the fishermen would come up and fill their bait boxes for the day. Once they had the bait needed for the day's work, the men in the boats would take the net back into the lagoon and release the remaining school. They were wise men who never took more than what was needed for the one day. They knew that the bait-fish were not there for them to waste, and as long as they showed respect the fish would always be there.

Many seasons passed and Jonah continued living quietly in his bamboo and thatched hut following the death of his father. Being the only child, the young man was accustomed to solitude and naturally preferred the freedom his lifestyle gave him. Thus he never took a wife, which was just as well. He fished alone after his father died. His friends in the village who belonged to larger families offered to let the young man join them and share in their catch, but he politely thanked them and declined. He preferred working alone. The long hours spent behind the oars helped him grow accustomed to the absence of his beloved father. He never expressed, nor did it ever occur to him to, the feeling of oneness he experienced during those times alone at sea. He only knew that he felt comfortable and at home.

The runs of bonita and dolphin remained good for many years. The village maintained a small surplus to get them through the slow times but basically they caught only what they needed. One time a man from the city came and offered to buy all the fish the village could supply. Some of the young men were eager to do business, but the proposition was sternly opposed by the village elders, and the man from the city was told to leave.

The old man watched the great frigate bird until it disappeared into the distance. Then he looked towards the shore and picked up his first landmark. A long stretch of white sand beach, interrupted by an ancient lava flow, marked the spot where the old man stopped rowing and began scanning the surface of the water for his second landmark. A vast coral head lurking just beneath the surface of the water marked the spot where he would begin working. The spot indicated a point where the reef ended going seaward, and then plunged to a fathomless abyss of crystal blue. These deep waters at the edge of the reef were well known to the old man. Many sharks, residents of the periphery of the reef and cruisers of the open sea, gathered here where the deep Pacific Ocean meets the wall of coral and basalt.

Boating his oars, allowing himself to drift freely about, the old man began assembling his gear. Taking a five-inch steel hook, he meticulously tied it with wire to one end of a link of chain. The other end of the chain was tied with wire to a length of rope, and then the rope was secured to one of the wooden kegs. He repeated this procedure with all six kegs and then tied them so that he had two sets of three kegs apiece. He spaced them so that they were ten yards apart and set at depths from ten to sixty feet. Working swiftly and accurately with hands rough and cracked from years at sea, Jonah completed the preliminaries of his task. He then walked to the bow and removed the lid from the plastic trashcan. Taking his baseball bat from under the bench, he used the handle end to stir and turn the foul smelling stew of fish head and fish viscera, all floating in a solution of water, crank-case oil, and fish blood. Selecting six of the largest bonita heads, he baited each of the lines, making sure to bury completely the hook so that no part of it showed. Having done this, the old man began setting the lines. He put one line in the water and watched the head slowly sink, the lifeless eyes catching beams of light through the azure transparency. As one keg entered the water the old man returned to the oars and moved off slowly, paralleling the shoreline for the ten yards before setting the second line. He repeated this for the third keg, then moved away some twenty yards before repeating the whole procedure for the second set of three kegs. Completing this part of the job, it was now time to lay down the slick. Taking the wooden bowl that he used for bailing water, the old man moved back to the plastic trashcan and began scooping out large bowlfuls of oily fish soup, and then poured it out over the surface of the water. He continued doing this, periodically moving about in a circle around the kegs until he had created a large oil slick which would permeate the area with the scent needed to bring the sharks in. The old man then moved off so that he could observe the whole area.

It was never a very long wait. As it usually went, the old man would drift about, watching the floating kegs until one of them began to bob up and down, signaling a shark on the line. With that he would row over to the kegs and start laying out more of the fish oil slick. The struggling and thrashing of the hooked shark and the fresh scent in the water would surely bring up others. He would then leave the area again and wait for the other kegs to begin bobbing. All he had to do then was wait for the sharks to exhaust themselves. Being unable to swim, as they were held in place by the buoyant kegs, the animals literally drowned. Once the kegs stopped bobbing it became time to harvest. He would row back to the kegs, and starting with the shallowest one, start pulling up the rope. The shark would usually come up without resistance. Most of them were in the four to six foot range, but occasionally a big tiger would arrive on the scene and swallow one of the smaller sharks. When this happened, the old man would immediately cut that line, having no desire to tangle with a shark that had the capacity to capsize his boat. Upon raising the first shark to the surface he would use the baseball bat to club the fish until he was certain it could do no damage. After boating the shark he would disassemble that line before bringing in the next. Once he had all six lines in and disassembled, the old man would take out his knife and begin the work he was growing to hate. It wasn't the act of butchering he hated; he was after all a fisherman, but this was different, very different. Butchering the sharks caused him to view the act with a loathing that he didn't fully understand, as though he were somehow unclean. He began by removing the jaws, being careful not to cut through the cartilage so that they would remain intact. Then with a few expertly applied cuts, he would remove the entire skin in one piece. Then he would carefully remove the eyeballs and put them in a wooden bowl filled with sea water. He would then heave the rest of the carcass overboard. This was the act he despised the most, but the old man had no choice.

While he sat drifting in his small boat, waiting for the first keg to begin bobbing, he looked up at the blinding sun now directly overhead and said aloud, "What kind of work is this for an old man? I was once a great fisherman, how did I come to this? The killer and waster of sharks." The old man put his head down on the oars and turned inward again. He traveled back, back to that morning eight years ago. The morning of the arrival of the first commercial fishing trawler in his home waters. That morning marked the beginning of the end for his small fishing village, and the end of the old man's life as a great fisherman.

The morning began with a great commotion. Jonah awoke to the clammer of excited voices as people ran through the village, heading for the beach. He emerged from his hut and began making his way down to the lagoon. The villagers had gathered on the wet sand. All eyes were fixed upon the gray waters just beyond where the low tide had left jagged peaks of algae-covered rocks exposed to the inclement atmosphere. It was a damp overcast morning, and a piercing wind sent a chill through the old man as he focused his eyes on the object just outside the reef. A great steel ship moved slowly along, paralleling the shoreline. Occasionally puffs of smoke belched forth from its exhaust stacks, and figures of men could be seen milling about on the deck. They seemed to be tending some sort of spool and crane apparatus that was towing something behind the ship. The villagers were too far away to really see what was going on, so some of the men got in their small boats and began rowing out across the lagoon to get a closer look. Jonah ran to where his boat was and pushed off to follow them. The steel ship had come to a stop and as the armada of small boats drew closer they could see the lines from the spool and crane were towing a huge net. Jonah was still several hundred yards away when the ship's stacks began belching smoke again and the clangorous whine of a motor was heard as the big spool on the deck began bringing in the line. The men of the village stood up in their small boats and stared in disbelief as the huge net emerged from the water. Anchovies, tons of them, had been scooped up by the trap. Millions of tiny silver flashes struggled for freedom as the net was maneuvered around over the ship's hold, some of them escaping through the mesh only to fall on the deck and be trampled by the crewmen. Then the net was slowly lowered, and as it disappeared within the ship, the old man bowed his head and began making his way back to shore.

It had started raining, and as the foreboding clouds gathered overhead, the old man had a terrible premonition. This would not be the last ship of this kind to come here he thought as he cowered under the driving rain. They were taking the bait-fish in volumes that would soon ruin the entire area. Once the anchovies and sardines were gone, the bonita and dolphin would no longer come this way. There would be no more marlin or sailfish. The fishermen would no longer be able to feed their families, and the village would perish.

None of the men went out fishing that day. The storm gathered in the morning grew worse through the afternoon. As the great steel ship moved off, trailing its huge net and belching black smoke, the villagers mingled about, talking of what, if anything, could be done to stop the vandalism that was now threatening their existence.

Of course nothing was done. Just as the old man had predicted, other steel trawlers came. As the schools of bait-fish dwindled, so did the daily catches of the fishermen. Within five years most of the village people had moved away. Some went to find jobs in the city and others moved inland to work on farms. The few that remained tried to adjust to the deteriorating conditions, but soon they too grew disgusted and moved away, leaving the old man alone.

As Jonah raised his head from the oars and stared up into the cloudless sky, he said out loud, "I should have left with the others, but where can an old fisherman go when all the fish are gone? Could I have gone to the city to live in the alleys and beg in the streets? Should I go inland to toil in some dirt field? No! That is not for me. I have lived my life by the sea and I shall die and be buried by the sea." As he looked over to his circle of wooden kegs, the old man remembered how he came to be the only shark fisherman on the coast.

Jonah had been sitting alone on the beach, staring out over the lagoon. The midday sun felt good as it beat down upon him. He had not been out in his boat for weeks. The live bait important to successful fishing was nowhere to be had. He found himself subsisting on wild fruits and the few animals that he was able to forage from the low tide pools in the lagoon. A great depression hung over the old man like some terrible dark shroud and he thought that soon he would leave the village that had always been his home. As he stared out over the tranquil water a voice came from behind him.

"No fish today, old man?"

Jonah spun around and raised a hand to shield his eyes from the sunlight. He didn't recognize the man who was standing some five yards up the sand in the shade of a coconut tree. The stranger was wearing a light-colored suit and dark glasses, and the way the shadows of the palm leaves played across his figure caused him to appear as though he were fading in and out of focus.

"No more fish here," replied Jonah. "The fish have all left this place," he continued. "The village that was once here perished when the big steel ship came and took everything away. I myself am preparing to leave this sad place."

"I have heard of your troubles, my friend," the stranger said as he emerged from the shadows and walked to stand near the old man. "And I believe I can be of some assistance to you."

"And how can you help me?" Jonah inquired as he stood up and inspected the stranger's face. He was dark-skinned and had a thick mustache that curled down at the corners of his mouth. His hair was blue-black, worn slicked back and tucked under a wide-brim, white Panama hat. When he spoke his teeth showed the glitter of many gold fillings.

"I represent a business concern that deals in shark by-products and I am prepared to pay a handsome price for such products."

"Sharks!" said the old man. "You buy shark?"

"Not sharks," the stranger replied. "Shark by-products. I am interested in shark hide, shark teeth and eyes, and as I said, I am willing to pay good money for these things."

Jonah thought for a moment, then asked, "But what of the rest of the shark, the meat?"

"I have no use for shark meat, my friend, it is impossible to sell at any price. All I want are the items that I have mentioned."

The old man stood silent, brushing one hand over his white whiskers, and considered the proposal. He didn't much like the idea of butchering any animal for its skin, even a shark, but the idea of once more being able to roam freely over the deep waters that he knew so well was more than he could resist. He thought that if maybe he could find some use for the shark meat it wouldn't be so bad, and he knew from experience that there were lots of sharks in the local waters. "And how would I go about catching these sharks?" asked Jonah. "All I have are simple handlines."

"I will supply you with the materials you will be needing," replied the dark stranger. "And I will instruct you in the proper method of extracting and preserving the items that I want. Do we have a deal, old man?"

Jonah thought for a moment, looked over his lagoon and the open sea beyond, then turned and spoke. "We have a deal."

"Good," said the stranger. "I will come here tomorrow with the things needed to get you started." They shook hands consummating the pact. The dark stranger then turned and left by way of the shadowy path from which he first emerged. As Jonah watched him walk away, he was overcome by a feeling that he had made a terrible mistake.

So Jonah became the first and only shark fisherman on the coast. With the help of the dark-skinned shark broker, he quickly learned the best technique for catching sharks and preserving the sellable parts. However, there was one very big problem; no matter where he went he was unable to sell the shark meat. He went up and down the coast, to all the marketplaces, and the response was always the same. Not interested. Usually by the time he got to the marketplace the meat had started giving off a peculiar foul odor and he couldn't even give it away. He tried using the meat for bait to catch more sharks, but quickly learned that even sharks will not eat the dead and decomposing shark meat. So Jonah was left with no other choice but to dispose of it by the simplest means available. Over the side at the end of the day, before starting the trip home.

The years passed and the old man became successful. The shark broker would visit twice a month to pick up his merchandise and pay Jonah his money. That was the extent of their relationship. There were no papers signed and they dealt in only cash. Jonah bought a small motorbike to take him to and from the market. He even purchased a radio for his hut, but he was not happy. He was plagued by a remorseful feeling with which he couldn't reconcile. The wasting of the shark meat went against every thread of his nature. He often thought of quitting, but the thought of once again being forced ashore was more than he could bear. So he continued his morbid routine and over the years grew calloused. His conscious mind rarely dwelt on his deeds, but when he slept, his dreams were of swirling shadows, thrusting jaws, and snapping teeth.

The kegs are all bobbing now. Six good sharks on the line. It won't be long now, the old man thought. They will soon grow weak and drown. Then it will be time. Jonah took out his knife and ran a thumb over the blade to test its sharpness. Soon he will be doing it again, the unholy work that he struggled daily to ignore. Six pairs of jaws for the tourists to waste their money on. Six hides of leather to make shoes and wallets for the rich men in the city. A dozen macabre eyeballs, to adorn the ears and fingers of the rich men's wives. Jonah brought his sharpening stone and began to hone the blade to a scalpel's edge. A thought flashed through his mind. "I will quit this evil work today." Jonah continued sharpening the blade, his eyes fixed on the circle of wooden kegs. They were barely moving now. He returned the knife to its sheath and put the sharpening stone away. Reaching under the bench, he brought out his baseball bat. He stared at it through eyes blurred by the sting of salt water, and with a desolate feeling in his heart he tried to envision his father's face. But no image came. He looked up to the sky, hoping to see the great frigate bird soaring proud and free above him. But the sky was empty. He was truly alone.

Jonah stood alone and looked out over the blue expanse. His figure cast a long shadow over the water. The day had worn on without him noticing, and the evening wind was beginning to gust. He would have to hurry now. He looked at the kegs and saw they were motionless. "Good," he said aloud. "Let's get this over with."

He got behind the oars, and rowed over to the first keg. Looking down through the clear water he saw the small shark drifting some ten yards down. He untied the rope from the keg and began pulling up the shark. As the head broke the surface the fish began to thrash weakly. It was still too alive to bring aboard, so Jonah reached for the bat. Holding the shark's head up with his left hand, he raised the bat with his right hand and brought it down hard. Again he raised the bat with his right hand and brought it down with a dull thud. The shark drifted, motionless now, its dead eyes staring back at the old man. Jonah dropped the bat, and using both hands hoisted the lifeless fish on board. A small remora released itself just in time and fell back into the water. It disappeared in an instant. The old man then lifted the keg aboard, but didn't bother disassembling the line.

The sun was now well into its descent toward the horizon. There wouldn't be time for neatness today. The next two kegs came up much like the first. The three sharks sat neatly piled at the old man's feet as he rowed over to the second set of kegs. The wind was really beginning to blow, pealing a spray off the churning surface. A chill ran through the old man as he wiped his eyes and began pulling up the first line. No resistance. He quickly pulled up the rope, and the severed end emerged from the water. "Damn," Jonah said as he inspected the tattered end of the rope. The small shark must have gotten past the chain and bit the rope. Jonah hoisted the keg and the remaining length of rope aboard, and then moved to the second keg and began pulling. "What, again?" The line was slack. He began frantically to pull in the rope, noticing that it was a bit heavier than the first. As the rope emerged from the water, so did half the length of chain. "Bitten through?" Jonah swallowed, then realized what was happening. He looked out over the water, scanning the surface in every direction. He saw nothing; no fin, no telltale ripple, no shadow caught from the corner of an eye. Nothing. One more line to go.

"Leave now!" a voice in his head shouted. "While you still can!" He looked down at the three small sharks. "Only three." The old man looked at the last keg floating next to the boat and thought, "Maybe he ate the two and left, maybe he's gone." Jonah reached down and took the rope with both hands. He lifted slightly. There was the familiar resistance. "Ah yes, a nice small shark." Not wanting to wait around any longer than necessary once the shark was up, he hauled the keg aboard and sat it behind the bench. He then reached down and with both hands began pulling in the line. "Yes, four good sharks. Today will not be such a bad loss."

He looked over to see where the sun was, when suddenly his arms pulled out from his body and he found his face underwater. He let go of the rope and felt something racing past alongside his right leg. He had not discon-nected the line from the keg and the rope was now disappearing over the rail. The old man stood and shook the water from his face. The rope came to its end with a snap, and the keg lodged between the bench and the rail. Jonah reached for his knife and turned to go for the rope, but tripped over the pile of sharks and the knife flew out of his shredded red palm. He watched the knife sink, the blade sending off flashes of light through the crystal clear water. The boat began moving sideways, being pulled by something immense. Jonah got back to his feet and reached for his keg. Just then the rope smoked across the length of the rail, catching the old man at the hips. He felt the bone in his thigh snap as he went sprawling to the deck. The plas-tic trashcan toppled and fell, spilling its contents over him. The smell of oil and fermenting fish gagged him as he screamed and reached for his leg. His vision blurred, and he fought to keep from blacking out. He struggled to his feet and fell in the direction of the bench. His hands landed on the keg, and he noticed that the rope had gone slack. Just then something rammed into the belly of the boat with a force that lifted the front half clear off the water.

Wood splintered and cracked, and Jonah looked with horror at the water gushing through a gaping hole in the bottom of the boat. He was taking on water fast and the boat began to list to one side. In a panic, Jonah grabbed for the wooden bowl and began frantically to bail water. His eyes darted in every direction. The dead sharks rolled passively around him. Then he glimpsed something moving towards him. The gray fin towered above the surface of the water, silently slicing a course directly for the boat. The old man sat frozen as he watched the awesome apparition glide past his eyes. It banked a turn and made a pass under the boat. Jonah spun around and saw the back of the dorsal fin moving away, then spun back to see the tail disappear under him.

Everything was floating. The kegs with their tangle of rope, the dead sharks, the fish heads, his baseball bat. Jonah lunged and grabbed the bat, just as the starboard rail dipped below the surface. The boat was going under fast now. Jonah scratched and crawled his way for the stern, trying to outrace the rising water, but it was hopeless. The stern went under and Jonah found himself awkwardly treading water, still holding the bat. He looked down and watched his boat disappear into the abysmal darkness. He panicked and kicked into a swimming stroke. The pain shot through his leg and knotted in his stomach. He rolled and screamed. Then he saw it. The monster shark swam past to his left, just below his feet. Jonah saw its pitch-black eye as it passed, lifting him up with the water column. He spun around, but saw nothing. He spun back, his eyes wide with terror. It hit him from the blind side and he suddenly found himself being propelled through the water, still clutching his bat. He felt the vise tighten, the pressure crushing in his ribs, and as his final breath left his body Jonah cried out, "Father, forgive me."

In the last seconds before his mind was consumed in the darkness, the old man bobbed onto his back, and stared up into the twilight. There in the sky above was his father's face smiling down at him and nodding.

Coming Back

VICTORIA NELSON

Pukoo, on Molokai's East End, has three ghosts. There is a woman in white who walks on the highway. A dead Chinaman swings from the rafters of the stone house once owned by the von Tempskis. And the creature who lives in the *haole koa* thicket on the mountain side of the road is a woman by day, a giant squid by night. In the old days this creature used to creep down to the pens by the beach to eat the pigs. There are no more pigs at Pukoo, only a bulldozed hotel site; how she manages these days is not clear.

The squid woman and the others come out on *pukani* nights when the moon and stars are blotted out by clouds.

The highway that winds around the East End stops in Halawa Valley, deserted thirty years ago when the people moved to town and to the pineapple fields on the West End. In the old days each trail in the valley had its own chant to be recited against bad spirits. The famous Twelve Winds of Halawa were known by name. Today the names are gone, the winds remain. But a driver who eases his car down the road into the overgrown valley may hear his name spoken out loud at the bend where the road crosses an ancient Hawaiian footpath. And in the empty tin-roofed houses of the valley a mirror fogs, a child cries, a white dog runs down a decrepit hallway.

One East End family allowed a brother-in-law who was not a blood relation to clean out the well. A few nights later the mermaid paid the brother-in-law a visit. The mermaid was very pretty. She had white hair and smoked a cigar. She liked men. The brother-in-law woke up to find her pulling the blanket off his bed. He jumped up and ran out of the room. The mermaid drifted next door, where she tried to suffocate the baby. Everybody got on their knees reciting prayers and obscenities. After the old grandmother had said the Lord's Prayer backwards ten times in Hawaiian, the mermaid went away.

Many people on the East End of Molokai return from the dead. The dead have many reasons for coming back. Mostly, it is to settle unfinished business. Sam Kalani's grandfather came back to his startled family because the cows from Murphy's ranch were trampling his grave. Mary Kahunanui came back to her three daughters as a loud wind in the night, but they were never able to determine her wishes. And Lena Kaupu came back.

Lena Kaupu was eighteen years old, a temperamental girl with a beautiful Hawaiian face and stocky Japanese legs. She lived with the Lum family, who took her in after she quarreled with her mother, a plump, flashy-type divorcee who worked as a receptionist in the island's only resort hotel.

Lena hated her mother's ambitions to live haole style. When she was twelve, Lena took the exams that would have sent her to the Kamehameha Schools for a high-class education. She failed on purpose. To her mother's screams of displeasure, Lena shouted, *"Ai kukae!"* and ran from the sound of that phony genteel voice ringing in her ears.

As she grew up, Lena discovered the best way to get back at her mother. She began to hang around with the bad boys—Steamboat, Bobby Wong, Kalei, all the twenty-year-olds who sat jobless on their family porches drinking Primo and shooting empty bottles for target practice. They liked to get ready for the monthly pig hunts. Then one day Bobby Wong slit open her forearm with his knife for no reason at all. It hurt Lena. The doctor had to sew big ugly stitches to close it up.

Her mother had Lena put on probation by the Juvenile Authority of Maui County. They made a special trip to Maui on the airplane, sullen bandaged Lena and sullen overdressed mother. After that, Lena moved in with the friendly Lums. She dropped out of high school and started work in the pineapple fields on the West End. If people asked about her mother, she always said, ''I nevah see her no more. Nevah. Lena keeps her word.''

Then Lena met Stevie Hupai, one of the East End boys she had not known before. He was a year younger; Lena's friends kidded her about that. Their laughter infuriated her. She and Stevie had loved each other from the very first moment they met, at a dance. Love melted her hard young face and opened it to the world. When she walked down the main street of Kaunakakai, the old wood-frame stores with their dusty verandas, sleeping dogs, and dying plantation workers squatting in the shade breathed gently in her direction. But Lena thought only of Stevie.

Stevie's mother and father did not like him seeing that good-for-nothing Lena Kaupu. He paid no attention. His parents grew insistent. They forbade him to see Lena again. If he disobeyed, they would kick him out of the house. And Stevie could not be accepted by another family in the old way, because of the curse on him. He was given to sudden tempers. When he was only a child, he had thrown his knife at his younger brother and killed him, by accident. Older Hawaiians avoided Stevie and did not like him to visit their homes.

Lena's mother stepped in. If Lena didn't give up Stevie at once, she would report her daughter to the Juvenile Authority and have her shipped off to reform school in Honolulu. Mrs. Kaupu was not really sure this would happen, but she felt the law was on her side. Lena would never know the difference anyway—her mother and the law were the same, as far as she was concerned.

After the ultimatum Lena and Stevie went driving in his brother's '51 Chevy. They drank two six-packs of Primo and discussed the possibilities. It was three years before they could marry without their parents' permission. How could they run away? Neither of them had ever been to Honolulu, except as little children. The rest of the world seemed very far away from Molokai.

"I hate her, I hate her!" Lena screamed.

Stevie said nothing. Suddenly he raised his beer bottle and smashed it on the dashboard in front of them. He stuck the jagged top under Lena's chin. "More better we finish it like this!" His hand shook at her neck. Tears ran out of her eyes and dropped on his wrist.

"Wait, Stevie." Lena's tight voice was a distant echo of her mother's. "Yes, we will do it. Not here. We go Uncle Richard's. We fix things up first so that people will know why."

Lena's Uncle Richard had a cabin up in the mountains above Kalaupapa. They would wait until the weekend to go up to the cabin. Stevie would bring his father's pistol with all the bullets in it.

Lena wanted to compose a farewell note. Every night that week she worked on it at the kitchen table. Whenever one of the Lum children would creep up and lean teasingly over her shoulder, she covered the writing with her hand. On Thursday she produced a final version which she copied over neatly on the lavender stationery her aunt had given her for Christmas. This is what Lena wrote:

> Dear Uncle Richard, By the time you read this Stevie and I will be dead. Our families will not let us be happy. But we forgive them. Because our love is bigger. We want to be married by the pastor and put in the same coffin. That is our last wish. Please bury me in my white muu muu in the closet, there is enough $ for a bridal veil too. Aloha nui loa, Lena.

She addressed the envelope to her uncle with the command "Open Monday!" printed underneath.

Pale and silent, dressed in their best aloha clothes, Lena and Stevie dropped off the envelope at her uncle's house on Saturday morning. Uncle Richard was a wishy-washy type who hated trouble. As he handed over the key, he avoided their eyes. "What you doing there? What you folks up to?" he asked nervously. Lena could see he had guessed something was up. But he did not want to be involved.

Uncle Richard did not want an answer, but Lena gave him one. "Stevie and I take one last holiday," she said, "then we break up." She threw the envelope down on the kitchen counter. "Remember—no open till Monday!"

She knew he wouldn't touch it.

They drove up the mountain road very fast. Stevie said nothing. All the fight had gone out of him. He followed Lena tamely up the path like a little boy and let her unlock the rusty padlock on the cabin door. The single room was dirty and hot. There was no furniture, not even a chair to sit on. A rat had crawled in through a broken window and left its refuse in the corner.

The pistol hung limp in Stevie's hand.

"Do it now!" begged Lena. "Otherwise no can do evah!"

Stevie started to cry. He sobbed so loudly the birds stopped singing outside. "Cannot, cannot!" he cried, sitting down heavily on the floor.

Lena unglued the gun from each damp finger of his hand and pressed the barrel to the back of his head. A strange little voice issued from his mouth. It said: "Lena."

"We got to do it fast!" she screamed. "No time talk story!" she pulled the trigger. There was a loud report and Stevie's forehead blew off.

Lena dropped the gun and ran out the door. By the time she came back, the ants had found Stevie. So she went ahead with it.

It was against the law for dead people to be married and put in the same coffin. Stevie was buried in his parent's back yard next to his aunt and his little brother. Lena was put in the Mormon cemetery. Lena's mother did not have to buy her a bridal veil. She was buried in her best dress instead. Lena's mother married the acting manager of the hotel and they went to live on Maui.

So Lena came back. Washing the family car one afternoon, Della Lum looked up and there was Lena, big as life. She vanished as soon as she saw Della looking at her. That night it rained so fiercely that the road to Kaunakakai washed out. For a week the weather changed wildly from sun to rain to wind, every hour of every day. Then a mysterious pink car ran over the Lums' dog, Albert.

All that was Lena, the Lums agreed. But no one heard from Stevie, sleeping with half a head out in the wet behind his parents' house. For weeks the East End people were on the lookout. Nothing happened. So they decided that Stevie was dead for good. Not that he was at peace. It was just that some people go so far away when they die that they never come back, not for any reason.

A Small Obligation

SUSAN NUNES

"You know what she did yesterday?" my mother asks. She puts her coffee cup on the counter. She has been nursing it while she watches me fix myself breakfast in her kitchen amidst the leavings of an earlier meal.

"I can't find the tabasco."

"It's in the icebox, on the door," she says, then asks, "What do you want that for?"

"The eggs."

"You put that in eggs?" My mother finds it extremely difficult to watch idly while someone else works. "Don't you want bacon? There's bacon in the chiller."

I have to be firm. "No," I say. But when I turn around she is standing proprietarily over the eggs, spatula in hand. "Mother," I say in the patronizing tones we acquire in adolescence when speaking to our parents, "I've been cooking eggs for years." I nod toward the dining room and tell her to sit down and drink her coffee. "I'll be out in a minute," I add reassuringly, "then we can talk."

Still she hesitates. "Don't you want some coffee?"

I look at her with ill-disguised exasperation. "I'd love some. Now will you please sit down?"

When I join her with a placemat and my eggs, she has cleared a space for me to eat. My coffee is there, the cream already in it. "Sorry about the mess," she says. She looks about her.

My mother uses the dining room table as a makeshift desk. Whenever we visit she apologizes for the mess and vows she is going to convert the spare bedroom into a proper office. But the clutter remains: two dictionaries, thick file folders with wooden clothespins protruding from the sides, legal pads filled with her crabbed script, old *New Yorker*s and Dad's *Maryknoll* magazines, a large bottle of aspirin, solicitations from Catholic relief societies, number one pencils, capless Faber-Castell pens, a salt shaker, and her ancient Smith Corona.

"You know what she did?" she asks again.

I offer her toast and immediately regret the distraction.

"No, thank you," she says. "I can barely manage half a piece in the morning."

"What did Grandma do this time?"

My mother begins with a great sigh. "She does the strangest things, Amy, the strangest things. In yesterday's paper, her paper, was a picture of some women demonstrating for the Equal Rights Amendment. They were carrying placards, large oval things on poles with 'Support ERA Now' in big block letters. The words leapt out at you. Graphically very effective. *Anyway,* she'd been studying the picture all morning—you know the way she does—the paper three inches from her face. Totally absorbed."

I know how intense Grandma's actions can be. My mother takes a sip of coffee. "After her nap it was the same thing. I even stopped writing at one point and asked if she wanted some tea or a cookie, she gets so hungry in the afternoon. No, no, she said, she was all right. So I asked her again, just to be sure. You know how she refuses out of politeness, then acts as if I've taken the food out of her mouth."

My mother is tapping the edge of the table with the fingers of her right hand. It began some time ago, the tapping. "I hate the obliqueness," she says vehemently. "Anyway," she continues, "it must have been around four, shortly before I planned to prepare dinner. I heard the walker, then her slippers. I always know when she has something she wants to tell me. The *urgency* of those little footsteps. So I stopped working and I waited.

"She sat down where you're sitting. The newspaper—somehow she'd managed to hold on to it—was tightly rolled up. She put it there, where your mat is, while she made herself comfortable, then slowly and deliberately she unrolled it. *Then,* Amy, she proceeded to tell me the most incredible story. It's so *strange* where she gets these things. I ask myself, where do they *come* from?"

Mother's stories often have long prefaces, her telling slipping into familiar cadences. In many ways her stories were the most affectionate connection we had after my sister was born. Long car trips, the hours she spent ironing my father's starched shirts, Friday nights after dinner, family gatherings, all were occasions for telling. When measured against each other, her tales far outweigh our battles. I can forgive her almost everything.

She was born in Hilea, a plantation town that no longer exists. It was located in the foothills of Mauna Loa, south of Pahala in the Kau district of the

Big Island. She was the second of four children and the only daughter. Following her father's wishes, she became a teacher, but just before the war, in what I believe was a fit of rebellion, she married my father, who is not Japanese. Later, Grandfather's language school was shut down by the authorities after Pearl Harbor, and every month she dutifully handed her paycheck to her parents.

Obligation runs terribly strong in some families. Perhaps it is an individual guilt. Her oldest brother did not have the same need to fulfill unarticulated debts. Even as a child hearing the story of the paycheck, I felt it unfair that she and Dad were the ones who had to support her parents during a time when everyone was hard pressed. After Grandfather's release from the relocation camp, he was able to earn a small living blockprinting Hawaiian designs on shirts, muumuus, and other souvenirs purchased by servicemen stationed in Hilo. Grandma sewed khaki pants for the Army and taught *shishu*, Japanese embroidery, which was not considered a dangerous art. I loved my grandparents, but $120 seemed an enormous sum. Would I have to do that one day?

My mother is not looking at me. Her eyes are fixed somewhere above my head, and her right hand is tapping the edge of the table. After a while, she says: "Her hands were black with newsprint. She asked me if I remembered Japan. 'No, Mama,' I said, 'I've never been to Japan.' But she went on in her schoolmarm voice as if she hadn't heard. She said, 'They are honoring the turtle, these women. See? They are expressing their feeling about the turtle. In Japan it is a sacred and auspicious creature. *Minasai.*'"

Mother's voice has taken on the character of Grandma's. "Look," she mimics, "the turtle shells are painted many colors. They are holding them on poles, and the crowds will bow with respect as they go by."

Mother pauses to clear her throat before continuing. "I said, 'Mama, why don't you *read* it. It's not about turtles, it's not even about Japan.' I didn't tell her the picture was black and white or that the women were Americans and not Japanese. But I did tell her that they weren't marching in honor of the turtle; they were marching in support of the Equal Rights Amendment. Then, as if I'd presented her with the most surprising news, she said, '*Sō?*'"

My mother's hand is still tapping. She is staring at my chair. "You're thinking it was cruel of me, Amy, to insist, because she knows nothing about such things. But she's *clever,* you know."

"What happened then?" I ask.

"Well, she sat for a few minutes looking at the picture, and then she said, 'I don't know about *that.*' Why didn't I send her to her mother in Japan? She was a burden, but *her* mother would take care of her. 'Mama!' I said, 'your mother has been dead for almost seventy years!' And you know what she said? 'Oh? Is that so?' "

"Do you remember the turtle, Mother?" I ask. Mother looks puzzled. "You know, the one I got for a gift when we lived on Piopio Street."

Her hand stops tapping, "Piopio Street? Oh, yes," she says, smiling, "Mr. Naito gave it to you."

"Right."

"You were five. I remember."

It was a tiny creature which fit in the palm of my hand. It looked like a little lacquer jewel box, the shell painted bright red and blue. My grandmother gave me a blue glass bowl. I put water in it, some smooth black pebbles, and carried that bowl around for days, ignoring the warnings that I would drop it and cut myself to bits. After a week I decided the turtle looked unhappy. In a fit of generosity I took it out to the shrimp pond, picked it up by its painted back and let it go. It sank like a stone and disappeared in a puff of silt. Gone. How I searched for that turtle! But I never saw it again. I dreamed about it, imagined it had drowned. Twenty-five years later, after my grandparents moved to Honolulu, I told Grandma about the turtle. She thought the story was hilarious, and when I asked her why, she said that after we moved to Villa Franca she had seen it sunning itself on a rock. Yes, of course she knew it was the same one, because the shell still had traces of red and blue lacquer.

We don't mean literally in this family. What you have to do is wait for the underlying meaning. It'll come eventually. Sometimes you can ask directly, but you risk making the person lose face. There's a word for it in Japanese which I don't recall, but I know what it describes. Imagine someone in a kitchen. Pots and pans are being thrown around, drawers slammed. Obviously, someone is angry. Now in the typical American household one would probably go into the kitchen and ask what the matter was. On my father's side, someone would yell, "Shut up!" But not in ours. No, we would know that someone was offended and someone else was responsible, but to ask what the problem was would make the offended party feel they were angry about something not worth your noticing, and they would lose face.

I have always tried to act as if I really knew what had offended. I have had to wait for the proper opening in which to make amends. Eventually the opening will come, but the signal is usually oblique.

My mother and I are sitting on the patio. The wisteria is in bloom, and purple clusters hang from the ceiling beams. My parents have been eating their meals here, now that Grandma is confined to her room most days. She has been finding it increasingly difficult to walk and complains frequently that her feet are cold, that her back and hips ache.

"I was talking to Ann Conant next door," my mother is saying.

"Oh?" I know that what my mother and Ann Conant have in common is the subject of aging parents. I also know the story. Ann and her husband Ben cared for both their mothers.

"Taking care of two old folks, it must have been terribly difficult," my mother says. The story goes that Ann Conant's mother was the invalid, and every morning they'd have to leave her lunch in a tray by her bed. She couldn't move. If she wanted to go to the bathroom during the day, she had to do it in her diapers. Mother had told me this more than once so I knew she was bothered by it.

"What about Ben's mother, didn't she help?"

"Nope." The no is emphatic. "She hated Ann's mother and wouldn't have anything to do with her. Actually, Ben's mother died first and a few months later they had Ann's mother declared indigent and put in a nursing home. It was just too difficult and too expensive."

I realize I am expected to say something. This is the opening, the story an illustration of something else. I tell my mother she's becoming housebound, that she will *have* to make a decision about Grandma herself, and how difficult that will be, but how necessary, after all she must consider her own health. Mother says nothing while I review the obvious arguments. When I finish there is a long pause.

"*That's* not the only thing," she says. "I don't mind having to bathe her, lift her, scrub her, listen to her. It's—Last week I found her in the kitchen trying to reach the telephone. She'd wedged herself between the walker and the counter. Frightened me half to death, I mean that whole thing could have given way. When I asked her what she was doing, she *demanded* that I tell her Megumi's number. *Demanded.* I asked her why she wanted to call him, he never called *her.* Oh, she said, there was something she had to discuss with him, very important. And then I saw she was holding a postcard, so I asked her what it was. She held it away from me, as if she were a child being forced to share. It was none of my concern, she said, none of my concern. I must have looked shocked, because she relented and said all right if I *had* to know, she'd gotten an important card from Japan and had to speak to Megumi about making arrangements for the visit. I asked her what visit she was talking about. She said—as if *I* were the child—that her nephew and his wife were coming. I'm afraid I insisted that she show me the card. Well! Do you know, Amy, it was written over eight years ago? *Eight years!* She'd unearthed it from that pile of old letters and photographs in her room and *seized* on it for some *inexplicable* reason."

Emotions play on Mother's face. Just as I did as a child, I have the strongest urge to protect her. She continues: "I told her that when Hironaka and his wife visited us, *I* made the arrangements, *I* fed them, *I* took them shopping and entertained them. Megumi did nothing but gift us with his presence."

"He's impossible—"

"Sometimes I get so angry, I—"

In our family, sentences have a way of fading away. We leave one another with unfinished thoughts while our minds race elsewhere. Here, take this and keep it until I get back. For a while Mother and I talk about the wisteria on the other side of the house, the one which doesn't bloom because the cutting was from the mainland. It takes a seasonal cold snap to jar the plant to flower, my mother says. She won't cut it down, however.

Before I leave Mother tells me one of Grandma's General Nogi stories. Grandmother has a keen sense of history—not so much an interest in chronology or in great events playing one upon the next—but a sense of the great personalities of her past, their idiosyncrasies. General Nogi was one of her favorites, a source of many moral lessons. Mother had been cutting Grandma's nails and commenting on how hard they were and how quickly they grew. As she talked she put the parings in an ashtray. Grandma looked critically at her hands and said that Nogi-sama had revered his mother so much he saved her nail parings and hair and kept them until he died.

"I suppose," Mother comments wryly, "this was to suggest that I save *her* parings. Or that I don't possess the proper proportion of respect."

"Don't laugh," I caution her. "It probably was."

"I'm not laughing. You know what else she said?" I shake my head. "Nogi-sama and his wife committed suicide after the Emperor Meiji died."

At ninety-two, my grandmother's world is terribly circumscribed. Bedroom and bath. Patio only once a day. I drop in unexpectedly late one afternoon and find her in her rocker on the back patio. She is staring intently at a spray of orchids a few feet from her chair. Her newspaper lies folded and unread on the floor. She is almost beautiful, softened in the late afternoon light, her little body tucked neatly into the cushions. When she hears me she turns and calls my name as if she hasn't seen me in years. Then she says, "Look. Pretty, *nō?* Grandpa make." She points to the pot. "You give me, this one." I move it closer to her. Very gently, she touches one of the blooms. "I like this one." The patio sits at the base of a terraced hill. Up the cement stairs and around the corner is where Mother found Grandfather, his limbs collected but the back of his head split open where it had struck the concrete. He had been fertilizing orchids. Mother is no longer fond of dendrobiums, but Grandmother still takes pleasure in them.

The telephone wakens me. "Amy? It's Mother. Grandma's had another stroke. I'm calling from the hospital."

My grandmother has given us all a scare, but she will survive this one, the doctor says, although he cautions that cerebral "accidents" of this sort often result in erratic behavior.

So begins a week of nightmares after they bring her home from the hospital. For three nights a fire burns in her room. On the fourth there's snow in the bamboo grove. On the fifth and sixth she cannot find the furo—at 3:30 in the morning—and on the seventh the fire burns again.

"Miho, Miho!" she calls out, waking both my parents.

"What is it, Mama?"

"Come, come," she cries, and when my mother comes, she says, "Look. A fire. There!"

"*What* fire, Mama. There's no fire!"

"*Mite goran!* Look, you foolish girl," she says, pointing to the closet. "Can't you see it?"

According to Mother, Grandma's body was turned around completely, her head where her feet should have been, her kimono half undone, her hair loose and hanging, the pins scattered on the floor. My father thought she was possessed.

"Where is my favorite aunt?" she demanded. "What have you done with her? Did you tell her to go away?" She had managed to pull herself up into a sitting position, and as Mother tried to cover her she cried, "Leave me alone. Where is Shizumi-san? Shizumi! Shizumi! What have they done to you?"

When my mother tried to turn her she snapped, "Who are you? What are you doing here?"

My mother is hurt as she relates this. You would think she might take in stride the rantings of an old woman crippled with stroke. But the woman is her mother.

"Mother, no one's going to blame you." It is late and I really should get home. I long for a bed and a junk novel.

"What are you talking about?" she says sharply. She looks at my face and her fingers start tapping the edge of the table. "This place is a mess. I should get all this stuff cleared away into the back room. It's just more than I can handle right now."

I am uncomfortable, as if the clutter on the dining room table represents something I was expected to do but have not done. "Mother," I say, "no one's going to blame you if you put Grandma in a nursing home."

"You girls," she says with conviction, "you girls will get *nothing* from Daddy and me. What little we have will be set aside for our old age. I will *not* allow you to be saddled with the responsibility."

Is it my imagination or is she attacking me? I cannot escape the feeling that I, that we, are being punished for something. But what is it, what is it we are supposed to have done? We are a family of unspoken obligations. I don't know why, but I am stung.

When it came, Grandmother's death was a surprise but not a great tragedy. Shortly after the week of nightmares, Mama walked into the bedroom with breakfast on a tray and found her curled up and quite dead. I was worried about Mama, how she would take the funeral, the trip to Hilo for the memorial services, the adjustment to a life relatively free of the day-to-day demands of someone who needed her. But she survived the "ordeal," as my sisters and I came to call it. In fact, Grandma's death brought the family closer together. For the first time in years Mama and Megumi were on friendly terms. And I visit more often. She seems to look forward to my company.

In the Buddhist tradition there is a series of memorial services following a person's death. The family repairs to the temple and sits through a special ceremony. Prayers are recited in Japanese. Even Dad lit a joss stick. After the one-month anniversary we had dinner at Mama's. We used the occasion to go through old photograph albums spanning the almost seventy years of Grandma's life in Hawaii. It was close to midnight when, with everyone gone, Mama and I begin to clear up the shards of the past—my sister's expression— scattered on the living room floor.

I am reminded of the task of cleaning Grandmother's room after the funeral and the dread I felt at what Mama's response might be. After all, Grandfather's death was still not that far in the past. That had been terribly difficult for us all, especially my mother, who felt his death acutely. Anyway, cleaning Grandmother's room turned out to be an occasion for laughter rather than tears. When Mama lifted up the mattress she uncovered a trove of ferreted-away junk: used paper napkins folded into tiny squares, brown candy wrappers, a half-eaten piece of what we thought was dried persimmon, pieces of balled-up kleenex, two handkerchiefs, an old coin purse, a store receipt, nylon stockings, and a not-so-junk twenty dollar bill. After going through her purses we collected a total of $8.43 in loose change. And the letters! She had saved everything. The photographs filled several boxes, and it was these that received our attention. There were so many.

I pick up a color shot of an old man standing in front of a house and holding what looks to be a book in his hands.

"Isn't this Grandma's brother?" I ask. Saburo lives in Japan and I have met him only once. He was an energetic man, close to eighty at the time, who walked around our house with his socks on.

Mother takes the photograph and looks at it. "Yes, that's Saburo, Grandmother's last living brother. He's about ten years younger than she. Hironaka's father." Grandmother's two other brothers died of tuberculosis during the war.

I point to the book. "What's he holding?"

"Oh, that," says my mother, smiling. "Didn't I ever tell you about the poetess? Grandma's great-grandmother. That's a book of her poems. Megumi took the picture the last time he was in Japan. He described the book as very old, insect-eaten. The family hadn't preserved it."

"You never told me about a poetess. Can I see it again?" The house in the background looks like the farmhouses in a Japanese woodcut. My grandmother was born in that house. Her family had occupied it for generations. "What a shame. What was the book called?" My mother shakes her head. "Damn," I say, "I wish we could make out the script." Saburo looks so formal. I can see the strong family resemblance, the raised brows, the low hooded eyes. "What do you know about her, Mama?"

"Very little," my mother replies. "She was a child of promise. *Gañ wo kakeru. Gañ* is a promise; *kakeru*, to obligate. It's a promise you make to the gods to fulfill a particular obligation if a certain wish is granted. Her parents had waited so long for a child. They promised that if they had one, that child would make a pilgrimage to some shrine. *Kami mairi wo shimasu.* That was the obligation. *Kami,* the gods, and *mairi,* to pray. *Shimasu* means to perform."

"Where was the shrine?"

"I don't know. Grandma didn't remember and we never bothered to ask."

"Did she make her pilgrimage?"

"She tried. She was a well-educated woman, even by today's standards. Grandma said she wrote many, many songs. Anyway, for one reason or another, it wasn't until she was an old woman that she decided to make the journey. Apparently her sons tried to dissuade her; it would be a difficult journey, they said. But she was determined to go. So she left with her two servants. Many weeks later the servants returned with a small box containing her nails and hair."

"She died on the way?" I ask.

"She died on the way," my mother answers. "She never reached the shrine."

"Kami mairi wo shimasu," I say quietly. "No wonder—"

"What did you say?" she asks.

"Nothing. But I wish I had known about her before."

Mama laughs. "Oh, Amy, there are so many stories." She hands me the photograph, which I had laid down. "Here, put this away in that box next to you. The one with 'Japan' on it."

The Man Who
Swam through Jellyfish,
through Men-of-War

ROBERT ONOPA

Kimo Akeo owned a cream-colored Cessna from which he spotted fish for his sons. In the clear Hawaiian air, he flew in an elegant, extended zigzag pattern over waters he had set nets in when young: those of the Kaiwi Channel from the westerly shore of Molokai to the easterly shore of Oahu; from Makapuu Point in the north, south to the Penguin Banks. In the moving waters of the channel—seas blue-green and brilliant whose vast bulk was furrowed by the wind and heaved by swells—his fifty-year-old eyes could distinguish schools of nehu, anchovies, swimming in shimmering circles just beneath the surface, or aku bonita, whose fins breaking water turned it foamy white in circles a hundred yards wide.

Seeing such fish, he would radio the position and direction of the school to his sons in family sampans below. Nets were set for nehu—close-meshed, surface float nets, twenty boat widths wide—and though a hold loaded with nehu might be taken to market, the Akeos caught nehu for aku bait and chum. Aku bonita was the prize. Nehu in the bait wells, Kimo swooped his Cessna and directed his sons to foaming circles of white, cruised by wheeling gulls, where the large fish fed toward Makapuu Point. Thrown washbuckets of nehu, the bonita fell into a feeding frenzy, broke the water, gorged two-inch unbaited hooks whose only enticement was that they shone. With big fishing underway, Kimo Akeo, who had swung fish back into the hold for thirty years himself, would circle once in a wide graceful arc, last glimpse money being made, and settle to cruising either island's coast.

From the air, the coastlines were patterns of coral, reefs outlined, rip currents and tidal pulls streaking the water—whose color changed from sky blue to violet, from ice blue to white, as the currents carried it over live reefs, past meandering sand spits miles wide, past points, through the surf break, and finally to the sea-green deeps where the aku swam. Some days, off Oahu, he could see two-hundred-pound ulua lolling in the shallow sub-reef, the sun

157

glittering off their silvery backs; off Molokai, vast stretches of empty sand peppered with the shifting shadows of crabs, vast flocks of birds, like dust in the sun off the roadless westerly coast; or, near the sea change between the islands in winter, schools of twenty or more blue whales, massive and graceful as swells, sounding as they rounded toward the leeward coast of Oahu, running toward open sea.

"There's a plane down there. A small airplane. You can see it," Harriet Kunen said, trying both to get her husband's attention and to keep her eyes fixed on what she saw from the oblong window of the huge aircraft. "Cy, you have to look. There are whales, in front of it. You can see them, you have to look."

Cy Kunen reluctantly stuffed his magazine into the seat pocket before his knees and undid the seat belt he had fastened when they had begun their final descent; gawking annoyed him. They were down to three thousand feet now, minutes away from landing in Honolulu, approaching over the Kaiwi Channel. "By Christ . . .," he muttered finally, craned to the window. "Christ, that plane is low."

"Like it's landing," said Harriet. "Those splashes are whales, aren't they, Cy?"

"No, I. . . ." Already the light plane and the fish it followed were passing from the middle of the window aft. "Did you see that stream shoot up? I'll bet those are whales. Christ."

"That plane is in the water, Cy."

"It must be a seaplane."

"Cy, you're crushing my dress. That plane landed in the water."

"I can't see, Harriet. In the water? Can you land a seaplane in that kind of water? Harriet, move, you're. . . ."

Already too far aft for Cy to see clearly, the light plane appeared to Harriet to stop forward motion, wallow, pitch, then yaw. It seemed to lose definition and blend with the sea-green water heaved by swells.

"Maybe you should tell the stewardess, Cy."

"Harriet, don't get hysterical." Cy Kunen settled back in his seat, refastened his safety belt, and made an indecisive motion toward his *Business Week*.

"Cy."

"Harriet, we're landing." Through her window the Kaiwi Channel slipped aft, and Harriet could see the point at Makapuu, Koko Head, and the high-rises of Honolulu stretching into view. The huge plane yawed to port and along its wings flaps separated from smooth aluminum surfaces with a high-pitched sound of rushing wind. "You can tell the stewardess what you saw when we land. Just don't get hysterical, for Christ's sake. Those . . . whales down there, it could have been . . . anything." Cy Kunen stretched around and saw the other passengers in the half-full aircraft for the most part gazing out the windows on the other side of the plane, where Diamond Head reared. "Look," he said, "if you want to look at something, there's Diamond Head." Now he reached for his magazine.

Three miles off the southeastern shore of Oahu, Kimo Akeo settled his Cessna into the Kaiwi Channel, stung with disbelief at the abruptness of the last two hundred feet of his descent. Low over the channel, looping a playful school of blues sounding and rolling in the sea, a flashing panel light told him his back-up magneto had gone bad, and then, before he had time to think about it, his working magneto cut out. He had time only to feather his propeller as the Cessna soundlessly eased toward the swells. With the engine cut he could hear the shift of the trades and the slosh of the sea; and it was all he could do to bring her nose around and settle squarely, bang open his door, scramble out on the wing. For a long moment he felt the Cessna wallow in the water, then a swell brought her tail up as the cowl dipped down. With one chagrined glance he took in the control panel, the nonoperating radio, and his new windbreaker on the second seat; then Kimo slipped into the soft bulk of the water, dunked his head, and swam slowly away. Ten yards off, treading water, he watched his Cessna disappear.

He was left with the hiss of the wind and the ticking of the sea. When the swells raised him, he could see blue-green mountains, diamond flashes of windshields on the Makapuu coast road, the lighthouse, the white spray of surf crashing outside Hanauma Bay. Two, perhaps three miles off. Despite the vastness of the water, the pull of the current, and the relentless rising and falling of the swells, he was not afraid. For thirty years he had spent as many as twelve hours a day in the water, setting nets—though this was not a part of the channel he had fished.

Before too long he could see from the rapid shift of a line he had been watching between the lighthouse and the ridge behind it that he was in a current taking him south with a speed unknown on the Molokai side. This would be the slip off Makapuu. He would have to start swimming, but if he did swim, say, straight for Oahu—it occurred to him—he would be carried past Oahu by noon, and to the open sea. So there was reason to be afraid, he understood, because his only plausible landfall lay behind him. He stripped off his trousers and T-shirt, turned in the water and looked for Molokai's westerly shore. He could see it only as a bluish mist rising on the water—twenty-eight miles away. Windshields flashing at his back, the current pulling him south, he began to ride the ticking soft bulk of the ocean, stroking in a wide arc that he hoped would take him close enough to Molokai for lights to swim by when behind him the sun had set.

Cy Kunen did this: spurning Waikiki as the merchandised wet dream of perverse, asphyxiated Angelenos (he was thirty-five, from New Jersey), he took his wife in a rented Vega past cane fields and pineapple-planted slopes to the sugar town of Pupukea, where—he had read—the big waves were. Those he saw: walls of water, house high, just off the road.

Cy said, "Now this is Hawaii."

Harriet said, "Cy, this is beautiful."

Cy beamed as if it was him she was speaking of.

They left their car on Kam Highway and walked across the sand, a thirty-yard stretch, to where the surf boomed in at the shore break. Fifty yards out, vast masses of ice-blue water rose twenty, twenty-five feet, moved forward—they seemed slow, their movement excruciating and ponderous, they were so large—till at the inside reef the swells broke, crashing into their own bulk, sending foam hissing onto the sand to where their feet were. Cy rolled up his trousers. Harriet took off her shoes.

"It's warm, Cy. We should have brought our suits."

For a few minutes they watched. Then Cy chased a receding wave, ran back from the rush of hissing foam. He did so again, then turned to smile at Harriet higher up on the beach. She saw the final and largest wave of the set hiss foam at her husband knee-high.

Cy Kunen's knees buckled, and he went down on all fours, sliding backward with the pull of the rip. Harriet, openmouthed, watched her husband slipping back across the sand. She began to scream when the rush from the following wave broke over him. She saw him pushed back up the sand—but as he tried to rise, the undertow of the same wave pulled him down again. Halfrolling toward the shore break, he was engulfed by the next wave, and then he slid up the sand on his back. Harriet ran to him, stepping high; lost her footing as the sand was sucked away in the rip; and fell, her dress in her face, rolling in the water. Two huge waves later the largest of the second set pushed and rolled them both high on the beach.

Eyes stinging, throat gagging, Harriet cried. Sand was in her underwear, her hair, her mouth, her nostrils. Staggering to retrieve his shoes, Cy Kunen dropped to his knees and vomited on the sand.

Behind them the shore break hissed and the sea made a ticking sound. A lone surfer, who had begun running across the beach when he had seen Cy fall, held Harriet as she cried.

Brown-black hair, face made up, a slightly heavy but attractive body, sun-pink skin, white bikini: Harriet Kunen sat in a padded canvas chaise on the lanai of the Hotel Halekulani. She was trying both to watch the setting of the sun and to comprehend the headline of the *Star-Bulletin* folded in her lap:

UAL-FAA TAPES SUBPOENA QUASHED?

A slight breeze moved coconut palms, date palms, and across the beach the sea rippled at the sand with sun-glazed laziness. A fat orange sun hung over the ocean, and Harriet watched it, wondering, well, UAL-FAA?, SUB-POENA QUASHED?, UAL SUBPOENA TAPES FAA QUASHED?, mightn't she go blind looking directly at the sun? But it didn't seem to hurt her eyes in the slightest. Could she feel anything? She turned the paper in her lap, started to read an article in a bottom corner of the page—then sat up and read from the beginning out loud:

PLANE DOWN IN CHANNEL

> Honolulu, Feb. 3. James Akeo of Piho, Molokai, was reported missing as a light plane which he was piloting apparently crashed in the Molokai Channel this morning. Shore fishermen and tourists at Makapuu, Oahu, said they saw a small aircraft down in the channel apparently with engine trouble at 9 A.M.

> Akeo, 54, a spotter for Limo Fisheries, had filed a Molokai-Molokai flight plan. He was last reported in radio contact forty-five minutes before the crash. A U.S. Coast Guard spokesman said that rescue efforts would concentrate off the southern Oahu coast.

Cy grunted. At first he had paid no attention to his wife's reading. He had been staring at a huge-bosomed girl sauntering up the beach, watching her breasts rise and fall, thinking, You must have a nice tush, too—but he caught the gist of the story soon enough. Embarrassed he looked at his wife.

"I wasn't the only one," said Harriet, pinker than she had been.

Cy nodded, thought he should stand up. But his limbs hung without energy. He looked at the sun: it was huge and liquid, orange-yellow, sus-pended but sinking into an endless sea that stretched flat—glassy, sun-glazed. At the same time he recalled the distant sea-green water they had seen in the channel, and felt the rise and fall of the swells as he breathed. A heat within him matched the heat of the sun on his skin. Dazed by the sun, the chemistry of his body confused by the length of the flight that had brought him to this island, he felt himself suspended where he sat. He looked down. He made circles with one dangling foot in the thin sand, which seemed everywhere to creep onto concrete.

The sun set at Kimo Akeo's back, unseen, as he stroked the rise and fall of soft swells in the calming sea. The wind at such times of day subsides; the sea settles. The water is warm and comfortable: it would be a time to fish. But soon Kimo swims in darkness.

A cloudless sky looms above him. From time to time he rolls over, rests on his back. Suspended in the water, he sees and considers the positions of the stars—the Southern Cross on the horizon, Cassiopeia's Chair directly above him. As yet, he can see no lights which he can positively identify as Molokai. He is swimming, he thinks, toward Molokai's roadless westerly coast, where lights would not be apparent. Behind him he can see distantly the domed glow of Honolulu, a light-suffused, blue-black atmosphere. The moon will not rise until ten.

He makes himself a proposition: if he can swim until sunrise, he will live to fly another plane. Floating on his back in the calm sea of early evening, he almost sleeps, dreams of watching the sea, of blue-green mountains, of sand beneath his feet.

By 10:00 P.M. the moon does not appear, but the seas rise. First light, he calculates, will be at five. He begins swimming in earnest again, encouraged by the invisibility of the moon, for that makes him think that it is tucked now behind Molokai. Before an hour passes he is touched—touched and stung. One jellyfish, one man-of-war: two. Touched and touched again. Men-of-war floating on the water, in a wind-driven school. How wide?

He parts the water with his hands, breaststroking, to keep the faintly glowing jellyfish from his face. He is tempted to double up and float. Jellyfish here? Perhaps he is as far south as Penguin Banks; if that is so, the current has carried him further than he has swum. He does double up, slips off his jockey shorts, rips them in his hands. Stuffs rolls of cloth up in his nostrils, swims again, stroking as powerfully as he can, his eyes closed. He cannot tell if he is still in jellyfish, for the stinging stays with him, swathing his body like electricity. Only when he must, he breathes through clenched teeth, halfrolling to his side. He dares not open his eyes.

Cy Kunen sits slumped in a chaise on the balcony adjoining the room he has tried to sleep in. In a clear sky, the moon is distinct, its craters discernible.

Stars shine. He had slept, he thinks, three or four hours before he found himself awake, before he slipped from the room to the lanai. Behind him, Harriet sleeps soundlessly. Before him, on a moonlit, deserted beach, the sea laps at the sand rhythmically. On the sea, neither boat lights nor buoy lights shine. Perhaps he sleeps again, unknowing. But he is awake to see in the east the blackness modulate and become a thin gray stripe. The grayness spreads slowly in the eastern sky, is washed with blue at the horizon. The sea assumes shape; directly east he can see the crater looming, outlined. He can faintly hear birds, and at first light, behind Diamond Head, he sees a ghostly rainbow, its shape diffuse, its colors slight. Before he can hear it, he sees illuminated in the southern sky a large helicopter canted forward, driving west. Against a background of birds he hears the sound it makes: flat flat flat flat flat flat. Its sound fades as mynah birds distantly scream. The beach becomes the color of sand.

He passes indoors, where all sounds cease. Harriet lies on her side; then, as he touches the bed, turns on her back. The covers lie strewn at the foot of the bed. For a long moment he watches her, then kneels down, kisses her stomach—soft, warm, rising and falling beneath her nylon nightdress. She sighs, her eyes barely open. Quietly, as if it is her breathing, he hears her say, "Cy."

Her knees rise, fall. In minutes she is naked. Cy Kunen rests on the lower half of the bed as behind him light streaks the sky. The air seems to him salt-rich, humid. Her vagina tastes of the sea.

In the channel Kimo Akeo swims, sunburned and skin seared by men-of-war. As he swims, he is lifted and lowered with the rhythm of swells sown in the South China Sea and grown huge off the westerly winter surf line of Molokai Island. But he does not see that the island is there; to his eyes swells approximate island approximate swells. Lately this is what he sees from a trough: water around him, sea-green, transparent, bright with sunlight and suspending microscopic worlds of air. Other sightings include seabirds, flotsam, and at sunrise a fin slicing water, flashing gray or violet (which, he could not say—shark or dolphin: which?). The sun, when it is higher, maps on his back areas of slight, severe, and somnambulant pain. He strokes slowly, evenly, each arm just falling, pulling when he can.

He trusts to some unchecked sense of direction. No doubt the sun. For a time he daydreams of flying and considers himself as gently pitched and yawed by the wind. Below him silver fish sail in the current, contract dorsal flesh, turn together in military ballet, descend further still to regions of black coral, cowries, and anemones heeled by some breeze. Kimo perceives weather: a hiss has risen on a ticking sea, and the swells are coming alive.

He is raised as in an updraft. His eyes register across the sun-glazed ocean a blue-green shore, mists rising in the valleys, sea spray. The swell rolls from beneath him, lifts higher as it rolls and crests into a transparent sheet of water topped by spray, obliterating the distant shore. Kimo considers that he hears the roar along the outside reef and feels it in the water. Even alongside him a mountainous winter swell breaks for an instant, settles, travels to another cloud of white. Shark or dolphin, swell or bonita, choose one, choose none, choose two. Seabirds. Kimo makes for the weather. Sun high, the seabirds wheel, making for the inside reef, the opihi-rich small surf, the crabsweet shore of Molokai.

Communion

PATSY S. SAIKI

It was quiet, deathly quiet, and that was strange, for Morio Tamura's life had always been full of sounds. There had been the crickets and cicadas on the Tamura farm in Japan, and the rustle of canefields and harsh commands of foremen on the sugar plantation on Hawaii. Here, in Honolulu, the sheathed thunder of cars, buses and trucks from below his locked and heavily draped bedroom window merged with his everyday life. Sound and noises were taken for granted, like the air around him, yet now there was this depthless, monotonous silence.

Was it time to get up? He had to be at the delicatessen by four if he wanted the coffee and doughnuts to be ready by five. A few faithful customers always came early for breakfast. What time was it anyway? He tried to open his eyes but couldn't. He then tried to reach for the clock by his pillow and again he couldn't. He didn't even hear the tick-tock tick-tock that put him to sleep every night. Am I dreaming? he wondered. Then he fell into motionless sleep once again.

The next time he awoke, he noticed not only the silence but the chill in the air. It was . . . it was . . . was there such a things as antiseptic chilly? As if one were being preserved in a tub full of alcohol?

The tub reminded him of his iron vat with bubbling oil in which he made his doughnuts. How many more cases of oil did he have in his storeroom? And flour . . . should he order another forty bags? The newspapers talked about a shipping strike in a few weeks. But if the strike wasn't called, then he would be stuck with the flour and somehow the mice always got to the flour sacks. The health inspectors didn't like that.

Time . . . time to get up . . . what time was it? Surely it must be almost four. Why was it so quiet and cold? Where was Mama? Where was the alarm clock? I must be really exhausted, he thought, and fell asleep once more.

Two nurses entered the room in the morning, one with some towels and the other with a tray of thermometers. The first one said, "Mr. Tamura . . . Mr. Tamura . . . I'm going to wash your face, okay?" The second slipped a thermometer under Morio's tongue.

The first nurse asked, "How many days is it since he's been in a coma? Forty? Fifty?"

"More like ninety," the second nurse said, examining the chart at the foot of the bed. "Ninety-seven today, to be exact."

"You think he'll ever come out of it?"

"Hard to tell. He's a tiny man . . . only five feet tall and weighed 110 pounds when he was brought in. He's 76 pounds now. But he looks like a scrapper, a fighter. The other day I was giving him an alcohol rub and it seemed like he tensed his right arm. First time I felt that. So he could be coming out of it."

"Sad . . . being pistol-whipped for a few dollars. Honolulu was never like this. I can remember when we used to leave our windows and doors unlocked all the time . . . even at night."

"I know. Now I don't feel safe even in my own garage. And I lock myself in the car when I drive."

"Kind of a shame, isn't it, someone in a coma lying in this private air-conditioned room. He can't even appreciate it, yet he has to pay for it."

"I think the police wanted him here. Anyone coming here has to pass through two stations."

"Must cost the family a fortune. I heard a rumor Admissions suggested the family take him to another hospital, when they found out he didn't have any health insurance."

"You can't blame the hospital. But we took him, didn't we?" She picked up her tray. "Hey there, Mr. Tamura, brave man, you in your secret world, have a nice day, huh?" She left, followed by the other nurse.

Morio Tamura, in his secret world, faintly heard Mama calling him. Or was it his mother in Japan? No, it was Mama. The paper cranes, he thought. The paper cranes Mama's making for my sixty-first birthday party. What fool originally thought of making a thousand paper cranes for a sixty-first birthday party, and what fools made this into a tradition? Fools with time, that's for sure.

I wish we had a daughter, he mused. A daughter-in-law is okay, but a daughter is different. Now I understand why Mama used to say that if we're going to have only one child, she would have preferred a girl to a boy.

He thought of Tom, his son, and Evelyn, his daughter-in-law. They were good kids, kind and considerate, but somehow not as close to them as a daughter would have been. His friend Shoda had a married daughter and always on Sunday afternoons this daughter brought some food over for her parents—"So you don't have to cook tonight," she said. Then she cleaned the kitchen and bathroom and sometimes the inside of the refrigerator while her husband talked to her father. How lucky the Shodas were!

It must be time to get up and go to the shop. Must be close to four. What would the workmen say if the shop wasn't open by five? They depended on him for coffee, doughnuts and biscuits. Where would these truck drivers and construction workers have their large but cheap breakfasts? I must get up. But I can't open my eyes. Am I drugged? How could I be? Am I dreaming? Wake up, Morio Tamura. You don't have time to be sleeping. But he fell into another deep, unconscious sleep.

A few days later, Mrs. Tamura sat folding her paper cranes in the hospital room, as usual.

"*Oto-san*," she whispered. "*Oto-san,* Papa, can you hear me? Wake up! Try! You've got to come out of this coma. You can't die without saying goodbye to us. At least to me. Wake up! Look, I already have eight hundred cranes. Only two hundred more to go, and remember your birthday is only a few months away. You've got to be well by then. I sewed your red kimono for the party, and we have the guest list. So wake up, *Oto-san,* for how can we have your party without you?"

Mrs. Tamura sighed. After three months she was exhausted with anger and worry. What would happen to them now? Should she sell the shop? Maybe the new owner would hire her. After all she was still strong at fifty-seven, and she knew all the customers. Would she have to depend on charity in her old age when she had worked steadily for thirty-five years, minus six months before and six months after Tom was born? Thirty-four years of hard work in America, the land of the free and the home of the brave, Tom used to sing. The land of justice, of plenty, of love. And a land where someone wanted to kill her husband for a few dollars!

"What kind of country did you bring me to," she asked. "I gave up a country where I had relatives and I could understand the language. In that country I don't think anyone ever pistol-whipped another person from the back, even in the feudal days of long ago. The Japanese fought man-to-man, from the front, with warning. Why did we come here? What happiness have we had, working from four in the morning to nine at night, every day of the week?"

She pounded her husband's body in anger, heedless of different tubes attached to his body. "They say this country has justice, but there's no justice. The police didn't even bother looking for the boy. They said they had no clues. They just wrote something down on a piece of paper, that's all.

They just accepted it . . . it wasn't anything unusual to them to have someone almost killed by another. When I try to talk to them they just move
away. *Oto-san,* how can you die now? You didn't have your party. You didn't
see the thousand-crane tree. What about that trip to Japan? You said we
would go back on your sixty-fifth birthday . . . when you retire. Lies . . .
all lies! You aren't even trying to come out of your coma. It's easier lying in
this air-conditioned room than working in a hot delicatessen and standing on
your feet all day. You don't care about us . . . you're taking the easy
way out."

"What? What?" her husband mumbled. "Four already? Time to get up,
Mama?"

Mama . . . Mrs. Tamura . . . was so shocked she forgot to ring the bell to
call the nurse. Instead she ran to the door and yelled, "Nurse! Nurse! Come
quickly. My husband just talked to me!"

Two nurses came running. "Mr. Tamura, Mr. Tamura, do you hear us?
Can you understand? You're in a hospital and we are taking good care of
you. You have nothing to worry about. Your wife is sitting right here. Mr.
Tamura . . . Mr. Tamura?" But Morio Tamura was back in his deep, deep
sleep.

"Are you sure he spoke?" a nurse asked. "It wasn't a moan? Or a
gurgle?"

"No," she answered. "He asked if it was four o'clock already."

"Four o'clock? Why four o'clock?"

"That's when he used to get up to go to work every morning."

"You're sure it wasn't wishful thinking? You didn't imagine it?"

"I'm sure. He spoke clearly." The nurses waited. But they had many other
chores, Mrs. Tamura knew. So she said, "Thank you. Maybe I did dream it,
after all." She picked up her bag from the floor, extracted some paper, and
began folding a crane.

After the nurses left she leaned over Morio and whispered, "So! You make
me look like a fool! Why did you stop talking? Listen, Papa, I know you can
hear me. By the time I have my thousand cranes, I expect you to be out of
your coma. You understand?" She scolded gently.

When, several days later Morio next awoke, he felt his mother pushing
him. "Morio-chan, Morio-chan, wake up. Wake up and work in the fields
for a few hours. Remember your brother is sending you to high school. You
must work hard before and after school since he's making this sacrifice. Be
grateful to him."

Be grateful to his older brother? But Morio knew why his brother was
sending him to high school. Ever since Morio had contracted diphtheria

when he was twelve he had stopped growing. Now he was fifteen and still so small he was of little use on the farm where strong labor was needed. His brother was hoping that with more education Morio would go to some city and not be dependent on his older brother.

"I would be grateful if I hadn't heard my brother discussing this with my sister-in-law late one night," Morio thought. "They were talking of ways to get me off the farm for good. They made me feel so unwanted. I wish I had never heard them talking about me."

So he continued sleeping although he could feel his mother pushing and pulling him . . . maybe even washing his face? Now why would his mother wash a fifteen-year-old's face? He wanted to protest, but instead he fell into his deep sleep again.

Five days later Mama said, "Well, that's the thousandth crane. Now I'll have to tie them to the tree branch Papa got from a friend. We have the invitations ready. . . ."

"Mama, did you get white print on red paper or red print on white paper?" Morio asked, as if he had been in conversation with Mama all along.

Mrs. Tamura trembled and dropped the crane she had been holding. It took her a few moments to say quietly, "White print on red paper."

"Good. It'll be easy to read. Remember we had an invitation once with red print on black paper and we had to hold it a certain way to read the invitation? Poor Mama, a thousand cranes! But now you can relax a little."

"I enjoyed making them," Mama said, hoping one of the nurses would walk in on the conversation. "Somebody come . . . somebody come . . . ," she prayed.

"Come to bed, Mama. We have to get up early tomorrow morning, as usual. I had a long day, standing on my feet, and they feel like lead bars attached to my body. I can't even move them. You sleep early, okay?"

"Sure . . . sure . . . as soon as I put my things away."

She pressed the bell. When two nurses came in she said, "My husband spoke again. Right now. He asked about the color of the print on the invitations we made for his sixty-first birthday."

The nurses looked at each other. "That's wonderful, Mrs. Tamura. That's a good sign he might come out of his coma. Now listen, there's nothing more you can do for your husband now, so why don't you go home and rest? We'll take good care of him."

So they still didn't believe her. But it didn't matter. It was a matter of days or weeks before he'd come out of his coma completely. Papa was getting better and look what a clear mind he had. "Yes, I think I'll go home and rest," she reassured the nurses.

It was a week before Morio spoke again. "Where am I? I dreamed I was in Japan with my mother."

"You're in a hospital, Papa," she told him. "Remember someone hit you on the head with a pistol?"

A muscle twitched in his face. "Oh, I remember. A boy . . . a man . . . came in and bought doughnuts. One-half dozen. He paid me and as I was going back into the kitchen I felt something hit me. That's all I can remember. How much money did he take?"

"All that I left in the cash register before I left. About six dollars in bills, nickels and dimes."

"Strange . . . he looked like such a nice boy. He talked so softly. I gave him two extra doughnuts because there were two left. He told me he wanted only six and I said the extra two were free. He said 'Thank you.' By the way, when can I leave here? I have to order some flour, in case we have a shipping strike later in the month."

"We already had a shipping strike, Papa, and it's been settled, so don't worry about the strike."

"We had a strike? But it was supposed to begin June 15!"

"It's September 9 today."

"September! How can that be? It was June 2 yesterday."

"You were in a long coma, unconscious, Papa. But thank heavens you're okay now. Listen, I'm going to call one of the nurses. They didn't believe me when I said you talked the last time. Talk to them . . . the nurses . . . so they'll know you can really talk."

When Mrs. Tamura returned with one of the nurses, Morio was again in his deep, motionless sleep. The nurse sighed in exasperation, but with sympathy. "Hang in there, Mrs. Tamura," she comforted her.

For another long ten days Morio Tamura slept, like an empty sack with tubes going into and out of him. Mama talked to him, pushed and pulled him, whispered, shouted, scolded, whimpered. Had he really talked to her? Even Tom wouldn't believe her, so she herself began having doubts.

"You know, Mama, when we wish and dream for something, it seems true," Tom told her. "You wanted Dad to come out of his coma and you wanted him to talk to you, so you heard him. It had to be in your mind, because how come he doesn't talk when anyone else is around?"

But the very next day he opened his eyes for the first time, although he couldn't move his head or hand. "Mama, forgive me," he said. "I lied to you. Well, I didn't exactly lie, but I didn't tell you how short I am, when I asked my brother to find me a wife in Japan."

Mrs. Tamura was surprised. He was now talking about what took place forty years ago. How his being short must have bothered him!

"I didn't want to tell you how short I am because I was afraid you wouldn't come to marry me. The white people on the plantation used to call me 'shrimp' and the plantation boss told me to work in the kitchen because I was so small . . . like a girl," he said.

"So what?" Mama answered. "I lied to you too. I told the go-betweens not to tell you I'm 5'3" tall. At all my *miai* in Japan the mothers turned me down because they said I looked big and clumsy. They wanted a dainty daughter-in-law."

"Mama, remember when we were first married? When we took snapshots, I always took them on steps. I would stand one step behind you so I would look taller. How it bothered me, being shorter, yet I was happy because I had a tall wife and I wanted tall sons."

Mama waited for his next words but he closed his eyes, sighed, and went back to sleep.

The doctor and nurse came in, just a little too late to hear Papa talk. By now Mama refrained from telling the nurse about Papa holding a conversation with her.

"How's my husband?" she asked the doctor.

"As well as can be expected," the doctor answered.

"When will he be completely out of his coma?"

"What do you mean . . . 'completely out of his coma'?"

"Well, sometimes when he talks to me he's clear about things, but then other times he thinks I'm his mother, I think. When will he not go back to sleep again for days at a time?"

The doctor and nurse looked at each other. "We've had cases where patients have been in coma almost ten years," the doctor said. "Then we've had patients who came out of a coma perfectly normal and patients who couldn't remember anything or recognize anyone. We don't know about Mr. Tamura."

"Papa's mind is clear, and of course he recognizes my voice."

"Remember, when your husband does regain consciousness, if he ever does, he may not remember much because of the brain damage and massive hemorrhage," the doctor warned.

"But he does remember," Mrs. Tamura insisted. "He even asked about the color of the print I used on his sixty-first birthday invitations."

The doctor looked at his watch. "Fine . . . fine . . . let's keep working and waiting and hoping and praying. Miracles can happen. Now would you mind waiting outside for a few minutes?"

"What about this case, Doctor?" the nurse whispered after Mrs. Tamura left.

"Damage was extensive to the brain area . . . plus the hemorrhage. . . ."

"It's a wonder he's still alive, isn't it?"

"He got hit two or three times in the back of his head, at the nerve center. I think the paralysis is permanent."

"Poor man. Better if he had died right away. Now maybe he'll be a burden on his wife for years and years, and they don't even have health insurance. Personally I'd rather die than be a vegetable fed by tubes."

"Sometimes you don't have a choice. Sometimes the next of kin don't have a choice too. Unless laws are changed." They left, and Mrs. Tamura entered to find her husband sleeping peacefully.

Seven days later Morio opened his eyes and said, as if he had not been unconscious for more than a week. "Listen, Mama, will you promise me one thing? Listen carefully, now. In case I turn out to be a bedridden invalid, if I'm completely paralyzed, promise me you'll help me to die."

"No, how can I do such a thing? . . . "

"Mama, please. Won't you help me?"

"Even if I wanted to help you, what could I do?"

"I don't know. A healthy man can die in a car accident or drown in the ocean or fall from some tall building. But if one is bedridden and especially if he's like a vegetable, how can he die when he wants to? I don't know, Mama. That's where I have to depend on you."

"What are you talking like this for, just when you're getting well. Every day you're getting better, you know. I don't want to hear anymore. Besides, visiting hours are over."

"Please, Mama?"

"No."

"It's my only request. From my only life partner. For the sake of my life partner."

"I don't know what you're talking about." But she reached out to him. His thinness pained her. How could a man's arm really feel like a stick?

"Mama, is it daytime or nighttime?"

"Nighttime."

"Could you open the window and please turn my head so that I can see out?"

"There's nothing to see out . . . only a few stars."

"Stars? Oh, I want to see the stars . . . I never had time to see the stars while I was working. Remember when Tom was in kindergarten and he had to sing 'Twinkle twinkle little star' all by himself for a Christmas play and we practiced and practiced together with him?"

"And the teacher scolded him because he sang 'Twinkoru twinkoru litoru star . . . raiki a diamondo in za skai.' "

Did he chuckle? Mama thought so, and she too smiled. But then he seemed to have fallen asleep again so she left.

Morio opened his eyes and saw the stars. As he gazed at their shiny brilliance they seemed to break into little pieces and slide earthward, together with his tears that slid down his cheek to the pillow.

The next morning the nurses called cheerfully, "Good morning, Mr. Tamura. And how are we today?" But instead of wiping his face, the nurse called the doctor right away.

"Too bad Mr. Tamura passed away without regaining consciousness. One hundred and thirty-six days in a coma so he's really skin and bones," the nurse said.

"It's a wonder he lasted this long," the house doctor agreed.

"Kind of sad," the nurse said. "You know, there was such love between them, Mrs. Tamura is sure Mr. Tamura spoke to her several times. But that's physically impossible, isn't it? His throat muscles were paralyzed as much as the rest of his body, so he couldn't have talked, could he?"

"Most likely not," the doctor agreed. "But then there's a great deal we still don't know. . . ."

The nurse pulled the pillow case from the pillow. Strange . . . it was wet, as if with tears.

Secrets

MARJORIE SINCLAIR

He got out of the van and waved at Janie. She blew him a kiss. He didn't notice the spiral of dust as she drove off. He seemed detached—already on his way toward the ridge.

The dirt road was much as he remembered, except that grass and a stunted growth of lantana encroached on the wheel tracks. He loved the grass the way it was now, tall and pink in seed-time. In the past he had watched its many moods—how the wind travelled across and darkened it in streaks, how the color changed from season to season. There were more guava shrubs now. The fruit was ripe and falling, the smashed yellow and pink rinds along the way—birds and rats had had a feast. The smell of fermented guava hung in the still air. It would be hot later without the wind.

On the edge of the forest, the first sweep of emotion struck him. In the chest and belly—a strong and airy presence, throbbing. A mixture of anticipation and fear, he thought. And a small trace of hope. He couldn't for a moment remember just why he was walking there. That is, what his real reason was. He knew only that he wanted to come, that he had been impelled by a secret force. Janie had seemed to understand. Perhaps she understood more, but she hadn't said.

In the trees, the old road dwindled away. He had to trust his remembrance and sense of direction. He walked on for twenty or thirty minutes, quite certain he was going the right way, although nothing seemed at all familiar, except the kinds of trees and plants—the eucalyptus, the small ohia, a few large old koa and a scattering of kukui. It had always been a curiously mixed forest.

Sweat began to drip into his eyes. He pulled out the red bandana Janie had given him and tied it around his forehead. For a few minutes he rested on a fragment of old Hawaiian wall—walls ran all through this country. The silence and heat were oppressive. He remembered that a heavy stillness often dominated the forest. The land in this particular place dipped into a hollow;

174

it held the air like water in a stagnant pool. Just the other side of the hollow and up the slope was an abandoned road. Years ago, farmers and Hawaiians had used it as a short cut to avoid the road which followed the precipitous and winding profile of the coast.

He took a sip from his canteen and started out again, climbing the slope. The earth, which was never quite dry in this area, steamed. Sometimes he slipped, falling almost to his knees. He realized he was winded—he was pushing too hard. He would be glad to reach the ridge and the sea air. About halfway up, the going became rougher because of pieces of *aa*, clinkery and crumbling. There were a few hard, water-smoothed rocks. He tried to hop from stone to stone to avoid the mud underneath. He steadied himself on the thick branches of guava. By the time he reached the ridge, the sun was lower in the sky than he had realized. The walk had taken longer; soon the one night he had allotted would be upon him.

At the top of the slope he moved toward the sea, some five or six miles distant. That was the way he remembered it—the old road and the village straggling along the ridge. After a ten-minute walk he saw a cluster of large mango trees ahead. His heart commenced a heavy painful beat, and tears came to his eyes. Strange that the emotion should be this strong after so much time. In the clump of mangoes there used to be an old house stained green. Inside the house were the splintered frames of a wooden sofa, a broken rocker and a table with one leg missing. He had tried to get his father to help him carry the table home. But his father had said with unusual roughness that the things did not belong to the family.

He planned to go straight to the house and set up his little camp there. It had been his favorite of the half dozen deserted buildings in the area. He used to sit on the dusty floor and imagine old men and women minding babies, children climbing mango trees to eat the green fruit, a young woman washing clothes, someone pounding poi. The only trace of these people was their empty houses with broken sticks of furniture.

The clump of mangoes was thicker and darker than before. Underneath the trees, the earth was bare except for a few shriveled brown fruit. Flowers which used to be kept neatly in beds had grown wild throughout the lawn. He looked for the house. He couldn't see it. Was his memory playing tricks? —surely this was the place for the house. He moved closer. The lava rock steps were there; the foundation was there. Beyond the steps lay a sagging heap of lumber through which weeds and grasses grew. He wanted to cry. But he sat on the steps and put his head in his hands. Why hadn't he thought of this—of the erosion of time? He knew that the other houses too must have collapsed. The lives which he had once imagined there could no longer exist.

When walls fell in on each other and only stone steps remained, the people had truly gone. They could walk up the stairs—but only to a jagged heap of lumber. They had no space. In the distance the sea hummed faintly. The dusk came heavily through the trees.

He removed his backpack and took out the thermos of coffee. He drank the sweet, bitter coffee slowly. Janie had made it just right. He then put his backpack by the side of the steps. He wanted to explore the village before it was too dark.

Where some of the houses had been, little was left; splintered termite-eaten boards, piles of stone. No walls remained standing. The banana and mango trees were lush. And the old soursop tree still stood in the yard of the red house. Years ago he had taken soursop fruits home, and his mother had made delicious chiffon pies. He had watched her cut through the snowy white pulp, he had smelled it cooking. There had been fruits then he seldom saw now, the surinam cherries, the starfuit. A strong inner feeling choked in him: he wished he hadn't come. Such places as the village are better off in memory; only there do they remain the same. He walked heavily back to the green house, hardly aware of what he was doing. The dusk thickened.

He moved his backpack onto an open grassy spot. Gladiolas and periwinkle gone wild sprouted all about. He took out the blanket and spread it on the grass. Then he opened the plastic container Janie had prepared. He munched on fried chicken and rice balls. When he finished, he cleaned up the trash and put it at some distance away under a rock. He scratched a bit of earth around and over it.

Returning to the blanket, he stretched out. The fragrance of the mountains was all about him—that special green-pungent smell. Only Hawaiian mountains had that smell. In California and certain parts of the south of France the pine dominated the air—sharp, sweet and resinous. In Greece the bare mountains smelled of hot, dry rock and wild herbs. He had never known the smell of snowy mountains. This green-acrid Hawaiian smell was in his memory and in his blood. In the Hawaiian mountains, waterfalls slid over moss and had deep, still pools at the bottom. The sound of birds was always there, yet one seldom saw the flutter of a wing. Ferns so deep a man couldn't walk through. . . . Ancient lava flows. Lichen, all kinds of lichen. Stone walls wandering everywhere.

He was afraid to allow too much to come back. It made him feel guilty all over again. And angry. Mother was always in the doorway peeking anxiously —her hands stained with fruit and earth. His father riding down the mountain slope on his horse, stinking of horse and saddle; his father like a giant, threatening at times and distant at others. . . .

A voice startled him. "Eh, Kimo! Long time you no come!"

He jumped up to peer through the darkness. The old man stood exactly as he had thirty years before. His white hair ruffled, his blue jeans stretched tight over the muscles of his strong thighs, his palaka shirt faded. "Mr. Kahalewai! I didn't know you were still here."

"I stay. Where you been?"

Kimo didn't know quite what to say. "Pretty much everywhere, I guess. But I wanted to come back."

"I hear you marry that Rapozo girl, then get divorced."

"Yeah, I did."

"Then I hear no more nothing about you."

"I go the mainland to university. Then work. I marry one other *wahine,* Janie."

"You get any *keiki?*"

"Only one, she died, she *ma-ke.*"

"Oh, I sorry."

"But look at you! Just the same."

"Sure, us old folk, we no change. Hey, you come my house tonight. Humbug sleep out here. Plenty mosquitoes. We get one extra bed. Come on, pick up your stuff."

Kimo stuffed his things in the backpack. Mr. Kahalewai started down the road. He flashed his light along the way. The path was rocky and sticky weeds grew at the side. Kimo recognized very little.

They went to a house Kimo could not remember, small and brown. Inside, kerosene lanterns cast a dim orange light on the table and chairs. One had a red glass shade over it. Old calendars hung on the wall, some with dried leis draped over them. On a small round table with a crocheted cover were the pictures of the family. Mr. Kahalewai pointed to them—"All *ma-ke* now. Only Roselani and me left."

Mrs. Kahalewai brought a plate of hot beef stew and a bowl of poi. He ate to please her, although he had already had Janie's chicken. Mr. Kahalewai wanted to talk.

"You know that house where I find you? Well, old Antone Freitas live there long time ago. He your father's uncle. You know?"

He didn't know. Father never talked much. Kimo had always been wary of the secretiveness. "When I was a kid, I used to go in that house. They left some furniture behind."

"After Antone *ma-ke,* his daughter Marie and her little girl live there. They call the little girl Violet. Then one day the two of them go away. They just leave the house like that."

"When I was a kid, no one lived in any of the houses in the village."

"Yeah, everybody move away. This place too far from everything. Nobody want stay."

"I remember meeting you once on the road. You look just like now. You no change."

"I been old a long time. A long, long time. Some of us just hang on."

"You know my father?"

"Yeah, I know him. From kid time."

"I was in Europe when he died."

"Yeah, you no come home for funeral." He paused. Then went on, "That Violet, now, she became a singer. She sing in the nightclubs in Honolulu. Make plenty of money. Big name. She call herself Nohelani. She get fat now, but she can sing."

"Mr. Kahalewai, they no tell me my father was dying. The funeral was over when I heard. That's why I no come."

"He smoke too much, he get cancer."

"I wonder why they no tell me."

"Your father no want, I think." The old man talked about Kimo's father, and Kimo saw him again, stern and rigid, remote. On his horse he was another kind of person—a part of the animal and of the mountains, the wind. "Your father number one paniolo. No one could ride a horse like him. . . . Only thing, sometimes he was mean. He get mad and shout. No can blame him. He got tough time in his kid time."

Kimo wanted to ask more, but Mr. Kahalewai said abruptly, "Time for us old folk to go to bed. You can sleep in the extra bedroom. Everything clean. Mother keeps everything too clean."

Mrs. Kahalewai kissed Kimo and turned down the white cover of the bed. The couple went into their bedroom, and he was alone. He heard the surf from the distant sea. Insects crackled against the screen. He lay down and stared into the intense darkness of a countryside with no light in a house or on the road. The sheets smelled of mold.

Antone Freitas. He spoke the two words. His father's name had been Anthony. Marie and Violet. Once father had mentioned Violet, with disapproval. But never Antone and Marie. He never talked of family. Yet he had taken Kimo to the Freitas house. He said he wanted Kimo to see an old place and that he wasn't to forget it. The tone his father used was like a whip cracking.

Kimo didn't forget the house. It became his secret place for years. He tried to remember the details of the first visit. They rode up on horseback. Father claimed that the only way to know a place was to ride to it and through it on horseback. You could feel earth and the air of it. At the green house they dismounted. "You go look in the house. I'll be back." His father walked off down the road, his boots clumping heavily in the dirt.

The house was a spooky place for a kid. I thought it must be haunted. I tiptoed up the walk and steps. The door was open. I stared through. A gekko dropped on my arm. I had to choke a shout in my throat. "You little shit," I said, glad to have something to talk to. I stepped through the doorway and saw the old three-legged table and the broken chairs. There were calendar pictures pasted on the wall, mostly pretty Coca Cola girls. I chanted to myself, "You little shit, you little shit." It made me feel braver to hear my voice while I walked through the rooms, and on through the kitchen to the back porch and steps. I sat on the steps and stared into the trees. The leaves moved and made small sounds. A bird trilled and another answered. I liked the smell of rotting mangoes. A strange excitement stirred in me—I wanted to capture this whole experience, to hold it as simply as one can hold a stone or a piece of wood. There was some kind of magic. It put me in touch with the trees, the earth, the house. And with the mysterious lives lived there.

When father came back, I asked who had lived in the place. "No one you know," he said.

"Why did you bring me here?"

"I brought you here. Now we go home."

After that visit, I returned to the house every time I could steal away from the family. It was where I started my "book." A scrapbook in which I put down things I saw and felt; where I made small drawings of plants, trees, birds, and the old houses. I needed to put things into words and drawings. Only then did I begin to understand meanings.

A sudden squall beat the walls of the Kahalewai house. Kimo sat up. He had not slept. Leaves scraped like small animals on the roof, loose shingles rattled. The moldy smell was overpowering, and more so with the squall. It was curious, he thought, that the smells and sounds were there, undeniably there—but the house itself seemed unreal. He could see nothing. Only blackness—not even the slightest thickening of the blackness for a chair or dresser shape. He would rather sleep in the open, even with the rain. He crept out of bed and pulled on his clothes. The floor creaked under his feet. He didn't want to wake his hosts. As he went down the stone steps, a thin branch of something brushed across his arm. His body shook. He was glad to reach the road through the village. At the Freitas house, he spread his sleeping bag on the wet grass and finally went to sleep.

The sun was beating on him when he woke; close to noon, he guessed. The mango trees had shaded him from the bright light until the sun came over head. He wanted to wash and wandered about the remains of the house to look for a container which might have rainwater in it. Near an old back gate was a galvanized tin tub with an inch of brown, leafy water. He cupped his hands and poured water over his face. The cold washed his sleepiness away. . . . The Kahalewais—he must go and apologize for leaving them so discourteously during the night.

He walked down the road. He was sure the path to the Kahalewai house started just a little beyond the village. The dusk had been thick; he hadn't seen a great deal. He remembered some sticky plants, a series of old fence posts and a sake tub with rusted wire holding the ribs together. The Kahalewai house was in a place where the trees were thick and overarching. He couldn't see any trees which looked like that. The trees he saw thinned considerably at the edge of the village. He walked on for half a mile or so until he came to the edge of pineapple fields. Strange that he couldn't get his bearings.

He returned to the Freitas house determined to walk very slowly and hoping that some small clue, even the feel of the ground under his feet would help him. He had begun to sweat, not from exertion but from anxiety. Last night was real—he had no doubt of that. Why couldn't he find the Kahalewai house?

Suddenly he saw an overgrown trail which he must have missed the first time. The grass was stunted and coarse. No foot had recently walked there, he thought. But he followed this vague green path into the woods. On a stump he saw an old tin cup and further along a coil of rusted chain under a lantana bush.

Finally he came to a house. The roof sagged dangerously. The walls tilted —it would not be long before it too became a pile of splintered lumber. He went up the stone steps and peered through the doorway. He could see nothing but the deep gray luminosity of air and the weeds which had grown up through the floor. In a far corner bits of red glass glinted. The house had been stained brown.

He thought of last night—it was true and solid and real. He did not doubt that he had paid a visit to the Kahalewais. The old couple themselves with their brown skin and white hair, the beef stew, the moldy sheets, the photograph of a small girl which had been isolated from the other photos on the round table—set apart for a special memory, perhaps a special love. He remembered that once his father had spoken of the Kahalewais. "They are a strange people. They stay apart. Some say that they have chiefly blood, the kind that must be hidden." When Kimo asked for more, his father said, "Everyone has secrets. We have no business to pry."

No business to pry. Secrets—any and everybody's. Here in this village were all those lives—lived and forgotten. The Kahalewais, in that little house with kerosene lanterns and stew and poi to eat, went on day in and day out knowing something. What? And father had never talked of Antone Freitas. Or of his own brothers and sisters. He had a picture of his mother, a photograph brown with age of a woman one could hardly see. She had on a full white skirt and her hair was in a bun.

Father, in a community where family was the center of life, seemed without family. He kept himself apart. He appeared from a mountain slope like someone from an old legend. An Oedipus, perhaps. He remained aloof.

Kimo hated his father for his cold secrecy. Once in a burst of adolescent nastiness he shouted: "You're not a real father. You don't give a damn about any of us." Mother had slapped his face. He remembered with shame that he had laughed at her. His father took his revenge. All through the years he moved farther and farther away. He didn't even allow them to tell him of the cancer. The distance between them remained intact, solid as a rock.

Back at the Freitas house he wrote in his book for a while. All about the crumbled village, Antone Freitas (there was little to say—he was father's uncle), the visit to the Kahalewais. He wrote about how he could still taste the sweet-sour flavor of the stew; the lamp with a red glass shade and the little pieces of broken glass in the old brown house; the stifling smell of mold and the feel of coarse muslin sheets on his naked body. Senses had their own memory. Senses don't lie. He had always believed this.

He packed his gear and hoisted it on his back. Janie would be waiting by now. He walked along the ridge and started down the slope. The heat slapped him in the face and wrapped around his body. The *aa* lava rolled under his feet. The wet earth had a fishy smell which he couldn't recognize. Finally he came out of the hollow. In the distance he saw the van.

Janie came running down the road shouting his name. She was in a panic.

"Kimo, Kimo!" she cried and flung her arms around him. "Where have you been? I thought you were dead!"

"Darling, I was where I said I would be."

She began to pound him on the chest. "You shouldn't do this to me! You shouldn't frighten me."

"Janie, what's the matter?"

She pushed back from him. "Kimo, you've been gone three whole days!"

"No! Impossible—just one night."

"Three whole days! I've been camping in the van, waiting. Last night I was about to get the police when an old Hawaiian came alone. He said he'd seen you. Talked with you. That you'd be coming."

"Mr. Kahalewai. I was with him in his house last night."

"Maybe you were with him in his house last night—but he was here too."

"That can't be. Janie, you're confused. I was gone just the one night."

She pounded his chest again. He could feel the force of her anger and love. "Don't tell me such stories. I know how many days have gone by. I had to do the waiting. What did you do up there?"

He took hold of her flailing arms. He didn't know what to say. "I didn't do much." He paused. "I just explored here and there. Ate your good chicken. That's all."

She laid her hand on his mouth. "Kimo, don't do this to me. You know how I hate your secrets."

Watching Fire

MARY WAKAYAMA

Must have been '52. On New Year's Eve when Sparky Takahashi was maybe twelve, and I was nine, he set the canefield on fire at the H.S.P.A. That means the Hawaii Sugar Planters Association which is all gone from Makiki now. Finally.

Spark had a lot of impetigo over his dark, skinny legs and arms. He sported one wild popeye and plenty of hair, short but thick. When the cane was blazing, something which the lane kids never expected since it was mostly green, he showed us he could run like hell.

Siren and all, the police came right away to Makiki Court. It was off Makiki Street, in the lower valley, the little lane running down the middle of about a dozen plantation bungalows and winding up to one big, carved-up mansion in the back by the wooden garage shed. Our gang led the way, but the officers already knew where Spark lived. They rapped on the screen door of his house. Turned out they were the two heavy-set cops. One was tall, Chinese-Hawaiian, and the other short, with a Pilipino name, who always kept at least one eye open wide over all the neighborhood children.

Sparky was scared, but he couldn't lie or run away easily since we were all hanging around the edge of the porch watching to see what would happen and if they were going to take him to the station to beat him up. We used to tease him, "Spock you laters," and wink because of the name Sparky. But we said nothing about seeing him now. Nobody even wanted to lie for him, to say he wasn't the one setting off sky rockets over there, because he never let anybody touch his stuff, not even look at one of his small cherry bombs. We knew he had them when he showed off by guarding his bulging Hawaiian Air flight bag. He always acted cocky, but he was just like everybody else.

I was thinking, "Good for you, Sparky. Now you gon' catch it."

Mr. Takahashi was holding him by the back of the neck. His voice was sighing and squeaking when he told the police, "I went find him under the bed. Whoa, bad egg, this one."

Mr. Takahashi was always calm, but what a thing to say about his own

183

son. Maybe he thought they would let him off that way. Spark looked like a fish with the mouth open, body squirming, arms trying to flap away, so maybe he couldn't even hear what the grownups were saying.

"Take him station. Teach him one lesson," Mr. Takahashi looked like a stern demon with bushy eyebrows. He had the eyes that bugged out, too. Even the new crowd in the lane, real outsiders who came to see what kind of accident it was, could tell right off it was a father-son case.

But the old man was even more sharp. He acted like he was going to turn the boy over to Officer Kawelo, the easy cop. One time, quick, he made like he went shove Spark to him, but he aimed his body right through the two men's. Big guys, fumbling around, they couldn't catch what happened.

"Huh? Hold it right heah, boy."

Slippery Sparky went for the chance. Officer Calaro tried, but he could only hold on to the back pocket which got ripped off from the rest of the moving body. Down the steps, shoving Old Lady Machado one side, stepping on Dennis' baby sisters and pushing right through the neighbor's bushes, Spark took off. Before you could spit on the ground, we couldn't see him at all. He knew it would take too long for the slow fats to charge him. Plus he had the advantage at night.

We jumped, whooping, off the railing and ran after our friend. "Spock you later. Good one!" He was a wild bugger, and we had a feeling he would show up down the stream. What a bimbo-chimpo. By now I was hoping he would make it.

Officer Calaro put his finger into his khaki shirt collar to loosen the necktie. Calaro was angry at the father, grumbling to him, "You send him over tomorrow, yeh?" He gave all of us the reak kukae stinkeye, as if we did something, and he smelled it, too.

People started to go home, back to the partying. You could hear firecrackers from up and down Makiki Street and popping sounds from the little yards in the Court. Back in their Dodge cruiser, Kawelo and Calaro took off to someplace else, maybe a roadblock for drunks, but they were quiet about it. Mr. Takahashi was behind his screen door again looking in the direction of the burned-out section of cane across the street. Some Pilipino working men were still hosing down the part of the fence that had been burning. A fine rain from the cloudy sky helped out: piu, it was over. Everything looked like normal, except for the night which was smoking red with fumes and once in a while, the fiery streak of a sky rocket. Somebody up in Tantalus had some real good ones going.

We would find Spark later when things got slow. He was minor. New Year's was the big event, the thing we knew was coming from the time we smelled Christmas around the corner.

Now I can remember how much I ran around in those old baby days. I was whatever the day was. I marked the pace with my whole body, breathing in and out to step up a good chase from sunup to day's end. I was in a hurry to taste it all. I flicked our house radio from the Cherry Blossom Hour to Boston Blackie to Tropic Melodies, dancing by myself to every lively voice and tune. And I waited for New Year's with unbearable patience.

Best of all was seeing my mother's husband drunk under the bed. He would always hide there. I could count on him. The patter of firecrackers drove him wild as he headed for cover, remembering the flying war bullets that haunted his brain. I watched her beat him with a wire hanger.

"Stand up like a man!"

I watched him turn into a screaming child. She would be crying, too. At those times I disappeared into the closet, walls, furniture. I was completely still, just a camera waiting. A skinny girl with big eyes.

When I had enough of them I made the spin into escape, back to the Court and the action around me. New Year's Eve was when I could count on a rhythm to meet my own, to swirl me on my way. The night was fast.

The sound of firecrackers whizzed and rip-popped through the air.

"Look up!"

Just before disintegration there was still the last colorful image frozen in watery aerial action, trailing fancy tails and shrieking whistles. Occasional rapid fire popping just down our street made me take notice of the ground. All the small animals, down to the last nervous mongoose, were suddenly burrowed in, hidden somewhere tight. They shuddered to the rattattat of a tiny string of crackers, followed by the boom thunder of an explosion in a garbage can. Smoke was heavy everywhere, hiding the excited scurries of movement in the night air. Familiar people, who looked like strangers, dark figures in milky darkness, moved wildly. They danced around flames on the cement. Fluorescent colors flashed, and gold was molten in redflame. Night jewels decorated our patches of grass while the whole edgy town reveled crazily.

Somebody's father, a big guy, shimmied up to string a long rope into a telephone pole eyelet hook. Small children, jumping up and down in excitement beneath him, willed the entire setup. The firecrackers hung down six feet in a braid that almost reached the sidewalk. One of the younger uncles held out a burning match. Instantly everyone cleared away.

"Ha-ha. Only kidding." He flicked the flaring sliver into the gutter.

This string was saved for the main attraction, ready for the moment it would become the midnight marker.

So much going on! I couldn't stand waiting. I hopped in a tight circle, hugging myself, waiting for the final explosion of the whole night fabric, when the crackling roar would erupt through the entire island. Light, color, noise, voices, and feeling would surge through all the living and even ripple out to touch some ideas that we thought were gone. Time was still. Everything melded into the general breathless waiting in the midst of so much sound. Even I was forced to anchor myself to quietness.

I spotted a cockroach. 11:57 P.M. Driven into frenzy by the constant din, it zigzagged around my feet, going for the telephone pole where the chunky line dangled. The roach was shaped like an overburdened Dodge, rocking back and forth, bent for somewhere out of the exploding light. It stopped short just in front of the pole. A quivering roach drunk with noise.

Leaping, I stepped on it. Crunch, slide. It was no longer afraid. But I shrieked and fell backwards, catching myself and racing up to our porch steps. I saw Raylene's uncle's hand reach out to set the long fuse on fire.

"Covahup your ears," she screeched at me.

Nineteen fifty-two left us in a roar, "Happy New Yeah!" The adults continued drinking, feeling good. Somebody shot off a gun, "Wheehah!" Voices were singing. Radios tuned up louder. The lane was violently alive, a distillation of our vibrance.

I saw it in red, yellow and black: the rocky new beginning. Pachi-pachi-pachi echoed on through the rest of the dark hours into the morning.

When everyone thought we were asleep we met by our marble ring in the dirt next to Spark's wash house. Some of the kids couldn't escape their families or their need to sleep. So three of us got set to search the stream to find Spark.

Lee and David were older and expected another boy, Wyn Silva, not me. They were not happy about letting me stay.

"Okay. You, girl. Go home now. Beat it. Go sleep."

"Lemme see, too. Come on. . . . Otherwise I-going-to-tell."

I tailed them as we ran to the garbage pit in the back of all the sheds and apartments. There was an open space and a barbed wire fence before the hillside slouched down to the stream.

The stream divided us from the places where haoles would care to live. They lived up in the bungalows at Punahou Cliffs and at Arcadia, which was home for a governor. I was in awe of that vast lawn. The mysteries of a manicured lotus pond and a weathered barn structure could lure me across the stream. People on that side had cocktail parties in slow motion and drank to the sound of tinkling ice and bubbling laughter. Some of them spread out beach towels to sunbathe by the hour. I had seen this myself, passing very near and silent in the glittering water.

As soon as we were there standing above the water on the stone embankment, Lee made the owl sounds which would alert Spark to us. There was no answer.

We knew he was hiding in the tunnel.

Lee said I had to go first since I had the flashlight.

"But David already took 'um, and I wearing only slippahs." I looked down at my feet, too scared to face the command to retreat. They decided they needed me then. David pushed the light back to me. The two of them made me walk ahead, instructing me to play the beam on the ground and the sliding dirt of the rocky slope. We held on to the roots of the big banyan at the edge of the canal. It guided us down.

Once we were next to the water, the mouth of the tunnel gaped darkly ahead. The arch wasn't higher than ten feet, but we had seen mountain water gushing through it, flooding it completely in a short time, and I had been warned to stay away from the bums and escaped convicts that were sure to be hiding in there. My own eyes had seen whiskey bottles discarded on ledges within the recesses of the first part of the tunnel. I never went further. The others were sure the tunnel would come out in Waikiki past Pawaa Theater. Raylene used to insist it would lead to the ocean at the end of the canal.

My nose told me it was a place of decay which waste water itself could not wash away. I believed my mother who said it was filled with rat piss. My hesitating feet were saying the no that my mouth could not. Or maybe I just didn't talk much in those days. Quietly I had edged back until the three of us were walking side by side. I wasn't going first.

The mossy slime on the concrete flooring which carried the stream bottom away from Makiki was troublesome to walk on. The color under the flashlight's moving arc changed from green to brown. Reddish parts of it, which made the tunnel sides look bloody, seemed to be rusty scum water from metal feeder pipes leading out of the dirty culvert walls.

That night there wasn't much real water at all, just the little that lapped in from the stream at our back and tugged us in, further and further. The slow, oozing water licked at our feet. I began to feel closed in and looked backwards often to make sure the opening was still there. Forward, the light showed more orange grayness from the walls lined at their sides by debris of every kind. Silt gathered in places where sickly weeds grew.

We could hear the faint sounds of a trickling waterfall somewhere deeper ahead. Where we were had a hollow quiet.

"Whaddat?" David stopped. Lee moved wildly, ready to run backwards.

I froze, holdng the light the way a statue would point a torch.

A rat skittered away on a ledge above our heads. I saw fierce red eyes which stayed suspended in my mind like the skyrockets a few hours before.

David whistled through his teeth in disgust. He did it again louder.

And then we thought we heard Sparky answer us. A half-whistle, maybe a wheeze.

We ran toward the sound, carefully avoiding hunks of bent metal, a rotten ironing board, broken bottles, and suspicious clumps of obscure rubbish. We passed too near an almost-forgotten and deep crevice which held the unspoken rumor of polio-water, the illness our mothers forever threatened us with.

"Ovah heah!" Lee yelled into the darkness.

"Heah, heah . . ." bounced off the tunnel in echoes. For a long time we moved nearer and nearer the outfall's patter. The light marked a hump in the wall.

When we saw him up in the niche, he looked like somebody else.

I flashed the beam directly on the crouching figure. Suddenly someone next to it moved up jerkily, half-awake.

"Anuddah guy. Two."

He leered confusedly into the light, his head cocked at a strange angle.

"Damn pilute. You piss drunk." David hissed scornfully. It was his brother, Larry, and Larry's side-kick, the high school boy with a mustache. They had been drinking beer in their hiding place.

When Larry realized who we were, accusing him with our light, he pelted us with beer bottles. He was furious but a junk shot. I dodged. He missed me, too. In panic I dropped the flashlight. There was no time to feel for it, to regret the licking I would get for losing it.

Then we were racing again, back to the tunnel entrance, hoping in cold perspiration to avoid the dark traps along the way. David's brother's fury followed us in echoes. We could hear bottles hitting the tunnel walls and the echoing of the hits and the glass falling like rain.

It was a long run.

My heart felt alive again when I finally saw the opening and passed through it immediately to scramble up the dirt hillside in murky, mottled moonlight. There was air. The banyan roots felt like a lifeline. The heaving relief of coming up lightened me, the last one out.

It was when we reached over the top of the wall, when our muddy feet touched the ground on the other side, that we heard the laughter. Spark was cackling at us from his nest high in the tree. He thought we were funny. He tilted his head back as he brayed and coughed and howled at us. He couldn't stop.

I was still puffing and too ready to bolt for home. I couldn't figure it out fast.

"Eh, jaggass, come on down heah," Lee shouted, ready to fight him.

Spark laughed even more, sputtering and heehawing.

Looking for him, I saw his bent silhouette above the tree's crotch; his head up higher looked trapped by the branches. He began to make his way down.

I was thinking. He played a joke on us. He made me scared. My anger flooded over me, and my voice found its way out, pushing past tightly held in tears and the fearful caution which kept me silent.

I spluttered, "I goin' squash you, good for nothing lo-lo."

When I went for him to obliterate him with my flailing hands and arms and feet, Lee and David had to drag me back, still choking angry. They had watched Spark's useless foot come down first. It was wrapped up in a bloody t-shirt.

Standing painfully Spark had to straighten his left side slowly. While in the tunnel he stepped on a hidden jag of glass.

He spoke to me. "Joking, okay?" And his eyes were looking into me. I had never seen myself that way before, reflected in someone's eyes.

I looked small and hopeless.

Somehow I got home, tearfully running away from those miserable boys and sleeping long into the first day of the New Year, forgetting the endless tunnel and the gashed foot, the fires and the anger.

Spark's punishment, my licking, Lee and David, the whole Court disintegrated slowly until years later I could not remember that they were once part of me.

In '74 I was digging in my 10' × 10' Makiki Park garden. Crouched down, dripping with sweat, I found out how the earth casually resists the would-be farmer's hand. No longer the H.S.P.A. headquarters, the ground was city property now. In the middle of softening the soil I had stepped on a sharp spear of growing sugar cane. It was still sending out stray shoots in the desperate way of a crop that has been banished from its former field.

The stomach of my foot ached.

When I hopped over to a water faucet, I saw the Pilipino man. I opened up the spigot to bathe the sore foot and watched with interest as the stranger swung a pick axe against the brick wall of an old laboratory.

Like a few other structures the remnant had already been emptied and abandoned, but the three walls, two of them wooden, maintained their old H.S.P.A. form. Bit by bit the heavy wall was crumbling, chink echoing after thump, with every blow.

The hardy old goat did not let up. His face glistened with moisture. All of the energy of his being concentrated on tearing down the wall. As he flailed and hacked, he grunted and swore continuously. He stopped to sing a verse of The Star-Spangled Banner. Was he insane? Stone-drunk? He looked like somebody's grandfather with all his shirt buttons neatly fastened. I was too embarrassed to stick around or reveal my fascination. I returned to my plot and heard him laughing joyously to himself.

When noontime arrived he was still at work. The sun set him afire with its glowing heat.

When I picked up my weeder and hose, ready to go home for the sweltering afternoon, only half the red wall was broken down. My discouraged eye found his face and scanned the unfinished work once more.

"Those bricks are for the garden?" I asked him and pointed at the rubble at his feet and then waved toward our plots. Some gardeners set up little boundaries and stepping stones in their areas.

The man got up from his squatting rest, straightening himself full length, his back to the glare.

He shook his head and wiped the sweat off his face with a handkerchief. He blew his nose.

When he was done he looked directly at me and smiled kindly.

"It is just time for this building to come down. I used to work in this place here as a laborer."

He turned away and continued to bring the wall down. His action made me remember Makiki Court.

"No . . . can . . . help. . . ." He released a word with each flashing whack and laughed again.

The Seabirds

SYLVIA A. WATANABE

Mr. Ah Sing, the vegetable man, told the Koyama store lady that Doc McAllister had finally come pupule as they watched him race past in his day-glo orange shorts, kelly green t-shirt, and yellow baseball cap at quarter to six on Saturday morning. With his face contorted into a determined grimace, and his legs pumping, McAllister disappeared up the red dirt road that ran through the center of the village, like a light throbbing in the rain-colored air before suddenly winking out. "Crazy old man stay fifty already," Mrs. Koyama agreed, smoothing the pleats of her plastic rain cap over her black-dyed hair. "Everyday run, run. For what?"

"For live one hundred years." The vegetable man laughed and continued unloading his truck. Lift, turn, stack. His arms moved, rhythmically, balancing the weight of the produce crates.

"Ai ya." Mrs. Koyama laughed too. "More better stay home sleep, I think."

Emi McAllister turned in an embrace of half-sleep toward the sound of the front porch door slipping shut behind her husband. Without opening her eyes, she drew the warm sheets close and pressed her face into the hollow where his head had lain on the pillow. The morning smelled of lavender from the garden, and rain.

As the sound of his footsteps crossed the wooden porch and moved up the gravel drive, she thought of how familiar she'd become with all the different views of his retreating backside—driving off in the middle of the night to deliver babies, walking away toward waiting airplanes, disappearing out the back door to avoid her anger, racing off on bicycles and skateboards, pursuing the perfect wave on the rolling back of the sea. He had taken up running two years before, on his forty-fifth birthday, when he decided that he was going to live forever. Aunty Grandma claimed that anyone who ran that much couldn't be up to any good; she was suspicious of an excess of anything, except cantankerousness. Emi wasn't entirely inclined to disagree. But whether McAllister was in retreat or pursuit, she'd never quite decided; it all

191

seemed part of his passionate, singular struggle to attain what he once called a kind of grace—moments lived so intensely that all of one's perception and skill were brought to bear on them. Now, as his footsteps vanished out the creaky wooden gate, morning seemed to open up behind him in a familiar cooling of the air—a release of tension, like hands letting go.

A window was suddenly thrown open. . . .

Morning took him in, like the sea. McAllister splashed through rain puddles up the center of the village, past the giant kiawe tree on fire with bougainvillea, the house with the hundred cats, the Prayer Lady's, and the weatherbeaten hulk of the temple cast upon the edge of the water.

At the Koyama store, the vegetable man had nearly finished unloading his truck. McAllister snatched a sidelong glance at himself in the window; You're not getting older, the cigarette ad behind his reflection said. It was coming easily now. The sleep was gone from his limbs, and the old stiffness in his right calf had worked itself out. The salt air felt good on his face and neck. He remembered her hands, the bold yes-look, the black hair spilling like sea grass on the sand. His blood sang. Five miles out. Five miles back. He'd run his fastest mile his last year in college during the regionals. There was only a lap and a half to go, and Joey O'Day was in first; he was in second. He kept pushing the pace, but O'Day wouldn't break. Then, they were in the final stretch, and McAllister made his move. The crowd was yelling. . . .

"Yakamashii!" the old woman was shouting out her bedroom window, in the room next to Emi's. "A person can't get any sleep!" Aunty Grandma had been wakened by the frenzy of barking, which swept through the dogs chained in the backyards of the Filipino plantation camp on the hill, behind the village. McAllister was headed for the upcountry. "Mo urusai! Urusai!" the old woman cried. Emi struggled from under the covers and got out of bed. "Aunty, shinpai shinaide," she called down the hall. "You will wake Tamayoshi Sensei." Mr. Tamayoshi lived with his blind wife and spinster daughter in the schoolmaster's cottage behind the Japanese language school, next door. Emi was too late. The lights were already blazing in the cottage windows. She could hear bewildered voices calling to each other. "Dooshitano?" "Are you all right?" "What's happened?"

"Mack! Mack mack mack!" the ducks joined in, from the Fat Man's backyard two houses away. The sparrows rang like bells in the herb bushes.

The light was changing quickly now, as the sun rose, burning away the rain. McAllister wiped the sweat out of his eyes with the back of his hand.

He struggled upward against the curve of the hill as it pulled at him, slowing him down. His chest burned. "You slowpoke!" the girl had called from the raft, dangling her legs over the edge. Her wet hair flowed over glistening brown shoulders. The water rippled outward from around her feet as they stirred up sparks of sunlight beneath the surface. Just as he reached the raft, she rose and plunged into the sea, laughing, all gleam and motion disappearing toward shore.

He reached the top of the hill and began to descend the other side. He resisted the downward flow at first, like he always did, until he was sure. "Come," she said, pulling him down. He yielded to the movement of the hill. "Come." Then, it was easy again. Her arms all around him. Her warmth like a gift. He ran faster—the hill and he a single dance. Time fell away . . . faster . . . fastest . . . became nothing. He soared.

When Emi got home from distributing apologies and homemade rice cakes to the neighbors, she settled Aunty Grandma under the mango tree with a dish of mountain apples and went to work in the garden. It was nearing seven, but McAllister wouldn't be home for another half an hour at least. "Mah, kore wa mezurashii," Aunty said, turning a scarlet fruit in her hand.

"They are from Mrs. Tamayoshi's nephew, Ernest," Emi told her. He had a farm upcountry. Emi reminded herself to cut some lemon grass for Tamayoshi-san's arthritis.

"Ah, so ka?" Aunty said. "I haven't seen such fine ones in a long time."

A seabird circled overhead, like a curved blade turning slowly in space. "Ii ko shite, neh, Aunty," Emi said. "If you need anything, I'll be in the garden, okay?"

Emi walked through the garden, as she did every morning, stopping now and again to scoop up a handful of soil or to pinch off a leaf and turn it over in her hand. She noted the mint sprawling toward the marjoram beds and the new siege of caterpillars attacking the sage. She pulled up the green onions that the old woman had planted under the allspice, the parsley coming up in the potted laurel, the snow radishes among the basil. "Why don't you grow some real food?" Aunty always chided her, for not having a proper garden.

Emi stopped to weed under the lavender. The plant breathed its scent into the air—reminding her of the old letters with foreign postage stamps, the pink satin in China chests, and the yellowing photographs of young women in heart-shaped lockets that she remembered from Aunty Grandma's *jochū* days in the Spencer house across the bay, where the new resort was now. It was a fragrance redolent with decay and the promise of emotion which always seemed to belong more to the young women in the photographs than it ever had to her.

"Umakatta yo," the old woman called out. She had finished the mountain apples and was wiping her mouth on her apron with satisfaction. Other sea-birds had joined the first, and they all revolved in union, like the parts of a clock, circling and circling in the bright air.

Emi dug deeper into the soil, and the smell of lavender rose from the damp ground and clung to her hands, her skin, her clothes. She went deeper still into the crumbly black earth where the roots reached tenaciously down. Under the mango tree, the old woman was singing. Emi thought of fresh-scrubbed young women in white cotton dresses. She thought of the girl. . . .

It had just been one of those things, McAllister decided all over again, as he turned onto the coast road leading back to the village. He smiled. A sense of well-being spread through him. Two miles to go. Emi would still be in the garden. Underfoot, the puddles were beginning to evaporate, and the road felt sure and familiar. The sky was luminous with sun. . . .

. . . Almost as if it were lighted up from inside, she remembered. It had been a morning like this, the way it never was, except in early spring. That morning, she had taken Aunty to be fitted for a set of teeth at the dentist's in the new shopping center next to the resort. The sky was clear and high; the sun a window of light, saturating the air with brightness, but giving off little heat. There was a sharp-edged clarity to people's faces, the goods in shop windows, the droplets of water spouting from the fountain. All the details that usually flowed past in a blur of color seemed to be chiselled out of the air. A young Filipino evangelist with pomaded hair and a black and red plaid jacket was shouting in the middle of the plaza. "Brothers and sisters, He is waiting with open arms!" His shouts echoed off the concrete walls, filling space. "Come to Jesus!" Emi turned to hush Aunty who was beginning to mutter about people making a spectacle of themselves in public places, when she glimpsed McAllister in the crowd across the square. . . .

"Hey, Doc!" Domingo Manlapit called, as McAllister approached on the other side of the road. "Looking good!" Domingo was out in front of his house polishing his purple Cadillac, as he did every Saturday morning, when McAllister passed. The metal body gleamed with points of light. McAllister slowed down and crossed the road. "How's she going, Domingo?" he asked. "The back okay?"

"Stay good," Domingo said. "But too much pilikia, I think. All this strike talk. Everyday, everyday I get headache."

"Come and see me," McAllister called, as he started down the road again.

"Maybe I can give you something. . . ." Another half mile. Breakfast smells and fragments of conversations drifted out the open windows of the houses. He thought of hot coffee steaming in a white cup, and slices of cold papaya, and biscuits melting with butter. . . .

. . . His back had been turned toward her, but she had recognized the tilt of the head, the attentive, listening stance—as if she were seeing a familiar but only half-complete reflection in a mirror. She knew that if she looked a little harder, she could not miss the girl.

The air shimmered with sun. She did not hear the shouting anymore; there was only the huge, prying hunger to see. McAllister moved away from the crowd, still bent toward the girl. Was he putting his arm around her? Emi moved to follow. She could not see. Suddenly, she became aware of Aunty Grandma pulling at her hand. "What are you looking at?" the old woman demanded. "What is there?"

Emi closed her eyes and breathed in. "Nothing," she said, willing the trembling in her voice to stop. "Nothing." She repeated the word firmly, then turned slowly and placed herself, deliberately, in the old woman's line of vision. "I was looking for that new sushi place that Mrs. Koyama was telling me about when I went to the store, the other day."

"But what were you. . . ?"

"I think it's in that direction," Emi continued, without looking back. "They have all kinds of good things there . . . tuna, squid, salmon roe. . . ."

Aunty was interested now. "And do they have sea urchin too?" she asked. . . .

. . . Now, the old woman sang. The dogs in the Filipino camp had started up again. Emi made one last thrust at the soil, then pulled. The lavender came out of the ground with a tearing sound. Emi laid down her trowel and went into the house to put on the kettle. . . .

McAllister turned onto the dirt road that ran through the center of the village, past the store where the vegetable man and Mrs. Koyama sat drinking coffee out of styrofoam cups, past the temple, the Prayer Lady's, the giant kiawe, and Tamayoshi Sensei's. . . .

Aunty Grandma was digging in the garden and did not look up as the wooden gate banged shut behind McAllister. Emi came to the kitchen door and silently watched him walk up the drive and cross the yard. "Hey!" he called. "What's for breakfast?" He climbed the stairs toward her. The faded cotton dress she wore was bleached white in places by the sun and did not conceal the gentle sagging of her flesh beneath. Then she was close, and he smelled the lavender on her skin. "You running fool," she said, but her voice was soft. "Hurry and change out of those wet things, or you'll catch your death of cold." Overhead, the seabirds circled farther and farther inland until they disappeared over the mountains.

What the Ironwood Whispered

CEDRIC YAMANAKA

What causes a man to commit murder?

That's what I was thinking about as I stood across from the hard, sturdy frame of Louis Kamaka—eye to eye—separated by the fading strip of white paint that represented the free-throw line on the ragged, wet, asphalt basketball court at Lanakila Park. It had rained the night before and much of the pavement was slippery and covered with puddles. Broken pieces of glass from beer bottles lay scattered around the court and when the sun caught the glass at a certain angle, they sparkled strong enough to hurt my eyes. I watched Louis's massive chest go up and down, up and down in quick breaths and then I looked into his eyes. Louis's eyeballs were large, round, and yellow, and if I looked hard enough, I could see the red, tomato-colored ends where they disappeared into the firm bridge of his nose. Beads of perspiration fell into the lines of his forehead and ran down his cheeks like tears. It was his ball and the score was twenty to twenty. The last basket would win.

He started dribbling slowly and deliberately with his left hand. I watched the ball bounce up and down, inches from Louis's feet and his thin, blue rubber slippers. I hand-checked him, putting my right hand on the damp white T-shirt that stuck to his sweaty back. He backed cautiously to the basket and, because of his strength, I found myself giving him room. He made a quick move to his right, and I bit. Then, palming the ball with his right hand as if he were doing a hook shot, he pivoted to the left, jumped high in the air, let out a savage yell, and slammed the ball into the basket. His hand banged against the loose, metal rim and the sound was like a can being blown down a sidewalk by a sudden gust of wind. The ball shot through the rim and bounced through the torn, dangling chain net with a swish and slammed into the surface of the court. Louis landed on top of my back and we toppled to the ground, his arms wrapped around me to keep me from falling. Particles of paint and dirt sprinkled upon us like rain from the still vibrating back-

197

board. I could hear a hum from the metal pipes that held up the basket. My mouth tasted of dust.

"Whew," Louis said, wiping sweat from his brow. "You all right, or what?"

"Yeah."

"Eh, dis game was too close foah me," he said. "You getting bettah." Then he rose and helped me to my feet.

The stories I had heard about Louis were the kind that stuck with you for a long time. When I was over at Kalakaua Intermediate, people said he once killed a guy in a fight behind the bowling alley across from the Kam Shopping Center. Choked the guy to death with his own two hands. They said he drove up to Kapalama Heights one night with the dead body and cut the guy up and buried him under piles of fallen ironwood leaves. I don't know if I believed the stories or not. I guess I didn't know Louis well enough to make up my mind. I don't even know if Louis was aware of what people were saying about him. But I do know one thing. Everyone seemed to know Louis's name, from the teachers in school, to the cops, to the ministers at church. I even remember my mom telling me to stay away from him. Like I said, I don't know if I believed the stories about Louis or not, but whenever he scratched his eyebrow or tapped his fingers on the desks at school, I watched his hands with the morbid fascination of someone standing around in a museum looking at a gun that was supposed to have killed many people. I tried to avoid him, but every now and then, he'd call me to play a game of one-on-one basketball. Most of the time I told him I had something to do. But once in a while—like today—I'd lie to my mother and tell her I was going to a friend's house to help paint his kitchen. Then I'd sneak out the backdoor, and meet Louis somewhere. The last thing I wanted was for him to be mad at me.

"We go mah house," said Louis, as we walked to the water fountain. "Still early, ah?"

"Yeah," I said.

"Good," he said. "Get someting foah eat." He turned on the fountain and stuck his head under the stream of water. The water splashed on his face and spilled down the front of his shirt. Then he drank long, hard swallows. I could see his Adam's apple moving quickly up and down. A little Hawaiian girl was jumping rope and when she noticed Louis watching her, she smiled and jumped faster and began counting aloud. Louis shook his wet, shoulder-length hair like a dog, pulled it back over his ears and took off his shirt. I walked to the fountain and drank. The water felt cool and crisp. The opening where the water came out was thick with dark-green moss and the drain was orange with what looked like rust. After I drank, we headed for Louis's house. The Hawaiian girl with the jump rope had disappeared.

Louis lived in a small, wooden house on Pohaku Street, a block or so away from the park. Across from Louis's house was the Kapalama Canal, a thin ribbon of oil and water and algae and metal and anything else that fell into the rain gutters of Kalihi. The canal, I guess, began somewhere in the rain forests of the Koolau mountains and tapered down through Kapalama, collecting water from gutters and puddles and ground wells, until it met the ocean past the canneries and oil refineries near Honolulu Harbor. Children from the nearby apartments often waded in the shallow water with their pants rolled up to the knees, slashing the water with scoop nets and catching the small, striped tilapia and the brown, slender medaka by the hundreds. While they searched the beds of moss for more fish, they left the ones they had caught in their plastic buckets to suffocate in the sun.

We turned into Louis's gravel driveway. An old man wearing glasses and a straw hat was watering a hedgerow that lined the beige house. He wore a white undershirt and a gray pair of short pants. The old man's hair was well cropped and his gold-rimmed glasses sparkled like mirrors in the glare of the sun. A thick, musty-smelling pomade filled the air. Turning to us with a sudden, anxious movement, he asked, "Where's your mother?" The tops of his thin lips vibrated nervously when he spoke.

Louis looked at the old man. I watched Louis's long lashes and the yellowish-colored eyeballs and the tomato ends near his nose. "You went sleep or what today?" he said.

"Yes."

Louis took out the house key that was hidden at the bottom of an old Thom McAn shoebox.

"I bought fish," the old man added, weakly.

"What?" said Louis.

"Fish. I bought fish."

Louis's mouth set firmly. "What kind fish?"

"Ahi. For sashimi."

"Sashimi? What da hell you tink? We rich or someting?"

"But—"

"Stupid." Louis opened the front door. The air in the house smelled musty, a mixture of varnish, old paint, wet blankets and the ammonia-like smell of a catbox. When we walked on the floor, the wood creaked and the framed pictures of flowers and waterfalls that hung on the walls shook. Louis headed for the kitchen and I followed. A pot of rice lay in the center of the dining table. I could smell coffee and the stench of meat rotting in a milk carton near the sink. Louis opened the cupboard, took out two small plates and a wooden rice scoop, and walked to the table. A small, brown cockroach the size of a raisin skittered on top of the rice. Louis swore and flicked it off with the back of his hand. The roach fell onto the wooden floor and ran into a stack of crumpled newspapers and a *Life* magazine with a picture of John Lennon on the cover. Louis put the rice on the plates; then he walked to the icebox. The bulb did not work. He took out a bottle of milk and offered me some, even though there was only enough for one glass. I refused, but he insisted I take it. He then took out a pink tupperware container filled with a dark, greenish-brown seaweed dipped in a vinegar and shoyu sauce. The seaweed was fine, like thick hairs. It smelled of salt water and vinegar. With a pair of chopsticks he put a generous portion of seaweed on both plates. "Picked 'em mahself," he said.

"Wheah?"

"Kailua side."

"Haven't done that in years. . . ."

"Limu picking. Das one art dat stays with you forever."

Louis sat down on an orange sofa and put his feet on the coffee table. Across from him was a small, black-and-white television. The sofa was dusty and when he sat, it made a loud groan. One side of the couch was covered with colorful cushions, the other side a neatly folded red futon. Louis picked up a copy of the newspaper and looked at the television section. He rose and turned the set on to *Gilligan's Island.*

"I saw dis one," said Louis, as he sat down. "Dis da one Gilligan gotta stay up all night and watch da orange seeds but he went fall asleep and went dream about someting. . . ."

The front door opened and Louis stopped talking. The old man walked in, wiping his feet carefully on a mat. I noticed he walked with his back bent and his head down. He smiled and waved sheepishly and disappeared into the hallway. He closed a door and the walls shook. Louis was shaking his head.

"Who's dat?" I asked.

"Who?"

"Da old man."

"Ass mah faddah. . . ." Outside the crickets whirred.

Louis's father walked out. Now he was wearing an unbuttoned aloha shirt —blue with pink hibiscuses—and his hair was parted neatly to one side. In his right hand was a dark brown mandolin. The metal strings were copper with rust and a thin layer of dust covered the polished wood. The old man was smiling.

"Put dat away," said Louis.

His father made a sad, disappointed face. His eyebrows sagged and he looked down at the instrument. He slowly sat down next to Louis on the couch and he began to play. His thin fingers moved clumsily and hesitantly over the strings at first, but in a few seconds he had picked up speed and began playing the opening strains of the "Hilo March" with the fluent and sensitive delicacy of a man who had played all his life.

Louis watched the television.

"Where's your mother?" the old man asked Louis. Louis rose quickly and snapped off the television. He walked outside and slammed the door. I could hear sparrows scream as they scattered off the telephone lines outside. I didn't look at the old man. I followed Louis outside and closed the door behind me quietly.

He was in the garage opening the door to his yellow pickup truck. There were shelves in the back of the garage filled with tools, plastic bottles of Prestone anti-freeze, garden hoses, cardboard boxes with engine parts, WD-40, mouse traps, Armor-All, and a stack of worn-out tires. "We go smoke some pakalolo."

"Wheah?" I asked.

"Da old graveyahd down da street."

"You crazy! My grandma stay buried deah. Besides, I ain't going smoke in no graveyahd with dead people!"

"Nothing foah be scared about," said Louis, looking away. "Dead is dead, brah."

Under the truck was a thick, black pool of oil. Crab grass and dust had accumulated in the puddle.

"We go beach, den," said Louis.

I got into the truck. The cab had a sickening smell, like somebody had stepped into dog crap and wiped his feet on the rug. Louis worked the stick-shift and released the hand brake. In ten minutes, we were cruising Koko Head-bound on the H-1 freeway.

Ala Moana Beach is a popular beach for locals because, if nothing else, it's convenient. I mean it's easy to get to, and it's like in the center of town. Over at the beach, there's a place called Magic Island where people gather by the hundreds to jog, toss frisbees, barbecue, sunbathe, bicycle, fish, swim and surf. I don't know what's so magic about the place, but that's what they call it. To the left of Magic Island, if you're facing the ocean, is a sort of pool created by a stack of boulders that serves as a breakwater. Louis and I swam to these boulders. I was pissed off watching Louis and his steady, constant strokes while I was left about fifteen yards behind swallowing water and wondering how deep the water was and pumping hard with my legs, feeling the cramp welling in my calves. We climbed upon the wall and sat facing the horizon. The wind felt cool against my skin.

"Rob-boy," he asked, "still working service station?"

"Yeah."

"Wish I had one job," he said, pinching his nose to remove the water. "But who da hell going hire me?"

"Maybe once you graduate, you going—"

"Ain't going graduate."

"What da hell you talking about?"

"Screw dat place. No ways I going back. . . ." A large wave slammed against the breakwater and I could hear the ocean sound rush under the boulders beneath us.

"Eh, brah," I said. "Gotta graduate."

"I no need do nothing," said Louis. The wind was loud and his voice seemed soft, distant. "I going play basketball. Be one millionaire with da Lakers."

"You crazy."

"Why?"

"Get planny guys who good, tink dey can play for da Lakers. Like da guy from Leilehua—Filipino guy—Bautista. And what about all da guys in New York and Chicago?"

"I scruff Bautista one-on-one."

"What if you no can play basketball?" I asked. "What if you ain't good enough?" There was a long silence and I felt bad about asking the question.

"Den you know what I going do? Hah?" He looked at me. He made a fist and the knuckles in his thick hand cracked. "You know da small pond behind Joe Ayala's Bar? Da nice pond dat dey lock up?"

I nodded.

"Get one catfish swimming around in deah. Just one. Big, strong and fast. I gotta catch da buggah. I promise I going catch em."

I hadn't been to the pond in years but I remember it as a very quiet and still place. The water was a dark green and the trees reflected off the placid surface. It was long, maybe seventy-five yards, but not very wide. It would take no trouble to throw a baseball from one side to the other. The water was cold as ice because it was fed by a small underground well. The strange thing about the pond was that as far as I knew, no one ever knew its name. It was just the pond with the catfish. All the kids in Kalihi wanted to snag that catfish. I once had him, too. I was fishing for some large tilapia that I could sell to the old Filipino men, when something caught my line. The monofilament shot out of my reel and buzzed like a hundred dentist drills. I knew I had the catfish. I fought it for about ten minutes, and I felt it tug and it was like holding a magnet in my hand in front of a large piece of metal. The fish jumped out of the water and wriggled in the air. I saw the thick body, and the black, dead-looking eyes, and the long, long whiskers. It was only then, when I saw it curl in the air and shine in the sun, that I knew I really wanted it. I fought it for another ten minutes, and then the slack of my line went dead. I knew that my bait, hook and lead were gone.

My boss, Mr. Oliveira, is a tall Hawaiian with curly black hair and a tiny wart, the size of a small bread crumb, on the corner of his left eye. When he smiled, his teeth looked yellow from tobacco. He was a fullback for one of the old high school football teams, and he always talked about the time in Honolulu Stadium when he returned a kickoff seventy-eight yards for a touchdown. Not too long ago he had lost his wife in a traffic accident and I only found out about it when I read it in the obituaries. "Why da hell dey gotta print dat kine stuff?" he told me. "Just leave us alone. We tell when we like tell."

I had worked for Mr. Oliveira for a little more than a year. I met him last summer in a pool hall on Gulick Avenue. We got together and shot several rounds and we got to talking about different kinds of scotch and what we read in the newspapers. I beat him in three games, won fifteen bucks, and he offered me a job.

"Howzit, Robbie," he said, as I came into work. He was under the hood of an old model Toyota SR-5. The metallic blue color of the car was the shade of faded denim jeans. Mr. Oliveira's hands were big and strong and the cords and muscles in his forearm twisted and danced when he turned a bolt with a wrench or loosened a screw. I walked over to him. He was sizing up the SR-5 for a new radiator. The grill was cracked and torn, and small flies and moths—white as if frozen in ice—were lodged between the spaces in front of the radiator.

"Mr. Oliveira," I said. "I like ask you one question."

"Look dis baby," he said, gesturing towards the car. "How you figgah?" He smiled and scratched the back of his neck with the crescent wrench. I laughed.

"Uh," I started again. This time he looked at me. "I was tinking I know one guy who work hard and looking for one job."

"Friend of yours?" Mr. Oliveira wiped the oil off the crescent wrench with a towel. "Go same school as you?"

"Sort of."

"I know em?"

"Maybe."

"What da name?"

"Kamaka. Louis Kamaka."

He looked at me. I saw a pencil stuck behind his ear. His brown eyes did not move and I saw the beads of sweat in the pores of his skin below his nose. "Louis Kamaka . . . Kamaka . . . I heard dat name someplace before. . . ."

He wiped his fingers on the towel and patted my back. I looked up the hill to Kapalama Heights and felt the wind in my hair. I imagined the breeze blowing around the fallen needles of the ironwood trees. I wondered if Louis would ever catch his fish.

It was the closest I ever got to running away from home.

I was fourteen and in the eighth grade and it was Halloween night. There were three of us—Keala, the oldest; Foster, the youngest; and me. It was about nine or so and we had finished the trick-or-treating. Keala was still wearing his mask, a glow-in-the-dark mask of the Creature from the Black Lagoon. I had covered my face with a thick, red liquid that they sold in drug stores that was supposed to look like blood. Foster went trick-or-treating without any mask. Keala said he didn't need one because he was ugly enough.

We were sitting down on the lanai at Keala's house. He lives in one of the low-income housing areas in Kalihi Valley. Keala was eating a Reese's peanut butter cup and I was sucking on a lemon-flavored lollipop. In the parking lot, Keala's father was buffing the fender of his Impala. The night was thick with quiet.

"One day we should go up deah," said Keala. He was pointing with his finger towards the dark mountains. "Das wheah supposed to get da guy Louis went kill."

"What guy?" I asked. I think it was the first time I had ever heard the story.

"You know da guy Louis Kamaka? Basketball dude?"

"Yeah."

"He went kill one guy. Right behind Kam Bowl."

"Nah," I said. "Why?"

"My faddah told me. He went choke da guy's neck and he drove up da mountain and he went cut up da guy and bury em in all kind places."

"One of my friends knew one guy who found some bones up deah," added Foster. He had a terrible scab on his knee from falling off his skateboard. He picked at the scab and some of the skin was green with pus. The black hairs near his knee curled and tangled in the softness of the raw skin.

"We go up now," said Keala. He was smiling and looking at me. "We go get one shovel and dig da guy up!"

"You crazy," I said. "Mah faddah would break mah ass if I went up deah at night."

"No need tell em."

"No ways."

"Why?" he asked. "Scared?"

"No, but—"

"Panty."

"Wheah we going get da shovel? No more shovel—"

"Your old man get one," said Keala. "I seen em—"

"You nuts," I said. "Mah old man would bust mah—"

"Panty."

The first thing I always remember about that night up on the mountain was how dark it was. When I put Keala's flashlight against the inside of my palm, I could see the bones and veins—all orange—right through the skin. And when I aimed the flashlight into the ironwood trees, I saw the beam of light reach through the shadows like those spotlights the airport uses on dark nights. It was cold and we kept warm by wearing two jackets each. Keala led the way with the flashlight. I felt secure being second.

There was no moon and no stars and once we were up on the mountain, no one mentioned Louis or the body. The ironwood needles on the ground were wet and slippery. Foster carried my father's old shovel over his shoulder. No one said a word but our footsteps were very, very loud. Keala was the first guy to stop. I could feel my heart pounding in my chest and throat. "Pass da shovel," he said to Foster. Foster gave him the shovel and Keala started to dig. He was strong and did not have much trouble breaking the soil. It had rained earlier and the ground was damp and soft. I could smell the soil. Foster held the flashlight and aimed at the deepening hole. Several pill bugs ran out of the hole and scampered beneath the fallen ironwood leaves.

"What if Louis watching us?" asked Foster in a whisper. "What if he like kill us?"

The air was getting colder. I did not say a word. Keala dug deeper.

Somewhere down the valley, someone was chopping wood. I could hear the hollow thud of the axe, steady and hypnotic like the sound of an old clock.

"What da hell is dis?" asked Keala suddenly. Foster knelt and picked up a small white fragment, maybe an inch long. Keala aimed the flashlight at it and dusted it off with his finger.

"Das part of da ribs!" said Foster.

"No," said Keala in a louder voice. "Ass part of da tree." He threw the branch away and we moved to another spot deeper into the dark forest.

We walked for another ten minutes and the grade of the mountain got steeper. We had to grab hold of roots and vines to keep from falling off the sides. I could hear Foster breathing heavily behind me. The spaces between the trees were pitch black. He stopped and stood at the edge of a cliff. We looked at all the lights of the city and we saw the dark ocean. "Can see mah house, or what?" asked Foster.

"Right deah," said Keala. "By da freeway."

"Wheah da freeway?"

"Dose row of lights. So bright! Blind or what. . . ."

Silence.

Keala looked at me. He had heard it, too.

"What da hell was dat?" I asked.

We stood silent and we heard the sound again. Footfalls in the grass.

"You heard em?" Keala asked.

I nodded.

We turned and scrambled down the mountain, falling and scraping our knees and arms and faces, tripping over each other's legs, snapping branches with loud cracks, and all the while, Foster screaming behind us, "Was Louis! I saw Louis! He had one knife. Hurry up! He coming after us. . . ."

I never learned what the hell those sounds were. Maybe a wild pig or one of those mountain men who plant pakalolo or the wind or maybe just our damn imaginations. Imaginations, shit. The next day I got dirty lickings and was grounded for a week because I had left Dad's shovel up on the mountains to rust and be buried under the needles of the ironwood trees.

I hadn't seen Louis for the next couple of weeks so I decided to walk over to his house and see if everything was all right. Several Filipino boys were playing Hawaiian-style football in the street. The main difference between Hawaiian- and American-style football is that with Hawaiian-style, you can throw the ball as many times as you want. I looked at the lawn and the mailbox and the house. A faucet against the wall dripped slowly, plopping water into a small puddle in the well-cut grass. The pickup was in the garage. The fenders and windshield were covered with red dirt. Through the curtained plate glass window of the house, I could see the black-and-white flickerings of the television set.

I walked up the steps and the wood creaked loudly. There was a small, white doorbell, but I knocked on the wall instead. I heard the television go off and then I heard footsteps through the house. The door opened. Louis wore a thick beard. He stroked it and looked at me for a while as if he didn't recognize me. His eyes were very red. After a while, he invited me inside. The air was cool because a breeze was coming in through one of the open windows but the catbox smell of ammonia still lingered in the house. I heard the crickets chirping outside and the faucet below the window dripping. Inside, the icebox hummed monotonously. "What's up?" he asked.

I sat down on the sofa. From a crack in one of windows, I could see the mountains of Kapalama Heights and the tall ironwood trees resting still in the breeze.

"Just seeing how's everyting."

"Still alive." He sounded annoyed.

Louis walked over to an embroidered flower design that was framed and hanging on the wall. He straightened it. "Nice, ah?" he asked. "Mah muddah did em."

"Yeah," I said. "Must take long time."

"How school?" he asked.

"Still deah."

Then I said, "Miura said foah tell you come back school. You can still graduate if you study up. He said you making one mistake." Miura was the school counselor. He was also Louis's basketball coach.

"Tell em I said no need school." Louis sat on the coffee table and picked up a forty-pound barbell and started doing curls with his right arm. The muscles in his forearm vibrated to the rhythms and clankings of the metal weights and the veins in his biceps pressed insistently against the dark skin. His fingers looked thick and firm wrapped around the metal pipe.

The sound of the mandolin came from the hallway. Louis placed the weights on the floor and the walls shook slightly. The music stopped and I heard a door open. I sat watching the afternoon sun high over the mountains. The air looked gray. The old man's shadow appeared from the hallway and fell upon a bookshelf filled with empty liquor bottles. Louis stood up. His fist was clenched. I stood up also.

"Louis?" said the old man gently. "Did your mother buy groceries today? I told her to pick up some—"

"What I told you?" asked Louis.

"I—"

"I told you foah fucking stay in your fucking room!" He was shouting. He punched the wall and the house shook. Several of the framed works of embroidery fell to the floor. "You deaf or what, you bastard?" He punched the wall again and the glass in the window rattled. The old man, with his head down, disappeared quietly into the hallway. Louis followed. I heard him say something. Then I heard him slam the door. Louis came back into the living room, his fingers twisted in his hair. He shook his head and sat down. I got up to leave.

Someone had vomited outside of the bathroom at the gas station over the weekend, and the pungent smell coming through the Kona wind made me gag. I stood over the bucket hoping that the Pine Sol would drown out the bitter, sickening smell, but my stomach still turned uneasily as the mop smeared the brown, sand-colored puddle into a mess of chunks of orange like carrots and green like lettuce. Then, when I rinsed the mop in the bucket, the puke caught and dangled in the rope ends. I swore at the bastard who did it, whoever he was. I saw the empty case of Heinekens in the back of the garage when I had to sweep up the broken, green bottles. I could tell that they had cracked the bottles by throwing them against the wall. The sun was high over the afternoon and I felt my back sticking to my shirt. I took out the bathroom key and opened the door. The floor was wet and slippery. The drain in the toilet had clogged with toilet paper and the water had overflowed. I swore and mopped my forehead with the back of my hand.

"Howzit," I heard. I turned around. Louis was eating a bag of li hing mui. It was a big bag—the expensive ones that run about a dollar—and I declined when he offered me one. "Hoooo, what a mess. What da hell happened?" He was carrying a fishing pole, a small tackle box, and a plastic bag filled with what looked like bread crumbs.

"Somebody went puke over heah." I explained about the case of empty Heinekens in the back of the garage.

"Jeez," he said. "You know what you should do?"

"What?"

"Next time, hide over heah. Then when dey come again, nail um. Punch da lights out. Just hide. Like in da bushes or someting. . . ."

"Wheah you going?"

He smiled when I asked him.

"I going catch dat damn fish."

I don't know what made me go over to the pond that day after work, but I did. The fence was locked with a bicycle chain, but it wasn't very high, so I climbed over. Once on the other side, I felt the soft mondo grass and I listened to the birds and the crickets and an occasional plop when a tilapia broke the surface of the placid water. It was a shame the pond didn't have a name. For the longest time, I thought it was the most beautiful place in the world.

On the bank adjacent to the canal sat Louis, wearing a baseball cap, a blade of grass in his mouth. Next to him was a small Hawaiian boy. Louis's hand was on the boy's head and the boy's head was resting on Louis's shoulder. The boy's smooth, sunstreaked hair looked reddish in the sun. Louis looked up and smiled when he saw me. I waved and walked over. "Any luck?" I asked.

"Naw," he said. He had a small Garcia reel, the kind my father uses when he goes shore fishing for oio or weke over down the Waianae coast. Louis's denim jeans were rolled halfway up his calves, and the curly black hairs were wet and stuck to his brown skin. The boy next to him was playing with a dark red crayfish, teasing the legs and watching them paw at his finger.

I looked into the pond. There were three large rocks in the deepest part, right in the middle. The rocks were covered with moss. Occasionally, sparrows and mynah birds sat on the rocks and picked at their feathers. I don't know how long we sat there, the three of us, talking about everything that came to mind: cars and beers and cartoons and cheerleaders. The sun started to sink behind the milk-white apartment houses. The laundry lines and antennae stretched against the darkening sky like the silhouetted legs of large insects.

"Next week da big day, ah?" asked Louis, slowly reeling in his line.

"Yep," I said. "Just bought da cap and gowns and all. So damn expensive and all you do is wear em once. Mah folks, dey pretty excited. . . ."

Louis smiled distantly. "Ass good." He opened the plastic bag and rolled a small piece of bread into a ball between his thumb and index finger. Then he put the ball into his mouth and wet it. He fastened the moist ball of bread onto the hook and cast his line into the green belly of the pond, the space between the three large boulders. That's the place I first hooked the catfish.

"What you going be doing from now on?" I asked Louis. I scratched my nose and I thought I could still smell vomit on my hand.

He pointed towards the pond. "I told you already. I going hook dis catfish."

"What happens after you catch em?"

There was a long silence. The boy let the crayfish go and it skittered into shallow water and disappeared.

"Ask me when it happens."

I have forgotten the name of the small Hawaiian restaurant on King Street that always looks closed. It has red-framed windows and dirty-colored bricks, and smoke from the kitchen flows through a smokestack on the roof. Behind the place is an apartment surrounded by laundry lines and old shrubs. Old ladies from the apartment are always washing their clothes in the basin near the parking lot of the restaurant. The parking lot is unpaved and when you drive through it, a lather of white dust billows in the air and you have to roll up your windows. Louis called me up the day before graduation and asked me to meet him at the Hawaiian place for lunch.

I got to the restaurant first. The air had a funny smell, strong and not very pleasant—the smell of pork and dishwater and coconut and fried fish and cooking oil and crushed taro leaves. Ferns hung from straw baskets dangling from the ceiling. Every now and then, a hum came from the soda machine. It was lunch time but I was alone in the place. An old radio on the wall played classical music.

Louis came in fifteen minutes late and sat down. An old Portuguese lady came out with a notepad and Louis ordered laulau, poi, salmon, raw Maui onions, and two Primos. He didn't even look at a menu. The waitress stuck the pen behind her ear, and repeated the order. I wondered who the hell was going to pay for all of this.

"Sorry I late," said Louis. There was a patch of dirt beneath his thick fingernails.

"Ass all right."

The beer and the onions came first. The lady placed two cocktail napkins on the table and set down the cold, brown beer bottles. Louis told her that we wouldn't need the glasses and she nodded without smiling. Then she put down the Maui onions with a side order of Hawaiian salt. Maui onions are the sweetest in the world. We sprinkled the salt on the onions and ate them raw, like apples. Louis smiled and drank his beer from the bottle. "Eat up, brah. Dis mah what-you-call, graduation present to you."

"Present?" I asked. "Wheah the bucks come from?"

"Nah mine," he said, making a face. "Just eat up."

The laulau came. The steam from the taro leaves rose like ribbons into the ceiling fans of the warm restaurant. Louis started eating. The food was good. "So what, school-boy?" he asked, between bites. "What you going do now dat you going be out of school?"

"Work. Fix car—"

"Clean up vomit."

I looked up. Louis smiled disarmingly. "Nah, brah. Take it easy. Only joke." He sipped his beer and laughed loudly.

"What about you?" I asked. "What you going do?"

"I get by."

"What you going do foah cash?"

"No worry about me," he said, finishing his beer. "Planny money."

"You tink you can live off your parents forever?"

He put the empty bottle down and peeled at the wet label.
"My parents," he said, quietly. "Shit."

I've known Louis for a long time, at least I've known who he was for a
long time. I think the first time I ever really met him was at basketball tryouts. We were both sophomores in high school but he was already starting
and averaging about ten points a game. The papers called him a dangerous
player because he was very physical and moved quickly. When you played a
zone and left him alone in the perimeter, he'd hurt you with his twenty-foot
jump shot. When you played a man defense, he'd move you into the key and
with his speed and aggressiveness, he'd get his position for the lob or the
dunk. Anyway, he was at tryouts, standing on the bleachers watching us,
popping his gum and spinning a ball on his finger, while the rest of us
grunted and sweated and swore and cried through sets of lay-ups, wind
sprints, five-on-fives, and rebound drills.

Once I played against Louis and he sent an elbow into my chest. I lost my
breath and had to gasp for air. My eyes were open but all I saw was blackness.
A small Filipino boy named Antonio something came over and helped me to
my feet. "Ass da guy who went kill somebody. He play dirty, yeah?"

I never made the team. I was cut in the last round. But I still went out and
watched the games now and then. Louis was listed as guard on the program,
but because of his large, thick frame, he often played at forward. I remember
a game against McKinley. Near the end of the game, with Farrington well in
control, a McKinley guard was driving down the floor on a fast break. Louis
sprinted down court and laid an elbow flush against the guy's head. The
McKinley guy fell and his head hit the floor. The trainer had to come out
with a towel and wipe up the blood. The crowd booed, even the Farrington
guys.

The next day I was in the weight room doing bench presses. Louis was in
the corner by himself doing squats. It was early afternoon, just before lunch,
and the air had a dusty, yellowish color. Louis came up to me and asked me if
I had a cigarette. I told him no and he walked away. Three guys came into
the weight room and asked me if I knew a guy named Louis. I pointed him
out. The three walked over to Louis, and when he saw them, he rose slowly
to his feet. The three boys jumped him. One guy got his throat, one guy got
his hands, and one guy tried to tackle his legs. Louis spun around, and with a
loud scream, picked up a long, thick weight bar. He held it, parallel to the
ground like a sword, and screamed, "What? C'mon you bastards! C'mon!"
The three made a hesitant circle around Louis. One guy pulled a knife. Louis
swung the bar and hit one of the guys square on the temple. It made a horri-

ble, dull sound and I heard a crack. The boy fell to the ground and he was bleeding from his ear. Once he was on the floor, he did not move.

Louis watched the two other boys. "Who next?" he said, quietly.

"You tink you big with dat pole, ah?" said the larger of the two standing boys. He was wearing a gray sweatshirt and a headband.

"Put em down," said the boy with the knife. "No need weapon, brah."

Louis threw the bar down. It made a high-pitched sound that echoed in the hot, small room for a long time. Like a tuning fork.

"What now?" said Louis. "Outside, you bastards."

Both boys laughed and the one with the knife charged Louis and stabbed him in the stomach. I didn't know what the hell was going on. Everything was moving in slow motion, like in a dream. A fucking bad dream. I saw the blood spilling from the spaces between Louis's fingers. It was a dark color, almost black. Louis's yellow eyes were on fire and his teeth were set in a tight, trembling grimace. He tried to reach for the bar but the boys ran out of the weight room. The dark blood was on the concrete floor, and the red splotches—the size of raindrops—fell like wet paint onto the benches and equipment. Louis stepped over the third boy, who was still on the floor, and slowly grabbed a set of weights for support and gently set himself down upon a bench. He put his head down and placed his hand on his stomach. He swore and a thin ribbon of blood began to spill out of the trembling corners of his tight lips.

"I going call Mr. Ahuna," I said. Mr. Ahuna was one of the physical education teachers.

"Nah, brah," said Louis, standing up slowly. He tried to smile. "I all right."

And he left, just like that.

I watched Louis walk out of the dark room and then I looked at the boy he had hit with the bar. He was still lying on the floor. His hair was dark and sticky and wet, but it didn't look red. It was like he had just gotten out of the shower. A custodian came in with a mop and bucket. He looked at the puddles of blood and the red fingerprints on the door and the weight machines and the benches. Then he looked at me.

"Damn you kids," I heard him say, as he shook his head. "Damn you no good kids."

"What's your problem? You no like poi?"

I looked up. I was jabbing my spoon into the brown mound of poi in my bowl. "I do," I said, laughing.

"Hope so," replied Louis. "You Hawaiian, ah?" A pretty Chinese waitress came out of the kitchen and Louis ordered two more beers.

"Half."

"What da other half?" He gave me a piece of his laulau and said he wasn't hungry.

"All kine. Portuguese, Japanese, little bit Filipino, some English. . . ." I raised my knee and it bumped the underneath of the table. Someone had stuck a piece of chewing gum there and it caught on my corduroy pants.

"So what," asked Louis. "All your folks going be deah tomorrow?"

"Yep," I said. "My old man going take pictures. Mah muddah stay picking maile with my aunty from Kauai. My uncle bringing couple cases of Budweiser. . . ."

"Lucky you get nice family."

I smiled. The Chinese girl brought the two beers and Louis gave her a dollar bill.

"Yep," said Louis. "You damn lucky."

Mr. Oliveira said that he would slap my head if I didn't take the graduation present he stuck in my hand. It was an old, white envelope and I opened it under the lightbulb that hung from a thin chain on the ceiling above his desk. In the envelope was a crisp ten dollar bill. "I knew you could do it," he said. "You get brains. You one good boy."

I smiled and he patted me on the back. "Now I can work real hard foah you," I said. "I can learn how foah fix car and do da body work like how you wanted me foah learn."

Mr. Oliveira was looking at me. He ran his hand through his hair. "I don't know," he said.

"Mr. Oliveira. You not going fire me, ah?"

He smiled and his grayish eyebrows sagged. "No, Rob-boy. No. . . ." I was relieved. "I was just tinking, good boy like you . . . you should get da skills foah work someplace else. No waste your time dis kine place. Maybe learn electronics. Das wheah da money stay. Electronics.

"But I like learn how fix cars. I like it here. You one good teacher."

"You tink I like seeing you clean up vomit? Scrub toilets? You better than dat, Robbie."

"But. . . ."

"You go out look foah another job. Wheah they treat you better, like one man. Wheah you can make one name foah yourself. Go wheah you can keep your hands clean and make planny money. If you no can find one place like dat, and you decide you really like fix car and get your hands all dirty and covered with oil, if you decide you like work ten hours a day, move around engines, den I'll be happy to take you back."

He put his large hands on my head and looked at me. I could see myself in his irises. Behind him was an old Playboy magazine calendar and a row of old boxing posters. "Dis is always your home," said Mr. Oliveira. "If you no can find anyting better, you can always come back."

I clutched the envelope in my hand and knew that whether I actually wound up with another job or not, the hardest thing in the world would be to walk once again into Mr. Oliveira's gas station.

Graduation Day was a shower of color and the air was thick with the smell of carnation, plumeria, rose and pikake. Eight hundred of us—the largest senior class in the state—cloaked in maroon and white, walked two-by-two in straight, disciplined lines as the band under a canvas tent in the corner of the amphitheatre played the strains of *Pomp and Circumstance* over and over and over again.

There was a light rain falling from the mountains and I remember thinking, as the flutes trilled and the drums rolled and the cymbals crashed, about the many times in study halls and cafeteria lines and homeroom periods that I had wondered and dreamed about this moment.

I was in line with a guy name Ben Puahi. Puahi, or Puhi as we used to call him, was my oldest and best friend. We went all the way back to the days over at Kalihi Kai Elementary when we used to raise pigeons and go hunting for hammerhead sharks under the bridge at Sand Island. Puhi was a big dude. He was the catcher for the baseball team and batted three hundred four years in a row. He was also the runner-up in the state wrestling championships. He lost in the finals against some Japanese guy from Pearl City who was a black belt in judo. The Pearl City guy swept Puhi's legs and then used a hip throw to slam Puhi to the mat. Then the Japanese guy pinned him, all in less than a minute. When Puhi got up, he patted the Japanese guy on the behind and smiled. That's one thing about guys like Puhi. They know how to win and they know how to lose.

There was a large crowd standing behind the roped-off areas of the walkway. Mothers and fathers and little sisters and calabash cousins and big brothers were snapping photographs and thumbing through programs and pointing and clutching sweet-smelling plastic bags full of leis. I felt the smooth gown on my arms and I remember fixing my cap nervously several times.

"Well, my man," said Puhi. "It's all over." It seemed strange to see him so well shaven. All the boys stood tall with clean faces and newly cut hair. It was the damnedest thing.

"Yep."

"No more waking up six-thirty in da morning. No more biology. . . ."

"Kind of sad, though."

Puhi looked around at the pink-colored buildings. "Yeah," he said. "I know what you mean."

I heard our names over the crackle of the loudspeakers. "Robert Kahoano and Ben Puahi." Puhi raised his hands in the air.

"Dis place going get some memories," he said. "Remember da game against Kaiser where I hit da tree-run homer over at Lanakila Park and da baseball went hit da bus?"

I smiled.

"Everyting going be different from now on," he added.

As we marched up the bleachers in straight lines, I thought about everyone in high school and what Mr. Oliveira told me yesterday and I wondered what the hell we all would be doing, say, a year or two from now. Puhi waved at a girl and I smiled. She was a pretty Filipino girl and she wasn't wearing makeup. None of the girls wore any makeup; they didn't want the tears to smear it.

The band played the alma mater and then everyone sat down. The principal was introduced and he started to speak. I could hear the wind blowing over the microphone. From behind the bleachers where we stood, someone called my name. I turned around. It was my cousin Kawelo. Kawelo was rich as hell because he was manager of several fighting chickens and he got large commissions off the cock fights. He even made the razor-sharp knives that they tied to the roosters' feet. I smiled at Kawelo and he held up a large bottle of Jack Daniels.

Then to the right of him, I saw Louis. His yellow eyes caught mine and he held my glance but he did not smile. He was looking at me and slowly nodding his head.

By the time the principal had finished talking and we were officially declared graduates of the Farrington High School Class of '78, everyone threw their caps in the air and firecrackers went off in the bathrooms. I turned to the spot where I had seen Louis standing next to my cousin, but he was gone.

An old Hawaiian lady with her gray hair in a neat bun was picking mangoes off the tree in her yard. She had woven some stiff wire into a round cup —like a scoop net—and connected it to a long piece of bamboo. She stroked the branches of the large tree and caught the fruit in her net. The Filipino boys were playing football in front of Louis's house. I watched for a while as one boy ran deep, stumbled on a rock and fell down. The ball landed on Louis's mailbox and bounced back into the street. I picked up the ball and threw it back to one of the boys. The boy who had fallen down saw me walking into Louis's driveway and shouted, "He no stay home."

"Wheah he went?" I asked.

"I don't know," the boy said. His knee was bleeding and he limped back to the huddle. "Everytime nowadays, Louis no stay home."

"Wheah he go?"

But the boy did not answer. He was in the huddle. Louis's truck was not in the garage and the curtains to the house were drawn tight. I turned around and left. They sent the boy with the bleeding leg deep again.

"Boy! Boy!" The old lady was calling me.

I turned around, smiled and walked over. Her property was separated from Louis's by a scattered row of lichen-covered rocks. She had a laundry basket full of ripe common mangoes.

"You looking for Louis?" she asked.

"Yeah."

"You one friend of his?"

I didn't answer.

"I no see da boy long time. All time he go out."

I thought about the bag of li hing mui and the ten dollar lunch and the tip to the Chinese girl. "Does he come home?"

"Night time he come home. Yell at da faddah."

"How come he yell at da faddah like dat?"

"Wha?"

"Da faddah. How come he yell at da faddah?"

"Louis?"

"Yeah."

"Da faddah pupule. Nuts. Da buggah crazy."

I looked at the shuttered windows.

"What you mean pupule?" I asked.

"When Louis was one small boy, da faddah came home one day and caught da wife screwing around with one other guy. Louis's faddah went take out one hunting knife and went chase da guy out. Den he went after da muddah, but she ran away and she came running into my house. I hid her."

"Jeez. . . ."

"She no come back. Been years. She ain't never going come back. Louis's faddah. Da buggah went crazy. Talk to himself all night. Waiting foah her. Sometimes I hear him crying and swearing. Give me da creeps. And all da time I hear dat mandolin. He play one mandolin, you know. So lonely sounding. I close da curtain and shut my ears. When he and Malia—das his wife's name, Malia—was in happier times, dey would sit outside with Louis and da old man would play his mandolin. Sometimes I pity Louis. . . ."

"But. . . ."

"Da old man is good-for-nothing. Useless. Pupule."

I turned around to leave and the lady asked me to take home some mangoes. I smile and refused. The Filipino boys were still playing football but the boy with the cut leg was nowhere to be seen.

Mom insisted that I go to the cemetery and drop off a carnation lei for grandma and tell her that I graduated. Grandma died when I was still in kindergarten. The two things I remember about grandma were her squid luau and the way she smelled when she walked past me. She taught me once how to dry squid and make the legs curl so that they would be more tasty in the garlic sauce. She held the squid and dipped the legs into a bucket full of white sauce. She would never tell me what was in the white sauce because it was a family secret. Now, only me, my older brother Mitchell, my dad and my mom know. The other thing about grandma was the way her clothes smelled when she walked past me. She always smelled like aloe because she tore the plant and rubbed the sticky liquid on the burns on her arm and on the blackened, rotten gums in her mouth. Now, once a year—usually near Easter when the ladies set up booths outside and sell lilies—I visit grandma and bring her a pot of flowers or a bottle of beer or a cigarette and I sit down with her and talk out my problems.

It was early afternoon but the graveyard was cool because it was shaded by tall, thick brushes of oleander and plumeria. I made my way through the heavy, yellow brush, past the short, barbed-wire fence, and found grandma's stone. The tombstone was nothing more than a foot-high piece of cement, shaped something like a washboard, with her name, birthdate and date of death. It was caked with red dirt and sparrow crap. I knelt down and placed the carnation lei on the dried grass around the stone.

How you doing, grandma? I graduated yesterday. Now I going be one good boy. No need worry about me.

I could feel the wind at my back. The birds were loud in the trees. Birds always sing loudest in cemeteries. That's what dad always tells me.

I not going be missing school too much. I mean, I still going be playing basketball with Joe and Willie and Mario and Sammy. Maybe we go out shoot couple rounds of pool, go on Grant's boat drink beer and cast for papio.

I ran my fingers on the tracks of the headstone made by slugs. The carnations still had a sweet, rich smell. Behind me I could hear the dull sound of shovel scratching soil.

Should have been at da graduation yesterday. With all da flowers and everyting. I marched with Puhi. Had one big bash over at his place aftahs. Drank one whole bunch of Lowenbraus and Tequilas. Drank da bottle and swallowed da worm. Got so wasted and fu. . . . I winced. Nah, Grandma. Wasn't dat bad.

A cardinal sat on the sharp edges of a chain-link fence.

Still working for Mr. Oliveira. But I don't know. He said dat da money stay in electronics. He like me make one name foah mahself. Electronics. . . .

The sky was blue and there were no clouds over the ocean.

What does Heaven look like, Grandma? Is it like in da books?

I could see a line of red ants cut through a patch of withered blades of grass, carrying a long, dead gecko.

On weekends, maybe, I can go over to da pond and try snag da catfish. You know da one I always tell you about? Da one I had on my line? You would have been proud if I snatched dat dude. Was bigger than da ulua dad caught on Lanai. I extended my hands about a yard apart. Nah . . . maybe not dat big. . . . Lots of guys trying foah snag da catfish. Get dis one guy, Louis? Remember him? I told you about him. He da guy who went kill one guy. I don't know how anybody would be able to do something like dat.

Kam Bowl was a block away from the graveyard and if I looked hard past the trees and the yellow flowers, I could see its white concrete walls.

Mom's all right. Still working at da delicatessen and complaining about her back. And dad stay working on one house in Moanalua, by da airport. He said he might take us camping next week. I kinda remember how you used to like to come camping with us. I remember da time in Kauai when was real cold and you went lend me your sweater. Where was dat? Haena side, ah?

I watched a white moth fly into the sky and disappear in the glare of the sun.

Someone tapped my shoulder gently and I turned around quickly. Louis smiled and tapped my cheeks. His forehead was smeared with dirt and his hands were caked to the elbows with mud. He was carrying an old, rusted shovel made of metal that had been painted red. "Dis your grandma?" he asked.

"Yeah."

Louis squinted and cleaned the dirt off the headstone with his fingers. "Eighteen eighty to 1965. She lived long. . . ."

"Yeah."

"She was happy. I can tell."

I smiled. Louis was wearing denim jeans and a torn, white T-shirt with the sleeves cut off. His big hands were wrapped around the handle of the shovel.

"What you doing heah?" I asked.

"Dis mah place," said Louis, spreading his arms. "Mah job."

"Yeah?" I asked. "Since when?"

"Last week or so."

"No scared, or what?" I asked. "Work graveyahd?" I remembered the stories people told me about the graveyard. Once there was this old man—an ambitious Korean who had two families and was blind in one eye—who sold bubble gum and cheese cake and ice cream and bowls of noodles in a small van parked alongside the cemetery. He was a greedy man, and he worked late hours. One night, people heard him scream and they heard the windshield and windows of his van cracking, as if someone were throwing stones and shattering the thick glass. The next morning, the old man was found curled in his van—his eyes open wide in death—the streaks of blood running parallel down his flesh and the white walls of the van. The slices on his chest were clean and precise, like claw marks. The cops burned the van in an empty lot on Sand Island and in the graveyard, the grass never grows near the place where they found the body.

"Come," said Louis, putting his hand on my shoulder. "I like show you someting."

I followed. Louis was whistling an old Hawaiian song that they always played on the radio. He led me to the ditch he was digging. The smell of damp soil filled the air: the smell of lichen and mold and humus and dried root. It smelled like mountains after a hard rain.

He put his arm on my shoulder. "Tell me da truth, Rob," he said, gesturing towards the pit. "Da ting straight, or what? One side look kinda crooked?"

"Uh. . . ."

"Tell da truth. Dis mah first job. Did em mahself. What you tink? I should fix da edges, or what?" The hole was shaped like the nameless catfish pond, long but narrow. In a neat pile next to the hole was a mound of dirt. On the dirt were cubes of cut grass. I looked deep into the pit. The dirt was rich and brown. "Nobody went help me on dis buggah. Did em mahself."

I smiled. Louis stared at the hole and closed one eye. "You sure not lop-sided?"

He took me once more by the arm. His fingers were hard and callused. We walked through the thick yellow grass with the smell of blooming plumeria sweet and milky through the air. I stepped cautiously, not wanting to walk on any of the markers. Louis was wearing his thin, blue rubber slippers. I read the names on the headstones. Many were Hawaiian, with inscriptions and oval, black-and-white photographs of grandmothers and little children and wives and husbands and fathers. I wondered who took all the pictures and what happened to all of the people and their sons and daughters.

"Nothing foah be scared about," said Louis. "Everybody gotta die. Ass da least ting for worry about. Da least ting. . . ." He bent down and emptied a vase full of dead flowers. Then he poured the putrid smelling water into the dried soil and emptied the flowers into an empty trash can. The smell of the old, gray flowers was as bad as the dark-colored water.

We reached a small, wooden shed with a corrugated roof. Louis opened the combination lock and we walked in. Inside was a chair, a table and a small basin. On the table was a transistor radio, a deck of cards and a thermos. The air smelled of sawdust, rust and coffee. "Dis mah office," said Louis. "Dis mah place. After I walk around and cut da grass and trim da hedges, I can come in heah and sit down and tink." Louis was nodding. He placed the shovel against the wall, next to an old manual lawn mower, broom and dustpan, hoe, hand truck and a wheelbarrow half filled with gravel. "Dis whole yahd. It's mah responsibility. Louis Kamaka's place. Rob-boy, you see what I'm saying? Dis mah place."

He smiled and looked at the corrugated roof of the shed. Then he picked up the shovel and we walked outside. The sun was bright. I followed Louis as we wound our way through the cemetery. I could see the muscles in his shoulders and back moving up and down, up and down.

"But what you going do foah da rest of your life?" I asked.

"What you mean?"

"You cannot go digging graves foah da rest of your life. . . ."

Sweat ran down his armpits and onto the mud on his chest and forearms. He squinted as he looked at me. "Why?"

"Nobody digs graves foah deah whole life," I said. I could not explain.

"What dey do?"

I paused. "Maybe electronics or someting. Wheah you can make one name foah yourself."

Louis was shaking his head. "I happy heah. With da soil and da worms and da shed. . . ."

"You crazy?"

"What da hell you talking about?"

"I mean . . . you young."

"I going wait foah you at da catfish pond."

"Wha?"

"Ass what I going do. I going wait foah you at da pond."

He stuck the rusted, brown shovel into the gravel and the shadow of it, and Louis's stooped back, pointed directly towards the ironwood trees swaying gently in the breeze on Kapalama Heights.

GLOSSARY

Most of the words and phrases in this glossary are in common usage in
Hawaii. Though they are from several languages, they have become familiar
to people in the islands because many cultures have coexisted and inter-
mingled here for several decades now. They are explained for those readers
encountering them for the first time. In general, the definitions chosen are
those determined by the stories themselves or by common usage; they are not
meant to be comprehensive definitions. Words sufficiently explained by con-
text, and those that are simply variations of standard English words, are not
included. Dialectical spellings and punctuation vary from one story to
another, and no attempt has been made to standardize these. Finally, words
from the Hawaiian language are spelled throughout as they were by the various authors, with and without diacritical marks.

Ah, so ka	is that so
Ai kukae	eat shit
Ai ya	what a pity
Akua	spirit
Ali'i	royalty
Aumakua	family or personal god
Dooshitano	what's happened?
Furo	bath
Grind	eat
Hanafuda	Japanese card game (among the terms of the game used in the story "That Was Last Year" are: gaji, the only wild card in the hanafuda deck; basa'd, shut out or skunked; yaku, a combination that scores points)
Haole	Caucasian
Hapa	of mixed race
Hapa-haole	part-Caucasian

Heiau	Hawaiian place of worship, often constructed in the form of terraces
Ii ko shite, ne	be good now, okay?
Jochū	maid
Kapu	taboo or prohibition
Kahuna	priest
Keiki	child
Keʻokeʻo	white
Kuula	shrine
Lee-see	gift money
Lo-lo	crazy
Mah, kore wa mezurashii	My, isn't this something?
Mahu	homosexual, transvestite
Maʻke (also ma-ke)	dead
Mauka	inland
Mo urusai	noisy; troublesome
Ohana	group of people bound together by common beliefs or kinship
Okole	buttocks
Opala	bits of debris
Pau	finished; done
Pilikia	trouble; problem
Po-po	grandfather
Punawai	water spring; reservoir
Pupule	crazy
Puʻuhonua	place of refuge
Sansei	third generation
Sensei	teacher
Shaka sign	hand gesture of greeting or approval
Shinpai shinaide	don't worry; don't worry yourself
Ti	a woody plant ending in a cluster of long, narrow leaves with many cultural and ceremonial uses
Tutu	grandmother
Umakatta yo	that was delicious
Wahine	woman; girl
Yakamashii	noisy